I0583297

THE TREASURES OF THE CLAN

A LEGENDS OF CYCONIS NOVEL

MARTINA B. RIVERS

tuliptypeset.com

Dearest Reader, this book contains elements of sexual assault, miscarriage, attempted abortion, emotional/physical abuse, and self-harm.

Cover design by Caitlin B. Miller
Maps design by Caitlin B. Miller

Tulip Typset
Washington, USA

First Edition: September 2025

ISBN: 979-8-9996290-0-5

Thank you to my friends and family,
in the here and after,
for your love and support.
This wouldn't be possible without you.

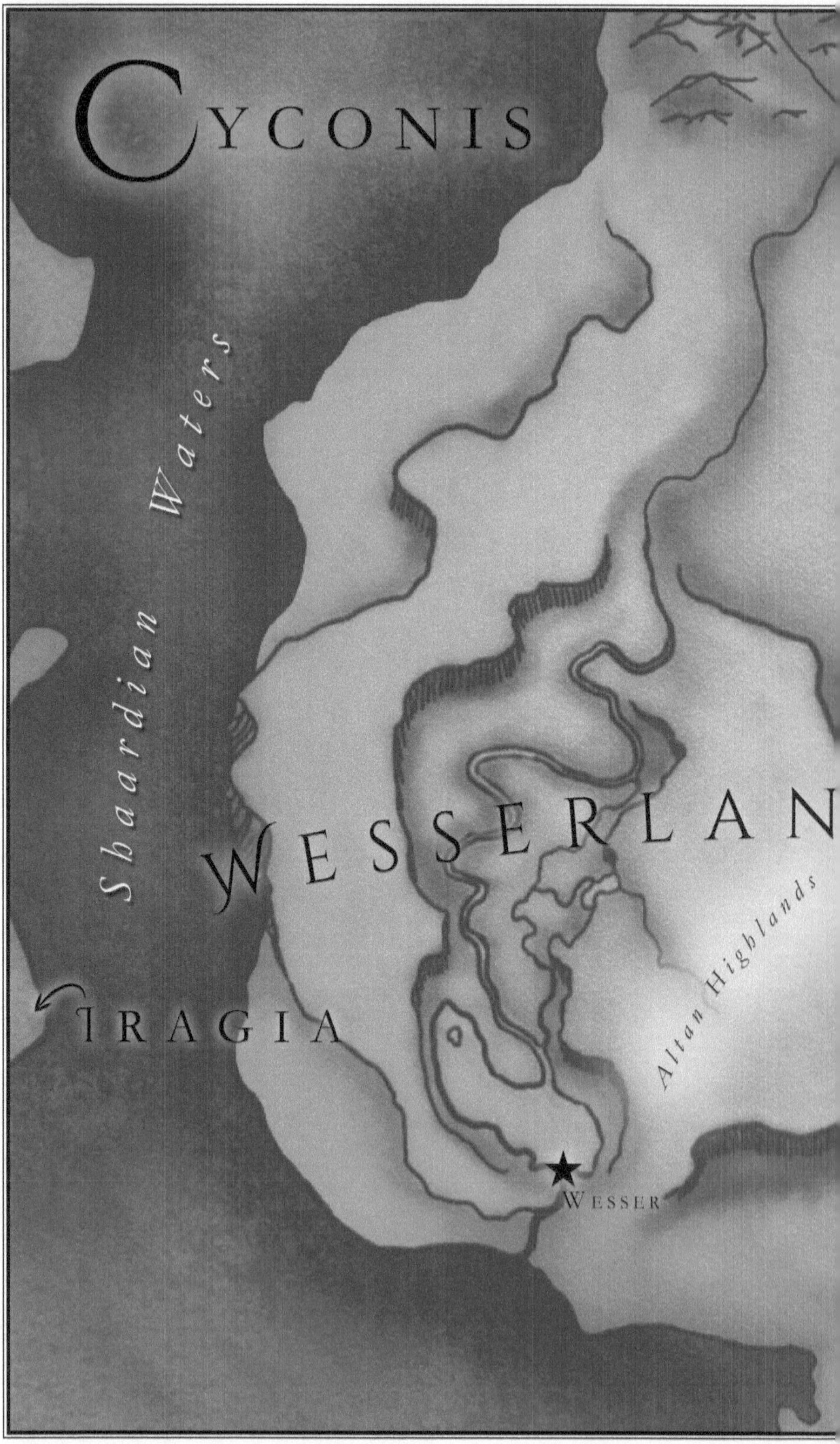

CYCONIS

Shaardian Waters

WESSERLAN

Altan Highlands

IRAGIA

WESSER

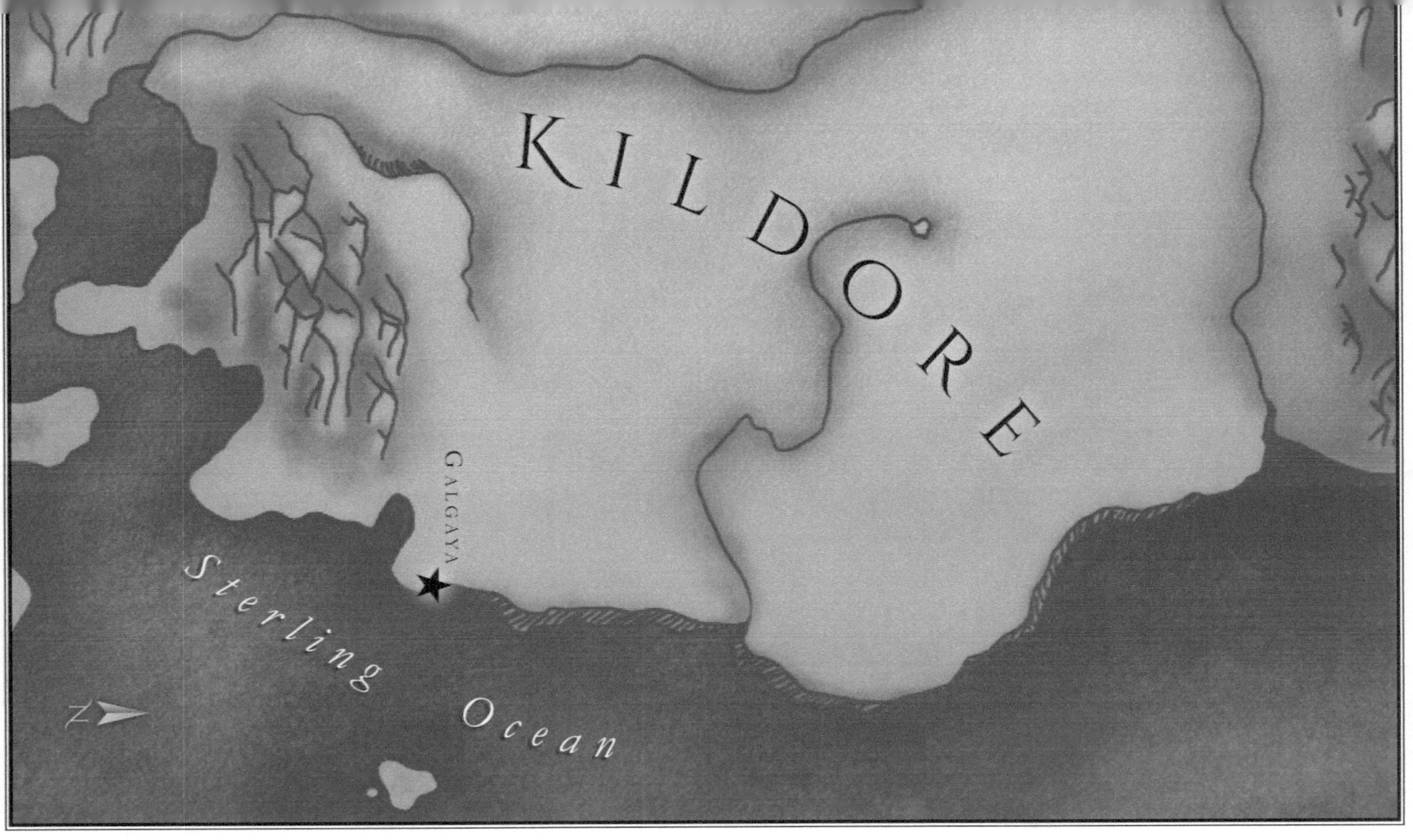
KILDORE
GALGAYA
Sterling Ocean
N

1

DAVAN PASSED THE BREAD SCRAP TO TREASTA and reclined beside her on the dusty floor against a wall peeling of faded yellow wallpaper. The silver moonbeams shifted as he adjusted his square frame, the failing shutters hanging crooked on their hinges rattling as he drew his knees into his chest. Almost winter, they wrapped their heads in torn linen scraps, found wasting away clothes in knocked over wardrobes they donned for extra warmth. Treasta eyed his dark, greasy locks poking through the fabric. The dirt on his face smudged across twin scars on his lips, filling them in a way that reminded her of their unmistakable deepness; wounds from years ago still struggling to heal left him with a crooked and cleft smile—an expression he hadn't worn since leaving Galgaya.

She held the meager bread scrap in her palm, assessed its weight—she may as well had been holding air. Near skin and bone, Treasta always was slender, but her frame had hollowed into nothingness after months of travel, save for a bloated stomach under layers of blouses and a dress. Achy bowels rumbled anytime she ate, and since the onset of whatever was causing her intense pangs, Treasta found not eating easier than dealing with the repercussions her body would suffer.

With Davan's wide and penetrating stare, she nibbled until the scrap disappeared down her gullet, the texture rough, the dryness sucking away what wetness survived her parched mouth. The empty cavity of her stomach growled, and sudden nausea set in. Treasta's face flushed cold and hot in a single sweep.

Davan took another bite, chomping and passing a look of bewilderment at his ill partner.

"I don't feel good," was all Treasta said as she waited for the feeling to pass, her complexion, reddened from days traveling under the early winter sun, washed white; her gaze fixed to the floorboards, the old wood preserved after decades of abandonment.

Davan's voice filled her head. Something about the bread not being stale. Something about her being dramatic. *Dramatic.* It wasn't the first time he said that in the past week. She heard him scoff. And had she been looking at him, she would have seen him roll his eyes. Still, his arms came around her to ease the chills.

"Start feeling better," he said, as if she could help it. "You're slowing us down."

"I'll be fine," Treasta assured. "Don't worry about it. It'll pass."

It had been hard to forage in this region, something neither had much skill in, and the season made resources scarce. Miles back they had rested in the cellar of an inn, camping behind stacks of barrels during the night. They wandered the streets during the day, taking what they could from unsuspecting folks. At the markets, Treasta was apt at distraction—well-spoken when she wanted to be and good at fooling just about anyone who crossed her—while Davan, though somewhat boxy in stature, would saunter coolly around the booths, swiping goods as he saw fit. It was a good set up while they recouped supplies and rested, but after a few nights, they had lingered a little too long in the cellar and were found. The watchmen were called, everything they had stolen was confiscated, and they were kicked from the town. They left with the little food they carried and with the weapons hidden on their bodies.

Treasta walked herself to a make-shift bed in another room, the mattress long splayed open, the hay scattered about. She patted down the old fabrics and dirty linens left behind decades or more ago by whomever abandoned the homestead.

Davan didn't follow. He threw his head back, looked toward the ceiling beams and watched the waning day's rays until the night blinked them away. He lit a candle, stood and watched Treasta from the threshold of the next room. Stopping at the abandoned homestead was meant to be for one night. They were not only fatigued, but the weather was unpredictable, some days raining ice; other days a light shower of snow coated the dry, rocky terrain only to melt the next morning as a frigid wind blew, warning of winter. If Davan had it his way—he turned from Treasta, disappearing down the rickety stairs and stepping outside—he'd continue without her.

On foot, it had been difficult. They needed horses, a task that ultimately was abandoned once the watchman barred them from the last town they had traveled through. Davan cursed himself for messing up. *He never messed up.* And now there was *this.* He rammed his foot into a fence, knocking the failing boards to the frost-kissed earth before picking them up one by one then to splinter them against the frozen ground. An angry scream escaped his lungs.

He didn't see inside the dark frame of a second-story window Treasta's moonlit face, her blue eyes wide and watching.

The next morning, the ice-cold air invaded their rest. Having curled into the other for warmth, neither Treasta nor Davan had slept well. His heartbeat in her ear would have once soothed her, but as dawn cracked over the horizon and the rays of a low sun splayed through the shutters, the beating echoed like war drums with his uneven breaths. Treasta shut her eyes, hesitant to move.

Davan held his hand toward the light. An orange streak cutting across his palm was absent of warmth. The cold of the night settled across the Altan Highlands, seeping into the day. Two mornings ago, they had awoken to a soft blanket of white outside. It had melted by noon, but the next snowfall could stick.

Davan nudged Treasta. "The weather's good."

She swallowed back air and exhaled.

"*Get up.*"

The sharpness of his words made her nervous, but she couldn't let him see that.

He pushed her from him. "*Now,* or we won't make it to Herra before dark. And then what, huh?"

What she wanted to say as she caught herself on the floor: *I'm so miserable. I'm sick and I hurt and I'm hungry and I'm tired. I'm so very tired, Dav. I should never have come. I'm only slowing you down. You hate me, don't you?*

What she did say: "How much further?"

Treasta stood, held her balance on the wall, and took a deep breath. Once she got her legs moving again, maybe she'd feel better. All this idling wasn't good for anyone. She needed to be better for Davan. He didn't hate her, she realized. He was just upset that they weren't as far as either of them had expected to be by now. They had pushed themselves too hard in the beginning to get ahead of the others. *She* had pushed him and herself.

Davan's silence spoke his uncertainty. He stared at the clean trail swept up from Treasta's standing. The disturbed gray dust floated into his vision; the stark division from its resting place on the floorboards and where she had lain appeared like a ghostly outline of his lover and partner in crime.

Davan gathered the tattered clothes they had been sleeping on as he wrestled with his thoughts. He asked her to join him on the mission. She didn't even hesitate. She knew the risks. *If she dies*, he told himself while slipping tunics over his head, *that's her fault, not mine.* He pulled a tattered gown embroidered with pinstripes over Treasta's head and then a long-sleeve shirt and a knee-length vest—its pockets would keep her hands warm.

Treasta shoved him away. "I don't need you to dress me," she said, her dried lips cracking. She pressed the sleeve against the wound; the little blotches of blood were near-invisible against the dark fabric. Allowing Davan to care for her would only add to his burden. "Ain't much daylight this time of year." She looked at Davan, and he saw a glimmer in her eye. "We'll get there, 'kay? Whatever it takes, it'll be ours," Treasta said, referring to the treasure they and their fellow guildmates were after. She sat down in a nearby chair, balancing on its three legs. "Remember what I said before we left?"

Davan cocked his head, taken aback by her shifting tone, but pleased to see his Treasta acting normal again. "Yeah, yeah, yeah. Promised we'd win no matter the cost." He was beginning to doubt this. Childish hope. *Her* insincerity. "I never forget."

Treasta began wrapping her hands and feet with linen scraps before slipping on her boots. She reassured: "Unstoppable you and me are, Dav. *You're* unstoppable." She forced her smile wider. "Everyone knows it. They can't stop you. They'd be fools." There was that smirk she hadn't seen in forever cutting into his cheeks, and as she chuckled a just as insincere chuckle, she added: "*They will fear you.*" Yes, that was what he needed to hear to ease him, to keep his ire at bay. When he turned away to gather supplies, she let out a slow exhale, having held her breath for too long.

She sipped water from a glass bottle and deposited it into a satchel she slung over her shoulder as he strapped a pack to his back lightened by a lack of goods. Davan carried two knives, one on each side of his hips. Treasta kept a small blade strapped on her thigh under the skirt and carried a phial hidden on her body, the nonfatal liquid inside with a potent smell that could make even a giant sleep.

On their trek, the rising sun's light was deceiving of warmth. Treasta's feet ached, her stomach ached, and her body ached, but she couldn't let Davan see her pain. They knew Herra wasn't much farther from what a vendor at the town they were thrown from had said: "If you're in a rush, you should keep the crag in sight, but the terrain's rougher off the road." It was rougher than anticipated, with narrow ridges in some places, dark rocky outcroppings from deep within the earth jutting through the soil. The more weathered spots left piles of broken-down, jagged stones that shifted as they climbed. Cresting the next outcropping, they spotted the white rockface of the crag that stretched for miles southward.

As the day continued, clouds set in. Davan and Treasta found a spot to rest.

In Treasta's mind the crag never ended: the bright cliffside stretched for eternity, wrapping the land until no land was left to wrap and then wrapping in on itself, wrapping in on her. The world turned hazy on the edges of her vision: Davan was just a shadow; the shape of her name muffled on his voice. Not his voice. A low female voice seeping from the edge of somewhere not here.

She came to.

"What was that?"

"Hmm?"

"It was like you weren't there. I was talking to you."

"You were?" A pause. "You were."

Her chest became heavier, and for a moment she felt like she was choking on nothing but her thoughts as an unidentifiable terror took residence in her body. "Maybe this was a mistake." The spiraling crag came to an abrupt stop, as Treasta realized she misspoke.

Davan's tone darkened, words spitting from his mouth: "We are not turning back." Then, a deep breath. "This is important to me—*to our future*," he reminded. "One moment you're fine, the next you're not.

And, frankly, I don't know what to do. You want to go back, fine. But I won't forgive you."

"No!" She lowered her tone: "No. … I didn't mean it."

"I'll get to be in charge under Fylle." This again. It was all he talked about. "And once Fylle is gone, the guild will be mine. Don't you *dare* fuck this up for me."

Treasta froze, inhaled, and then nodded her head. This wasn't the Davan she knew back home in Galgaya. After they got their hands on the treasure and returned to the guild, this would all go away, she told herself. Something about this wilderness was making him like this.

"Look," he began with a sigh, trying to cool his temper, "once we get to Herra, let's recoup, yeah?" He started counting on his fingers. "I'll find you a goddamn feast. Horses. Wine. Name it, it's yours."

The feeling in her chest didn't fade. Maybe it was because she had never left the coastal city they called home before now. Maybe it was her doubt. Maybe it was just her aching stomach. But nothing seemed to settle quite right—the food, anything she drank, even Davan's words brought little hope. It had been almost two months since they left. Their boss, Fylle, sent them with nothing, and now the mission felt like it was for nothing so long as Davan couldn't be appeased. Legend spoke of a flute that turned its player to gold, crafted by the dwarves of old. The yellow glimmer of the instrument was burned on Davan's brain. His hands itched.

What if we don't win? she wanted to ask. Instead, she said, "Once I get a proper meal in my stomach, I'll feel like new. I'm not giving up, Dav. I'd never give up on you. Swear it." Her words sounded convincing enough that Davan's expression softened.

A couple weeks ago, they had run into a cohort from their guild—the Dubilee Tribe, as it was called. Aeran was alone. Elsie was arrested miles back, and he had continued to Wesser without her. They learned from Aeran that Kim killed Kleri. Pleased to know his guildmates were failing, Davan chortled when he learned of Kleri's death, a reaction that Treasta had at first ignored, but since then, she had been thinking about. She couldn't imagine doing that to Davan. While she would only kill when necessary—and she had more than once—he gave little thought to human life.

Treasta looked around. The Altan Highlands of Wesserland—dry, vacant, yellow grasslands absent of forests—were unforgiving and so very different from the coastal city they called home.

Davan broke their last loaf and passed it to Treasta. She cautiously ate, prepared for another stomachache, trying to distract the feeling by remembering how fellow guildmates often whispered about Davan's brown-nosing. They called him weak. Treasta didn't know whether Davan knew this. Either way, Treasta loved him—that's what she told herself—doted on him, despite his orneriness. She reminded herself about how he protected and saved her many years ago.

She watched the muscles in his face contract and retract as he chewed.

"Are you happy?" she asked.

He continued eating and sucked back snot with a sniffle as his nose dripped in the cold. He didn't answer right away, and Treasta wasn't sure whether she should have risked the question. It was too complicated, too deep—Davan didn't do "complicated" or "deep" well.

"What do you mean?" he asked.

She eased, glad he didn't dismiss her and thought about her question, trying to understand why she asked it. "I … I don't know." The question was less for him than it was for her. "Are you?"

"I guess," he said with a shrug. "I'll be happy when we get our hands on the treasure and when we get home." With a mouthful of food, he scoffed. "What is happiness anyway?"

What is happiness anyway? Treasta stared at the golden crust. *Of course I'm happy,* she longed for Davan's words. *I'm happiest when you're by my side.* Flakes of bread collected on the ground as she picked at the loaf. *What is happiness anyway?* She sighed as she replayed the words in her head again. Not even a "yes" or "no"—an "I guess."

"Once I'm marshal"—as the thief-king's right-hand man was called—"I'll get to call the shots," he said. "Then, well, you know, I'll get what I deserve, no matter the cost."

Davan flashed a grin. She humored him, exchanging a toothy smile and forced a soft laugh. She could count past her fingers the number of times Davan reminded her. "You've always called the shots in my book." She winked—the tease, it was what he liked.

He leaned toward her, eyed her lips. "Yeah? You know, if I become thief-king, you'll be my thief-queen."

Treasta stopped him from kissing her. "I want a crown."

His laugh was airy and hot. "A crown, huh?"

"You heard me. I deserve one, don't I, if I'm going to be your thief-queen?"

"Does milady prefer gold or silver?"

"*Ahem*. Does *Your Royal Majesty*," she corrected.

His eyes rolled inside his head. "Excuse me, Your Royal Majesty, Highness, Excellency, Great One, *my Queen of Thieves*."

A laugh escaped her lips, and his weight pressed heavily into her through his kiss. For a moment, excitement roused her. Davan and Treasta—their names together always had a special ring—future king and queen of Dubilee. But the thought was cut short, as she shoved him and flew to her feet.

Treasta heaved over a rock, her body bent over its sharp edge as if the earth were ready to rip through her insides.

She heaved again, as if to feel her soul leave her body.

Treasta stared, hazy-eyed, at the bile and bread pooled just inches away.

THE WIND CUT THROUGH THE LAKESIDE TOWN.

Treasta, lightheaded, grasped Davan's arm as their feet left tracks behind them in the thin layer of fresh snowfall on the cobble street. It was dusk when they arrived, but gray clouds had swept over the land in the past hour, leaving the setting sun absent. The only indication of night was the fading of light from a diffused daytime glow to a soft steel blue. Herra, nestled between jagged hills, was larger than they expected, with docks stretching over water coated in a thin sheet of ice, boats unmoved in the stillness.

The market closed before their arrival, many shops shuttering with the falling of darkness. A lamplighter carried on from one lamppost to the next, igniting the last wick at the center of the town square. That's where Davan and Treasta rested along a fence, their bags cascading off their bodies onto the ground. Treasta examined their surroundings, always surprised at how similar everything was to back home. Truly, Treasta didn't know what to expect leaving Galgaya, but she found most interactions with locals to come with ease, save for her foreign accent, which had and hadn't always worked in her favor when trying to con.

She hadn't the energy to play criminal with her skull painfully throbbing as she held her head. The sound of a creaking sign caught her attention.

"Let's get a room for the night, yeah?" Treasta said, pointing toward the yellow-walled Laughing Crow Inn across the square. "Come on, Dav," she tugged his arm, trying to pull him that direction, "we deserve it for getting this far, don't you think? *You* deserve it, my future thief-king."

Davan's pockets were empty. "We don't have any coin."

The gray-and-blue-painted sign continued teetering in the wind. Treasta had an idea.

She removed the long vest she had been wearing, bound it into a ball and placed it under the skirt of her gown. A lump appeared as if she were pregnant. Then she ordered Davan to give her another article of clothing. He stripped himself of one of the layers he was wearing, and she balled it up and stuffed it under her gown.

"Come on," Treasta said and started toward the Laughing Crow Inn, walking with an exaggerated hobble.

Davan followed her lead.

Lingering along a tight alley not far from the Laughing Crow Inn, a hooded figure watched as Treasta stuffed her dress with fabrics and plumped up her thin frame with the roundness of the moon before she and Davan disappeared inside.

The door opening and closing alerted the innkeeper at the counter that someone had entered the establishment. A bright, "Welcome in," and a gentle smile greeted the figure, but the figure exchanged no pleasantries, instead completing a quick scan of the surroundings before giving Davan or Treasta a chance to glance the sweeping of a cloak passing by—though they seemed rather preoccupied maintaining their own ruse.

Inside the restaurant, the figure found an empty table, tugging on the hood of her cloak to better conceal her face in shadow, but she hadn't gone unnoticed by some of the locals. Greasy men gaped in her direction, taking notice of the secretive stranger sitting alone. The figure wiped her nose on her sleeve, sucked back snot dripping from being outside in the cold too long. Briefly catching the men's glances, she spat on the floorboards and reclined. From here she had a good view of Davan and Treasta, watched how they worked the innkeeper, saw how the innkeeper fell for their little scheme. The hooded figure enjoyed having the upper hand, and an even more satisfying was realizing how easy it would be to "take care" of them, just like she did with the others she had crossed since leaving Galgaya.

The figure watched as Treasta wooed the innkeeper with her woeful story, rubbed her fake belly, but the woman was too taken by the tale—even as plainly exaggerated it was—to notice the dimpling in the gown each time Treasta's hand pressed on it.

The hooded figure rested her head in her palms, leaning toward the direction of Davan and Treasta. But the idleness of the restaurant made blending into the room difficult, and the unwashed men who she had caught ogling her minutes ago had yet to mind their business. They whispered among themselves, threw glances in her direction, and exchanged words. A quick flash of silver glinted as a man pulled money from his purse, sliding it across the table to his friend, making bets on what she looked like, whether she was actually a woman—her boyish figure often left men confused—and whether the figure was worth something in the sack. She tried to sit back, tried to be less suspecting, but it was clear their curiosity wouldn't waver. The figure came to her feet and retreated to the bar, losing sight of Davan and Treasta.

She called the bartender over, ordered ale in a somewhat raspy voice, deeper than what most would suspect of her size. She set down a half bit coin; the bartender's eyes came alight impressed at how well polished the copper was. "I can practically see my smile in it."

When he set down a beverage and walked away, she rolled her eyes and sipped. It was more bitter than she preferred, but at least she looked less conspicuous. Anything not to draw the attention of others.

"Why hide that face?" a voice oozed from her left side—one of the oily men.

She inhaled, held her breath a moment to collect herself. Admittedly, she knew she could be reactive, especially against men's advances. Pigs. She had thought she was dressed masculine enough to avoid situations like this.

She turned toward him and when he caught a glance of the scars on her pale face and her dark hair cut close to her scalp, he stood up, said, "Pardon me," and walked away. As he retreated to his table, as he forked over the stack of sterling bits he had wagered, the hooded figure let out a low laugh as she drank, taking pleasure in the grotesque creature's reaction. Good, she thought, hearing him say, "No, I won't fuck that," because she'd kill him before he had the chance to even try.

From over the rim of her mug she caught a glimpse through the open doors of the kitchen the outline of Treasta's faux pregnant stomach. She and Davan were following the clerk down a hallway on the other side of the inn.

As the door shut, Treasta shook out her dress; the bundled-up fabric cascaded to the floor. A proud smile flashed on her face as she set the satchel on the small bed. Having taken pity on a false tale of a dying mother and Treasta's faux pregnancy, the clerk gave them her cheapest room near the kitchen. The room itself wasn't large, its ceiling rather low. The last light of the day faded and the lamplight from the back alleyway provided a soft glow inside from the window.

"That," Davan pulled her toward him, "was brilliant." He held her close, ran his hands through her hair and brushed the strands away from her face. As she parted her lips to invite a long celebratory kiss, his nose scrunched tightly, and he swiftly concealed it in the crook of his arms.

"Gods, Treasta, your breath." A disappointed sigh escaped his lungs, and he instead lit an oil lamp resting on a small table in the corner of the room. He sat in the chair next to it, trying to take in fresh air seeping inside from the cracks along the poorly sealed window.

Hunkering into herself, Treasta brought her hand to her mouth, smelled her breath stained with the sour remnants of puke. Her eyes lowered, feeling the cold draft lingering on the room.

A knock at the door startled them. Treasta tucked herself under the covers and turned away from the door as she curled into herself to hide her nonexistent stomach.

Davan pulled the door open a crack to see the clerk standing with a tray.

"It's on the house," she said, and passed it to Davan. "I'm sure you're famished. Got to keep the baby well fed if you trying to get to Wesser. Long way, isn't it?"

Such kindness wasn't unexpected, but Treasta didn't allow the gesture to bring any guilt into her heart, instead concentrating on Davan's goals and his future, thinking about Dubilee and remembering the ocean, the smell of salt on the breeze, the noises of gulls and the business of the streets. Get the bounty. Go home. Bounty. Home.

Two bowls of chowder, a side of potatoes and vegetables in colors Davan had never seen before were nicely placed on the platter. The innkeeper held up a bag and gestured for him to take it. Its weight had knocked him off balance, and the tray nearly slipped from his hand.

"I hope it's not too much," the woman said as Davan planted his foot to catch himself from falling.

He hesitated to thank her, but he managed to say, "Thank you for this." It didn't feel genuine, but he did sound surprised, because he was, and that was maybe enough.

"I'll pray for your journey."

And as she walked away, Davan nudged the door shut with his foot.

Treasta sat up, examined the tray, and then ruffled through the bag while on the bed. At least a dozen and a half of apples, loaves of bread wrapped in cloth. Digging deeper she found a scarf, hat and coat fit for her faux pregnant body. A knitted cowl and two pairs of gloves and thick wool socks were also there. She grinned.

"We don't deserve this," Davan said as he set the tray down and leaned on the wall with crossed arms. He wiped his nose on his sleeve. What he meant: *You, Treasta, don't deserve this.* If he left tonight with the goods, then he'd have double the supplies for his journey. He'd be able to get twice as far—no—thrice as far on his own.

"Since when do you care?" Treasta let out a laugh finding a purse. "Dav, look." Her face came alight, and she started counting the sterling bits across the mattress. One, two, three … ten, eleven, twelve … thirty. Thirty silver coins at their disposal all because she pretended to be pregnant—a trick she would be sure to remember.

She told him to pass her his pack, and in the silence, she transferred everything the woman gave them into it, then examined the failing threads along the seam of the bag's flap, sucking on her teeth, holding back feelings of inadequacy spurred by his dismissal of her kiss. Davan never turned her down like that before. She tried to let it go, but she couldn't control the sadness. He, she realized, was making her feel this way. He thought he was better than her. No! No … get that out of your head, she told herself. Davan was good, he had always been so loving, always took care of her and put her first. … Right?

Treasta cleared her throat, hoping he wouldn't hear her choked back emotion on her voice. "We just need transportation now. If we can get a couple horses, we could get ahead of the others."

"We don't know who's left," Davan said. Frowning at the thought others could be ahead of them, he sat back down. Old, it nearly buckled. "Aeran I doubt will get far. Elsie was arrested. I can imagine at least four others who gave up. Probably never made it out of Kildore. Kim, well, she's got that limp. It'll slow her down."

Treasta agreed. And then thought she should at least try to eat something, even though she struggled to hold anything down. Starting with the potatoes, Treasta waited to take a bite, then continued eating when she realized her stomach wasn't reacting. She found herself biting into an apple—its juices, sweet, gushed over her lips and down her chin—and then went in for more potatoes and vegetables. Groaning, she said with cheeks full and still chewing, "A feast, Dav, just as you promised." A spoonful of chowder followed by another crunch into the fruit's flesh. It was a combination she didn't expect to pair well but it did, and it satisfied. The anger and frustration Treasta had been feeling just moments ago vanished.

Then she realized Davan was staring with disgust.

"What is it? Did I do something?"

Davan picked up the other bowl and quietly ate, shrugging off her behavior. The chowder's warmth on his palate brought him at ease, and as he ate, his felt the muscles in his body loosen. An unexpected moan of satisfaction escaped his lips, and the draft in the room seemed to fade. He couldn't remember the last time he had a warm meal, but the pleasure he was experiencing—the flavor, the texture, the heat, the fullness he felt within his stomach—made him forget his guilt. Neither Davan nor Treasta had room for it anyway.

"You're right," he said with a casual shrug. "I don't care. And on the morrow, I'll get us horses, couple of strong and powerful beasts that can ride for days and days. You won't have to worry about walking ever again. You have my word."

Treasta had fallen asleep not long after eating, and Davan was too awake to rest. So, he stepped into the cold night; the pavement was slick with a thin layer of ice that had formed from the misty air, and he caught himself slipping, grabbing onto the door frame, then carefully walked with hands in pockets.

The city-state of Wesser was still maybe a few weeks or even a month out. Could have been sooner, he scoffed and cursed under his breath.

Davan eventually wandered to the town's south side, found his way down an alley, where hermits curled under awnings desperate to escape the cold.

A couple exiting from a door nearly collided into each of Davan's shoulders. He made a nasty comment, but neither paid him any mind, distracted by one another. Somehow, despite being a foreigner, he felt invisible. He supposed he didn't look much different than the locals; his accent could be discounted as one of a poor and impoverished fellow, and like most people from Wesserland, his skin was naturally a golden tan; his brown hair and hazel eyes were what set him apart from the locals' dark brown to raven-black locks and dark eyes.

Davan passed through a red-framed door, where the couple had exited. No sign indicated the business's specialty, but inside it was clear that it had a specific type of clientele. An image of the couple walking outside flashed through his mind, and he realized this tavern doubled as a brothel upstairs. For a moment Davan, thought about turning around—normally he would have, a bit abashed by such things, but he took another step and then another until the door felt yards behind him. Davan was twenty-one, and sex wasn't something he ever shied away from, but this was different. So many women, beautiful women with beautiful faces and figures sauntering around the room and interacting with their delicate touches and smooth voices to soothe patrons.

The woman at the bar waved. He took a seat at the only empty, red leather-padded stool. Her nails tapped on the countertop in perfect succession—one, two, three, four, one, two, three, four.

"Hi, sweetie," she said. "Fancy a drink? Only one sterling bit."

He slapped a coin on the counter. She took it and in return she poured a whiskey.

"You seem bothered," she said.

Davan didn't recall anything about his demeanor that would have given him away, but the woman somehow saw right through him.

He wasn't too interested in talking. She took notice and left him alone to sip his beverage. But he didn't sip it; he shot it back in a single gulp and then slapped another sterling bit onto the counter.

She smirked, amused and intrigued. And as she set down another drink, she said, "Ah, so *nothing* is bothering you, huh?"

Davan flashed her a look and lifted the glass to his lips. He maintained eye contact with the woman as the cool rim touched his mouth. His gaze fell to her lips as she licked them, and she watched him with a knowing gaze. He shot his drink back, slapped another coin on the counter, and then shot back a third.

"I'm Oda," she said. And he felt a beating inside his chest guided by an excitement he had never felt until her introduction. She held out her hand for him to take, and he drunkenly kissed it.

"Davan," he said. "I'm Davan. Just Davan."

"Well, Davan *just* Davan, I imagine something must be …," and she looked him up and down with her night-dark eyes, "… ailing you. Perhaps I can help."

"I don't know if you have the remedy."

"I keep a wide assortment of medicinal goods in my … office. Some are more potent than others. They say I'm quite the healer."

"Potent?"

"It depends." Oda's hips swayed, and she cocked her head with a sly, taunting smile difficult for him to look from. "Some people can only handle certain varieties, while others like the *harder* stuff."

She leaned over the counter, her soft breasts revealing themselves just enough. "Oh, Davan," she said. "Oh, sweet, sweet Davan just Davan." And she walked her fingers across the bar and up his arms until her hand cupped his face. She rubbed his cheek with her thumb and watched his lips and then his eyes, lulling him into a trance.

He couldn't keep his breath steady, felt a tightness in his chest that could be loosened only one way. He wanted her lipstick to stain the fabric of his trousers and collar of his tunic. He was so desperate to have her feel his body the way Treasta did before she had fallen ill. He wanted to crush her under his weight, for her to cry out to him to stop stop stop, but he wouldn't stop, couldn't stop. He needed her, and she clearly needed him. Oh, Oda. Sweet, sweet Oda—a name so soft couldn't be owned by anyone else.

"Oh, Davan." Oda, she was at least twenty years his senior, but his desires cared not to differentiate between a woman in her forties and someone his own age. She rubbed his hand. Swayed her hips some more; her voice increased pitches at the end of her sentences. "Come on, love," she said and tugged at his hand. "Let's talk in private."

Once on his feet, the room spun. Oda guided Davan to the back and up a set of stairs. There she led him into a room lit with candles and where a fireplace was burning. The heat inside was overwhelming against his already flushed cheeks hot with desire and drunkenness.

Davan felt a sweat come over him, and Oda sat him down in a sofa chair, situated a pillow behind his back, and stood over him.

"Sweet Davan." The air on her breath was like roses.

He felt her weight on him, her hands running up his shirt, working it over his head. This, Davan thought, was freedom.

She untied his trousers and knelt to bring his erection into her mouth.

Davan couldn't put to words the daze he was in, but he felt higher than the clouds, like he could talk among the stars and make any dream he had ever imagined into reality. Oh, Oda. Oh, sweet, sweet Oda. Just the echo of her name in his head ignited a dangerous blaze within him. Her eyes, her mouth taking in every inch of him, the motion of her body, the chills she brought his body when she touched him haunted him in all the ways Treasta never could.

Stumbling his way down the street, he caught himself falling and leaned against a wall.

He rubbed his eyes and looked around now second guessing whether he was going the right direction.

Tired, Davan slid onto the pavement and nodded off.

Over the next couple hours, Davan came in and out of sleep. Davan knew he needed to get up, but finding the strength was difficult, so he opted to rest a little while longer. The next he awoke, he could barely open his hands or extend his legs; the cold night worked its way into his joints and claimed the spaces between his bones.

He struggled to his feet, solely driven by the thought of freezing to death, and felt a lingering drunkenness weighing him down as he wavered in the direction of the Laughing Crow Inn.

Davan stumbled inside, the door shutting heavily enough to cause the building to shake some, and his steps echoed down the hall to the room where Treasta slept. He thought about what he would tell her. Needed a reason for why he was drunk and out late. No. He stopped himself from looking for any more excuses. He refused to feel guilty, wanting nothing more than to feel the thrill of tonight again. Such excitement had long escaped him until now.

"Hello, Davan."

He had yet to look up after opening the door but knew it wasn't Treasta's voice. Then he saw her face, scars lit in the lamplight, a polished blade glimmering at Treasta's throat. Davan suddenly sobered.

"Aeran said you were arrested," he said.

"Piece of shit left me there to rot."

Davan's gaze passed from Elsie to Treasta who held her composure.

"Don't do anything stupid," he said, his words slurring some.

Elsie's laugh revealed a chipped tooth Davan didn't remember there being. "You think I'm going to just let you get to Wesser before me? Please."

She pointed with her nose to a loose bundle of rope on the bed.

"Tie her ankles."

Davan unraveled the rope and just as he knelt at Treasta's feet, Treasta threw her head back into Elsie. Elsie fell backward, catching herself on the table. The lamp wobbled off and shattered, fanning a puddle of oil across the floor, which ignited instantly.

The three scrambled.

Elsie kicked Davan in the face.

Davan managed to get a hold of her legs, dragging her toward the bed and tying her to its post. Racing against the spreading flames, he bound her hands.

"We got to get out of here, Dav," Treasta called as she gathered everything. They needed to escape not just to avoid being caught in a fire, but also to flee town. The clerk knew their faces.

Davan and Treasta raced out of the room, hearing Elsie scream after them "to get back here!"

Outside, from down the road, they looked back, waiting for the red blaze to come aglow in the night.

The colors of fire began to flicker in the crystallized fog.

Neither said another word.

3

THE SOUND OF A BELL FILLED TREASTA'S HEAD—the town awaking in its entirety, residents rushing to help douse the blaze as they lined up from the inn to the well and from the inn to the lake, hauling and passing buckets of water for naught, the shouting, the crying, the innkeeper who watched with horror, the guests inside the inn fleeing hungry flames, the smell, the falling ash … Treasta scanned the people gathered, her stomach in a knot, as she searched for Elsie, but she wasn't anywhere to be found, and Treasta, while somewhat relieved that she was dead, couldn't stop wondering what it must have been like to suck in fire as a final breath.

Until sunrise, the duo lay low, slipping from town, then camping about ten miles out where they found a shallow cave along the walls of a rocky ravine. Below, a river cut through the earth; above, a long, wooden bridge spanned from one side to the other. Davan and Treasta could relax just out of sight from anyone traveling along the highway.

Before fleeing the inn, Treasta had managed to gather everything. The hat and cowl, the scarves, socks, and gloves kept enough of the cold off their skin that it made traveling by foot more bearable. She massaged her sock-dressed feet, trying to ease the soreness.

"What happened to getting us horses?" she asked. "We *need* horses. Or we're not going to get anywhere. And the last set we had you got them stolen."

Davan drew a long breath, listened to Treasta yap and complain, as if she were ungrateful for everything he had done for her in the past decade. As he stood, he demanded, "Shut the fuck up about it," and bumped past Treasta to take a piss over the ravine.

Treasta shrunk as he slammed into her and rubbed her tender breasts that seemed to only get worse as they traveled. They had been aching for weeks, and she thought bundling up enough would help relieve the soreness, thinking the cold had something to do with it.

Davan returned and sat down where he could look out into the ravine to watch the rushing river below. They decided to stay there for the rest of the day. It was a safe spot for a fire and just out of the elements enough that, should it snow, they would have somewhere to hunker down for a while.

"Do you think anyone has gotten to Wesser yet?" Treasta asked. She just didn't know what else to talk about with him anymore.

Davan hoped not. That bounty was his—he already claimed it and would do anything to get it should someone else beat him to it. "I doubt it."

Silence.

"Do you think we'll be the first ones there?" she asked, trying to fill the quiet.

He shrugged not in the mood to talk.

The wind's howl cut into the cave.

When Davan had asked Treasta to join him on this mission, she thought how foolish he was to even consider it. She thought him foolish, of course, but at least she could keep an eye on him. Sometimes Davan's decision-making got him into trouble, got people hurt. Treasta would often have to talk him out of an idea that she thought was too rash, so staying in Galgaya never really felt like an option. She imagined how it would feel to continue about her life for months before possibly seeing him again, likely to become trapped in her own mind, living out their lives together in her fairy tale house as the wife of a cobbler with two kids, while her awake self would worry whether Davan would return. The not knowing—that was what brought her to saying yes, but Davan also didn't take "no" for an answer.

Treasta took in the silence between them, looking him over and searching for anything to tell her to stop loving this man. She couldn't find anything. He was perfect. She crawled to him, placed her head in his lap and took his hand. With his free hand Davan combed his fingers through her hair and looked upon her with a softened expression. She kissed his palm and placed it over her heart so he could feel how he made it beat. Treasta shut her eyes.

That night, Davan and Treasta drifted to sleep with the campfire burning. Davan awoke a couple times to stir the coals, but eventually he fell into a deep sleep; the embers dimmed into a low burn.

Treasta's eyes shot open. She didn't move, thinking of having heard the shuffling of feet. Davan lay asleep next to her. She could feel his breath on her neck as he snored. The flashing of light from a lamp being set down at the cave's mouth revealed a long shadow of a figure.

Her knife was still attached to her thigh, but any movement she feared would startle the stranger into attacking her. She kept still. The figure rummaged through their bags and then picked up the lamp and wandered off.

Treasta carefully stood not to disturb Davan and quietly followed the fading lamplight through the dark. She crept, keeping her distance in the moonlit night. The jagged terrain was a bit rough to manage, but she noticed the figure led her down a path toward the river. The sound of its rushing masked her footsteps as she closed some of the distance between them. He had Davan's pack. She could see his bright hair, far lighter than her own, was chopped shorter in the front and longer in the back. Treasta thought about how she would retrieve their goods. The man didn't seem all that bigger than her. He was kind of small but had wide shoulders. She could probably take him if she sneaked up from behind.

Treasta reached for her knife and crept a little closer. She adjusted her grip, repositioned herself, and took another step.

The man stopped. "I know you're there."

If she didn't move, maybe he would disregard her presence as an animal.

He turned around, held the light in her direction and searched the dark with just his gaze.

She got a better look at his face: pale, somewhat hollow, his scruff was nearly translucent on his chin.

Just wait. When he turns to carry on, attack. Shove the blade right through his neck.

Her grip on the knife tightened as she prepared for her next move.

But he didn't carry on.

Instead, he set the pack down and sat cross-legged on the ground.

Treasta wasn't positioned well to move. The rocky ravine didn't give her any options to get around him, and if she returned to camp, he would spot her.

There was a third option.

Treasta hunkered a tad deeper and aimed. But when she threw the blade at him, expecting it to stick into his chest, it bounced off landing an arm's length away.

He rolled his eyes—that wasn't the first time that had happened—and grabbed the blade, looking it over, and then laughing said, "A blade for a child?"

Treasta stared wide-eyed, frustrated, and now scared. She didn't know whether to stay where she was or step into the light.

When she revealed herself, cautiously with her hands raised, he smiled.

"I wasn't sure which one you were, but I figured it was you. Your friend back there wouldn't have waited so long to attack me."

"I just want our bag back."

"Of course you do," he said.

She carefully stepped closer.

"I'm not going to hurt you. If I wanted to, I would have back there," and he motioned in the direction of her camp. "Your friend snores loud, you know."

Treasta had a hard time relaxing. He was uncanny, and it unsettled her how confident he was. "What was that?" she asked.

"What? Oh," he realized, "you mean why you couldn't hurt me?" He laughed lightly and shook his head. "No."

"No, what?"

He stood up, grabbed the bag, and kept walking down the path. "No. I'm not telling you my secrets. I trusted a girl with a secret once and it nearly got me killed. Maybe twice."

She chased after him and grabbed one of the straps, pulling until her arms were sore. He stood there, waiting for her to give up. And she did.

"Give me the bag," Treasta demanded.

"Or what?"

"My friend is a lot stronger than I am."

"And now he doesn't know where you've run off to. Smart."

Her face turned redder than it already was in the cold. "Look, that's all the food we got."

He paused. "And now it's all the food I have."

"I won't leave until you give it back."

The man looked over his shoulder momentarily and then shrugged.

Anger arose from within, and she acted faster than she could think. Treasta grabbed a sharp rock and chucked it at the back of his head with as much strength as she could muster. It struck him; his white hair stained with a blotch of red.

"Gods!" he grabbed at his scalp, winced, and bent over to collect himself. "You really do have good aim."

Treasta stood there shocked the rock did damage after the knife couldn't. She grabbed a larger stone, ran, and toppled over him, trying to smash his face.

He managed to block and dodge her attacks, but barely.

He shoved her off.

"Enough!" He threw the pack in her direction. "Fine, take it. But can you give me at least three apples."

She grabbed it, held it close, and held her ground. Three apples? Annoyed, she rolled the fruit in his direction. At the very least, it was a peace offering.

"How did that hurt you, but a blade couldn't, huh? What are you? Some kind of *gifted*?" she asked, referring to those who are born capable of harnassing magic.

The man sat there rubbing his head. "No, I'm not a damn gifted. I wish. You know how much easier my life would be?"

"Well, what are you then?"

"I'm human like you," he said.

She looked him over, saw his rounded ears. He wasn't even half Eldei? Surely with hair that white. Treasta realized at that moment that she had never met a half-elf before. Maybe they wouldn't have white hair like the Eldei of the Diresha Empire. Maybe they wouldn't have pointed ears either. The thought stumped her.

"When you look like me," he said, standing, "you got to carry a charm to protect yourself. Had one guy try to add me to his collection. What was it he said?" He pondered, the pause somewhat annoying Treasta. "Called me a 'perfect model' and 'specimen.'" He shuddered at the thought.

She didn't understand, and when he realized, he stepped closer.

His eyes were pale violet and carried a faint red hue with white eyelashes framing them. They had a slight wobble as he held her gaze. He grabbed her hand, degloved it, and held his cold palm flat against her warm palm. Such a pallor made her light complexion appear sun kissed.

"You're the first, I got to say, to try and kill me with a rock though. I'll remember that."

"What are you doing out here?"

"Surviving," he said. "I do better on my own anyway. You should go."

"Wait, no. Maybe you can help us."

"Help you? How?"

Treasta looked around, though her vision was limited to what the moonlight allowed her to see. "Do you know the land here?" He picked up the lamp, waiting for her to continue.

"I can pay you," she said. "Ten sterling bits."

"Ten? That's pennies. What do you expect me to do with ten sterling bits?"

"Fifteen."

He rolled his eyes, crossing his arms. "Fifty."

"Thirty-five."

He started back down the path. Treasta followed.

"Please, we don't really know where we're going. We're just trying to make it to Wesser. And we need to get there fast. I got word from my grandmother that my ma isn't well. I'm just trying to get there before she passes."

"I can get you to Wesser," he said. "But I need fifty sterling bits—scratch that. Fifty gold bits would do better. It's generous, but not too generous for such a job."

Fifty gold bits—she held her composure at the egregious request.

"You'll help us, then?"

He exhaled. "Yes, I'll help you."

"I don't know your name."

"It's Darius," he said. "But you can call me Chimes. How about we meet at the bridge at sunrise. How does that sound?"

Treasta nodded, and then shuffled, kicking a small stone. "One more thing," she said, her voice quiet, as if nervous. "Can we act like we never met before, then?" He eyed her with an inquisitive look but didn't ask. Instead, she said, "I just don't know how Davan—um, *my friend*—will react. He doesn't really like it when I talk to other men."

"And he's your *friend?*"

Another nod. "He's good. But I think it would be better for both of us if we pretend we're strangers."

Chimes tossed an apple, catching it, tossed it again, and it landed in his palm with a thud as she waited for him to say something. "Yeah, sure." He shrugged. "You've got a deal. Fifty gold bits, though," he said as he pointed his finger at her with a sly smirk.

Walking away, she heard a crunch as Chimes tore into the apple's flesh with his teeth.

4

BREAKING THE HORIZON, THE SUN WAS WELCOMED to a cloudless cerulean dome, the air less cold, the breeze having swept southeasterly. Treasta bent in half, held herself up by leaning on her knees as Davan continued to climb. He peered down from the top of the ravine, tilting his head, waiting. His voice echoed down the scarred earth, "You coming or what?" Then said, "You ain't going to puke again, are you?"

Yes, Treasta had puked again. The walk back to camp last night, while the gradual grade had taken its toll, and as soon as she returned to the cave, she vomited. Her insides splattering their supplies, waking Davan as some of it struck his face. He had jumped to his feet, drew his blade reflexively, but as soon as he realized what had happened, he cursed at her, wiping his face with her scarf and walking outside to rest against a rock nearby. "Make sure you clean everything up," he had told her.

You ain't going to puke again, are you?—his words sent a wave of shame over her. She had sat in the dark, the fire too dim to see at that point, and had wiped everything down with the scarf the nice woman at the inn had given her. Treasta didn't look up at Davan, who contemptuously watched from the ravine's edge, afraid to meet his gaze, knowing that look he would give her anytime she did something *wrong*—wrong to him. "I'm sorry. I'm sorry!" she had cried last night, but Davan had crossed his arms, set his head back, and shut his eyes.

"Hurry up!" he called, looking over the ravine.

But Treasta knew if she took another step, she would faint. She needed to sit, so she did, and from above she heard a groan, and from within she felt chagrined. Taking a deep breath, she caught her head in her palms as coldness seized her and her vision filled with a bright white light.

"Trea! Let's go!"

"I just need a minute!" she shouted, but even that was too much. A bout of nausea set in, her head spinning.

She needed food. She needed water. But Davan had taken the satchel and backpack with him.

She needed him.

To soothe herself, Treasta imagined Davan crawling into the ravine to tell her it would be okay, to give her something to nibble—his large hand on her back, his deep voice in her ear, saying, "It'll pass. Hang in there. It'll pass."

It'll pass. It'll pass ...

At the spell's fading, Treasta warily stood, balancing on the rocks. Carefully, she climbed, watched the placement of her feet, thought how easy it would be to slip at one misstep.

She collapsed over the edge.

Davan's boxy frame stood over her a dark shadow. He grabbed her arm, yanked her to her feet, handed her the satchel, and without a word, continued toward the bridge.

Slowly, Treasta dragged herself behind him, face hiding behind her wavy hair, eyes searching the dead grass under her feet, until Chimes' bright voice rang in the air.

"Ho, strangers!" he called, standing alongside a covered wagon attached to a brown horse. Oh, right, Treasta remembered, *him,* their deal. *Fifty gold bits.*

Davan paused shy of the road, observed the white-haired stranger chomping on an apple, eyed his wagon and goods.

"Need a ride?" Chimes' smile beamed. "I can get you where you need to go."

"Oh, I'm sure you can," Davan said, his voice low and snakelike. Just as Treasta placed her hand on his shoulder and before she had the chance to say anything, Davan rushed him. Hands on his throat, he pinned Chimes to the ground. He loosened his grip just enough to give passage to air. But the stranger, unfazed, lay in mud.

"Dav! Don't hurt him," Treasta said. She tried prying Davan away, but what little strength she had failed her. "Stop it! Stop! He can help us."

Davan let go, shot her a confused look and jumped to his feet. "Help us? Who is he?"

Chimes rolled away, coughing and catching his breath.

Rushing to the white-haired stranger's side, she helped him up and examined his neck, the tips of her fingers brushing with a gentleness across his skin. Her breath shuddered as the mark of Davan's grip took shape; Chimes bruised easily.

Davan drew his knives. "Who is he? You're acting like you know him."

"You need to calm down," she said, coming between them. "I've never met this man. I just thought maybe we could ask him for help."

"We don't need help."

Chimes stood, mud clinging to his clothes. "You don't seem like you're from around here." The ruse of not having met Treasta the night before may have failed them, but Davan didn't press any further. No, he'd deal with that later.

Davan belted his blades. "We don't need your help."

"You need my horse," Chimes said. He polished the apple clean and took another bite. "And my wagon." Bits of flesh flung from his lips as he spoke, some of it landing on Davan. "Whoops. Sorry," he said with a light laugh. "I just really like apples."

"I could kill you, you know," Davan said, and he meant it. Before he was planning on choking the stranger unconscious, but now more determined to take his horse and wagon, killing this stranger wasn't off the table.

"Look, I'm heading out," Chimes said. "If you want a ride, fine. If you don't, then that's also fine. I'll carry on my way."

Davan redrew a blade and pointed it. "Give me the wagon."

"Davan, *stop*," Treasta called.

Chimes' gaze shifted from Davan to Treasta and back. He smirked. "She said stop, didn't she?" Sharp silence. "Okay, tell you what. You kill me with that blade, and you can have everything I own. Including this apple," and he tossed the core in the mud between them.

Davan waited for the catch, but Chimes, smacking his lips and wiping them clean on his sleeve, didn't say anything more.

Davan lunged at the stranger. The stranger dodged his attack. Davan lunged again, and Chimes grabbed his arm, twisted it around, and took the knife right out of his hand.

"I'm more of a sword kind of guy," he said.

Davan drew his other blade.

"No." Chime tossed the knife his direction. "I said you have to kill me with this one."

Davan picked it up and went in for the kill. He expected Chimes to move, but he didn't. He just stood there with his hands folded behind his back, and when Davan thought the knife would surely strike the stranger's gut, he fell back, rebounding off some kind of invisible force.

Davan's gaze darted from the knife in his hand to the man's untouched stomach to his face. Chimes gave him a knowing smile. He's done this before. He's made bets on his life knowing no one could kill him, at least not with a blade.

"What in the name of the Forgotten are you?"

"Just a normal person like you," he said. "Anyway, do you want a ride or not?"

Davan and Treasta loaded their belongings onto the wagon and then took a seat inside. Chimes kept the front flap of the leather cover open to chat. And chat he did. After he introduced himself and asked where they were headed, he carried on in meaningless conversation. Davan and Treasta learned Chimes didn't like staying in one place too long. He had a hard time holding still—that's what he told them at least. Then, they learned Chimes didn't have any family, or if he did, he wasn't in contact with them. "I like being alone," he said. "It's easier this way. Don't got anybody to worry about and nobody to worry about me."

"Davan's my only family," Treasta said. "I mean, he feels like my only family living so far away."

"So, what are you doing here, then?"

Ah, right, Treasta nearly had forgotten. They weren't supposed to know one another before this morning. She almost caught herself saying something like, "You already know," but instead repeated the same story about the letter from her grandmother and her dying ma.

Davan squeezed her wrist. He mouthed the words, "What are you talking about?"

Treasta pulled her arm away from him, rubbing it, and mouthed, "Don't worry about it."

Don't worry about it? Davan threw his hands up in defeat, sat back and let Treasta keep talking.

"So, you're from Kildore, then?" Chimes asked.

"That's right."

"What part? Yeras?"

"Yeras?" Like the province? Treasta looked at Davan for answers.

"Yes, Yeras," Davan said.

"That's not too far from here," Chimes said. He appeared to being thinking aloud, and Davan wondered what was going through this stranger's head for him to be so eager to help.

Paranoia crept into his soul. He watched Chimes from his periphery suspicious of the stranger's intentions. Could he have been from one of the other thief tribes? If he were, he wouldn't have known about the mission unless Fylle sent news of the challenge.

Davan wanted answers, but he needed to be cautious of his approach. "Where are you headed to?"

Chimes shrugged. "Oh, wherever. This wagon is my home. I find it easier to keep moving than settle anywhere."

"How do you get by then?"

"I'm a scavenger, I guess you could say. And a trader of sorts. I get by how I get by."

Vague answer. Davan said nothing more. It was clear Chimes was leaving out information despite his chatter, surely hiding his true objective. Never had Davan met someone who could say a whole lot of nothing.

Miles they traveled until, by midafternoon, they came to a fork in the road. A sign read left to Burk Gorge, right to Grenna and when they didn't follow right to continue down the highway that would eventually take them to Wesser, Davan grabbed Chimes by the collar.

"Where the hell do you think you're taking us?"

Chimes lost control of the horse; the wagon jerked as it veered off the road and into a gully. Davan was knocked out of the wagon; Treasta rolled with it down the embankment; the horse let out the most terrible noise she had ever heard come from an animal; and Chimes grabbed a patch of tall, browning grass deeply rooted in the earth. He let go and slid down the gully, first running to his horse.

The beast kicked icy-cold mud into his eyes, and he fell backward, wiping them clean. "Sh, shh," he said, trying to ease his horse. "It's okay. Shh …"

Chimes unlatched the horse from the wagon. She didn't appear to be injured, just shaken. Treasta came to help him and held the chestnut mare still. She petted her nose, watched her eyes turning from fear to peace. The horse slowly blinked as if to tell Treasta she was okay.

"There, there, sweet girl." The horse nuzzled Treasta's stomach.

The wagon was completely on its side; its contents spilled across the gully.

Chimes, surprisingly calm, began gathering supplies, setting upright the one barrel he owned. Luckily it hadn't come open, but the small crate he carried that held his camping gear had emptied. He looked around, trying to locate where everything went, grabbing items one at a time and ignoring Davan who lay on the ground wincing.

Treasta stayed with the horse. They couldn't have her running off.

Davan sat up and held his wrist as it throbbed in pain. He sneered when his gaze briefly met Chimes'.

Chimes strapped bags to the horse. "Do you think you can get her up the embankment?"

Treasta nodded, but she wasn't sure. It was wet, slippery from freezing overnight and thawing during the day.

"Unload her and bring her back down. We'll have to abandon the wagon."

She did as Chimes asked. Luckily the gully wasn't too deep. She and the horse slipped a couple times, but eventually made it. She unloaded the bags and guided the mare back down.

Chimes strapped the mare with a saddle and rolled the barrel over. He asked for Davan's help with the barrel. It wasn't large but it was full, and there wasn't anyway Davan could assist with a freshly sprained wrist. Treasta volunteered instead, and while she struggled with the weight, with her help, Chimes tied it around the saddle so it hung on the mare's side. He then strapped the crate to her back, and Treasta took the last load up the embankment.

Chimes offered Davan his hand, but Davan hesitated. Watching Chimes with eyes burning with embers, he refused to show any indication of trust and came to his feet on his own.

"Think you can climb?" Chimes asked, ignoring the behavior.

Davan scoffed, stalking past, boots nearly peeling from his feet in the viscous mud until his next stride sank deeper, and he fell forward onto his injured wrist.

Chimes assisted him to his feet, but Davan shoved him away.

"I don't need your help."

Leaving Davan, Chimes climbed the embankment and watched with

Treasta as Davan toiled with his uninjured limb to grasp roots and claw into earth, nearly losing his balance and rolling down the slippery slope.

When he reached the top, he lay on the damp ground before coming onto his knees to catch his breath. Treasta dropped to his side, examining his swollen wrist. As she concentrated on wrapping it, Davan held Chimes' gaze. He needn't say a word for Chimes to know what ire brewed within him.

5

A blurry room spun. She shut her eyes, but the darkness behind her lids was like a rocking ocean in a moonless night. The scent of burnt flesh seared her nostrils. She tried sitting up but hadn't the strength.

"I think she's awake," said a voice.

She moved her fingers as a testament to her consciousness. Elsie opened her mouth to speak, but her throat was sore. The last thing she remembered was she had managed to break free from the rope, then a blaze overwhelmed her.

"Water," she managed to mutter.

Cool liquid eased down her throat and over her cheeks.

She opened an eye—something wasn't right—to a still somewhat blurry room.

"Hi," a soft, matronly voice.

Unable to see the woman from her left-side periphery, Elsie turned her head to locate a small nurse in pale-yellow robes, sitting with her hands neatly folded over her lap.

"You are a living miracle," the nurse said. "The vicar didn't know if you'd make it. We had to call on the pharmacist to treat you. Prayer only goes so far."

Elsie raised her arms, stiff lying in bed for who knows how long, and she felt her face: the left side bandaged, wet with a salve.

"I don't want your prayer," Elsie said with a sore throat.

The nurse ignored the comment and continued explaining how they treated her wounds. "Blessed Alia saved you."

Elsie found more bandages on her arms and legs as she tried pulling herself up. Too weak, she collapsed onto her back. The nurse pattered her arm, then fluffed the pillows.

"Where am I?"

"In Herra," the nurse said. "At the temple's infirmary."

There's a temple here? Elsie didn't remember seeing one, though she hadn't taken the time to explore the town once she spotted Davan and Treasta at the inn.

Her eyes narrowed, remembering. And the nurse saw the change in her demeanor.

"You need to rest," she said.

Groaning with frustration, a vengeful fury entered her heart, and angry was she that she couldn't throw the bedcovers aside and run after Davan and Treasta, tie them back-to-back on a pyre and set them alight, hear them *scream.*

"How long have I been here?"

The nurse began unwrapping Elsie's dressing to reveal blistering skin. "About a week." She handed Elsie a mirror. The blaze burned deeper than Elsie expected, destroying her left eye. Whatever was in that salve was preventing her from feeling anything.

"You should rest here until you're healed," the nurse said.

"I can't," Elsie said. "I got to be somewhere."

"You go out in the conditions you're in, and I can't imagine you'll make it long without our medicines and without Alia's divinity. Give it at least another week. We can see how you're fairing then."

Elsie held back the rage brewing. Another week? And even then, they might not let her leave? Fine. Her one good eye searched the ceiling, and she accepted her fate—punishment for killing Aeran.

Nearly two weeks ago in Waylin, sitting in a jail cell with her hands bound, her weapons confiscated, her satchel of goods out of reach, Elsie chewed through the ropes wrapping her wrists with a delicate patience, as the guard—a scrawny boyish man who could barely hold still—paced the room, coming and going from outside with a high-pitch whistle that alerted her whenever he neared. She spat rope bits onto a dirt-packed floor too dense to dig through and wiped trails of saliva from her chin on her sleeve, thinking about how Aeran had deserted her after they were caught robbing a wealthy fellow. Aeran, a man of too-much confidence, had held the knife to his back; the sound of his coat tearing was heard in the air as the blade dug into the fabric. He had his neck with his other hand as Elsie swiped his purse and pulled the glimmering rings from his digits.

"Take us to your home," Aeran's voice lingered with a bite of malice. But the man had hesitated, and Aeran dug the blade, the point of it pressing into his skin. "I said take us."

Elsie had stepped in, shoved Aeran back, standing a head shorter between the two men. "Not today," she told him.

Aeran belted his blade as the man took off running, but before they could react, a town watchman had appeared with the man, and Aeran had jetted to the nearest alleyway, leaving Elsie trapped. She saw Aeran's shadow from the corner of her eye, catching a glimpse of him running as the watchman took her into custody.

Wrists breaking free from the ropes, Elsie stood inside the jail cell, creeping to the bars and peeking around the room to assure the guard wasn't nearby. The watchman had failed to check all her person, not realizing the long earrings dangling from her earlobes weren't meant to be fashionable but rather a means to break through locks.

The cell door swung open; she took a quiet and cautious step out. But as she gathered her things, a prisoner called from another cell.

"Please, let me out. Let me out!"

She hooked the lockpicks back onto her ears and continued without paying the prisoner any mind.

"Hey!" he called. His voice carried in another direction outside the barred window on his cell. "Guard! Guard! She's getting away!"

She held her items close, tried zigzagging through the streets and alleys of Waylin, and jumped into a hay pile on the back of a wagon hoping to have dodged the scrawny, boyish guard—a tussle she was confident in winning, but valued her time and energy, and didn't want to draw more attention to herself than she needed.

The wheels creaked as they began to turn; the driver carted her to the next town on his delivery.

Rolling over jagged rocks jutting from the roadway, the wagon shuddered and shook, tossing Elsie beneath the haystack, a small crate toppling over her. Wincing, she rubbed her head and shoved the box away.

After a half-day's journey, the wagon came to an abrupt stop; the noise of hooves and turning wheels were replaced with the sounds of a busy town. Elsie unburied herself to meet eye-to-eye with the driver.

He jumped back. "What in the Forgotten!"

"Thanks for the ride," she said as she dropped a well-polished silver coin into his hand and headed off.

She didn't know where she was, at first wondering whether the man had brought her in the wrong direction, and she set herself back an extra day or two of travel to Wesser. But, after inquiring with some locals, she learned the small town she had found herself in was called Geer. Geer, but a half day's travel on foot, relied on Waylin for its goods, and in return the village provided crops from the nearby farms during harvest season. Elsie suspected Aeran couldn't have gotten far.

She began asking around. "Have you seen a man with long red hair tied at his neck? Freckles. Paler than I am. Ugly face." Aeran would be easily spotted among the dark-haired, warm-skinned people of Wesserland. But no one seemed to have an answer.

After procuring a horse, Elsie hurried along the road toward the next town, again asking the locals whether they had seen an ugly-faced man with red hair, pale skin, and freckles. A woman caught a glimpse of the scars on her face, shuddering and backing away. Another threw up her hands, forcing Elsie to take a step back and spook the horse. Elsie calmed the beast, exhaling with frustration.

"He's my friend," she said with concern to the next person she crossed. "And he's not"—she tapped her temple—"all there. I'm all he has."

The man pointed toward a tavern.

Inside, Aeran sat at the bar, his hand firmly around the mug as he lifted it to his lips.

"I hope you're enjoying yourself."

Elsie's cool, dark voice crept inside his head from behind, and Aeran jumped, with no time to spin around, as she slammed his face into the counter, pressing with all her weight.

"You left me," she hissed through her teeth.

"It wouldn't have done either of us any good if I stayed behind."

"You *left* me," and she pressed harder.

The cold metal of a blade ran along his ear. "Give me a reason not to kill you."

He stuttered, searching for the words, as the barkeep took notice and barked: "Get the hell out of my tavern!"

Elsie grabbed Aeran by the ear. His flailing knocked his drink to the floor, the glass shattering.

Outside, she dragged him into the dark of a dead-end alley and shoved him into the corner.

"Give me a reason not to kill you," she said again.

He raised his hands, cowering into the corner. "Look, you would have done the same."

Elsie would have kept him around so long as he benefited her, at least. She only asked to partner up with him because he was a good marksman. Bow, crossbow—it didn't matter: Elsie was a bad shot.

"I ran into Davan and Treasta back in Geer."

She tilted her head, intrigued enough to listen. "And?"

"They're not far ahead of us. We could easily catch up to them in Herra if we leave right now."

"Why would I want to catch up to them?"

"Because," he said, "Davan is after the same thing you want. He wants to be marshal of the Dubilee Tribe."

"Whoever said I wanted to be marshal?"

"Don't you? Isn't that why we're doing this?"

Elsie sucked in a breath through her nose, then let down the blade and hugged Aeran as she exhaled a long sigh.

"Oh, Aeran. See," looking him in the eyes, she massaged his cheek, "this is why we make such a good team. But why wait until I threaten to kill you to tell me something you knew this entire time?"

She plunged the knife upward through his stomach and behind his sternum, twisting it. He coughed blood over her shoulder.

"I don't give a fuck about impressing Fylle, you stupid imp."

6

"WHY?" DAVAN ASKED TREASTA, the one syllable sharp on his breath under the long and endless shadows of Burk Gorge. Alone and away from camp, the echo of their voices bounced between the other as they broke branches off bushes along the rocky walls. "Who the hell does something like this for free? Who the hell does he even think he is, huh? *Chimes*, kind of name is that? You need to stop batting your eyes at him, you know. You're always smiling and batting your lashes, like"—and Davan mocked her then scoffed.

Treasta swallowed as she snapped a twig, cradling it with the bundle of kindling growing in her arms. She focused on Chimes, trying to ignore the accusations. "Maybe he's bored." Fifty gold bits, a promise Davan didn't need to know about.

Davan laughed in disbelief. "And you *trust* him?"

Considering she was paying him, yes. Treasta was careful with how she answered. "We don't have any other choice. He knows the quickest way there. You think anyone else would know to take this road? Dav, you know I only have eyes for you. He can get us where we need to go, and we can ditch him."

Treasta always being right was like an old wound slowing peeling open, and Davan, to calm down, had to draw in a long breath. A rock skidded across the ground as he kicked it. Sure, he recognized how foolish this route would seem to their guildmates had they come across it, but, gods, how he wanted Chimes to be wrong about everything just so he could gloat, rub his pale face in the mud, hold him there long enough to drown.

"And what's with the," he rubbed the air in front of his chest where the blade should have struck Chimes. "You sure he's normal? He doesn't look normal."

Treasta rolled her eyes, having answered the question a dozen times already.

It took five days to cross through Burk Gorge. But on the night of the fourth day, they stopped to rest in a grotto, a well-known spot for travelers braving the road cast in unending shadow.

Unpacking supplies, they settled down for the night. Flames ignited inside the cave—no, a hovel, like it was once an outpost. At some point in the distant past someone had cut slender windows small but large enough to keep watch in a place along the gorge maybe thirty feet above the ground, reached by an eroding stairway carved into the stone and hidden behind an outcropping in the rock wall. Here, they could go undetected and rest safely, unlike the other nights when they slept in the open.

"So," Davan looked to Chimes from where he kept watch through the windows, "what's you're secret, anyway?"

Chimes pushed the embers around. "I'm sure you're just dying to know."

And that was the end of the conversation. Chimes continued talking on about the canyons, dam, and a lake so large you couldn't see across it. He drew in the sand to show Treasta what it looked like, but his drawing was too poor beyond simple lines to understand. She nodded her head and smiled.

"So, it's like the ocean," she said.

"Ocean? Well, no."

"But you can't see across it."

Chimes thought on it. "I suppose you're right, but the ocean is bigger."

Treasta took the stick from his hand, drew in the dirt the outline of Kildore on the water to the best of her memory and marked an X for Galgaya's location. She then drew several squiggles to represent the ocean's waves, a circle for the island of Kaire and more squiggles in the direction that east would be.

She pointed along the shoreline. "All of this—these are cliffs. Galgaya is here. It's a big city."

"You get around, don't you? Where's Yeras?"

She felt the underlying layers of her skin turn hot. Yeras. Yeras … he means the city, not the province. She gulped louder than she meant as she drew another X toward the bottom of the "map." It was along the southern shore somewhere, but she didn't know exactly where and hoped her guess was close.

Davan watched the two. Treasta leaned toward Chimes; Chimes leaned toward Treasta. Treasta's laugh turned into a girlish giggle, and she either agreed or acted surprised with just about anything that came out of Chimes' big mouth. He took a deep breath and attempted to self-sooth by rubbing his thumb and index finger together in his pocket over and over again until his skin turned raw.

Underneath a freshly dawned sky, a lodge, painted in the colors of the blazing sunrise, appeared after five days of traveling through the gorge. The rising morning glow cast a cool shadow from the east, frost coating dead grass thawed into dewdrops twinkling where sunbeams touched the earth. Smoke puffed from chimneys from the multileveled establishment, its angled roofs steep and pointing skyward. As they arrived, Chimes asked Davan and Treasta to wait at the front door as he boarded his horse in the stable. Treasta, bending over, let out a long and tired sigh, ready to get off her feet.

"What the hell was that last night?" Davan asked when Chimes was just out of ear shot.

"What was what?"

"You were flirting with him."

She scoffed. "No, I wasn't."

"Yeah, you were," he said, his words sharp and accusatory. "You need to stop smiling so much around him. He's going to get the wrong idea. You don't want him to get the wrong idea, do you?"

Treasta caught his nostrils flaring and his seriousness struck her. "You really think that was flirting?" She forced a laugh, stepped closer, running her hand around his waist and hooking her finger around the tie holding his pants up. She lowered her voice, and said into his ear: "You think *that* was flirting?" She chuckled, placing a long sensual kiss with a nip to his bottom lip. Pulling away with a sly smile, she slid her had between his legs to take in his hardness. It never took much to get Davan aroused, but Treasta, even though she exhaled a low moan in his ear as she massaged him, felt no excitement.

"Dav, don't mistaken friendliness for flirting." She patted his check and shot him another peck just as Chimes returned. Treasta slung her satchel across his shoulders. "Might want to hide that," she said, placing the bag over his bulge, and winked.

Davan cleared his throat and adjusted his trousers.

Chimes pretended not to notice, but he did, and he caught a glimpse of the two holding hands—not just holding hands: Treasta wrapped herself around his arm, so his bicep wedged between her breasts, as she soothed him by rubbing her thumb along his hand with their fingers interlocked. Treasta rested her head on Davan's shoulder, her eyes wide and melancholic. She gave him a half smile, but it faded, her gaze dropping to the earth. As Treasta shrunk behind Davan, Chimes said, "We can stay here for the night," and he flashed a key.

"They just gave you a key?" Davan asked as they followed Chimes inside.

They crossed through the foyer, past a stone countertop and up a set of stairs.

"No. I told you, I'm a trader of sorts," Chimes said.

"So, what did you give them?" he asked.

Chimes smiled. "All your dirty secrets of course."

Coming to a room, Chimes unlocked the door and gestured for his fellow travelers to enter. Inside, the room had four beds, the walls were tall, the windows wide, and on a table was a welcome basket of cheese and bread. Davan eyed Chimes, concerned over Treasta's "friendliness" as she flashed him a toothy grin and thanked him for securing a comfortable stay. This stranger, he was up to something. He could feel it in his gut.

"I think I'll wash up." Davan gathered his things and left the room, not wanting to look at the white-haired man a moment longer. A hot bath would do him good anyway. If he couldn't get his emotions under control, trying to assess Chimes' intentions would come with more difficulty, and he couldn't act rashly.

Treasta rifled through Davan's pack. They were lower on food than she realized. "How far are we from the next town?" she asked.

"Should the weather stay fair, it should be an easy ride."

She sighed with relief.

"I'm sorry about your ma," Chimes said.

Treasta looked at him puzzled and then remembered. "Oh, yeah. I don't think we're going to make it."

"I'm sure she'd understand," he said and sat next to her on the bed. "How are you doing?" he asked, and she saw in his eyes a compassion she had never recognized in anyone. He wasn't simply asking about her day; he truly wanted to know if she was faring well with the condition of the mother that didn't exist.

Her lips parted open unsure what to say. "I'm … I'm okay all things considered."

Chimes' expression softened.

You were flirting with him, Davan's accusation rang in her head as she caught herself unable to look away. She cleared her throat. That was enough. No, she wasn't flirting. But was he? Or was he just being friendly? Treasta's stomach fluttered.

No. Not butterflies. She ran for the window, threw it open and puked into a garden container emptied for the winter months.

"Are you okay?" he ran after her, brushed hair from her face and helped her to chair at a table.

"I think I'm just hungry," she said. "Too many apples, too much bread," when, in actuality, it was the sharp scent of the cheese making her queasy.

Chimes insisted she lie down. "Perhaps some grits will help."

And he went and fetched her breakfast. She sat up in the bed and slowly ate. The bland meal eased her stomach.

"Sorry," she said. "I just haven't been feeling well for a while. I'm not used to traveling and it's been so cold."

"Whatever you need, I can get it for you."

She didn't expect anything more than what little she'd give a stranger met in the wilderness. But the thought was kind. *Kind.* Chimes' kindness, welcoming, was foreign.

After he left, Treasta's heart was as empty as the room, and she stirred her grits, the spoon's metal clink along the ceramic bowl helped to fill the space. With each bite she swallowed, a butterfly broke from its chrysalis.

"DARIUS IS BRINGING STRANGERS BY AGAIN," Chimes heard his Aunt Marnie say as he came down the stairs.

"They look like troublemakers," his Uncle Atlas added.

"He likes the troublemakers, doesn't he?"

"He gets it from you."

"Oh, stop it."

And he nuzzled into her neck, kissing it.

Chimes walked past. "Will you two cut it out? You'll make me sick if you keep going on like that."

"Sorry, honey," said his aunt, who kept her graying hair tied back in a tight bun.

"She's just too," his uncle slapped her a kiss, "tempting," and pinched her ass cheek.

"I really don't want to hear it," and Chimes went into the parlor and sat down.

Marnie followed him and sat on the sofa. She crossed her legs and leaned forward.

"So, who are they?" It was a two-fold question. Marnie wanted to know, but she also needed to know. The only way for her to get news on the happenings of the world was from chatty travelers or Darius.

Chimes shrugged. "They're headed to Wesser. Treasta's mother is dying."

"Oh," she leaned back, "the poor dear. You've got too kind of a heart, my boy."

Chimes sighed and buried his face into his hands. He fought back tears thinking about his own mother when he was just five years old, of his last memory of her lying in bed.

"Your ma would be proud of you, you know," she said, hoping to bring him some comfort. "Always thinking of others before yourself."

Chimes sat up and wiped his eye. He felt stupid for crying. Two decades it had been, and it didn't feel any easier.

"She doesn't think she'll make it before she passes."

"You'll do your best," Marnie said with reassurance.

CONDENSATION GATHERED ON THE DIAMOND-PANED WINDOWS too high for any average-sized person to be able to look through. The bath attendant lowered the flame and checked the temperature before leaving. It was a private room with a screen between the tub and the door.

The woodwork was of a crafty hand, the walls of cream tiles detailed with orange flowers painted in the middle of each one. Too expensive for someone like Chimes to afford. He rubbed his face with bathwater. Be grateful, Treasta would tell him should she hear him complain, and don't ask questions. He knew better than to ask questions, of course, but none of it made sense. No one could possibly be this foolish and naïve to help a couple of strangers found on the side of a highway. He tried shaking it off. Forget about it, he told himself. He splashed water out of the tub, agitated. Treasta had to know him somehow.

Davan reclined with the memory of Oda. It was the only way he could push the image of Treasta's giggling as she smiled at Chimes from his mind. Forget about it, he reminded himself again. Be grateful. *Be grateful, dammit.* What Davan could remember from the night he spent with Oda he recreated: red lips, her body on his, the way her breath felt on his neck as she moved with such practice. Davan sunk deeper in the water and nodded off.

"You'll come back, won't you?" Oda's image lingered as he awoke sometime later.

Davan popped the cork on the tub, stepped from the water, and wrapped a towel around his waist—his excitement prominently showing through the fabric, the primal craving for a woman's body was like an imprisonment from which he needed to break free.

The urge guided his feet into the hallway, and he rushed to the suite where Treasta lounged, throwing the door open, coming to the bed, thinking only about how her small hand felt over his pants, the firmness of each rub, the slight squeeze and brief tug, how Chimes had noticed them—and yes, he noticed them—Davan had caught his gaze just as Treasta pulled her hand away. She belonged to him, and Chimes needed to know it.

Dropping the towel to the floor, he crawled over Treasta, running his hands under the cover and up the skirt of her gown, whispering in her ear, "I'm going to fuck you so good," and sliding his fingers inside her, massaging at first with care, as he placed kisses along her neck, running his tongue along her flesh. The pressure of her insides around his fingers—*the heat*—he tore the covers and inserted himself, thrusting as he tugged on the golden locks of her hair, taking in her smell as he buried himself deep inside of her.

He collapsed, letting out a satisfied groan, his breath hot on her bared neck.

Treasta groaned. "Davan," she said and turned onto her side, curling into herself and holding her stomach. "I think …" But her words faded, and that was when he noticed the grits spilled at the bedside, and saw her face beaded with sweat, pallor the shade of winter.

"Hey," he patted her cheek, "Treasta?" He nudged her, lightly shook her, then took a step back as a coldness washed over him, realizing her lack of attentiveness too enraptured by his own arousal. "Treasta … come on. Get up."

Davan didn't have time to grab the towel or dress himself when he rushed out of the room, calling for help.

A woman with graying hair pulled into a bun came running. "What is it? What's happened?" She ignored his nakedness, following him to the suite.

"She's ill," he said. When they got to the room, he grabbed the towel. "Can you help her?"

The woman came to Treasta's side. Marnie rolled up the cuffs of her sleeves, felt Treasta's forehead and cheeks kettle hot. "My dear, can you hear me?"

A low whimper.

She was somewhat conscious. Good. Marnie set a second pillow behind Treasta's head, helping her sit up, and ordered Davan to get dressed and find Darius.

Feet kicked up on an ottoman in the parlor, Chimes sank deeper into the sofa chair, eyes shut, and taking in the peace of the slow in-between season that winter brought to the lodge. In the spring, the days were temperate; people flocked to the Milnar Valley for weekslong equinox celebrations to the goddess of spring after enduring another harsh winter. The season was always gentle, the land giving of life and fresh, the rivers and dried beds flowing until the blazing heat of summer scorched the highlands.

Davan's heavy footsteps reverberated through the lodge, disrupting Chimes' meditation. "You," his voice was sharp.

"Me," Chimes replied, waving his hands, yet to open his eyes.

Davan clinched his jaw, held his breath and let out a controlled sigh. One word. Just one simple word. *Help. I need your help. We need your help.* "Treasta needs your help."

Chimes' eyes flashed open. He sat up. "What's wrong?"

Davan shrugged. "She's been sick. Not feeling well for about a month now. I …" No, don't say it. *I've been pushing her and pushing her and pushing her.* "She pushes herself too much."

Chimes motioned for Davan to follow him and led him to the kitchen. "I'll run towels while you fetch water. Bring one here and a second to the room," Chimes said, and he hurried out the room.

"No, I can take the towels," Davan said.

Chimes picked up a metal bucket; he shoved it into Davan's chest, forcing him to take it. "You got stronger arms and will move faster than me. Two buckets. There's another one outside. Have you seen Marnie?"

"She the woman with the …" he gestured around his head, unsure what to call the style of her hair, until Chimes nodded.

"With"—a long sigh escaped him—"Treasta."

Chimes noticed the way Davan's stone gaze bore into him. "Hey," he said, placing a hand on Davan's shoulder, "Marnie's good with herbs and knows a thing or two. She'll take good care of her. I swear on my life."

7

TREASTA'S EYES FLICKERED OPEN AS SHE FELT the dampness of a towel run along her forehead and down her cheeks. Marnie dipped and wrung it, moving on to scrub Treasta's hands and saw how dirty she was. She cleaned under her nails.

"Who are you?" Treasta asked.

Marnie introduced herself as the lodge manager, nothing more. "How are you feeling?" she asked and passed her a teacup steeped with herbs. "It'll help with the nausea," she said when she noticed Treasta giving it a sniff, cautious of the concoction.

Treasta thanked her. She looked around and saw neither Davan nor Chimes in the room but felt a soreness between her legs and the memory of Davan's pleasure vocalized in her ear.

"Darling," Marnie leaned toward her, "your friend says you've been feeling sick for a while."

"That's right."

"And your," Marnie pressed her own breasts with her palms, "are tender?"

"Well, yes, but it's so cold out, and I'm just not used to traveling. We've come so far."

Pausing, Marnie exhaled as she hesitated to say the next words.

"Darling … you know … when women are pregnant, what you're feeling, what you've been feeling … it's quite similar."

Treasta's mouth opened but no words escaped. She shook her head, waved her arms. Then, she looked around for Davan, expecting him to be hiding somewhere waiting to jump from a hiding place like it was just some awful joke he put this stranger up to.

"That's funny," she finally said. "*You're* funny. I'm not *actually* pregnant. Davan probably just told you that."

Marnie stood, gathering supplies. "I'll let you rest," she said with a thin smile casting pity and left the room.

After a moment: "You can come out now," Treasta said to Davan. "I get it. You're trying to be funny. Trying to make me feel better."

…

Silence.

…

Her gaze darted around the room.

…

"Dav?"

…

Fumbling from the bed, Treasta ripped her clothes from her body, throwing them to the floor and hobbled to the mirror where she saw a swelling torso on a gaunt frame.

Treasta collapsed.

8

Damn nurse. Elsie pulled back on the horse's reins. The strength it required to ride was almost too much for her healing body, but she couldn't stay in that temple another night.

Morning, noon, and evening the nurse prayed at her bedside and expected her to pray with her. Elsie would close her eyes and try to ignore the low whisper, but it was nearly impossible. After the first week passed, the vicar and pharmacist insisted on another two weeks. When they gave her the news, she thought about smashing their heads together. But little good that would do her. Two more weeks. Fine. She thought it would be good to exercise her patience anyway.

So, she spent her time polishing up what money she had left and when she had enough energy, she explored inside the temple walls. It was a small compound, so it wasn't hard to find where they kept donations. Every day she would grab a couple coins, never enough for anyone to notice anything missing. Elsie was always careful. Aeran, however, would have taken the chest in its entirety. She was grateful he was dead, and grateful to herself for killing him.

"One more week," the nurse said one evening after prayer.

Elsie watched her with an emotionless gaze until her mouth fell into a disappointed frown.

"Nurse," she called as the nurse was about leave. "One more prayer?

I can feel the spirits of the gods healing not only my wounds but my heart."

Delighted, the nurse knelt at Elsie's bedside and together they whispered the prayer that Elsie heard recounted morning, noon, and evening for the past twenty-one gods forsaken days.

And just as the nurse closed the prayer with the traditional "*naman-lo*" she fell over onto Elsie's lap, the earring-pick lodged in her neck.

"*Naman-lo*," Elsie lowly echoed.

Blood sputtered after she pulled the pick from the nurse's flesh. She put it back on her ear, got up, grabbed her things, including the donation money now well polished, and walked out.

Now, Elsie found herself riding toward Wesser and caught at a fork in the road. Going left would take her through a gorge into lower lands, right would lead her to Grenna. The sky had darkened with storm clouds, so she veered her horse toward the nearest town.

It had just begun to snow when Elsie trotted into Grenna, a quaint ranch town of perhaps a few hundred souls. She dismounted and walked closely next to her horse with her head low as she approached a wooden gate.

A guardsman stepped forward, preventing her from crossing into town. Something about this stranger was unsettling.

"What's your business?"

"I'm looking for shelter for the night."

He looked her over and then the horse.

"If you could direct me to the nearest lodging, I would be deeply grateful," she said.

The fire from a nearby brazier whipped in the wind. The guard caught sight of her face—half of it had been seared and was still healing.

"Like what you see?"

The guardsman let her pass—perhaps out of pity or perhaps out of fear—and pointed down the road and said to turn left at the first crossing and right at the next. "There's a small inn next to a well."

As the day turned to evening, the storm cut through the region, blasting through the night. The inn wasn't much. It was small, as the guard said, just a handful of rooms attached to the backside of someone's barn. It would have been easy to miss had the guard not directed her. The room was big enough for a bed and barrel on which a lamp rested. The window was cutout from the wall poorly—its panes shaking with each gust.

Elsie planned to ride out the storm here. She'd pay for the room like an honest patron and lay low. How the laws and politics worked in Wesserland she didn't know. Word would probably reach Grenna about the nurse found dead in the temple in Herra. She liked the idea of a bounty on her head, imagined how the printmaker would depict her face or what the description would say. They didn't know her name because she had refused to give it.

She dimmed the light, watching the wailing storm through the window.

Morning roused Elsie with a snowball hitting the window, a white scuff of powder left on the glass.

Children. She dreaded children. Their giggling and merriment permeated the walls as they played in the fresh powder.

Today seemed a little warmer than previous days, but something about snow always made the cold more tolerable. She packed up her things, ready to carry on toward Wesser.

As she trod through the snow to fetch her horse, a stray snowball smacked her on the head. She faced the children to shoot them with a nasty scowl. They fell silent upon seeing her scarred face, no scowl needed. Elsie looked at them with a perplexed expression and when she realized the burn scars, combined with an eye that barely stayed open, more blemishes from knife fights and her chipped tooth, she smiled. How fortuitous, she thought. Maybe she should thank Davan and Treasta when she finds them. She decided it would be the last thing she says before she cuts their throats.

9

DECLAN'S BODY CUT THROUGH THE SNOW. Cal anchored his foot into Declan's side, and he and his friends towered over the felled boy, their shadows stretching over him.

"Come on, rat, get your ass up," Cal said and nudged him.

But Declan curled tighter into himself, shielding his head with his arms, shaking, not because it was cold but because he braced for another impact. By day he was bullied; by night his father did his drunken dance, throwing his fists into his mother, whipping Declan with his belt and grabbing him by his hair, yelling in his face. For Declan, yelling wasn't a sound but an expression. His father's mouth, always close to his face, wide, wet, and smelly, blasted his hot breath, and Declan would wince as clumps of saliva laced with phlegm landed on his cheeks.

Then his father would say something. Declan didn't catch it the first few times, too scared to look his father in the eyes, but eventually he realized he was repeating something about Declan "faking it."

It's what Cal and the other boys said as they walked off. But Declan didn't hear. He lay there for several minutes before peeking. They had run off, kicking up the freshly fallen snow, and began crafting artillery, packing balls tight before throwing them at one another.

Declan sneaked away, hid behind some crates to watch Cal and the others from a safe distance. They laughed, and Declan frowned.

Cal found a shovel and began cutting sheets of snow, lifting and stacking them into bricks to form a wall. He had finished building his fort before the others. It was three against one—a challenge befitting Cal.

Declan sighed. He dreamed of inclusion, of friends of his own; he wanted nothing more than to feel like he belonged among his peers and within his own home.

Last night his father drank more than usual. Anytime the temperature dropped he'd double up the shots to give his body the illusion of warmth. He kicked open the front door just as the snow began to fall, ordered something from his mother and slapped her a sloppy kiss. Declan caught the shape of the word "bitch" on his father's lips. His mother shrunk within herself and carried on doing whatever he had asked of her. Declan's father waved a partially emptied bottle. Its golden liquid sloshed. And at the sight of alcohol, Declan felt a sickness in his gut. He could smell his father—the sourness of his sweat overpowered the air. As he often did when his father got like this, he put on his jacket, gloves, boots, and hat and retreated to the neighbor's barn.

Cal's father was always patient with him. He would speak at a pace Declan could follow and fed him often. And while Cal and Declan had grown up together, something about his father treating Declan kindly made Cal bitter.

Declan had fallen asleep last night in the barn, sleeping alongside the horse of a woman who arrived from out of town. He preferred the company of horses anyway. They didn't have any expectations or demands. They never screamed in his face to see if he was "faking" his deafness. They were sweet to him, and he would name them, because he never knew what they were properly called by, and he thought he couldn't befriend the horses if they couldn't introduce themselves. Carrot, he decided on the horse's name. The names he chose were usually food related, something he knew the horses enjoyed. He spelled on the horse's back his name, C-A-R-R-O-T, and then bowed before the steed.

As Cal played with his friends, he caught a glimpse of Declan watching. Cal stopped what he was doing, faced Declan, and ran his finger across his throat in a cutting motion, before continuing his game of war. The first major snowfall was always exciting. Everyone would rush outside to throw themselves into the powder and make snow fairies together. Snow forts occupied alleys; mounds would be constructed to craft slides. And on occasion, daring children in their teenage years would climb to the steepest roof in town with a board and crash into the earth; bones were typically broken, but no one had ever died.

As he watched the other children play, he contemplated finding a board and climbing to the roof. Declan wondered what peace being close to the sky must bring away from Cal and the other children, away from his father. If he climbed to the roof, if he glissaded its slope and crashed into the earth, maybe the impact would fix him.

As Declan watched, he fantasized himself among them, crafting forts and slugging snowballs, laughing and laughing and laughing until his throat was sore and hoarse.

Carrot's owner emerged from one of four guest rooms attached to the back of the barn. She was small, hooded, and walked with purpose.

One of Cal's snowballs whacked her on the head. She whipped around, and without saying a word, the children cowered back, couldn't even get out a word as simple as "sorry."

When she turned around, Declan saw why. Captivated, he followed her. She prepared her horse and left.

Declan didn't know where she was going, but what he did know was that he wanted to be just like her—he wanted to shoot Cal a glance and for Cal to cower in his presence.

Declan rushed home to a father passed out from a night of drinking and a mother taking advantage of the momentary peace to sleep. His mother kept knives hidden in various places throughout the home: under the mattress for accessibility when she's sleeping, in the cellar, any place she knew her husband wouldn't have interest accessing. It was the only way she felt she could safely—if such a word could describe it—rest.

But Declan couldn't do this anymore. Grenna was small. No matter where he went, his father would be there, Cal would be there. He needed to be somewhere none of them would be. So, he gathered supplies. He didn't know what he should bring but he knew he needed the necessities. He raided the cellar. His father would blame his mother, but Declan didn't care. He was done finding bottles of whiskey buried behind their home. And he packed clothes for warmth, grabbed the thickest blanket and wrapped his bags within it and fastened the blanket into a sack to make it easier to carry everything.

Declan chased after Carrot and the woman not realizing Cal had followed him curious for why Declan was running out of town with a make-shift sack and dressed for the peak of winter. Declan didn't make it far out of town when Cal caught up and tackled him to the ground.

They wrestled, and Cal pinned him down, patting his face and pointing at his own lips. "Where do you think you're going," he said.

Declan struggled to wiggle free. He didn't answer him and instead began fighting back, flailing his arms whichever way, hoping he'd land a hit.

And he did.

Cal fell backward, holding his cheek. When he realized he was bleeding, he shot to his feet and charged Declan, but Declan braced himself and threw Cal to the ground. He sat on him, swung, and clobbered Cal with his fists while screaming as loud as he could until his throat was sore and hoarse.

As Declan towered over him, casting his shadow across his body, Cal curled tightly into himself.

Declan gave him a goodbye kick, spat on the road, and left Grenna.

10

THE TERRAIN HAD BECOME ROCKY ALONG THE HIGHWAY.

Elsie spread a map alongside the horse's body and looked it over. She estimated her current location. A few more miles, she figured, would take her to a road winding down the canyon wall. She folded the map and continued, walking alongside the horse for a ways before riding.

She brought the horse to a trot when she noticed the sky had overtaken the earth. A watchtower, constructed from the same vibrant colors of the canyon was positioned on the canyon wall. As Elsie came closer, she took in the vastness that lay before her. Endless, it seemed. But through the distant haze she saw water—a river so wide the land beyond it was but a blueish-red strip. It was still far. Further than she could comprehend. The snow didn't seem to fall this far southwest. The earth was jagged, the depth and width immense. And for the first time since she left Galgaya, Elsie felt a deep sense of overwhelming.

The outpost was abandoned, or at the very least not occupied. It would be a good place to stop before beginning the descent. So, Elsie unpacked, gathered wood from dried brush growing nearby, and started a fire inside the hearth. She rubbed her hands and held them out at the flames and took in the heat.

She stepped back, stared into the blaze as it lapped the air, and felt a tightness in her chest. Elsie tried shaking the feeling, but she became lost in her head, and disoriented, she remembered Davan tying her to the bedpost, she remembered the sensations: the roar, the cracking, the way the rope rubbed into her wrists until the flesh turned raw and she broke free. But what she especially remembered was the heat and the way it wafted into her nose.

Elsie looked around. A noise brought her out of her trance. She held her knife and started checking all the hidden spots in the room. She crept up the stairs where there was a table and under it a boy. They watched one another, neither taking their eyes off the other.

"Get out," she said. "Get out or …," she pointed the knife at him, "or I'll …"

The boy tossed something in her direction. It skidded across the floor. Elsie nudged it with her foot, flipped it over and saw it had a strap and buckle.

The boy crept forward, peeping from under the table. He was maybe eleven or twelve. Elsie couldn't tell; she was awful at recognizing ages, especially in children.

She picked it up, still holding onto the knife, and inspected what was a mask. She looked at the boy who held onto the table's leg.

"You should leave," Elsie said and tossed the mask his direction. "Get out." She pointed toward the stairs. But he didn't move. "Fine. Do as you will, but I don't want to see your ugly face again. You got that?" He watched her with large brown eyes framed within his russet visage.

Elsie belted her blade and returned to the ground floor.

She knocked everything off the shelves. Loud clattering disrupted the silence, and an unpleasant scree disrupted the air as she dragged the heavy wooden case to block the doorway and trap the child.

The boy, where did he come from? She didn't want to think about him. She didn't care. She wanted her peace.

A cold gust whipped the front door open to reveal cloud cover that, in the time since she arrived, had obscured the low-hanging sun. Elsie secured the door shut with a chair and then sat down, with legs and arms crossed, perplexed over the boy now penned away.

11

DECLAN STARED AT THE WOMAN, TOOK IN HER FEATURES—the scars on her face, the chipped tooth; her eyes were recessed, hollow and dark. Her presence was as ominous as the abandoned, drafty tower. As the window shutters slammed periodically against the bricks, he gaped, awed and frightened, feelings he didn't know could co-exist. This woman, her skin pale but face red from the cold, was clearly from the East Lands, just as he had suspected. Cal's father described them as having hair of many shades and complexions fair—Declan always imagined like a potato's insides—but this woman's, hers was like the skin of a garlic bulb.

The woman picked up the mask, looked at it with her icy blue eyes. He read her expression as one of anger and confusion. She glared at him. The mask skidded across the floor as she tossed it.

"Get out," she said, pointing toward the door.

He looked at the door and back at her. Declan held onto the leg of the table, unsure what to do. Get out and go where? He came this far; he wasn't going back.

The woman threw her hands in the air, giving up, and left down the stairs.

Declan loosened his grip around the table leg. He watched through the threshold for several minutes before standing and creeping to peer down the tower. The curves in its walls made it impossible to see the ground floor, but a light that was reflecting along the bricks slowly faded. He went to the window to look for the sun. It was cast behind clouds since he arrived.

He had trailed the woman for several days and kept his distance. At times he would lose sight of her. Following the highway was his best option as he hoped she didn't veer in any other directions along the way. He'd catch up, camp nearby, put on every layer he carried with him and wrapped himself in the blanket, head tucked away for extra warmth. He didn't know how he survived. Early on he made the mistake of eating too much. On the nights it was especially cold, he'd sneak into the woman's camp as she slept to warm himself next to the fire. What would happen if she woke, he didn't know, but the heat was worth the risk.

On the final day, he followed closely. The snow had begun melting the day earlier as a warm front eased into the region. But as the final day carried on, the weather began to cool again, the slush and puddles began to freeze. He had to eventually drop his distance. He understood anytime he slipped or took a wrong step, he risked her hearing him, and he didn't know how much noise he was making. The woman folded up a map, mounted Carrot, and trotted off. Declan lost sight of her again.

When he arrived at the watchtower, the sky had begun to darken. A soft golden glow flickered from inside. He sneaked around outside, looking through the window to see the woman stirring the embers. The heat radiated and was relieving on his winter-nipped cheeks. Before leaving Grenna, he had never felt so drawn to a flame. But after spending days in the cold, he saw himself falling into the flames.

Declan searched around, found a spot to climb up to the next floor, and fell inside its window with a heavy crash.

The floorboards vibrated: *the woman.*

He rushed under the table with no time to think, and as he poked his head out from underneath, he met her stony gaze.

Now, after having come face to face with the woman, Declan didn't know what to do. He tossed her a mask he made from bark and a belt while on the journey; it was one of the only ways he could keep his mind occupied. And she rejected it. He didn't understand why. His father would have beaten him if he turned away any gift. This woman, though, she was different.

Declan struggled closing the shutters. He latched it, but they rattled in the increasing wind. It was cold inside, but warmer than outside. The outpost wasn't large, and not far off were the ruins of an abandoned stable. He explored up another flight, got a better view of the canyon, and its massive expanse faded with day.

He plopped on one of three beds, their frames barely holding, the burlap of the mattress tearing and exposing old hay. Instant relief washed through him, and his eyes grew heavy.

Elsie woke in the middle of the night to a knocking. It started as a constant beat but developed into a pattern. She sat up, searching the dark. The fire had faded. The moon absent. The wind's howling cut through the cracks in the door and shutters. She drew in a long breath, holding back that dark feeling she felt inside whenever irritated.

The boy continued knocking, gradually increasing the tempo and volume until he was pounding with his fists. Elsie let out a grunt as she struggled pulling the shelves down. Then, when they finally toppled over, there he was just staring up at her holding a make-shift sack and that damn mask.

He held it for her to take. She looked at the mask and then back at the boy. Declan insisted she take it and held it up to his own face to show how it covered one side. And then Elsie realized he had followed her from Grenna. When she met with the man who lodged her at the barn, the boy was in the barn with the horses. She had caught a glimpse of him when the man showed her to her room.

The darkness Elsie felt within disappeared. She grabbed the mask, looked it over. It was made from tree bark, no hole to see out of. The boy assumed with such a wound on the left side of her face that she was blind in that eye. Observant. She slipped it on.

Declan smiled and nodded approvingly. He walked past her to the fire and tried to get it going again. He tossed in some boards from a nearby broken crate. Finally, it came alight. He wiped his runny nose and extended his hands to absorb its warmth.

Elsie slowly approached the boy, unsure what to do. "Hey, boy," she said from behind. "Boy, hey!" And she grabbed his shoulder.

Declan whipped around and stood. He motioned with his hands.

"Why did you follow me?" she asked.

He continued moving his hands and then shuffled through his bag.

As he turned around with a stick of graphite and stack of papers bound together with twine, Elsie clapped in his ears to see if what she suspected was true.

Declan shoved her arms out of the way and pushed her. He threw down his things and clapped violently in her ears and shot her a disgusted look.

Sure enough, Elsie backed off.

Declan picked up the pad of paper and his graphite stick that had broken in two pieces when he dropped it. He let out a sigh, annoyed, and then scribbled something on paper.

When he showed Elsie, she struggled to read it but could make out some of the words. Either the kid couldn't spell or the people in the area wrote in a different dialect.

Y em Declyn.

He handed her the paper and utensil.

Admittedly she wasn't very good at writing either.

I am Elsie.

He cocked his head looking at the difference in spellings between *Y em* and *I am.*

Then, she asked him why he followed her.

And Declan acted it out. He tried explaining that he saw her, the way she looked at the other boys, and how they cowered. He pointed at her and then himself and wrote:

Help me.

"No," she said. "Absolutely not." Help with what she didn't know. Something about the bullies, something about those kids playing in the snow, something about his parents. He was lost. "Go home, kid."

He shook his head, planting himself at the fire. He wasn't going anywhere.

THEIR VOICES FROM BEHIND THE DOOR ECHOED INTO THE SUITE. Treasta curled onto her side, hiding under the covers and holding a pillow over her head to drown out the arguing, but their muffled words still intruded her thoughts.

She wanted to be alone, shouted at anyone who would enter the room who wasn't Marnie. Davan never knocked. On one occasion he had crept inside, sat at the bedside, the weight of his body—it was like she could still feel him on top of her—creasing the mattress had jolted her awake. She kicked him, forcing him away.

"Treasta," he had said her name like it was a chore, "you don't look sick anymore. Let's go."

"Go away," she said, refusing to look at him, too afraid to meet his eyes after he invaded her ill-stricken body and too ashamed to tell him about the baby—*his* baby. She imagined how that conversation would play out: *who else you been sleeping with? Huh? Tell me! Was it [so and so] or [what's-his-name]? You said you only love me*—he would have picked any male guildmate he had seen her talking to the days before they left Galgaya. It didn't matter who, so long as he wasn't to blame. And what would she say? What could she say? Treasta never had the strength to argue back—once, maybe a couple years ago, she could have, but Davan didn't like losing arguments, and he would find ways to hold them against her if he didn't get his way.

As he left the room, malice laced his words: "If I don't get my hands on the treasure, I will *never* forgive you."

The room shook at the slamming of the door.

She heard Chimes say: "What happened? How is she?"

"*You*," Davan echoed, "don't you *dare* go near her."

A gentle knock.

Marnie.

"May I come in, dear?"

Silence.

"It's been three days. You can't stay in here forever."

Treasta pulled the covers over her head, hiding in a dark cave warmed by her breathing.

"Well"—footsteps carried across the room—"I've brought you fresh water to wash up—the sound of the pitcher resting in the porcelain basin—"and something to eat"—Treasta heard the metal tray slide along the wooden tabletop at the bedside.

"Why are you helping me?" Treasta asked from under the blanket.

She could feel Marnie's presence next to her. "Why wouldn't I?" she asked. Marnie sat beside her, and Treasta allowed the woman to pull the covers to reveal a redden and swollen face beset with tears. The woman exchanged a kind smile—perhaps the kindest smile ever bestowed upon Treasta. "We women, we are all each other truly have, aren't we? Listen," and Treasta sat up, wiping her eyes on her wrists, "I …," Marnie's voice lowered, "… was in a similar situation as you: with child, scared, unwed, plainly unprepared. I was younger than you are now."

Marnie poured Treasta a cup of green tea and passed it to her.

"What happened?"

Drawing in a long breath, Marnie looked to the ceiling. "My sister—Darius' mother—we left in secret to see a witch. After I paid her …," she paused, as if she were looking for the right words, "… a *hefty* price, she gave me a remedy. I drank it and bled for days."

"Wh—what price?" she asked, wide-eyed.

Marnie shook her head. "Dealings with witches are verbal contracts that must not be repeated."

More silence.

Treasta stared into the rippling liquid sloshing along the teacup's rim. Her gaze, turned serious, shot toward Marnie. "Where is this witch?"

Marnie held onto the silence a bit longer, giving Treasta extra space to think on her question before saying, "In the canyon."

The canyon. The Great Canyon, where the Great River and its tributaries carved deep through vast earth farther than the eye could see; the Great Canyon, where the Great River emptied into the Great Lake, so large one would think it were a fresh-water sea; the Great Canyon, where the Great Lake was contained by an incomprehensibly miles-large dam, where on the dam was the Great Lake City of Wesser. The canyon. The witch. *Wesser.*

Treasta swung her legs over the bed, the hot tea spilling on the linens as she placed the saucer on the bedside table. On her feet, she hadn't realized the strength she had regained—the tea, the meals, Marnie's care, and her determination to find this witch.

But Marnie's hand grabbed hers. "There's something you need to know."

Treasta faced the woman who rose to her feet, keeping hold of her hands.

"Your friend, Davan, he took it upon himself to take one of our horses and left last night."

Left? Treasta shook her head, pulling her hands back. Her body turned cold as the sudden realization of being pregnant and alone in an unfamiliar land set in.

13

SHE WOULD UNDERSTAND. Treasta knew how important this was for him. Right?

Davan was kicking himself for leaving, felt a tinge of regret entering his heart, but he couldn't waste another second knowing others would be after the treasure—*his treasure.* The beast's hooves kicked through snow as they strode. *You should always go after whatever you want,* Oda's voice rang. Then Treasta's: *Since when do you care?* Always, he thought to himself. And maybe, he wondered, he cared a little too much.

You're right, he had told Oda, his head heavy in his drunken stupor, *I should go after whatever I want. She's so clingy, has been ever since we met. Always by my side. Always saying I should do this instead of that, and then someone goes and kills the only person I care about, and it's like she got worse, treated me like a child, like a baby, like I couldn't handle my grieving without her ...*

The horse reared.

Disappearing into himself, he didn't realize the anger that had possessed him, pulling on the beast's reins with an uncontrollable strength.

The snow caught him, and he lay, arms and legs sprawled, staring at clouds, and the memory of nine-year-old Treasta lying near a wall behind a decrepit building in the Galgayan slums, where she had suffered a beating from some boys in their teenage years. At the time, she wasn't affiliated with any one guild, but she learned to steal and sell her goods on her own. She was good at it. But when she tried scamming the wrong people, it didn't end well. Davan, then ten years old, had knelt and rolled her muddy body over. A stern gaze was cast in the shadow of his face, as for a moment, he thought he had seen her eyes flicker open.

Later that night, Treasta woke up in a boarded-up tavern. He was sat next to her, staring with wide eyes, warm like sunlight. It was his home or—as he put it—hiding place away from the warring thieves' guilds. He showed her the scar on his forearm, the "III," and he asked what gang she was from. He learned she was a year younger and already knew how to work the streets, and he remembered how impressed he was the more he learned about his new friend. In hindsight, Davan didn't know how Treasta could have survived without him, alone and so vulnerable.

They shared the "III" on their forearm—a mark associated with the since defunct Triple Gang—and now they shared the same "C"—its tail curving down into a hook almost like "Ç" on their upper left arms—branded.

Davan wasn't sure what was better, but he knew staying with his old guild would have ruined Treasta. They had treated her like a puppet, a toy for years, and she accepted it because that was all she had known.

At thirteen, Davan grabbed her shoulders, looked her square in the eyes, and said, "I refuse to let them touch you ever again. I promise on my own grave, I'll protect you until I die."

Davan then went to the strongest guild in the city, the Dubilee Tribe, and spoke to its leader. Fylle had yet to appear in Galgaya. (At the time, he was affiliated with Dubilee through a sister tribe in another city.) It was Lodan who had owned the shadows. Over the past few years, the smaller guilds had been either absorbed or irradicated. Anyone who opposed Lodan wasn't allowed to live, and the former thief-king would lock them in the hideout's dungeons deep below the city, feeding them crumbs—just enough to keep them alive, just enough that they would suffer. It was how he liked it. Order and in power. So, Davan turned on his guild, told Lodan he would pledge his loyalty for life, promised he would say "yes" to anything he would ask of him and that he would never question it. Lodan agreed, and Davan became his most loyal follower until his death.

Davan stood, knocking clumps of snow from his clothes and shaking out his cloak.

Since when did you care?—forever, he wanted to tell Treasta. He had cared forever; everything and everyone and every decision he made was for them. And she never thanked him. *Never.*

While fetching his horse, he noticed in the distance a town—Hatchet, he remembered seeing the name on a signpost some miles back. Focus on today, he told himself as he took in the faraway and unfamiliar lands and the settlement near the canyon, its shadow coddling fog in the late afternoon.

Atop the beast, Davan trod down a hill and into the town surrounded by rock formations seemingly cutting toward the sky like hatchets.

A whistle broke through the crisp air. Then another from the opposite side of the road. A man stepped in his path, arms crossed. Two more came behind him holding blades.

"Ain't nobody getting into Hatchet without the king's approval," the first man said.

King? Davan took a gander at the buildings in his line of sight: poorly kept stone structures, a small water well, and a single manor house—that must have been where this king ruled—down the way spoke of an impoverished town.

Davan's suspicions were confirmed when the man guided him to the well-kept manor surrounded by a stone wall crafted from polished red granite with an impressive and large courtyard that in the spring would bloom a bright garden. On a stepladder, a boy was knocking icicles from the soffits with a broom. His eyes met with Davan's, and he stopped what he was doing to watch the stranger.

The man yanked a silky red rope hanging to the left of the tall dark doors carved with motifs of crawling ivy and twisting branches, and a bell echoed.

A woman answered, a young servant whose eyes hung with tiredness.

"We are here to see His Excellence."

The woman, face long and expression flat with apathy, exhaled without saying a word and opened the door. As Davan passed, she averted her gaze, staring at a rug, green like a deep forest that raced from the entrance and up a grand staircase. The cold air was shunned from the warmth of inside, as if Davan had walked through some kind of portal when the woman shut the door and latched it. Silently she crossed the room to pull on another silk rope, sounding another bell.

Several moments passed until a man, garbed in a long fur robe with rings across his fingers and large jeweling hanging around his neck materialized at the doorway at the top of the staircase. He took each step with extravagance, his feet soft on the rug running from the landing to the front doors. As he spoke, the paintings lining the walls absorbed the echo.

"Gareth, you always do well," the flamboyant man said. He circled Davan, touched his greasy hair clumped with dirt and oil and felt the decaying, old fabric of his tunic.

"I'm Davan. I hail from Kildore," he cut in, giving Gareth no room to speak.

The potentate's face came alight. "Such a journey." And it truly seemed as if he were excited to be in the presence of a Kildorei. Hundreds of miles Davan had traveled to reach the Great Canyon of Wesserland; he felt a great sense of accomplishment and pride, but something about this man's demeanor disrupted that feeling.

"And what do I owe this …," he eyed him, starting at Davan's boots stuffed with tattered linen wraps and working his gaze to the unmatching layers of his clothing and the mess atop his head as if he didn't just spend the past minute walking circles around him like a predator intimidating his food before the kill, "… pleasure, Davan of Kildore?"

"I'm trying to reach Wesser," Davan said, doing his best to smooth out his words to sound well off but struggling with the cadence. While he thought to lie, he wanted to keep his story as true as possible. "I was just passing through and looking for lodging. But your fellow here, Gareth, said I couldn't enter the town until I see you first."

"Hatchet doesn't see visitors often, Sir Davan."

"I can't imagine why," he said, then realized his comment was taken as an insult as the kingly stranger paused and pursed his lips.

The king dusted his hands off and rotated his rings so the light of nearby candles caught the gems just right to radiate their vibrate and otherworldly glow. "Leave us."

Gareth swallowed on air and shuffled as he lingered. He slowly held out his hand, but the king's eyes dramatically rolled in his head; he snapped his fingers and motioned for the servant to do away with the man. The woman, her long raven hair caught in the air as she rushed at the king's command, escorted Gareth outside, off the estate.

Just as the door shut behind Davan, he heard a faint complaint: "But I'm supposed to get paid."

Stoic, Davan's hard gaze didn't leave the king as he pretended to pay no mind to the strange quibble from Gareth, but he certainly didn't let such a comment slip by. He focused on the ruler, who watched past Davan with bright green eyes framed with bushy lashes under thick, but well-kept brows. His long face and long nose were offset by glossy hair dark like midnight, cut clean at his chin and bangs running flush along his brow.

"You may call me Sir Bastan," he said with a bow. "I prefer a less formal title around my visitors. You are staying, aren't you?"

Davan shook his head. "A kind offer, but I don't think I could accept. I cannot ask such a thing from a stranger and one of your …," he searched for just the right word, "… grandiosity. It is far too much for a lowly traveler like myself, umm … Sir Bastan." Davan's fake upper-class accent was failing him as he nearly forgot the potentate's name.

But Bastan placed his hand in the small of Davan's back, giving him a gentle, yet forced, nudge forward as he offered his new visitor a tour. Davan understood "no" wouldn't suffice. His skin crawled at Bastan's touch and the too-smoothness of his voice a little too close to his ear as he said, "Nonsense."

Portraits of different people at various stages in their lives lined the halls of the manor. It didn't matter where they were: the paintings were everywhere, fancily framed, but many old and worn, as though the art hung for decades. It wasn't easy to look away as they rounded corners and climbed stairs and passed through various rooms for various activities. No matter where he went, the faces of many watched.

Bastan seemed to take notice of Davan's curiosity. "A Kildorei fellow wandering Wesserland. Pray do tell, for why are you here?"

"A curious adventurer," was all he said. But he noticed Bastan didn't follow up with another question as if waiting for Davan to say more. "A nomad, you could say," Davan said—thinking about how Chimes used the same word, vague yet somehow suitable. "I prefer not to call any one place home."

"Different souls, you and I," Bastan said. "I much prefer the sedentary lifestyle, personally." He opened a door. The next hall they came into looked like many of the others, yet the paintings didn't change. "Hatchet is a homely place, don't you think? Perhaps you may choose to stay awhile, at least through the winter. Storms here, they can be violent, the air like ice—colder than anything you've likely experienced in Kildore. 'Tis the nature of the Altan Highlands."

Choose, an interesting word choice, Davan thought, because something about how Bastan said it, long, slow, with a slight pause flanking each side of the syllable, hinted that this king liked to dance around his intentions.

As they passed through one of the many sitting rooms, Davan broke his gaze away from the art and gave his attention to the king. "Have you been to Kildore, Sir Bastan?" Keep the conversation light, he told himself; he didn't want this stranger to know more than he needed about him.

"I have not," Bastan said. "But I have kin who travel to Kildore. Vast is it not? Maybe too vast for one king. I do wonder how one manages so much power across such acreage. I could never.

"Wesserland, do you know, has not a single ruler? Towns govern themselves; some govern others. Feuding is common, but there are years of peace, like now. Kildore is a young kingdom still, a weak and susceptible disposition for a nation. A peace treaty with the lands to its north, it can only go so far."

"You know more about our politics than I do," Davan said.

"Like I said," Bastan flashed a smile, "I have kin in the region."

They entered a dining hall, the table set with dinnerware for two, the hearth, framed with white tiles painted with green images of common scenes, flashed alight as the door opened and shut. Above the hearth, a mirror, and above the mirror ivy growing up the wall and across the ceiling beams—but not real ivy, Davan realized: sculpted reliefs so lifelike, he felt those vines could reach and grab him any moment. Then he saw such a horror in his mind: tied to a chair, tangled in vines, immobilized and choking back on nothing but fear.

Davan shook his head, blinking to wipe away the strange vision—an experience he didn't quite know what to do with, except second guess whether it really had happened at all. This place … this manor … this king … something didn't seem right. A waft of smoke from an incense burning nearby filled his nose; Davan felt a little woozy but maintained awareness.

"I'm a painter," Bastan said. "Well, it is a hobby, really. I enjoy painting in my downtime. But it can be quite difficult getting supplies. The summer months are when it is best to forge. Weeks before the solstice the rains wash through the basin, and the dry riverbeds flow. It is magical how the wildflowers know to bloom. There, along the banks, azure poppies sprout in great abundance. It is the only time of year I can forge for them. It is the only place in all Wesserland they grow.

"They make a beautiful blue pigment," Bastan continued as they carried on up a flight of stairs. Davan could see from a window what looked to be a lush, overgrown courtyard of spring's ripeness at the center of the manor. His breath snagged on his inhale, taken aback by the misplaced beauty at winter's genesis.

Davan blinked.

The large square fountain in the middle had iced over, the branches of trailing vines along the trellis naked of foliage. Clearing his throat, Davan followed after Bastan, thinking surely his eyes played tricks.

Bastan carried on: "I save the color for my most special subjects. Those who I admire, love the most, with whom I want to share my heart—they are the ones who don my favorite hue."

"I would think," he looked around, "green is your favorite."

"Green … is beautiful, but it is not rare. Where I am from, the sky dawns and sets with an emerald shade, the day like a bright chartreuse. But it is this sky's cerulean I admire more. It is remarkable that your sky, at the sun's rise and set, can be any color but green."

Bastan's voice trailed as Davan took in more portraits. The handiwork was remarkably detailed. These portraits were newer, the colors brighter, the varnish yet to yellow and the paint yet to crack. But of all the portraits that they had passed, none carried that beautiful blue Bastan described.

"You're very talented," he said with a yawn. "I've never seen anything like it."

"You wear kindness well," Bastan said. "It suits you."

In his tired stupor, Davan smiled at the thought of wearing kindness, and he chuffed, pleased by such a compliment, even blushing. He realized the tiredness he was feeling was beginning to weigh unnaturally on his body.

"Oh, you poor thing," Bastan said, catching Davan from falling over. "You are simply exhausted. Come now."

Bastan led Davan to a private room with a balcony overlooking the courtyard still winter laden. Woozily, Davan wobbled inside; the fine décor and furniture a tilted blur. The awake world was dreamlike now, and as Bastan helped Davan to his bed, Davan's mind melded memories with the present, the room fading in and out of yesteryears of manors he burgled in Galgaya.

"You may stay here as long as you like. I insist," Bastan said. "Please, ring the bell if you need anything. Dana is at your call."

Davan didn't remember hearing Bastan leave—no sound from the door opening and closing, no footsteps. Neither did he remember crawling under the covers on a mattress heavily layered in the softest bedding he ever before had laid, nor had he any memory of drifting into a deep sleep. So, when he awoke, who knows how many hours later, he jolted to his feet, alarmed and disoriented, having forgotten where he was.

He caught his breath as his heart raced behind his ribs, looked around for the king, and assessed where he had awakened. The room was large and airy, the bed centered between two windows draped with thick velvet curtains. The hearth eased to life from dim embers, and there were two mirrors: one near the privacy screen—he hadn't realized how disheveled he had become, perhaps magnified within a room contrasting of wealth—the other, gold and oval decorated with the same vine motifs like in other parts of the manor, hung over a wash basin crafted from jade.

Davan looked around, first turning up the covers and peeking under the bed, then opening drawers and cabinets, and tapping the mirror positioned in the corner of the room near the privacy screen.

Nothing seemed right about this place. No visitors? Why? It wasn't that far off from the main road coming out of the gorge. Perhaps he should have carried on the other direction when he came upon a crossroad.

From where he stood, Davan couldn't see beyond the roof laid with terracotta shingles. But the sun was coming to a set, apparent by graying skies paling into night. Even if he could see beyond the town, it would be impossible to confirm in the night whether any other roads reached Hatchet. And for Hatchet to be conveniently located along the canyon, certainly this would be a common place for travelers to stop on their journey.

"You're overthinking it, Dav"—that's what Treasta would have told him. She was always the level-headed one. Davan took a deep breath. He didn't want to think about Treasta. But it was difficult.

A soft knock came from the door. Dana, the servant from earlier, handed Davan clothes. He held up the doublet embroidered with patterns that matched the landscape, abstract yet angular.

Dana—Davan could barely piece together the day, but he remembered the king saying her name because of how similar it sounded to his own.

"King Bastan has invited you to dinner," Dana said. She was soft spoken and came across somewhat shy, or rather she just didn't make eye contact. Then he thought: was that a look of shame? "There is fresh water in the pitcher on the vanity and clean garments behind the screen."

Then, without waiting for him to speak, she left. Davan looked at the jade pitcher resting in the wash basin on the vanity. There wasn't water in there moments ago when he was looking around, nor did he recall clothes behind the screen. He shook his head. Or maybe there was; he couldn't remember all of a sudden which was true.

Oh well, he sighed and thought he should take advantage of the free meal. But Davan never trusted the wealthy, and he was fighting every bit of himself not to leave.

At the thought of leaving, he became dizzy. Davan grabbed his head and balanced himself on the wall. Treasta would have insisted they should stay, to "take what we can while we got the chance," or something to the likes.

"Treasta ...," he muttered her name with a guilty grievance.

Forget about her, he told himself, and focus on the mission.

14

HE LEFT. Treasta's head felt heavy. He really left …

She walked the lodge with an emptiness hollowing her chest, as she mentally searched for answers, trying to understand how he could ever place the treasure over their relationship … their love. And now—she caught a glimpse of herself in the reflection of a window—a baby, *their baby.*

How far along she was, it was hard to say, but she was showing, and she must have been for a while, because for weeks—maybe even for months—she had noticed a feeling of being bloated. But pregnancy? It wasn't on her brain. Her monthly bleeds were typically absent—somewhat rare even. Of all the sicknesses to consume her, it had to be this. Treasta felt utterly helpless, alone, and lost in lands unfamiliar and far from where she called home. It was like her body was no longer hers but *its.*

Boy or girl, it didn't matter; she refused to accept it as something human.

This is what Treasta knew: she needed to get to the witch.

A high price is what Marnie said she had to pay, but the woman never clarified, and when Treasta tried asking again, she didn't get any answers. Davan had what money they acquired since Herra—she was unaware of his frivolous spending at the brothel—and she needed to catch up to him somehow, thought maybe the witch just needed gold. But how much, exactly? Fifty? A hundred gold bits? Mounds of it? Heaps of jewels?

Sullen, she continued wandering, thinking about the feat it would take to travel such a distance on her own and in her condition.

Helpless, alone, vulnerable . . . abandoned—Treasta wanted to disappear into nothingness, to become the void between the stars.

Treasta found Chimes drinking at the bar, where he stared into the mirror behind rows of liquor, as if he were searching for something within his own gaze inside a face flushed vibrantly red. When he realized she was there, he lowered his eyes and took a long drink.

She sat next to him.

"You're feeling better?"

"Much better. Does my offer still stand?" she asked, thinking that she would worry about how to pay him and the witch later.

Chimes took another swig, set down his glass and walked around the bar to pour himself another. "So long as I get paid," he said. "Fifty gold bits." He retrieved another glass from the shelf and poured Treasta a drink. He slid it across the counter. "You need to relax."

"Excuse me?" she said and investigated the amber liquid. "I don't think I need to relax."

Chimes still didn't know about the child—it was clear in how he acted around her. Marnie was a good woman to keep her secret safe. For a moment, Treasta contemplated telling him. She took a sip; it was bitterer than she expected. Why tell him? While she was drawn to his aura on the days she felt her best, she hadn't known him long enough to trust him. And she worried about how he would react, because she knew how Davan would have reacted.

"You seem tense. Ever since Davan left, you haven't said much, barely left your room. This is the most I've seen you since we got here."

"Well," she set the glass down with enough force for her drink to splash onto the counter, "of course I am. Wouldn't you be if your guy just disappeared while you wasted away, alone and scared in some faraway country? I'm in the middle of nowhere with complete strangers and the man I loved—*love*—has run off after . . .," she trailed off, catching herself from saying anymore. She buried her head in her hands and tugged at her hair. "Look, I don't know what to do other than I need to find him, and I know he's headed to Wesser, and you can get me there. So, for the love of the gods, help me."

"What was it about your mother dying?" he asked. Something about his tone said he knew she had been lying. "I thought *you* were the one who needed to get to Wesser. Why is he headed there without you?"

Sniffing the alcohol, Treasta winced, her stomach feeling knotted at the aroma. She brought it to lips, tasted it with her tongue, and set it down.

"My ma's not dying," she said, keeping her head low. "Actually, I've never had a mother."

Chimes took a swig right out of the bottle this time, a sign of clear disappointment. But he had expected it. Something about their story didn't add up but turning her away after hearing such a tale would have been cruel whether true or not, and Chimes was anything but. He just didn't want his gut to be right.

"What about your dad? Brothers? Sisters?"

She shook her head. A rush of emotions overtook her, and Treasta found herself trying to hold back tears.

Chimes' expression was stern. He didn't react, just took another swig, and waited.

"Are you even from Yeras?"

"No," she said shamefully. "I'm from Galgaya."

"Galgaya? By Alia, Treasta, you came all the way from Galgaya?"

She nodded, hiding her face.

"Look, the only reason why I was helping you was because you had a dying ma."

Treasta folded into the counter, face tucked in her elbow as she began sobbing.

Chimes sighed. "Why should I help if you're just going to lie to me? I don't want to travel with someone like that. I don't want to help a liar."

Treasta looked up. She wiped her tears on her sleeve. "I promise I won't lie to you ever again. I promise on my heart so long as it beats, *if you just help me.*"

Chimes stared at her for a long moment, searching her cerulean eyes for any deception.

"Okay," he finally said. "Starting now, I want you to tell me everything."

She held her breath. "It's a deal. From here on out, I will be nothing but honest with you."

Chimes set his drink down, held out his pinking and flashed a child's grin. "Come on. Shake my pinky with your pinky, and it'll be official."

Treasta hooked her pinky finger into his, they shook, and she kept her finger locked a moment longer than she should have. A strange feeling entered her chest; she attributed it to the pregnancy and moment of vulnerability that came with a bit of relief. No more secrets—it seemed much easier than hiding the truth.

Chimes held his hand up with an open palm. "This is what we'll do," he said and began pointing to each finger as he spoke. "You get to ask me a question. If I don't answer, I drink. Then I ask you a question, and if you don't answer, you drink."

"Wouldn't that still be lying?"

Chimes shrugged. "Maybe. Maybe not. I don't expect you to spill anything and everything about yourself to me. That wouldn't be fair, would it? And how can we learn to trust one another if there's nothing to build from?"

Treasta nodded—an agreeable sentiment. "I ask first?" And when he gestured her to go on, she said, "Why are you called Chimes?"

"It was a nickname my mother gave me when I was young. Marnie says it's because my voice rang like windchimes on the breeze in early spring."

She noticed his eyes lower, and his expression softened.

"My turn," he said. "Why is Wesser so important to you?"

Treasta inhaled. "Not me," she said. "It's important to Davan. There's something there that he wants."

"And that's—"

She cut him off. "My turn. Are you actually a nomad or whatever?"

"Yes and no," he said with a shrug. "I come here when I need to, but, like I told you, I don't like staying still. What is Davan looking for?"

"Treasure. Why don't you like staying still?"

"I wasn't lying when I said someone has tried to kill me because I look different."

"You said people."

"Ehh, po-tay-to, po-tah-to." He tapped the counter, looking her over while he thought of what to ask next. "What kind of treasure?"

Oh, he was actually curious. "Why?"

"No no. Answer or drink."

Staring at the drink, she couldn't bring herself to raise the beverage to her lips, and answered, with a hint of reluctance: "A golden flute." His expression brightened as he smirked. "Now *that's* interesting."

"Why did you say you didn't have any family?"

Chimes froze with his hand around the glass as he stared downward. He didn't answer right away, but much to his own consternation he said, "It's not something I care to talk about much," and he shot back a large gulp, signaling he was done. "Marnie and Atlas are all I have. That's all you need to know."

"It's more than I've ever had," Treasta said.

Chimes walked away.

Marnie helped pack the wagon with supplies that should last until Wesser. "No tipping this one, you hear? They're not cheap." It was meant as a joke, but Chimes wasn't in the mood, too deep in concentration for the days ahead.

She walked to Treasta who was petting the mare. Marnie adjusted the collar on Treasta's coat, a gift from her wardrobe along with other articles of clothing to provide warmth and comfort until they reached the canyon. She patted the collar down then gave Treasta a long embrace.

"My darling, are you sure this is something you want to do? I would be happy to help care for you and the ...," she checked to see if Chimes was near enough to listen before continuing, "... babe. I worry."

"Oh, please don't worry. Your kindness has lifted my spirit, and I feel good as new. I haven't felt ill in days."

"And you have the directions I gave you?"

"Yes, Ma'am, I do," Treasta said. "I cannot thank you enough for everything you've done for me. I don't know if anyone before now has ever extended such generosity. But I can't stay. I don't know if I even could stay. Davan would surely return and, Miss Marnie, I don't want him to know. He can't know. It would be too much for him."

Marnie smiled like she understood. And Treasta knew she had her blessing.

Marnie kissed her cheek and then helped her onto the wagon bench. Treasta plopped down next to Chimes, adjusting her dress beneath her.

"I will see you, Chimes. Stay safe, as always," Marnie said.

"As always," Chimes said, and he lightly snapped the reins.

Hooves kicked up snow, and the wheels on the wagon creaked into action, cutting through the weekold powder. Treasta pulled the hood of her coat over her head to shield her face from the wind, and she looked onward toward the horizon wondering if ever she could shake herself from feeling dread.

15

THE CLANKING AND SHARP SCREE OF DINNERWARE cut into Davan's mind. He didn't know the proper etiquette, such as how to sit at the table—except he knew to keep his back straight—nor did he know which cutlery should be used with what dish, or where to place the napkin. He only knew to set it in his lap by watching Bastan. The best Davan could do for himself in this moment was to mirror the king. And dinner? It was a feast worthy of a solstice celebration.

Davan had joined Bastan in the dining hall, where the hearth's woody scent filled the room. Multiple courses were set out before him, large and colorful and so delicious that his tongue didn't know what to make of such flavors—sweet, tangy, soft, bitter—so otherworldly. For why Bastan would be so interested in feeding a stranger a well-made feast wasn't something that had slipped Davan's mind, but as the flavors enraptured his senses, and he leaned, eager, into his next bite at the very thought of starvation, he remembered how accustomed he was to feeling hungry.

"Are you enjoying your time here, Sir Davan?" Bastan asked from the other end of the table.

By now, a hen, cooked golden brown and piping with steam fresh from the oven, was set between them along with other large dishes and pies. Davan stretched his neck upward to see better over their feast. No, he wanted to say, but instead said, "Of course."

"Excellent," the king of Hatchet said, and he clapped his hands.

"But," Davan set down his fork and wiped his lip, "if you don't mind, I have been wondering why you've been so hospitable toward me?"

"Why wouldn't I be?"

There were several places Davan could start, but it wasn't what Bastan wanted to hear. "Excuse me, please, I'm not meaning to be rude. It's just that, I don't get treated so graciously by strangers very often and by a stately king at that. We're just so … different."

Bastan let out a boisterous laugh, amused. He lifted a brow, pointed his fork at Davan and then carried on eating. "Oh, of course. Of course I understand why people are wary of travelers and why travelers may extend the same kind of concern. I am a curious man," he said. "I enjoy meeting new peoples. It isn't often I get to meet someone from Kildore, though. So, you can imagine I just want to pick your brain. Please, tell me about Kildore. I must know everything."

Davan didn't know where to begin. "Umm … the ocean is blue."

"As large bodies of water are," Bastan said.

"I live on the ocean," Davan said. Maybe this is what he wanted to hear. Blood inched into his cheeks, as small talk with someone out of his class came with great difficulty. "In Galgaya. It's the capital city of Kildore. We have a king, too."

Bastan's eyes lit up. "Yes, I know about your king. Tell me, what is he like? Surely a regal fellow."

"Kingly, I suppose. I don't know. I've never met him."

Bastan nodded. "Of course you haven't." He chewed and set down his fork. "Sir Davan, I have a very, very important question for you."

Davan set down his own fork, assuring Bastan had his attention.

"May I paint your portrait? You have such a beautiful jaw. With the light striking it just right, I could capture dramatic shadows like never before. Oh, what a somber portrait you will make. And your scars," he sighed at the thought of laying Davan's features down, "it will symbolize pain, history, and perseverance—*a perfect model.* Or," he shrugged, "if you prefer, I can make your scars go away. What do you think?"

"Umm …" Such a strange man, that Davan wondered whether he was in his right mind. He thought about it for a moment, not about the portrait, but Bastan. His features were youthful, with his dark hair neatly cut, and his face cleanly shaven and powdered to hide the shadow of stubble. "How could I refuse," Davan finally said. "I'd be honored."

Excited, Bastan stood. "Dawn's first light through the south window will offer a wonderful glow on such handsome flesh should there be no cloud cover.

"I shall retire for the evening now. With what joy I shall sleep. Please," and he motioned over the table, "eat whatever your heart desires."

The crackling of the fire was all Davan had to keep him company as he sat alone at the table. The rooms shadows seemed to manifest on their own, the mirror above the hearth reflecting the paintings hanging opposite glistened.

Dana walked in and stood aside with her hands folded neatly over her lap.

Davan reached for a dish but caught her gaze. She was saying, "Don't," with her expression—lips pinched, eyes wide. It was the most expression he had seen her give in his time within the manor.

Davan withdrew his hand. He sat back, twiddled his thumbs around and around until finally he stood. "Perhaps," he said, looking at Dana from the corner of his eyes, "I should retire, too?"

She smiled. "I can show you to your room if you like."

"That'd be good."

Dana held the door, and she walked ahead of him, showing him back to his quarters. The hallway seemed different than before, as a single portrait was not the same as he remembered. A feeling of dread seeped through his body, a chill seizing his senses as the hair on his arms perked into an alert stance.

Just as Davan parted his lips to ask a question, Dana hushed him.

"We do not disturb the portraits," she said. "Let them rest."

The slender servant woman glided up the staircase, holding her pale skirt so she wouldn't trip. Something about the manor's silence wasn't silent at all but haunted by low whispers as if hidden figures gossiped about the stranger in their halls.

"Your room." Dana opened the door. But before Davan could cross the threshold, she stopped him, grabbing his hand. His hazel eyes met with her brown eyes wide and forewarning. Something was in her hand, and she gave an disingenuous bow, saying in a low whisper, "Do not trust the mirrors."

And whatever it was in her hand remained in his as she slipped away and floated down the hall.

Davan kept his hand wrapped around what felt like folded paper as he shut the door. He looked at the mirror briefly. Dana's warning echoed. Davan wasn't sure what was going on, but he knew something about Bastan and his home didn't sit right. The warning seemed to give him a sense of reassurance about how he had been feeling since his arrival. He kept his hand clutched, securing the note within his closed fist, daring not to open it until he was out of the line of sight of the mirrors.

Davan found a nightgown at the bed. He picked it up and went behind the privacy screen. He slung it over the accordion partition and noticed for the first time since he arrived within the manor a sense of privacy in this one corner.

He unfolded the paper out of sight of the silver glass.

"He is watching you in the mirrors," the note read. "Meet me in courtyard at midnight. Tread carefully the living halls."

Davan crumpled the paper, held it in his fist unsure what to do with it. The mirrors, he realized were positioned in such a way they saw nearly every inch of the room save for the privacy screen. He stuffed it in his mouth; the sour taste of the ink on the page bled into his tongue.

Davan left the nightgown hanging over the privacy screen when he left the room just shy of midnight. The mirrors … the mirrors had eyes, and the halls were alive. More alert than before, Davan kept watch for any silver glass as he searched for a way to the courtyard. The hallways had twisted into new paths since Dana brought him to the guest room, but after some time Davan found his way to the ground floor. He recognized the door to the dining room, remembered the mirror over the mantel, and chose to walk another way instead until he found the courtyard that was situated at the heart of the manor, four walls surrounding it with a door from all direction. The snow had been freshly cleared from the cobble walkway, barren branches hung low. Dana was at the fountain, holding her sweater closed over her nightgown, her hair pinned back.

"I didn't know if you would come," she said, quietly.

"I don't—"

"Shhh …," she hushed. "Whisper."

"I don't understand," he said quieter. "Why did you want me to meet you here?"

Dana stepped closer to him. "It is the only time we can meet without him watching. He is his weakest at this hour."

Davan tilted his head, waiting for her to continue. She explained: "For a few hours each night Bastan falls into a deep sleep, because he spends all waking hours in control. He's constantly expending his magic, but when he is asleep, his mind returns to his home world, and the mirrors, too, rest." She grabbed his hands. "Please, help us. You're the only person here who isn't under his curse."

"I wouldn't know how," he said.

"We are wasting time. If we do not do something now, he will paint you, and you will be trapped like the rest of us. Don't you understand? I cannot do anything because I am under his spell. When he paints our portraits, he *owns* our souls. All of Hatchet is imprisoned."

"No," he said, pulling his hands away and shaking his head.

"No?" Dana stepped toward him, reaching, but he took a step back. "You *must* help. You're *not* under his spell. You're *not* cursed. You *need* to help us."

Davan darted from the courtyard and down one of the many snaking halls, searching for the exit. When he came into the foyer, he threw open the door expecting a snowy gust to blast inside, but instead Davan froze. Where he expected to find his horse, he found another foyer. No, not another foyer: *this* foyer. He stepped through the doorway, except it felt like he had never left the room, like he had walked through a mirror.

Dana quietly entered and placed a sheet over a nearby mirror. "See? You can't leave."

"What the hell is this place?"

Dana acted calm, but there was a sense of urgency about her demeanor; Davan being there became her now-or-never chance to do something.

"You're the first visitor here in a decade," she said. "We've been stuck here as we were for nearly ninety years now. That is when Bastan arrived. He isn't like you and me, you know."

Ninety years? Davan looked her over. Not a wrinkle in sight. She looked his age.

"If you let him paint you, he will take your soul, do you understand that?" But when Davan didn't say anything, she added, "And you will be stuck here for eternity or until the curse is broken. Please," she begged, "you must help us. I don't know when another traveler will come through."

But Davan didn't know how. He searched her face, seeing the fear behind her eyes. What choice did he have without any way out? If what she was saying were true, then come morning, Davan would be stuck in Hatchet indefinitely.

His voice was flat as he asked, "What do I need to do?"

Dana's face washed with relief as tears filled her eyes. It was the first time she felt any kind of hope. Such inspiration guided her hand to take his, and she led him down the halls, understanding how they connected after years serving Bastan within them. They climbed to the second floor then the third and then came to a winding staircase inside a tower. At the top was a locked door. But Dana didn't have a key.

Davan examined it. Just an ordinary lock. He asked if she had anything sharp and slender. Her black locks fell over her shoulders as she pulled the pin from her hair. She passed it to him, and he straightened it, then knelt and began fiddling with the lock.

Click.

A sigh of relief escaped Dana. She pulled Davan to his feet, anxious to enter the attic.

The door eased open; the moon's light passed through an open window. Inside, paintings stacked one on top of the other, none of which were framed, except one.

Dana and Davan couldn't look away, captured by the mastery and sheer horror of Bastan's self-portrait. It was old, worn. The board on which it was painted was in a state of decay.

"This is it," Dana said. "I can't touch it. The spell prevents me from touching the paintings. I've tried before, decades ago when it hung in the foyer, believe me, but the oils burn my skin." Holding out her palms she revealed fingers discolored and scarred, like the pads of the tips had been seared.

Davan looked the self-portrait over, examined Bastan's countenance: the skin on his face hung loosely, his eyebrows unkempt and white, skin gray, his ear carried a double point, his hair gone, his eyes sunken deeply within his skull—he was nearly skeletal, something unhuman. Davan looked at Dana. She was staring unblinking at the portrait, her eyes filling with tears.

And he recalled the portraits in the hallways and the expressions they captured—fear, sadness, dismay—they reflected their souls and their truest selves.

Davan had never felt such deep sorrow.

"You've been trapped like this for nearly ninety years?"

Dana averted her gaze from Bastan's decrepit portrait. "I've always wondered what it would be like," she said, "to destroy it. What would happen? Why else keep it here away from the world?

"What is the world like, now?" she asked, briefly looking at Davan.

"I—I don't—" he paused. "It's beautiful."

As she sobbed, she managed to smile. "Please destroy it … before he wakes."

"What will happen?"

"I'm not sure. But eternity must be worse than whatever it will be." Davan turned the painting over, examining the rusted over nails holding the decaying wood within the frame. He felt the need to be careful, at first. Something about destroying a painting, cursed or not, brought upon him a strange feeling. But Dana began shouting. "Do it!" she cried. "Please!" she begged, falling to her knees, grasping his pants.

Adjusting his grip around the frame, Davan braced himself as he held it above his head and smashed it over his knee.

The wood splintered with ease.

Then, silence.

And the dust that had been floating went still.

Davan's gaze met Dana's.

And a shriek echoed through the manor.

The ground quaked.

And the door behind Davan flung open.

Bastan, who had been reduced nearly to his skeletal frame of decaying, gray flesh, and ears long and low with double points sagging, appeared before them an inhuman creature. He grasped the emerald jewel hanging from his neck, but he had become too weak to mutter anything of significance.

Dana took a piece of Bastan's portrait in her hand, its end jagged and sharp, and with all her strength charged, driving the board straight through his body.

Blackness encased Hatchet.

When Davan came to, he awoke within the manor ruins, its walls looked as if they had long since crumbled, not moments ago when Dana struck Bastan, but decades ago. He sat within what looked to be the foyer. The staircase he remembered as grandiose had long been gone. Remnants of an old runner below him were coated in ice. Davan stood, catching his balance on the slippery surface. Dana was lying nearby. Then he noticed others in the town appearing at the ruins. They looked around as if in a daze and coming out of a centurylong trance.

Davan knelt to Dana's side. In the moonlight, her skin seemed more vibrant, alive.

He nudged her.

Then, a gasp.

Her eyes flew open, and she cowered backward, away from Davan, momentarily forgetting all that had happened. She looked down at her hand. The emerald jewel Bastan had worn around his neck was tucked within her palm. It hummed with a soft vibrations pulsating through the pads of her palm. Warm. Cold. Warm. Cold. ...

"Is it over?" one townsperson said. "Are we free?"

"I …," she looked at the jewel. "Yes, we are." She stood, repeating the words with greater zeal.

And many fell to their knees around Davan and Dana, wept and praised them.

Ninety years under Bastan's curse. Ninety goddamn years. What sadness, what relief the residents of Hatchet expressed. Davan couldn't comprehend what they had gone through under the alleged king's sway. A faux king, a warlock, maybe even a demon—an *Andrili*—Davan thought, recollecting Bastan's gray skin and strange ears. But he had only heard of tales of the Andrili, those of the shadow realm known as Drynis.

Collectively, everyone shared an expression of "now what?"—including Davan. He hadn't yet been in Hatchet for an entire day's time; now he was their hero. Such a description was unbefitting, and he couldn't bring himself to stay a moment longer.

Davan rushed to find his horse near where he remembered leaving the beast.

As he started down the road, Dana hurried after him. "Wait! Please, wait."

He expelled a sigh, cleared his throat. "I don't want this kind of attention. I'm nobody's hero, you understand?" And, he wanted to add, *this place is too strange to stay in, anyway.*

"But I want to come with you," she said. "I can't stay here a moment longer."

She took Davan's hand and placed the emerald jewel still hanging on its chain on his palm. "Consider it yours."

The hum lowly vibrated through his skin—a honing crystal carved into a beautiful jewel. Mages and sorcerers used them to channel magic. He carefully inspected it. But this was a demon's stone. For the right buyer, it could fetch Davan more than a fair amount of money, enough money, in fact, his journey to Wesser and back would be without fraught.

Davan eyed Dana. "You're going to travel in that?"

Dana's face came alight at his words with an ear-to-ear grin.

Moments later, townsfolks were bringing him supplies, including a cart and proper harness for his horse. In silence they strapped the steed to the cart, loaded it with everything a traveler would need journeying in the cool, winter weather and fastened lamps to poles.

A deep discomfort gathered in the pit of his stomach. It was too much, but this time he had done something to deserve the supplies, unlike in Herra. Treasta's laughter rang in his head. *Look at you, Mister Hero Man. You shouldn't be feeling guilty. Why do you always feel guilty, huh?* He needed to get her voice out of his head.

A light was dawning in the east, ribbons of sunrays from beyond the horizon caught on distant clouds reflected pink and orange. And Davan, with Dana at his side, headed out of Hatchet. The echo of townsfolks waving them off lasted until they could no longer be seen in the early morning.

The darkness had begun to fade, and Dana snuffed out the flames in the lamps. She was nervous but didn't show it. She opened a hundred-year-old map.

"Where are we going?" she asked.

"Wesser."

She repeated the name with a sense of awe. "The Great Lake City."

16

DECLAN AWOKE BESIDE THE HEARTH AT THE OUTPOST, a blanket over him, the fire having long faded. He stood and sucked mucus back into his nostrils, wiping his nose. Looking around, he couldn't find Elsie. He flew to his feet, worried he had been abandoned, and raced up and down the tower, then outside. Elsie was loading Carrot.

He threw himself around her greatly relieved she hadn't left. Elsie pried him off, looked him over with an expression of disgust and pushed him away. She tightened the strap around the horse and without a word or any indication to the boy, she started following the path down into the canyon, walking alongside the beast.

Declan raced after her, trailing closely. That she was wearing the mask brought Declan joy, but he kept such a feeling to himself, thinking it would be best to keep his demeanor closer to hers. So, he pouted, let his mouth hang into a sharp frown and furrowed his brows. It was too painful of an expression to keep on his face, and he relaxed his muscles.

They had traveled a good distance into the canyon, reaching the first bend in the switchback when Declan's stomach grumbled. He tapped Elsie.

"What is it?" she asked after she faced him.

He patted his stomach and signaled with his hand at his mouth with what must have meant "food." Elsie copied him. He nodded and smiled. And she realized in that moment he could communicate with his hands, a visual language he and Cal's dad knew only with one another because no one else bothered to try.

She made the motion again, and he nodded again, then pointed to himself and added some additional context that Elsie didn't quite understand.

"So, you're hungry?"

He clapped.

Elsie supposed this wasn't a terrible place to stop. Enough space along the path gave them a prime location to build fire and enjoy a warm meal.

She showed him a stick. "Can you find more?"

Declan did as she asked, broke branches from dried brush and returned with a large bundle in his arms. She wouldn't admit it, but she was somewhat impressed at how well he did. Maybe this kid could be of help after all.

After sparking a fire, she situated a pot with water within the kindling and poured in some oats. He watched her carefully, like he was trying to absorb everything she did, eager to learn the ways of the world beyond the walls of Grenna.

Elsie was still eating as Declan slurped down the last of the hot meal.

She observed him with wonderment. He was maybe twelve at the oldest, had long black hair he kept tied back and was scrawny, but not so scrawny that he seemed like he was starving. The story he acted out about his father, mother, and other children, was a familiar one to Elsie, except her father killed her mother in a drunken stupor and then she killed him.

Elisandra was thirteen, scared, and didn't know what else to do, but she knew that if she hadn't killed him, he would have eventually killed her with his hand around her throat. But her father hadn't always treated her that way. Before coming of age, he coddled her, wanted her to be "one of the boys," but when she had her first bleed, everything changed.

"What did you do?" Her younger brother, Ida, was in the entry way. He was seven when he found her next to their father's body spilling blood from the deep gash in his throat.

"Get out of here," she told him, but he just stood there, too frightened to move.

"Dad?"

"In the name of the goddess," she begged, "leave."

Ida didn't know where to, but he ran until his legs were too sore and his lungs burned. Gasping, he collapsed. Three city guards noticed the child and rushed to him. They helped him to his feet. The child fell into their arms and wailed.

When the guards arrived at the home, they found only the boy's father. Elisandra was gone.

Elsie waved, getting Declan's attention. Declan set down his bowl.

"Do you speak with your hands?" she asked.

He answered with a nod, then retrieved his graphite stick and paper and wrote something out for her to read.

Y can teech yew.

"Yes," Elsie said, "teach me."

They rested, taking in the warmth of the fire as Declan taught her various hand symbols for the items around them, starting with the bowl and fire, then moving to the sky and sun. It was more than she could remember, but she repeated them, hoping with time she could communicate better with the boy.

As they continued down the switchback, so did the lessons. Two days passed by the time they reached the bottom. The warmer air came with a relief to them both.

"Hot," she said with her hands.

"So-so," he replied. "Warm," he corrected her.

"Warm," she repeated.

The breadth of the canyon was so vast, it was impossible to see to the other side from their current position. Outcroppings, crags, plateaus, and other various formations dominated the landscape. Here, pines and aspens called the terrain home, growing in healthy numbers to produce several groves. From here, Elsie and Declan lost the road. The brush had long overgrown, and it was clear this wasn't a road traveled enough for traffic to keep the path exposed.

Elsie unbuttoned her jacket to let the warmer air cool her body as a gentle breeze brushed under her cloak. She opened the map, flattening it on Carrot's side. Where on the map they were, she couldn't quite identify, but from what she could see, they should come to a river at some point.

They needed to get there while the sun was high, lest lose their bearings in the dark.

Declan looked around in awe as they continued, taking in greenery he had never before seen. This place was magical, he thought, so magical that he couldn't imagine ever returning to Grenna. Why live in a walled off town close to your enemies when you could have this? The canyon avoided winter with grace. And the more they traveled, the more layers they removed from their persons.

Where was the snow? Declan wondered. Something about the weather pattern and the depth of the canyon created a juxtaposition between the two terrains. Both regions were desertlike—the summer months blazed with intensity—but in the lands around Grenna, the dead of winter was unbearably cold, and surviving the winter months was difficult. But here, Declan would never have to worry about winter again.

As they walked, Declan signed what he observed and explained the differences between here and where he was from—though much of what he was saying Elsie couldn't understand, but she tried taking in new symbols and learned in that moment how to describe the trees as beautiful. His excitement warmed her soul, and a smile snuck onto her face.

"Beautiful trees," Elsie said as she repeated after him. "I agree. It is beautiful here."

And as they reached the river, Elsie realized she hadn't used the word "beautiful" since before her mother died. She remembered her mother's smile, the roundness of her cheeks when she tucked Elisandra into bed, and the softness of her kiss as she wished her goodnight. She remembered the yellow flecks of gold and brown ring of her eyes. Elsie hid her face from Declan to wipe away her tears. Collect yourself, she thought. The kid can't see you this way. She readjusted her mask, hoping Declan wouldn't be able to notice she had been crying. He had, but he continued unpacking Carrot to set up camp to give her a sense of privacy.

They built a fire, set up a tent, and retired for the rest of the afternoon and evening.

Come morning Elsie and Declan followed the river southward beneath graying skies. The water cut wide and deep through the landscape with intense force, exposing the orange layers of the earth. And yet, this wasn't the Great River that flowed into the Great Lake. Imagining such a landscape was nigh impossible for Elsie. Wide for miles, it was described to her. The river itself, she had heard, was like a lake flowing into a freshwater sea, except this sea was landlocked and humanmade thanks to the dam on which Wesser was built.

Traveling with a horse on such rocky and unpredictable terrain was becoming increasingly difficult without a road, but the beast was useful, and well loved by the boy. Declan guided Carrot carefully behind Elsie, who was yards ahead. She climbed a boulder, looked over its edge, and saw the river cutting for miles until it was out of sight. At some point, they'd need to cross the river. Surely an old bridge would manifest at some point along the way, but it wouldn't be so.

Miles passed and nothing. Elsie sat with Carrot while Declan explored on his own. She bit down on bread; its hard outer shell nearly cracked another tooth. They were lost. She didn't want to admit it and didn't need Declan to know, but she had a hunch that he suspected it.

Elsie exhaled, frustrated and defeated. She did not know where Davan and Treasta were, whether they were lurking somewhere in the same portion of the canyon, or whether they had already arrived at Wesser. She kicked herself at the thought and then felt a hot fire come alight in her body as a rage boiled thinking about how they left her to die at the Laughing Crow Inn in Herra. She supposed it was fair. She was ready to leave them there bound and gagged like she did to Kim. But now she wanted to make them pay. Her healing wounds itched. The aftermath of the fire, having to suffer while within the temple's walls and listen day and night to that nurse whispering prayers, her wounds—she wanted Davan and Treasta to suffer.

Davan and Treasta—the two were a well-known pair within the tribe. Wherever Davan was, so too was Treasta and vice versa. And what better way to make Davan squirm, she thought, than to tear out Treasta's throat before his eyes. She smiled at the idea, but her smile faded when Declan reappeared. This kid, she realized, wouldn't have followed her had she not held back in Herra, had Davan not tied her to the bed post. She wouldn't have felt the need to stop in Grenna because she would have beat the storm.

Elsie took a drink, trying to calm herself. Being hotheaded wasn't going to get her anywhere right now.

Declan began signing and pointed toward the cliffside of a crag that looked about a half-mile out of their way. She didn't quite understand him. Her gaze darted between the cliff face and the boy, clearly confused. He sighed, annoyed, and grabbed her hand, trying to pull her.

"Okay," she said, and got up. She wiped her hands on her trousers. "Gods be damned, you need to relax."

He rolled his eyes and pointed again. Declan packed the supplies that were strewn onto the ground and loaded Carrot without another word from Elsie and started toward the crag without her.

She took the final bite and followed him through the trees until an abandoned settlement appeared underneath an outcropping. Remnants of a road, old cobble and felled stone fencing, were before her. "Huh," she said, somewhat impressed, "good job, kid." But he was already unpacking the horse beneath the outcropping near one of the ruined buildings.

The air was cooler, staler in the shadow of the cliff. She wondered for how long the town had been abandoned, tried to imagine what it was like to live in once upon a time. The map yielded no clues, no markings of a town, no road, nothing. Long enough to be forgotten.

Elsie and Declan took shelter inside what seemed to be the most stable structure. In the firelight, Declan hunkered against a wall, slouching with his pad of paper and graphite stick on his lap. His gaze moved from the paper to Elsie and back again as the day waned into night.

Declan fell asleep with it at his side, revealing lines and shadows overlapping to form Elsie's high cheek bones, mask, and short straight hair. He captured the highlight from the fire on her brow ridge and even the deep cracks on her dry lips. But it was her expression that made it hard for Elsie to look away: one eye, wide and cast in dramatic shadow stared from the page; bags hanging told the story of a woman tired and who experienced a great deal of pain—and she felt that pain within herself. Elsie set down the paper carefully and quietly retrieved a blanket to lay gently over his body. Declan clutched the wool and pulled it toward his chest, holding tightly. He began to snore.

17

THE SNOW CONTINUED FALLING LIKE A VELVET CURTAIN. The horizon had since turned gray, the sun—the blazing heat—absent. Silent was the snow, apart from the turning wheels of the wagon and clobbering hooves of the horse crunching over the fresh powder. How, then, were they to know where they were going? Such a thought chilled Treasta, worried over traveling with Chimes—still a stranger—who refused to turn north at the fork toward Hatchet. It wouldn't be until they descended into the canyon they would come to another town. But he assured her they would be fine continuing in this direction and made little mention of Hatchet beyond the town's impoverished state. She needed to trust him. She had no choice but to.

Treasta tightened the strings on her jacket and crossed her arms for warmth. Winter was upon them, and it seemed here to stay in the Altan Highlands.

"It'll be easier once we're in the canyon," Chimes said.

But she didn't believe him. The land was coated white for days. *Trust him.* They were well stocked, and he was well traveled.

As she searched for comfort, Treasta found herself sitting closer to him as the days went on, so close that the warmth radiating from his body eased her some, and she would shut her eyes and pretend for a moment that Chimes was Davan and that Davan had never left her. But Chimes was kinder, gentler, and more attentive. When they camped, he served her meals first, always asked how she was doing, smiled with his eyes whenever she answered him, allowed her to sleep in the covered wagon while he sought shelter in a tent on a bedroll on the ground even as it snowed. Maybe it was the weather. Maybe it was the mood swings—trying to keep her emotions in check was becoming increasingly difficult. Several times she had caught herself crying over trivial things, such as when the tie snapped as she picked up a wood bundle from the back of the wagon and the logs scattered the ground. She hid her face in her hands and began sobbing, when normally she would have just cursed under her breath and began picking up after herself. Thinking about it now, she knew how ridiculous she looked. But Chimes didn't react. He knelt, gathering the spilled bundle, and made a fire. It was difficult not to compare Chimes with Davan, and she wanted to believe that Davan would have reacted with the same patience. But Davan wasn't a patient man.

Treasta jumped, threw her hands on her stomach and just as fast removed them, trying not to bring attention to it. What was that? Surely the terrain had become rocky, unseen beneath the layer of snow.

There. She felt it again. *Movement.*

Dread returned to her body with the same intensity as when Marnie told her she was with child, and now that child had rammed its tiny heel into the wall of her stomach. She was entirely lost within herself, the world becoming a distant haze on the edges of her vision. Lightheaded, she felt her forehead, held her hand there momentarily, hoping she could collect herself. But instead, a wooziness seized her senses, and her heart beat as if it would thump right out of her chest—the *ba-dum-dum* of its rhythm steadily increasing. And the more she thought about it—*ba-dum-dum, ba-dum-dum*—the faster it raced.

Treasta gripped Chimes' wrist. He pulled back on the reins to bring the wagon to a stop.

"Chimes," she said between breaths breaking from her lungs with such force she felt she would faint, "help. I feel like I'm going to die."

He touched her forehead and then cheeks with the same gentleness as Marnie's touch.

Her body temperature was rising, yet a terrible chill was taking over all faculties as numbness set in. Treasta couldn't control her breaths.

Chimes hushed her. "Close your eyes," he suggested. "Just listen to my voice, okay? I'm right here with you."

The darkness behind her lids spun. And she did the best she could to listen to Chimes' voice, to focus on the smoothness of his tenor. But as she tried not to think about how detached she was from her body, it somehow made it worse, and she began to float inside her own flesh.

"Take deep breaths," Chimes' voice echoed. It sounded like miles away. "Breathe with me. Can you do that?"

She nodded. And as he inhaled, she inhaled, and as he exhaled, she exhaled. They repeated the process until she felt safe inside her body and the numbness disappeared.

Treasta opened her eyes. He looked at her deeply worried, and then sighed in relief.

She didn't know what to say, but she felt another kick from the baby as he held her gaze.

"I'm pregnant."

Take it back. Say you're lying. Say it's all a bad joke to try to make him laugh after such a terrible moment. No, don't say any of that, you fool. Treasta's mind raced. But it was Chimes' silence that was driving her mad. She waited. She needed him to say something. And when he didn't, Treasta unbuttoned her jacket, took his hand, and held it on her firm stomach.

He flinched, feeling movement. But instead of pulling his hand away, like Treasta had expected, Chimes gently pressed, and the babe returned another jab. A smile grew on his face, one that expressed amazement and wonder.

"Is this why you were sick?"

Treasta nodded.

"Does he know?" Chimes asked, referring to Davan.

She shook her head and frowned. Treasta cupped Chimes' face in her hands to ensure his eyes locked with hers. "He *can't* know."

"You don't want him to know?" Chimes scratched his head. "He's going to be able to tell, you know that right? You're not …" his eyes fell to her stomach now able to see the roundness that had been growing under layers of clothes.

She leaned back and exhaled. "I'm fat. I know."

"Not what I was going to say."

"But you were thinking it. I saw the way you looked at my stomach."

"No," Chimes tried correcting himself, but it was futile, "that's not what I meant. What I meant was …" He stopped himself. What he was going to say next wouldn't have been any better. "You're gorgeous. But it's okay if you don't feel that way right now."

Treasta crossed her arms and scoffed. "You're just saying that to save yourself." She nudged him and motioned toward the horse. "Well, are we going to sit here all day?"

Chimes, without another word, snapped the reins.

As they continued, Treasta watched the falling snow, hoping a single flake, in all its complicated details, could make her feel something.

18

TREASTA DIDN'T NOTICE THEM AT FIRST, two smallish figures creeping along a wall.

They had reached the cliffside town of Hayam within the next day, a well-traveled town situated part way down the canyon's side, nestled within the cliff's face. A fog had settled in the canyon within the time they arrived, keeping the vastness of its expanse a secret from Treasta.

The two figures turned to one another and whispered, then carried on into an alley, disappearing into the shadows of the recessed structures.

Hayam wasn't small by any means, but it was neither a city. Chimes was talking with a stableman when Treasta crept away. The figures were familiar, but their faces had been obscured just enough that she wasn't sure whether they were who she suspected. Quietly she followed them into the dark recessed passage between slender stone buildings carved from the cliff. The air cooled in the shadows, and their echoes reverberated. She hunkered behind a crate, watching as the young members of her guild knelt next to a lamp. In the light, Treasta could make out beds and piles of personal items. It was apparent they had been living in the back of this alleyway for a long while.

The Pats, as they were known, twins named Patrick and Patricia, barely in their teenage years, who separately went by Pat and Trish. What the hell were they doing here? Treasta didn't recall the Pats had signed up for the mission.

A knife pressed into her jacket from behind. "Hiya," she heard in her ear.

"Come on. Let's get up."

Treasta listened. The Pats looked up, hearing the movement. Treasta appeared in the light with Laine behind her. This was beginning to make sense, she realized. Laine often offered the younger guildmates promises he could never keep, and they always believed him because of their eagerness. Pat and Trish scowled when they recognized her.

"Are you kidding me?" Trish said. "I thought we were the only ones who've gotten this far."

The twins were looking over the goods they had stolen, some supplies to help get by, and lots of trinkets and jewels and treasure that could fetch good money if they found the right buyer.

Treasta pulled away from Laine. "Really think that's necessary?" She eyed the tarnished dagger in his hand. The blade was blunt—did he know?

Laine used it to pick his teeth as he shrugged. "Looks like you've been doing well," he said, noticing she was not just dressed for the weather of the Altan Highlands, but her clothes were nicer than she typically wore. "Where's Davan?"

"In town," she said.

But he caught her hesitation, that break in her breath between words. He raised his brows. "In town, huh?"

"How long have you been here?"

"Long enough to have a hold on a couple of the vendors in the market. Pretty good, yeah?"

She wasn't impressed. "You ought to establish yourself here."

"I've thought about it."

"Davan left me," she said.

Laine pouted his lips and buckled his dagger. "Pity." He tucked his red hair behind his ears. "You should join us instead."

"Oh, not uh," Trish said as she came between them. "I'm the woman of this band."

"You've barely any breasts," Treasta said. Trish stood a foot shorter next to her. Her brother was maybe a few inches shorter, yet to be much affected by puberty. "You could be mistaken for Pat easily."

Trish's face turned red. Sure she and her brother were twins, but their curls were different shades of brown—hers kissed with gold, his ashen—and she had more freckles than him across the bridge of her nose. Trish landed a kick in Treasta's shin.

"*Bitch!*" Treasta yelped, and then shoved the girl. She rubbed her leg, feeling where her skin was tender; a sharp sting shot into her thigh when she found the bruise.

But before Treasta had a chance to straighten herself upright, Trish slammed herself bodily into Treasta and held her against the wall. Treasta grappled with the girl, and they tumbled to the cold ground. Trish ripped the buttons from Treasta's jacket, then tore into her tunic before landing a punch across her cheek, right under the eye.

Trish froze. Treasta managed, in between hits, to snag Trish's blade from her waist. A single trickle of blood dripped from her neck as the tip of the knife cut into her flesh.

Pat rushed to his feet, but Laine stopped him.

"The difference between me and you," Treasta's voice lowered in a forewarning tone, "is I'm not afraid to kill."

Trish swallowed back a gulp, carefully came to her feet, and backed away with her hands up.

"I swear to the gods," Pat said between his teeth, "if you touch my sister, I'll kill you myself."

"Go ahead," Treasta said, brushing dust from her clothes. The child moved inside her body, and Treasta felt the sudden urge to gut herself, to get it over with. Wouldn't that be the show the Pats wanted anyway?

She picked up the buttons, saddened Marnie's jacket was ruined. "For what it's worth," she said, "I don't care about the bounty."

"Then why are you out here?" Laine asked.

"I'm going after Davan. He left me. You think I'm going to just let him get away with that?"

Laine smirked. "Davan and Treasta, the notorious duo no longer a duo." He chuckled. "How do I know you won't take the bounty for yourself?"

Treasta shrugged. "I guess you'll just have to believe me. Laine, you and I, we've never had an issue with one another, have we?"

He shook his head. "Guess not."

"So why would we now? Tell you what," she said, "if I get my hands on the golden flute, I'll give it to you. But when I say I have no interest in it, I really do mean that." She eyed the sack Pat was holding at his side. "What I'd be more interested in is those lovely trinkets and treasures you've managed to nab." Then, Treasta had an idea. "I'll get you the flute if you give me everything in that in return."

"You want us to wait around here?"

"You said it yourself you thought about setting up base here. It's a good location, Laine. And a town this size, you get the right person in charge, someone who's greedy and wants what you want, well, you'd basically be running this place. Wouldn't that be ideal?"

Laine thought for a long while before answering. He held out his hand. "Fine," and Treasta shook it. "This will save me the trouble anyway."

Treasta gave a wry smile. "We both get what we want. I'll be able to find you here, then?"

Laine nodded. "This is the back entrance," and he pointed to the door. "I plan on taking over the pawn shop on the front end once the shop owner *falls ill*."

"You always were a clever one," she said.

"When can I expect you back?"

"Hopefully within the coming month, I would think. We're about a week or two from Wesser, yeah?"

Laine nodded. "Seems right."

"I'll see you then."

"Golden flute in hand."

Treasta smirked. As she left, she could hear the Pats complaining. Something about "giving up," and "we already have come this far" and "why the hell are you trusting her?"

She was still wearing that smirk when she emerged from the alley into a busy street. Then her expression turned serious as she thought of the endeavor. She'd need to get to the bounty before Davan if this was going to work, lest deal with his zealous nature. She didn't know where he was, though—likely miles ahead, maybe even days.

She found Chimes at the stable.

"How fast can we get to Wesser?" she asked.

Caught off guard, Chimes spun around and shot her a perplexed look, then his eyes widened, and he grabbed her face, looking over the welt forming under her right eye. "Who did this?"

She saw rage forming on his face, and something told her if she answered him, he'd have gone after Laine and the Pats. "No one."

A long silence fell between them.

"No one important," she added.

His lips tightly curled inward as he held back his anger. His nostrils flared as he exhaled. "We said no secrets."

"How fast can we get to Wesser?"

They had talked about it before. Two weeks by road, at least. Something about Treasta's demeanor was different than before. He allowed the change in subject … for now. Her brows furrowed with a seriousness he hadn't seen from her. "What's got you in a sudden rush?"

"I changed my mind," she told him, relieved he stopped pressuring her about the mark Trish left on her face. "I need to get my hands on that flute."

"I thought you needed to catch up with Davan, and that was it."

Trading the flute for the treasure Laine and the twins horded would fetch her a generous sum of gold and sterling bits, maybe even sacks' worth, and maybe it would be just enough for the witch's mysterious price.

"Like I said. I changed my mind," Treasta said.

But instead of answering her, he took her hand—and she should have pulled away, but the ridges of his callused palm were a curious feeling against her own skin. He kept her close at his side as they passed down the crowded street.

Inside the meadery the aroma of sweet honey laced with alcohol filled Treasta's nose. The windows were cut in the shapes of honeycomb, the tabletops and seats also held the same shape.

They came to the bar and sat at two stools.

As Chimes leaned against the bar top, placing his hand under his chin, he saw his aunt's jacket, the missing buttons and then the torn tunic. He held his breath long enough to bite his tongue. It was obvious Treasta wasn't going to explain what had happened. Not now, anyway. He'd have to find another way to get it out of her but couldn't shake the thought from his mind that she had been cornered by a couple of thugs and mugged.

Treasta held the jacket closed, shrinking into herself, ashamed, as she noticed Chimes peeking the torn fabric. Marnie's kindness was truly a virtue that Treasta held dearly, and now she ruined the things Chimes' aunt had given her to keep her warm—to protect her and the babe. Treasta rested her forehead on the table, a sudden surge of tears erupting from her eyes. She covered her head with her hands and wanted to disappear.

Chimes dragged his hands down his face. Now what? Now what? Now. What? He kept his cool by knocking his knuckle on the counter to grab the bartender's attention and not acknowledging Treasta as she wept—mostly because he didn't know what to do.

The man who walked over was someone Chimes knew—of course it was someone Chimes knew. Treasta listened from inside the cave she created within her arms.

"Little Darius," he said. "It's been a while."

"What did I tell you about calling me that?"

"Ha, well, you don't like Little Dee either. What's brought you out here?"

"We're headed to Wesser," Chimes said.

The man realized the woman sobbing next to him wasn't just some random patron from off the streets. "I see. Well, you know the rules.

"Hey, miss," the man patted the counter near her ear. "Hey, are you hungry?"

Treasta peered from inside her cave. She had stopped crying at some point, but her eyes were puffy and red as she looked at the older fellow with a long gray beard, darker skin, and dark eyes. She nodded, sitting up and wiping her eyes on her wrists.

"I'm Darius," the man said. "Call me Dee." Dee walked off to fetch meals for the two.

Treasta looked at Chimes and then at the doorway where the other Darius disappeared. "You have the same name?"

Chimes shrugged. "You feeling better?"

"Heh"—it wasn't quite a laugh, but it got the point across. "I'm a mess. I'm sorry. Marnie was right: I shouldn't be traveling under my condition."

"You're doing great," Chimes said. "Really, you are," he added when she flashed him a disbelieving look, unamused by his humoring her. "But, going and getting yourself mugged is going to put stress on the babe. Don't need you losing it. I feel like I'm protecting two of you."

"I don't need your protection," she snapped back.

He touched the mark on her face; she winced. His hand lingered on her cheek a moment before she forced his arm down. "I don't know," Chimes said. "Seems it. You going to tell me what happened?"

"You going to tell me why he's got the same name as you?"

"I'm his father's closest friend," Dee said as he returned with two plates steaming hot with food.

Chimes stabbed his fork into the plate. "My father's dead."

"He's good and alive," Dee said, looking at Treasta.

Treasta moved the food around on her plate: steamed carrots, potatoes, and chicken. Combined with the scent of mead wafting in the air, the smell made her nauseous. She took small bites, easing into it.

"He's dead to me," Chimes said.

"I got a letter from him just last week," Dee said. "He was asking whether you had come by."

"And what'd you tell that bastard?"

"Oh, I told him I saw you just the other day. And now my letter won't be a lie. Chimes, he worries about you, you know that right? With the way you look different than others, he's afraid you're going to wind up mounted like a trophy on some disturbed man's wall."

"Hasn't happened yet," Chimes said as he stuffed a large bite into his mouth.

"You said you didn't have any parents," Treasta said.

"I don't."

Dee rolled his eyes.

"What happened?" Treasta asked.

"I don't want to talk about it."

Dee's expression softened. "So, what's in Wesser for you?"

Chimes gave Treasta the opportunity to answer as he continued stuffing his face.

"My friend," she said. And that was all the information she was willing to give.

"Let me guess, Little Darius is your guide," he said.

Treasta nodded.

"And he asked for a hefty sum?" When she nodded again, he said, "Of course he did. That boy."

Dee went to the other end of the bar and poured three mugs, all carrying the same honeycomb motif.

Treasta looked the mead over, sniffed it. The strong scent nearly brought her stomach into her mouth.

Dee took notice, cocking his head confused. "Everything all right?"

"She's pregnant," Chimes said.

She nearly knocked him out of his seat—but instead Treasta turned away, trying not to take in another waft lest puke. She certainly wanted to knock him out of his seat, wanted to say, "Hey! What's the deal?" but was too busy collecting herself.

Dee nearly spat his drink back into his mug. His voice lowered. He was clearly trying to ask without Treasta hearing, "Is it yours?"

But she heard him, and still, she felt too sick to react. Treasta stood from her seat, turning away, doing her best not to leave the bar. But standing in the room another moment would put her out. She excused herself and went outside for fresh air.

When she was gone, Chimes answered: "No. It's her friend's … or whatever he is to her."

"Where do you find these people?" Dee asked. "A woman pregnant out of wedlock traveling alone?"

"She wasn't traveling alone when I found her," Chimes said. "Her friend, or whatever their relationship is, left her. We were staying at Marnie and Atlas' lodge, and she got really sick, and he just up and left her there."

"And now you're following him to Wesser? Why?"

Chimes thought about what to say. Anything Chimes would say, Dee would tell him to leave her, let her continue the rest of the way on her own, let the wild decide her fate. Chimes knew about the flute. Confliction seized him. The way she came to him, telling him her change of plans, she spoke like she expected his help, the goddamn golden flute …. Why did it have to be the golden flute of all the treasure they could chase? That was it: he needed to be done. He'd get her to Wesser and that would be the end of their time together. But the idea of leaving Treasta wasn't settling well. He worried about her, even if she thought she didn't need him.

"I …," Chimes hated lying, "… don't really know."

"Well," Dee took a swig and wiped his lip, "that sounds like something you need to figure out. You're still wearing that charm your grandmother gave you, right?"

Chimes patted his chest where it was tucked under his tunic and hanging around his neck.

"Dee," Chimes set down his fork, and pushed away his empty plate, "am I an idiot?"

"Of course you are. But all young men are idiots."

His stomach fluttered nervous to say what he had been thinking for a long time aloud. "I think I'm falling for her."

Dee's expression fell, serious. "Well, don't," he said. "You don't want to get yourself involved with a pregnant woman like that."

The comment was somewhat sobering, but Chimes wished he hadn't said anything after hearing Dee's wisdom. "You're right. I *would* be an idiot to want to be with a woman like that."

"Get her to Wesser and leave her."

"That's the plan," Chimes said, though he wasn't sure if he was being completely honest in saying it.

When Chimes found Treasta, she was sitting with her legs crossed on the wall that separated the main roadway cutting through town from the steep drop below. The jacket was in her lap, and she was weaving a needle and thread through the buttonholes.

He carefully sat next to her, letting his legs dangle over the edge. The fog had lifted, the Sarnak River below ran through the canyon with a smooth flow bending southwest toward the Great River. A boat with two smoke pipes cruised upriver carrying goods and passengers but looked the size of an insect from Hayam.

Treasta rethreaded the needle, breaking the yellow thread with her teeth. She moved on to the next button, careful not to poke herself. Too concentrated, the grandeur of the Great Canyon of Wesserland, the country's defining feature, was but an afterthought. As she weaved in and out, she thought about Marnie's words, the witch, the infant growing day by day; she thought about how Davan left her, the way she felt abandoned when she found out; she thought about Elsie burning to death, how horrifying it would be to drink of flames. And she wiped a tear thinking about everything, trying not to acknowledge Chimes sitting at her side; she was too upset at him for spilling her business.

After she left the meadery, she went and found a tailor. Used the few bits of copper she had on herself to purchase the needle and thread. It was perhaps the most honest purchase she made in who knows how long. She sat down, overlooking the canyon, feeling a sense of peace, alone with her thoughts as she repaired the jacket Marnie had given her. It was, after all, the least she could do for such a kind-hearted woman.

Chimes opened his mouth, but Treasta cut him off before he had the chance to speak. "Don't," she said. "I don't want to talk to you right now. I don't even want to see your face."

He didn't understand what he had done, so he stepped down from his perch, but before he walked away, he said, "Are you going to tell me what the hell happened to your face, or what?"

Nothing.

"Suit yourself," he said, and walked away.

Treasta held up the jacket looking over her handiwork. It wasn't great but it would do. She admired the brass buttons, how they shone in the midday sunlight, then folded it and set it in her lap to look across the canyon and admire the mesas and layers of color: reds, yellows, oranges—she imagined at the rising and dawning of the sun how the canyon must glow. She took in the view, drank in the peace away from Chimes, and focused on the inhale and exhale of her breathing. A flock of ravens swooped nearby; a vole skittered along the cliff's cracks and crevasses as a goat climbed not too far from where she was sitting and paused to lick the rocky wall. How it stayed balanced on the near vertical wall, she did not know, but she admired its courage and skills.

From behind, Laine appeared. He spoke in a low voice. "So, who was that strange-looking fellow?"

Treasta continued observing the canyon. "What do mean? What strange-looking fellow?"

Laine leaned against the wall, facing the opposite direction of her, observing the town. "That white-haired fellow."

"You're seeing things, Laine. A ghost."

The colliding of her two worlds—the thieves' guild and Chimes—was something she had been trying to avoid. Chimes didn't need to know about Laine or the Pats, nor why she needed the golden flute. It would be better this way for the both of them.

"Trish and Pat are following him as we speak. You think I'd not want to see what you're up to out here? I really needed to know whether you and Davan had actually split."

She didn't need Laine to notice how he got under her skin. She looked at him, composed herself in a way that expressed no worry, and said, "Do what you want."

"So, you're with that white-haired fellow, then? Never seen anyone quite like him before. He's human or Eldei or something else? Hair like that I'd think he'd at least be a half-breed. But," he trailed off, musing, "I don't know if a half-breed would be so … pale. Never seen a snow-colored half-breed Eldei before. Have you?"

"He's human," Treasta said. "A perfectly normal human. That's just how he was born. Now will you leave me alone? Or are you going to keep talking nonsense about nothing you know about? Snow-colored half-breed … you should hear yourself."

Laine smirked. "Here's the deal, because I want to make sure you get me what I want, Pat and Trish will be keeping an eye from afar. They won't intervene with your task, but if you stray from it, I will know, and they have strict orders if you don't bring me what I want."

"And those orders are?"

Laine turned his body toward her, leaning closer, and examined her bruised and welted face where Trish landed a solid punch. He made sure he had her attention and said, "Your white-haired friend, consider him dead."

"I should have cut Trish's throat when I had the chance," Treasta said rather coolly.

He laughed. "Well, it's your loss you didn't, isn't it? Though I suppose I wouldn't have been able to keep Pat from going after you, then.

"What I don't understand," Laine continued, "is why you don't want to keep the bounty for yourself. It's worth far more than any of the treasures we have."

"I have no interest in it," Treasta said. "It holds no value for me, but those jewels I saw in the Pats' sack—the crown, the pearls—those will be easier to sell, and I need the money."

"Sell the flute."

"You think that will be easy?"

Laine sneered. "You want to bring me something I can't fence?"

"I want to bring you something that you can use to your advantage to get in a place of power here, you idiot. It's not always about money, you know. You're smart, Laine. You're probably one of the smarter thieves in the tribe, maybe even the whole syndicate. You just get too hot-headed sometimes. Think before you react."

Laine crossed his arms and thought about what Treasta was saying, though he wasn't keen that the wisdom she imparted was actually good. What she was saying finally hit him, and he smiled. "Ah, I see. Are you sure you don't want to just join me here? You're far more clever than the Pats. Brains like ours," he tapped his temple under strands of red, "we could do whatever we want."

"And serve under you? No," she said. "I'll get you the flute, and you'll give me what I want, and that's the end of our relationship, you got that?"

"Yeah, yeah, yeah. You know, Treasta," and he stood straight ready to leave, "you're far better off without Davan."

"I really don't want to hear it," and she didn't. Her heart hurt thinking Davan cared more about treasure than her.

"Want to know what they've been saying around the guild?"

"No, I don't."

But Laine liked the way his teasing bothered her. He could practically see the anger manifesting. "Davan's got a girly in Galgaya. One who's not with the tribe."

"I said I don't. Want. To hear it."

Laine whispered in her ear, "Just remember our deal and your friend."

"You're trying to intimidate me," Treasta said as she swung around and came to her feet. She held the jacket against her stomach, hoping it was enough to hide the bump. "I'm not worried about my friend, Laine. I'd be more worried for that Pats if I were you. You better hope they keep their distance."

Chimes sat in the meadery talking with Dee at the bar. Treasta didn't give either man a moment to greet her when she slammed her fist on the counter and threw her finger in Chimes' face.

"You listen to me," she said. "You do not go telling *anyone* my business. Do you understand?"

Chimes stuttered and finally said, "You're right. I'm sorry."

"Good. Dee," she said, "thank you for the meal, but we have somewhere to be."

Chimes shot a glance at Dee who threw his arms up and shrugged.

Treasta took Chimes' hand, and as she walked across the room, she caught a glimpse of the twins sitting at a table near the wall. She held their eye contact until they were no longer in her line of sight.

"We're leaving now," Treasta said.

"Now?" Chimes yanked his hand away. "Dee can give us a place to stay for the night. Wouldn't that be better than on the ground? Especially with—"

"Especially with what? The thing growing inside me? Do *not* bring up my pregnancy. I don't want to talk about it."

Thing. Chimes crossed his arms and took a deep breath. She didn't want the child. How could he not realize that before now?

"I'm sick of being coddled. Your aunt, *you*—treating me like I'm porcelain. I am my own person, you understand that, right?"

Chimes knew not to answer. But he didn't like how a passersby began looking in their direction at what appeared to be a bickering couple.

He tried reaching toward her, but she pushed him away.

"Do not touch me."

Treasta stormed off.

She barged into the stable, throwing the door open and spooking the horses who kicked back and whinnied, alarmed. She found their wagon and sat in the driver seat refusing to move until Chimes readied the horse for travel.

But instead, Chimes climbed aboard and sat next to her. He could feel her anger in the silence.

She stared ahead.

"Trea—"

"*Uh-uh.*"

"Look—"

"*No.*"

Chimes threw his head back, defeated. "Will you just listen to me?" he said, speaking over her as she tried interrupting him for a third time.

Treasta glanced at him from the corner of her eyes, and when they made contact, she looked away.

"We're leaving the wagon here," Chime said. "We're not going to need it. We'll load a couple bags we can carry ourselves and walk to Maward. It's at the bottom of the canyon. We can get there by noon tomorrow and catch the next ferry to Wesser."

That got her attention. "A ferry?"

"It'll take a week to get there, but it'll be faster than hoofing it."

Treasta threw her arms around him, squeezing tightly. "Thank you, thank you, thank you, thank you."

"Now can we go back to Dee's?"

Treasta nodded. "I'm sorry. It's just once you found out I was …" she didn't say it aloud, partly because she hated hearing the words coming from her own mouth and because the Pats could be nearby. "You were treating me different."

"I'm concerned about what happened to your face. Can you blame me? You disappear and reappear with *that*," he said and pointed at the welt.

"I'm much tougher than I look," she said.

Frustrated, Chimes came to his feet and offered his hand to help Treasta down. She took it, and they returned to the meadery.

Dee chortled upon seeing them, but it faded when he noticed their fingers interlaced. He gave Chimes a disapproving look and subtly shook his head.

"Back again, I see," Dee said.

Chimes pulled his hand away and placed it in his pocket. He rocked on his feet, a little embarrassed after having been dragged out of the building and for hanging onto Treasta like a pup.

"Back again," Chimes said. "We'll be leaving first thing in the morning, if you don't mind us staying with you."

"Not at all," Dee said. "I only have one spare bed, though. After we close for the evening you can take the sofa in the lounge," he told Chimes. "I'm sure Miss Treasta here wouldn't mind some peace and quiet after traveling with you. I know he can be a chatty one," he added with a wink.

Chimes belted a forced laugh and scratched his head. He knew what Dee was doing: separating them like they were a couple of handsy children. It was an offensive assumption on Dee's part, but Chimes took it as the warning his father's closest friend intended it to be.

DANA TURNED THE MAP OVER thinking she had been looking at it upside down. No, that's not right either. She turned it back the other way. She and Davan had wandered into the canyon days ago. The warmer weather was pleasant and welcoming. After nearly a hundred years trapped in Hatchet, she didn't know what to expect beyond its boundaries, but this wasn't it. Dana, annoyed, folded the map. Something about using a hundred-year-old map probably wasn't ideal. They had passed several locations that were once settlements, since abandoned and lost to the years. An old gold mine was to their south, but that too was long abandoned. They had veered in that direction yesterday to find nothing worth taking except an old pickax. Davan gave it a hit against a boulder. The pick didn't break, so he decided to keep it, though it was rusting over. The only thing useful about the map was its landmarks: the rivers and those rock formations distinctive from the rest were named, marked, and mostly unchanged.

Davan returned with fish from the river. They were following along the Sarnak; its water moved with gentleness; its surface, clean and clear, made finding where to fish easy. A town situated on the cliffside could be seen from where they camped. The map showed it was Hayam. And it looked to be a bustling place even after all these years.

Dana folded the map and put it away.

"Any idea where we are?" Davan asked as he laid the fish across a flat rock. He cut its head off and ran the knife under its skin.

"We're near a town called Hayam," she said and pointed toward the town.

Going into town would slow him down, though it was the first town he had seen since Hatchet. As for the honing crystal, he didn't know what to do with it other than try to find the right buyer. The way it felt in his pocket, that buzz it gave off, it was causing him a great deal of agitation.

A horn blared, echoing from the river. From behind the tree line, two smokestacks billowed black plumes. Davan stopped what he was doing. He had never heard such a sound before nor seen smokestacks moving on their own. Dana also stared; this was just as new to her. They moved through the trees, Davan still holding the knife coated in fish scales and guts.

Standing at the riverbank, they watched a boat pushing through the water at a steady speed, large paddlewheels moving it forward. The horn echoed through the canyon as if acknowledging their presence. From the pilot house, the captain waved.

"Times sure have changed," Dana said as she waved back.

"We don't have ships like this where I'm from," Davan said. "Everything is driven by wind on our waters or by hand."

"I wonder what else has changed in the past hundred years," she said.

Passengers on the deck noticed Davan and Dana standing near the river. They waved.

A woman with long blonde hair, held up partially in a bun at the top of her head, walked along the deck. At first, Davan thought it was Treasta. He watched the woman until she disappeared to the other side of the ship. But the woman was dressed far too well to be her. Sadness overcame him; he fought the feeling of regret from entering his heart.

They returned to camp, and Dana got a fire going as Davan finished prepping the fish. The smell wafted through the air.

Together, Dana and Davan sat on the back of the wagon, eating.

"Why doesn't it snow here?"

Dana didn't have an answer. She chewed and said between bites, "I don't know. I've never left Hatchet, but before our town fell under Bastan's control, travelers would come through and talk about it. At least then, it was like this year-round."

The temperate conditions year-round sounded too good to be true, but the weather pattern since they entered the canyon had been pleasant—neither too hot nor too cold. Not much was known about Wesser except for the stories traders carried on their routes. It wasn't easy to get to for the average traveler and, frankly, most people didn't travel. If Davan made it back to Galgaya alive, he'd be the talk of the tribe. Everyone would gather around him to hear his stories and admire his fervor. The idea brought a childish grin to his face, one Dana took notice of.

"What's got you smiling?"

He wiped his mouth. "Nothing. Nothing at all."

Since they left Hatchet, Davan avoided answering Dana's questions regarding what awaited him in Wesser. She didn't understand why someone from Kildore would travel so far, and to be on his own seemed more dangerous. Even traveling with him seemed dangerous, but after nearly a century trapped in Hatchet, trapped with that godsforsaken warlock, watching for decades as he stole people's souls and held them hostage, she couldn't stay there one moment longer. Should she have stayed behind, it was hard to know what would have happened. Maybe the town organized itself in such away its residents came together to rebuild and reestablish itself as an honest, good place for travelers. A small band of locals, however, were devout to Bastan, they'd be furious at his demise. Dana wouldn't be surprised of the trouble that lot would cause. Yes, leaving regardless of what was to happen in Hatchet was for the best.

"You really won't tell me anything, will you?" she teased, though there was an air of seriousness to her question.

Davan broke a loaf of bread and passed her a piece before taking a bite of his own. "I think it's better that way."

Well, Dana figured, she would have to stop telling him anything about herself henceforth. Talking too much early on their journey was something she did. But she couldn't help herself. Davan was exciting, new, an outsider. And not just an outsider, a *real* outsider from a faraway land. She wanted to tell him everything about herself, Hatchet's history, her parents and siblings, and how well-trained the family dog was beyond herding. But Davan gave minimal responses, and Dana thought the more she revealed about herself, the more he'd be willing to open up to her. But there was nothing she could do that could make the man vulnerable.

So, she sat in silence with nothing but the sound of bread tearing between her teeth.

The smell of cooked fish slithered into Declan's nostrils. He hunkered in the bushes, followed the smell in the direction he thought it was coming from, and felt twigs crunch beneath his feet. He realized he needed to watch the ground more carefully, lest be heard.

Declan had a creative imagination. He liked to pretend a fox traveled alongside him, hunkered low, able to hide in the shadows of shrubs. He liked to pretend he was a fox, too, that he had pointed ears and red fur and whiskered cheeks, that the pads of his paws and feet offered stealth, and he could creep undetected. The fox liked fish, just like Declan.

He felt his stomach rumbling. Ever since he and Elsie arrived in the canyon, their supplies began running low, and Elsie began tightly rationing food. He had caught a couple of squirrels along the way, but that was as good as it got. Declan climbed a rock and peered over it.

A man with shoulder-length brown hair darkened from days of not washing it stood over the fire waiting for the fish, its meat strewn across stone, to finish cooking. A dark-haired woman was nearby, and then he caught glimpse of their wagon packed with days'—no—weeks' worth of supplies.

The man cut the cooked fish into pieces to share with the woman. He watched their mouths as they ate, waited for any kind of information he could get reading their lips, but they were quiet.

The woman: "What's got you smiling?"

The man: "Nothing. Nothing at all."

A minute or so passed before they exchanged more words.

The woman: "You really won't tell me anything, will you?"

The man: "It's better that way."

Interesting. Declan was intrigued. And that was it. Nothing more was said between the two. The boy lingered for a little while longer hoping to garner some more information, but nothing more could be learned.

As Declan stepped down, he slipped, tumbling to the ground with a heavy thud. He yelped and groaned as he rolled onto his side. Sitting up, he found he was bleeding: blood soaked his tunic where a sharp rock had cut into him. It wasn't deep enough to cause any serious damage, but painful enough that he needed to get back to camp. Elsie could clean it and wrap it for him.

But as Declan went to stand, he looked up to see the man hovering over him. He crawled backward until trapped against the rock he had fallen from.

"A boy?"

Declan watched his lips.

"What are you doing out here?"

He was too scared to move.

The man, confused, continued talking, but Declan stopped paying attention, looking around to find a way out. Nowhere to run, he jumped to his feet and tried shooting past the man, but the man stopped him, grabbing his arm. Declan tried pulling away, but he winced, feeling the strain on his side.

The man examined the wound, muttering something while doing so.

Declan again tried yanking himself away, but it was too painful tugging.

He caught the man saying something about his injury, and the man apparently could tell it was fresh.

Declan was dragged into camp.

The woman rushed over to see what was going on. She looked at the boy's side and went and fetched a bottle of liquor. She returned, popped the cork off, and after lifting the boy's tunic, poured it over the wound.

A scream escaped Declan, and he shoved them away. But just when he thought he was free, the man grabbed ahold of his arm again. Declan's gaze darted between the man and the woman, and he watched the woman say, "He's frightened. You're scaring him."

The man argued something back, speaking too fast to understand.

"Calm down," the woman said.

The man grabbed a handful of hair, holding Declan in such a way he couldn't move.

The woman demanded he let him go. But the man didn't listen. He ordered something at her, and her face said everything Declan needed to know in that moment: she was scared too.

The scary man's hand loosened a little, offering some relief on Declan's scalp.

Declan grabbed the man's wrists and pressed his thumb deep until he could feel the tissues and sinews move and until he felt the man's bone. The pressure forced him to retract his hand, and Declan made haste.

He ran as fast as he could, not looking back, not caring whether his feet snapped twigs or broke branches, not caring whether he disturbed nearby critters of their peace. His imaginary fox raced alongside him, and after racing back to camp, he collapsed, and his make-believe fox curled under his arms.

"What is wrong with you?" Dana asked, keeping what seemed like a safe distance from Davan.

Davan snuffed the fire and gathered everything into the wagon, failing to put anything in its proper place. He readied the horse and situated the wagon toward the road.

"What was that?" Dana asked again.

"We need to get out of here," he said.

Dana didn't understand. She ran in front of the horse, preventing Davan from going any further. "What was that?" she demanded, each syllable heavier and more serious than the last. "He was just a child. He was hurt."

"I don't trust no one," Davan said. "Including random children in the wild."

Dana scoffed. "Random children in the wild? Do you hear yourself? You sound mad. Davan, there is a town just miles up the road," she said while gesturing toward Hayam. "Surely there are ranches nearby. Surely those ranches could have children. Or maybe that child is lost and needing our help. You're awful, you know that? Just plain awful."

Davan climbed onto the bench, grabbing the reins. He held the horse from moving forward. "Are you coming or not?" he asked.

"Absolutely not," she said.

It wasn't what Davan was expecting to hear. He looked at her with disbelief, like she was just being difficult. "Get on."

"No," she said.

"No?"

"I think you heard me."

"Wait, you're being serious? You want me to just leave you here?"

Dana shrugged. "I guess so."

And he did without another word. As soon as Dana moved out of the way, he commanded the horse with a *"ya"* and he rolled out of the woods and back onto the road.

Dana stood there dumbfounded, yet relieved. She looked in the direction the boy had disappeared and went to find him to see if he was all right. The wound didn't look serious but if she could help dress it and get the boy back to his parents, she'd feel better, especially after such a traumatic experience. Good riddance, she thought as she followed in the direction the boy had run. Dana didn't know whether she could have handled another day with Davan. Afraid of a child? She huffed. Some hero.

After finding the boy at a camp, Dana hid behind the trunk of a standing dead tree. A slight woman wearing a mask was at his side, examining his wounds. The woman said something. It was too quiet to hear. Dana watched the two interact, the tenderness, a clear bond between them. A mother and her son? Siblings?

She remembered her own siblings and her parents; after nearly a century, the pain of losing them didn't come any easier. Bastan was wicked in how he treated the people of Hatchet. Her two older brothers and father had tried to go against him, spurred a rally of townsfolk, and marched to the manor with battering ram at hand. But as soon as the ram hit the doors, an invisible ward blasted them backward. Her father stood, grasping an ax, as Bastan stepped outside. The Andrili's face appeared half human, half demon—one yellow eye surrounded by gray, silvery skin bore over the crowd felled at the threshold. The townsfolk scattered, leaving behind Dana's father and her brothers. First Bastan took her mother as punishment, locked her in a painting—not just her soul, but her mind, too. Then he burned it, forcing her father and siblings to watch. When Dana arrived, Bastan didn't know who she was. She had told him she admired him, asked to serve him, hoping she could learn his weakness in secret—get revenge on what he had done to her family, to the town. She had spotted the portrait hanging in the foyer the moment she stepped inside; her eyes locked with the two-dimensional gaze of a young face painted in idealized human perfection—high cheekbones, slender nose, smooth skin, soft lips, except for that one yellow eye surrounded by a silvery complexion. Years continued to pass; the painting continued to change, revealing an aging warlock, exposing the demon beneath the mask. Yet Bastan had remained as youthful as the day he arrived. One day, Dana passed through the foyer to notice the portrait disappeared. Weeks, months, maybe years later—she didn't know how long it had been—she went into the attic to gather supplies when she noticed a sheet draped over what appeared to be one of

Bastan's pieces. Pulling back the sheet, a decrepit and decaying demon's visage met her gaze. Startled, she stumbled backward, nearly knocking the candlestick onto the floor. Then she remembered how he had burned her mother's portrait, erased her from existence. She grabbed the candle, held it below the frame, waiting for it to catch. Nothing. She clutched the artwork, felt an intense heat scorch her hands, and drew them away to examine the burns that she would keep hidden within lace gloves going forward. Visitors to Hatchet had become fewer. Then, years would go by, and no souls dared cross into the town. Rumor must have reached nearby settlements of a town from where no one returned. Bastan paid a handful of followers to bring him travelers. When Davan appeared, the potentate seemingly sprung to life.

"This town is becoming rather boring," he had told Dana one morning as she prepared the hearth in his chamber for the day. He began mumbling to himself after that, trailing off as he spoke: "I'm bored. Entertain me, woman"—whining like a child.

The town suffered no matter whether Bastan was pleased or not, but even more so when he was "bored."

Dana had told Davan some of this, of course, excited to recite what would become part of a hero's tale. "Think of all the stories," she had said. "It's all the people of Hatchet will have for hope." It was all she had. But as the feeling of hope dwindled, the excitement of the Great Lake City went with it.

It wasn't long before the boy noticed Dana watching him from behind the tree; her long hair caught in the wind surely had drawn his gaze. The same fearful expression returned to his face when his eyes met hers, and she felt herself crumbling—no child deserved what Davan did.

"Let go of him!" she had yelled, trying to shove him away from the child.

It was like he was distraught, paranoid—all that for a boy. Her heart raced at the thought, and she wondered whether Davan had at some point felt the same about her, that she was some kind of threat. Would he have grabbed her by the hair and threatened to kill her, too, if she happened to fall into his camp never having met him? She was relieved to be done with him.

The masked woman spotted Dana watching them. She came to her feet, her expression menacing under scars, and grasped her knife at the ready.

Upon seeing the blade, and the way the woman walked toward her shouting for her to "stop hiding, you coward," Dana went rigid. Bits of bark collected under her nails as her grip on the tree tightened. Move. Move, dammit. Finally, she broke away from the tree and found the bravery to step forward.

The masked woman was shorter than her, had choppy hair, and a mean face. She got close to Dana, holding the weapon near her neck. Something about how the woman carried herself, was enough for Dana to know the woman has used it before.

"What did you do to him?"

Dana tried taking a step back, but the woman took a step forward. "*I* didn't do anything," Dana said. "I wanted to make sure he was okay. He was hurt."

The woman looked her over with her one visible eye. Maybe Dana didn't seem like a threat—at least that's what she hoped when the woman put her knife away.

"He said someone hurt him."

Dana went to step around the woman, wanting to rush to the boy's side and address his wound. But the woman threw her hand up, pushing her back.

"Said it was a man and a woman, and now here you are."

"I was trying to help him," Dana said, her eyes locked in the direction of the boy who had since retreated out of sight. "He was hurt. I was trying to clean his wound and dress it so it wouldn't get an infection."

The woman kept her hand on the blade's hilt, ready to draw it if needed. "Where is your man friend then?" She looked around to see if anyone was hiding nearby, no one she could notice at least. "Where is he?"

Dana saw in the woman's expression she intended to hurt him for hurting the boy. "He left. I . . ." Why was she telling her all this? It wasn't that she needed to protect Davan—she didn't care what happened to him now that he was gone. In her time with him, she learned she overshared, and now she worried she was doing the same. It wasn't this masked woman's business who she was or with whom she traveled. "I'll be going," she finally said.

The woman threw Dana against the tree. Her blade swiftly drawn and at her throat.

"Where I come from," the woman said, "we have a rule: an eye for an eye. You know what that means don't you?"

Dana held her breath and nodded.

The woman sliced into Dana's side, not deep enough to cause any significant damage but enough to make her bleed. And she was bleeding a lot. She held her side, collapsing to the ground, fighting the urge to cry because she didn't want the masked woman—whoever this awful person was—to see her fear.

"I better not see you again," the woman said.

Dana ran off, pressing her palms into the wound. She ran until she reached the road, and she could again see Hayam. She lost the strength to run when she saw the incline of the switchback road leading up to the town. When she realized the woman wasn't following her, she removed her blouse, pulled the stained chamise underneath up, and wrapped her torso tightly with her shirt. A gentle breeze brushed her skin, and she started the walk to Hayam, hoping someone there could help her. The woman, Dana realized as she climbed, thought she or her "man friend" had something to do with the boy's wound. The revelation that someone would think she could ever do harm to another living being was a stab in and of itself.

Declan, while hiding in the safety of the trees, watched the two women interact at a safe distance. He shuddered when Elsie cut into the woman's side with no hesitation. The woman rushed toward where she came from, holding her wound. Even after she disappeared, he stayed in his hiding spot. His imaginary fox friend was at his side, standing on guard with teeth bared. Declan crawled beneath low-hanging branches beneath a pine, watching as Elsie began looking for him. He bared his own teeth as he winced; crouching was painful.

Declan tried to disappear within the shadows of the tree's trunk, shrinking as low as possible despite ache radiating from the wound in his side. He shut his eyes, held them closed with such force, the muscles in his eyes began to hurt. Flashes of everything that just happened reappeared in blips behind his lids, and the man's face—scarred with similar knife marks as Elsie's—the woman pouring liquor over his ribs, Elsie deliberately slicing into the woman overlapped in his mind. As he quaked, he tried controlling the meter of his breaths. Then he imagined the fox, placed the critter in his mind. It sat on its hind legs. Its tail flicked against blackness. Declan found himself in a place neither here nor there. He floated to the creature and petted its head. The fox smiled and kept its eyes, the color of deep forest, on his. It was as if the fox knew his every desire.

The fox stood on his back feet, his body and limbs elongating into the arms and legs of a boy, his paws became hands, and his face held a wildness to it: mouth fixed in a smile, nose long and pointed with a dark ombre spreading up his face from the middle until fading into red.

"Hi, Declan," the fox boy said as he communicated with his hands.

Declan's face lit with excitement. "You know my language," he replied.

"Of course I do. Do you know who I am?"

Declan shook his head.

"I'm your guardian."

Declan tried opening his eyes but couldn't seem to awaken from the trance.

"You can't wake up until I allow it," the fox boy said.

"You're not real," Declan said. He pinched his arm, felt nothing, and remained in the black ether of his mind.

The fox boy stood perfectly still, waiting.

"What do you mean *guardian*?" Declan finally asked after realizing he was truly trapped. "You are a fox."

"I am your fox. I look like a fox because you wanted me to appear like a fox. Pay attention, now. You do not want to go home, do you?"

"No. I don't want to see my father ever again."

"All is good," the fox said. "Your leaving will lead your mother to leave him. Cal's father will care for her and help her. What do you want for yourself?"

Declan's heart was racing as he remembered Elsie was somewhere in reality searching for him. He didn't know what he wanted; he just wanted out and didn't give it much thought after that.

"I want to be tough."

"Like Elsie?"

Declan nodded.

"Elsie isn't tough," the fox said.

"She's super tough. You don't know what you mean."

The fox laughed. "You saw what she did to that stranger."

Yes, and it's why he hunkered in fear beneath a pine tree. He could feel the needles against his skin even now. The wind picked up, brushing its branches along his back. A strange sensation it was to feel the world outside his head while being trapped within his own mind.

"You have much to learn about yourself," the fox said. "The man who held your hair, he carries something precious on him. He keeps it in the left pocket of his trousers. I felt it. Didn't you feel it? That buzz. You could awaken your abilities, and with them you could deliver what your father deserves, you could protect your mother, you could"—a smile curled over his face—"put Cal and his friends in their place. Show them who's really in charge." He folded his hands.

"Abilities?"

But the fox said nothing more.

Declan awoke under the tree to Elsie nudging him. He jolted, crawling away as fast as he could in the tight space. Everything looked like it was spinning; he blinked, trying to reorient himself after such a strange experience. The fox sat behind Elsie who was on her knees and keeping her distance to avoid startling him again.

She reached out. "Hey, it's okay. Everything is going to be okay."

But Declan stood with fury, communicating with such speed, Elsie couldn't keep up. She didn't understand what happened to upset him, but she saw his wound was bleeding through his dressings.

He threw his arms down, expelled a heavy sigh from his chest, and stomped his foot. Declan returned to camp, paying zero attention to Elsie as he passed her; the fox walked alongside him. Declan wasn't sure whether the fox was real or not—he really thought he had conjured the creature from his own imagination, needed to feel close to something and safe. But it was clear Elsie couldn't see it.

Declan sat near Carrot, took out his graphite stick, and began drawing the fox, the woman, and the man who hurt him.

Elsie sat next to him, looking over the drawings: the fox's face was nearly humanlike in its eyes; the woman was sad in her portrait; but the man expressed indignation on an impossible-to-forget face. *Davan.*

Elsie tapped the paper, holding it up to where Declan could see, but the boy didn't think she deserved his attention, so Elsie forced him to look.

"I know him," she said, tapping the paper repeatedly until Declan understood what she was saying. He cocked his head. Elsie pulled the mask off her face and pointed to the burn. "Him. He did this to me. Do you know where he is?"

Declan wrote in the white space around Davan's portrait: *ar yew goyng to hert hym?*

"Declan," she said, hands firm on his shoulders, "you're too young to understand, but people need to pay for what they do to other people.

He tried to kill me. Does that seem fair?"

Declan's eyes lowered. After a long pause, he shook his head.

Elsie began packing their supplies; Declan helped. And they climbed aboard Carrot, Declan sitting in front, grasping the horn of the saddle as Elsie wrapped one arm around him to ensure he wouldn't fall, and they dashed through the woods to find Davan.

When they got to the camp where Declan had found the man and woman eating fish near the river, all that remained were remnants of a campfire and discarded fish guts. Elsie saw the wagon tracks in the dirt and found the road nearby. She looked toward the town on the cliff. Davan wouldn't have gone to Hayam—he wouldn't have backtracked.

So, when they came to a fork in the road, one that ascended the cliff and another that followed along the Sarnak, they continued along the river toward the port village of Maward.

20

WHAT IS WRONG WITH YOU? Davan pushed the woman's poisonous words from his head, pushed out anything he knew about her: Bastan, Hatchet—gone. And good riddance, because he hadn't the energy to deal with yet another emotional woman with Treasta haunting him. No, don't worry about Treasta—*stop* worrying. *Stopstopstopstopstopstop.* She was safe. At the lodge. With Marnie. With Atlas.

Davan drove along the road with a permanent scowl, kept the river that moved with a glassy sheen in his line of sight. He pulled on the reins when he entered Maward, a village with a deep dock along the Sarnak. Passengers deboarded the steamboat he had spotted earlier; supplies were unloaded. Drivers waited with their carriages near the dock for customers looking for a taxi. Then, he saw the sign.

DEPARTURE
WESSER: 5 O'CLOCK

It was a good cart he was driving and a good horse that pulled—leaving the horse and supplies behind wasn't an easy decision, but the cart was slowing him down, and the road conditions made driving difficult. Davan packed his bag, threw it on his back, and unhitched the horse. He left the cart near the dock. It would go unnoticed for a little while, maybe even a day or two. But what to do with the steed was another issue. After some asking around, Davan learned of a ranch up the road, and the owner gladly bought the beast, saying, "She's young, strong. Will be good for breeding," and left it at that.

Davan pocketed the low sum; he didn't have time to haggle. And walked the mile back to Maward.

A blaring horn warned of departure in fifteen minutes as deckhands carried supplies onto the bright white vessel, its red lettering spelling "Sarnak Sarra Keen." Davan slid into line, helping a deckhand carry a large crate aboard, and disappeared. After some swift searching, he found a secluded spot within the shadows of tall creates and haystacks.

Declan ran ahead when he spotted Davan's wagon. He waved Elsie over. She stepped down from Carrot.

"Are you sure?" she asked, surprised Davan had been traveling with ample supplies. She rummaged through it and took what they needed, including food and liquor, and two bed rolls. The woman she encountered earlier must have been traveling with Davan. Strange.

Elsie sat on the back of the wagon and looked at Declan, who stared wide-eyed and curious at the ship. She tapped his shoulder.

"How many were with the man," Elsie asked.

Declan held up "one" with his hand. Then he noticed the fox slinking underneath the cart, sniffing around and following the smell toward the steamboat. The fox sat, facing the men loading cargo aboard. And for just a moment, Declan saw him. The man who held him by the hair disappeared aboard.

Declan pointed toward the ship; Elsie followed with her gaze.

"The man," he signed, pulling the hair at the crown of his head: the name he had given Davan.

"You think he's on the ship?" Elsie hopped down from where she sat. Declan's confidence was enough for Elsie to believe him. Then, in the dimming light of dusk, she saw the sign for the five o'clock departure.

She told Declan to wait with the horse as she hurried to the office to speak with the ticket master. She didn't have time to find another way aboard, so she purchased two tickets—first class tickets, because that was all that was available. She counted out her polished coins, slid them across the counter, and inquired about livestock.

"How much to board a horse?"

"Another fifty."

She flashed him a look.

"Livestock isn't cheap. We feed and tend to your horse, too. It's money worth paying, if you ask me."

She let out a defeated sigh. The money she had stolen from the temple was at least going to good use.

The horn twice blared: five minutes until departure.

"You better hurry."

Returning to Declan, Elsie handed him a ticket and he hesitated to move, thinking Carrot wouldn't be able to come, but as soon as he saw Elsie grabbing Carrot by the halter, pulling him toward the loading dock, he followed. Elsie left Carrot with the deckhands, and the two raced up the ramp.

"Right on time," said the man taking their tickets, punching holes into them and handing them back. "First class?" He looked the travelers over, eyeing them with suspicion. "Might want to reconsider what you're wearing."

Elsie snatched the tickets from his hand with a huff. As she climbed to the top deck where the first-class cabins were located, she realized what the man meant after seeing how well dressed everyone was. A woman eyed her as she passed and whispered to another woman: "That poor child," as if taking pity on Declan for "traveling with such a deformed mother." Elsie fought the urge to shove them over the railing. But instead, she and Declan found peace inside their room a few more doors down. The space was larger than Elsie deserved. But Declan, she wanted him to be as comfortable as possible, and as his face came alight, paying the egregious amount made it worth it to see him happy. They had been in the wilderness for far too long. And at times she worried they would never find civilization again.

Declan threw himself on the sofa, the dirt on his boots leaving a dusting on the cushion. Then he rushed into the only bedroom where on a metal frame was the nicest looking mattress he had set his eyes on. He rolled into its covers, burying himself like a fox in its den.

Elsie lifted the covers to see Declan's smiling face. "It's nice, isn't it?"

He nodded.

"We should probably lay low until we reach Wesser."

"Why?" he asked.

She sat next to him on the mattress. Elsie had never wanted to protect someone the way she wanted with Declan. "We don't want Davan"—she tugged the short hair at the crown of her head—"to know we're here." But really it was to keep those nasty gossipers from casting judgment. She didn't have a change of clothes for either herself or Declan, and there was nothing she could do about her appearance. Her short hair, the scars, the burn still somewhat visible despite the mask, her chipped tooth—all of it made her a target for the wealthy to shun her. And by all means, Elsie thought, shun away, just leave the kid out of it.

21

Aboard the Sarra Keen, Treasta was alone in the cabin, her shirt open, examining her rounding body, watching the babe's movement create momentary hills. She ran her hand along her skin, trying not to let the feeling of dread overcome her as it had several times before, trying to ease her heart racing with irregular palpitations.

As her head fell back, she stared at the soft white of the ceiling, its coat of paint thick, yet brittle like an eggshell. She wondered whether inside their shells chicks knew of peace, what it must feel like to break free, to instinctively peck away the very walls that protected them, to experience the chaos of existence so willingly as nature assigned. And what of her own nature? Treasta frowned, thinking about how trapped Davan had made her feel, how trapped she still felt now—yet somehow it was different to feel entrapped by her own failing mind. Ever since she learned about the child, she began a slow descent into madness. This madness—this craze—what else could nature be but cruel to give her this body, to force her to carry this child like fucking was some kind of punishment despite the pleasure. And what of her own mother? Did such thoughts plague her? Did she fuck a man too many times because it was what he wanted, and she just wanted him to be happy?

Treasta pressed her palms into her eyes, the pressure like a tourniquet on her ailing mind. Whoever the woman was who bared her those twenty years ago, Treasta pitied and forgave her.

Marnie's directions to the witch's location were hidden on her person. She had examined it several times, committing the route to memory:

> *From Hayam, follow the road into the canyon.*
> *Continue past Maward until you find a bridge.*
> *Cross the bridge and follow the riverbank back toward Maward.*
> *You will know you are there when the land is covered in art.*

She repeated it under her breath, thinking about the ways the child would suffer, just as she did, in an unbeknown world.

Treasta stood. Stretching her arms and back, she caught a glimpse of herself in the mirror: her body, it was unrecognizable. Treasta washed up, brushed out her hair and braided it. She looked herself over one more time, saw how her stomach had grown in the time since they had left Marnie's, and sighed.

She walked out onto the deck, hoping the fresh evening air would ease her soul. Treasta was beginning to worry about whether she was showing through her clothes. They seemed baggy enough; maybe she'd be mistaken for being fat instead, but her gaunt facial features gave her away. Despite the warmer weather, she opted to continue wearing layers, anything to keep herself from seeing what was underneath. The less pregnant she looked, the more normal she felt in her skin, but the growing infant remained a nagging thought, clawing on the back of her brain. Even as the lowering sun tucked behind the horizon, the beauty of the canyon basked in twilight couldn't be admired.

ELSIE, CURLED BENEATH HEAVY COVERS, HAD DRIFTED ASLEEP. It had been a while since either of them had gotten decent rest, but Declan was finding it difficult to keep his eyes shut. The fox sat in the corner of the room, its tail flicking, its bright eyes locked on him.

Declan spoke to the fox as he moved his hands, keeping his signs smaller and closer to his body as if he were whispering. "Go away," he told the fox. But it continued to sit there. Declan didn't know what to do. He wanted the fox gone, but he was scared that should he fall asleep, the creature would reappear in his dreams in the form of a boy again.

The treasure flashed through Declan's mind—an emerald gem he had never seen before. It was as if the fox had placed it there; then the fox showed him Davan's pocket, and then imitated the buzzing of the jewel—he felt it along his skin, the hairs on his arms standing.

You could awaken your abilities, and with them you could deliver what your father deserves, you could protect your mother, you could—he remembered the fox boy's wicked smile. Declan didn't finish the thought. To harm Cal wasn't something he wanted. Cal's father had been so good to him. But his mother, he was angry toward her: mad she never left his father, mad she let him treat them the way he did and for so long. Of course, it wasn't always that way, but when it was, a darkness swallowed their home and his father was uncontrollable. He remembered the good moments forged early in his toddler years when his father didn't stay out so late, when his breath wasn't poisoned by the stale stench of booze, before he did his nightly drunken dance and when that dance was play and Declan slid down his legs and he rode his father's shoulder's pointing to go forth. When the drinking started, he didn't know, but he wondered if his father had been like that his entire life, that when Declan was younger, he couldn't remember the bad because his mind suppressed it. At some point in Declan's short life, his father grew to resent him. Maybe, Declan thought, just maybe, it would be better to remember the bad, anything to keep him from going back. Nothing would change—that's something he was certain about. His father's face, its deep acne scars and wrinkles, flashed into fleeting memory. Declan felt a rage growing inside.

The fox bared its teeth into a smile, walked across the room, and peered over its shoulder, waiting.

Declan followed, carefully stepping with bare feet, and slipped into the twilight evening.

His eyes fixed on the fox as he meandered from the top deck down to the bottom deck. The fox lowered itself; Declan followed suit. At night, most of the activity was in the salon. He did not need to worry too much about running into someone here aside from the occasional deckhand, none of whom seemed to care about the boy sneaking about—a child suffering of boredom, a common occurrence aboard.

Two curly-haired workers, probably not much older than him, donned in uniforms and hats walked past. They didn't seem to notice him hiding behind a barrel. Declan peered around, making sure no one else saw him snooping, then continued when he thought the coast was clear.

But one of the workers blocked his path. Declan went to go a different direction and found the other one in his way, also. They were twins—and what he thought were two male figures were brother and sister.

The wind in the open air cut through the cargo hold. Declan searched for his fox, found it with its head peeking from behind the mountainous haystack. These two, Declan quickly realized, meant trouble—a couple of stowaways like Davan—and here Declan was moseying about obviously up to no good.

Declan began climbing the haystack, kicking bales behind him, knocking the twins down. Declan slipped away—at least he hoped.

He found himself in the livestock hold. Carrot dug his front hoof with delight upon seeing Declan. The boy smiled as the beast nuzzled its nose into his arms. He gave Carrot a good scratch between the eyes and continued after the fox.

Declan tiptoed. Just around the corner, hidden between stacks of crates and other various dry goods, was Davan, just barely visible in the shadow. Declan couldn't tell from his current position whether Davan was asleep. Observing the man's chest expanding as he breathed long and slowly, Declan inched closer to confirm Davan's eyes were shut.

The buzz tingled along his arms and up his neck, and the closer he became, the deeper it hummed.

The pocket wouldn't be difficult to get to from his current vantage. What worried him was whether he'd be able reach into the pocket and pull the jewel out without Davan waking. Declan realized the only reason he thought there was a jewel in there was because an imaginary fox told him so. But the longer he lingered, the more enticed he was, as if the jewel was beckoning.

The fox paced around Davan. Declan crawled toward him. Closer. Closer, closer closercloser ... his heartbeat thumped harder, harder. Okay, now, just reach—he thought as he eased his hand into Davan's pant pocket, so concentrated that he began to see a hazy glow on the edge of his vision.

It *is* real, he realized as he felt the cool gem's power leeching into his fingers' tips.

Once he had a good grip, he eased his hand from Davan's pocket. Declan, too mesmerized by its sheen, sat beside Davan until movement from nearby caught his attention. He cautiously investigated the open space. The twins must have found him, but where they were lurking he didn't know.

Declan decided to make a run for it, knocking over a crate in the process. Its thud reverberated through the floor and into his feet—loud enough, he knew, to have awoken Davan. And sure enough, when he looked over his shoulder the twins were no longer after him. They had turned around.

Declan hurried from the cargo hold, through the livestock hold, and up a flight to the second deck, where he collided with a blonde woman with braided hair who had been leaning on the railing and watching the sunset.

Pain radiated from his tailbone, and somewhat disoriented, Declan collected himself before looking up to see the woman standing over him.

She knelt. "Are you okay?"

Declan's hand tightened around the jewel; its buzz reverberated through his bones. He nodded, slowly. She helped him up, and he waved as a "thank you" and went back to his cabin on the top deck.

He locked the cabin door, then shut the door to his private room and opened his palm to reveal the emerald amulet set in a gold bezel. It shone in the dark, emanating a slight green glow. The fox circled around him, rubbing on his legs, pleased.

Declan slipped the chain over his head. The stone hung heavy around his neck. He tucked it into his shirt. And then the fox appeared to Declan in the full-length mirror as the boy.

Declan walked to the mirror.

The fox boy grinned.

Davan didn't believe it at first, the twins caught in his gaze. The Pats, perhaps the most hazardous duo from the tribe, were standing before him. He really didn't think anyone else had gotten this far, especially after so much snow had blanketed the highlands. The Pats mirrored Davan's expression, just as confounded.

They booked it.

Davan pursued.

Trish was a little slower than Pat, but Pat was clumsier. He tripped over his own feet, falling and sliding under the metal railing. He held on. Trish reached to grab him, but it was too slippery. Pat fell into the river.

Davan grabbed Trish by the collar.

"He can't swim," she said. "Let me go, or he's going to drown."

"Why should I care?" Davan asked.

"Let me go."

"Give me a reason."

"If I tell you why we're here, will you let me go?"

"We know why we're all here," he said.

"No. No, that's not it. We're following Treasta. Laine told us to."

Treasta? Laine? Trish must have been lying.

The boat rocked.

"Now let me go," Trish demanded.

Davan pushed her overboard, and Trish swam after Pat.

When the boat rocked again, it jerked with such force the dried goods it was hauling slid to one side and then back. A sudden fog settled in. Something didn't seem right. The air, the smell, it was like Hatchet. He noticed the stone in his pocket was gone—its incessant hum no longer there. The Pats took it, was his first thought. But they wouldn't have known he had it. No, the only other person who knew was Dana. And just as quickly as the fog laid itself over the river, it carried itself away. He had never quite seen anything like it before.

Elsie jerked awake. The sharp movement of the ship had her on her feet and throwing the door to Declan's room open to make sure he was okay, but what she discovered was a man with dark hair and cleanly cut bangs. He was naked aside from the emerald jewel hung around his neck.

"Who the hell are you? Where's Declan?"

"You really thought he'd stay with you?" the man said, speaking with a smoothness. "I just needed someone with any hint of ability to hone magic to touch the crystal. It worked. The boy doesn't know it, but he's got potential. He seethes with anger."

"Where is he?"

The man moved out of the way so Elsie could see the mirror and Declan inside the glass.

"What did you do to him?" Elsie went to grab her knife, but it wasn't on her person. She had stripped herself of any weapons when she had laid down to rest.

The man looked over Elsie's shoulder to examine his features. He tapped his face and adjusted his hair. "Do you want him back?" the man asked as he continued to look himself over with admiration.

Elsie fell into the mirror, holding it by the frame. Declan's fist hit the glass. Impenetrable. The boy screamed, but she heard nothing.

The man wandered around the room, waiting for an answer. He sat on the bed, crossing his legs and took up Declan's graphite stick and paper and began sketching. "I can give him back to you," the man said. "In exchange, I would like trousers, at the very least. Yes, trousers would do. Its drafty, I dare say."

"Where do you expect me to find you a pair of goddamn trousers? We're in the middle of a river," Elsie said.

The man eyed her legs.

"These won't fit you."

"I can make anything fit me, my dear," he said, smugly.

Elsie slipped off her pants and kicked them his direction.

With a flick of the wrist, they came to rest on his legs; she saw that he could indeed make them fit. The man again looked at himself in the mirror, smirking at his perfect form.

"Give me Declan," she said. "I gave you what you wanted."

The man handed her a sketch. Sadness was on Declan's visage in the portrait. It was striking how lifelike the drawing was, so much so that she swore to see his eyes move. She caught him blinking a second time.

Elsie looked at the mirror. Declan was gone.

"You said you'd give him back," she said.

The man smirked. "I did. You'll want to protect that," he said, tapping the page. "Paper certainly is fragile."

Elsie snatched a chair by its back and flung it. But when she thought she hit the man, he had stepped inside the mirror.

No, no, no … She rushed to the mirror, pounding on the glass until a crack split it. No. She refused to let him get away. Elsie picked up the chair, swinging over and over again, until it began to splinter and until the mirror shattered. Its pieces fell with her onto the floor, cutting into her bared legs. She held the portrait close. Her heart crashed into her chest.

Elsie sobbed.

The artist had signed his name.

Bastan.

22

Frantic to find Chimes, Treasta flew into the salon once the boat steadied itself. In the tall-windowed room, patrons set tables and chairs upright, others helped one another to their feet, checked to assure people were well, and the barman tended to the broken glass of fallen liquor bottles.

Chimes spotted Treasta before she had spotted him.

"Are you all right?" he asked as he rushed toward her. His hands went from holding her shoulders to her waist, and that's when he looked at her stomach. Gods. It wasn't even his child. Why should he care? Treasta reddened, ignored his gaze. "I'm fine," she said. "What happened?"

Whispers of a fog laying itself over the river and lifting itself away wove through the room, passing from one person to the next as everyone looked for answers no one seemed to have. Nothing would explain what happened that evening.

Then, a woman's shrill scream echoed from outside. Evermore curious, anyone and everyone who heard the shouting, rushed to see what was happening, saw down the deck a woman, donning a mask, being dragged to the next deck below. No amount of warning from the crew could get anyone to stay inside.

Another scream, more shrill, more violent, like her voice was blood-laced. And that was when Treasta saw her. No. It couldn't be. She took one step toward the brig. Thought her eyes deceived her. Thought her mind was playing tricks—it wouldn't be the first time.

Normally, Treasta would have avoided her guildmate, but Elsie's being alive ... well, she couldn't not follow, and Elsie's behavior, unlike the woman, perturbed Treasta.

"Wait!" Treasta called after the crewmen who hauled their unruly prisoner. She followed them into the brig where there was one holding cell. Elsie stumbled inside, falling to the floor like she was a doll, and the crew locked the cell door.

"Miss, you should leave," a crewman said. He stepped toward her to force her from the room, but Treasta was unmoved.

"I know this woman. What happened?"

One of the two crewmen answered: "We found her in a first class cabin destroying everything in the room. She's incoherent. Something about a boy trapped inside a mirror. You can talk to her if you want. Maybe you'll be able to get her to explain herself."

The other one laughed. "Good luck."

And they left her alone with the woman.

Treasta, cautious to step too closely to the iron bars, noticed Elsie's bare legs red with streaks of blood. "Elsie? Hey, it's me."

Elsie sobbed into the floor; her hand clutched around a crumpled piece of paper. Treasta's voice was familiar, but she didn't care. She turned away, curling into herself and holding the page closely.

"Elsie. What happened to you? I thought you were dead."

Flames flashed in Elsie's mind, a phantom waft of smoldering timber filled her nose. But the grief in losing Declan overpowered any rage she had for either Treasta or Davan. Elsie had been beaten, survived knife fights, and even fire these thirty years, but Declan, just shy of puberty, was torn from the world. She didn't know from where the warlock Bastan came, or why he was there, or what he wanted with Declan. *I just needed someone with any hint of ability to hone magic to touch the crystal.* Was Declan a *gifted*? It was possible. Many children grow up never knowing they have the ability to harness magic because they lack the guidance and resources. And it was rare for a gifted child to draw magic without a honing crystal. The amount of energy it required drained the average mortal masters.

The door creaked open. Chimes knelt beside Treasta and saw the pantsless woman dripping with blood.

He whispered: "What happened? Who is she?"

"Someone from home," Treasta said.

Elsie didn't recognize the male voice. She hadn't the energy to care why Treasta was there or whether she was with Davan. She sat up, wiping her eyes, and cleared her throat.

"I don't know what you want from me," she said. "I would think you'd be happy to see me in a cell."

As Elsie faced her, Treasta examined the mask and the hand-carved marks, that it didn't have a hole from which to see, and the worn-down leather strap. Elsie pulled the mask from her face, revealing the healing burn disfiguring her visage from lip to forehead, her left eye stuck partly open and fixed. She stared at the mask. The sorrow she carried on her face, the trembling of her breath, the way her lip quivered—Treasta grasped the iron bars on the cell and fell forward. It was like looking at a stranger. This wasn't the Elsie she knew.

"I don't know what to do," Elsie whimpered. It was the first time she had felt that way. Ever since she killed her father those years ago, she always knew the next step, always had an answer for herself.

"Can we help?" Treasta asked.

A terrible wail escaped Elsie; she folded in half. In one hand the drawing, in the other the mask—is this what it felt like to love and care for someone? Is this what it meant to have purpose? Uncontrollable were her tears as they ran long and deep with such force she could create valleys. *Declan!* She wanted to scream. Would the universe hear her if she shouted his name loud enough? Would her voice reach the stars, and would the stars have pity? *Declan! Declan! Declan!* Elsie wanted to turn back time, to force the boy to go home after he refused to leave her side.

Treasta reached through the bars. As she gripped the paper, Elsie's hand loosened. Smoothing its crinkles, Treasta revealed a portrait shimmering of graphite. A boy stared at her with large eyes cast in shadow. Was he crying?

Chimes drew a long breath after looking over her shoulder to catch a glimpse of the name signed in the bottom right corner. He exhaled a sigh, and put his arm around Treasta's waist, holding her for his own comfort and, in a way, for Elsie's.

"Bastan …," he muttered the name.

Elsie's eye flashed up. She pressed her face into the bars, desperate. The way this stranger said his name, it was like he knew him. "You know the warlock?"

Chimes nodded. "He's not just a warlock. He's from Drynis, or that's what they say."

"Drynis?" Treasta said it slowly, taking in each letter, trying to remember why she knew the name. Drynis—the shadow world? "A demon?"

"Is that what you call them in Kildore?"

It was a common way to refer to them to most the world, except the people of Wesserland interacted far less often with the nations to the east and north; it seemed appropriate that the those who resided in these lands would have another name for demons.

"What do you call them?" Treasta asked.

"Dark ones."

But formally they were the Andrili.

Dark ones … demons … either or, the people of Wesserland and the world beyond its borders agreed such creatures were trouble.

"You want to help?" Elsie's one eye was locked with Treasta's gaze. "Get me out of here." She removed her earrings and handed them to Treasta.

Treasta looked at the lock, and then at the earrings, their long and slender points would easily open the door. She closed her hand around them and pondered deeply about what to do. She remembered when Elsie found her at the Laugh Crow Inn. Treasta was asleep. Elsie would have picked the lock with these earrings to get into the room. The sound of the door opening returned to her mind. She had expected Davan to materialize, but instead a cold metal met her neck and Elsie's voice oozed the words "get up."

Treasta's fist tightened around the earrings. She stood. Hapless, Elsie's eyes widened. She reached for Treasta, but Treasta had taken a large step backward. With what power Treasta felt over Elsie, it sent chills through her body. Her lips curled into a smile, flashing wicked satisfaction.

And Chimes didn't know who Treasta was at this moment, but he knew he needed to back away. He melted into the wall, holding the door handle ready to step out.

"*Treasta*." Elsie's voice deepened. "What are you doing? Let me out. Let. Me. OUT."

Treasta crumpled up Declan's portrait. It rolled from her hand and landed just out of Elsie's reach.

Treasta pushed passed Chimes, exiting into the night. Elsie's shouted after her until her throat, sore, couldn't carry her voice.

A rush filled Treasta; for a moment she felt like herself again—the "herself" who existed before she incubated another living being in her womb. But Chimes had taken her by the arms, his fingers digging into the muscle as he pushed her into the wall. The palpitations of her heart drummed through her bones. She bit her lip, looking at his.

"What the hell was that all about?" Chimes demanded.

Treasta sobered. Elsie's earrings had warmed to the temperature of her skin, and she had forgotten she was holding them.

"You're going to answer me," he said.

Treasta's mouth opened but she didn't answer him. What was there to say? Anything he wanted to know she didn't want him to know. When she refused to meet his eyes, he let go and without another word stormed off.

She stood there searching for the right answer and avoiding it.

Treasta looked at the earrings. She threw them into the water. So light were they that not a splash was heard. She wanted to scream. Instead, she folded, holding onto the railing, and silently cried.

23

Morning, noon, night. Treasta knocked on Chimes' cabin door. It had been three days. And when he wouldn't answer, she went to the salon to find him sitting among three other gentlemen he befriended playing cards and dice games. Gambling through the night, they shared in drinks and laughter, but when Treasta came in they lifted their brows, stared down at their cards, smacked their lips or puffed on their pipes; because each time this had happened the nights before, she stood at Chimes' side, said a few words to get his attention, and Chimes carried on like she wasn't there. He tapped the table.

Treasta disappeared to her cabin, defeat appearing on her slumped shoulders.

"Your wife seems concerned," MK said. It was how he had introduced himself, though Chimes figured MK didn't like talking about himself too much, including giving away his name to a stranger on a boat, even as fleeting of a friendship as it would be.

"She isn't my wife," Chimes said, and he drew a card. Fanning the cards, he saw his hand yielded no wins. He folded.

MK showed his hand, splaying his cards on the waxed tabletop—the other two with whom they played followed suit—and he dragged a mound of sterling bit into his lap, catching the pile in his tunic.

The other two got up and left, accusing MK of being a cheat and a crook.

MK laughed at the accusation as he shuffled the cards—they flipped and cut with ease in the hands of a man who had been dealing cards for decades. He held his pipe between his lips as he delt.

"She isn't your wife, yet she's begging for you to forgive her?" MK laughed, the pipe bobbing under his silver mustache. "If she didn't care about what you thunk, she wouldn't be bothering you playing cards with your mates. Seems you got a wife." The man sighed. "Oh, to be young and in love."

Chimes picked up the cards and sorted them.

MK set down a pair.

Chimes picked up and discarded.

Did he feel like he had known Treasta since childhood? Sure. Was he going to let MK know that? Absolutely not.

"We wedded under the stars," Chimes said, reordering his cards and speaking in long, slow exaggeration. "It was spring. Early spring. We wanted our consummation as fresh as the first wildflower's bloom." He laid down a card.

MK matched his card with another suit, lightly chuckling amused at the fable.

"My mother was her maid of honor," Chimes said, "because her mother couldn't make it. And my father …," he paused, "he officiated our wedding."

MK discarded. "Where?"

"Hmm?" Chimes set down a pair.

"Where was your wedding."

Chimes smiled, his gaze growing distant as he conjured the fictitious wedding in his mind. "On the ocean." And he set down his cards, a perfect hand. "At the vineyards on the Shardian Waters. It was a small wedding. Private. She looked beautiful, hair in elaborate Wesserian braids, knotted and tied with pale blue lace to match her pale blue gown. I cried when I saw her."

MK threw his hand down, defeated. He smiled, motioning for Chimes to claim his earnings.

"No man's imagination can dream with earnest a story as beautiful as yours for a woman he doesn't love. Maybe she isn't your wife, but why should that matter? I've spent decades with my woman, and we've been nothing but faithful without the proper courtship."

Chimes pocketed the money. He had known Treasta for maybe a month or so. To be able to love someone with the depth MK described, the same depth Marnie and Atlas shared, in such a short period of time, didn't seem logical, but matters of the heart were oft without reason.

He stood, done playing for the night.

MK leaned back, folding his hands over his lap. "She's pregnant," he said. "Pregnant women, they're difficult. But it's because they're pregnant, you understand? If you can handle her at her worst now, imagine how she is at her best."

And with that sliver of wisdom, if one could call it that, Chimes went to the bar, ordered a drink, shot it back, and left the salon.

The echo of his boots' heels clacked on the deck. He took a deep breath. Maybe he should order another drink. No. He was already a little tipsy after drinking and playing cards for a good part of the night.

Knock, knock, knock.

Treasta had been lying in the dark, curtains pulled shut. She had given up, thought Chimes was done with her; maybe she should abandon her endeavors. Who cared whether the Pats were trailing them? This should be it: the end.

"It's unlocked," she called.

The door opened and shut. It was dark inside with the drawn curtains and no lamps or candles alight. So dark was it that Chimes struggled to see, and when he couldn't locate Treasta in his tipsy stupor, he almost left. But when he turned around, he fell into a chair, then the wall.

"*Ouch*," he winched, grabbing his side and sat to work through the sharp jab from the corner of the table.

She stirred, the covers rising and lowering as she turned over. Treasta pulled them in tight, resting on the cot. "What do you want?" she asked, sounding exacerbated.

He stood, instinctively wanting to step toward her voice. Unsure of whether he should come closer or not—partly because he couldn't quite judge the distance of where she rested from where he stood—Chimes instead leaned on the door, folding his hands, and twiddling his thumbs.

"Can we talk?" he asked.

Treasta pulled her covers into her body tighter. "I don't know if we have anything to discuss."

Chimes threw his head back: *thump.* He rubbed the back of his skull, his fingers digging into his scalp to satiate his nerves. "How about I ask you something and you can ask me something, with utmost truth."

Utmost. She agreed.

Chimes slid down the wall, resting on the floor as he held his knees in the dark. "Who was that woman?"

"I already told you," she said in the dark. "I know her from home. Why are you estranged from your father?"

"He abandoned us while my mother was on her deathbed. Can you blame me?"

She supposed not, but not having experienced what it was like to have a father made it difficult to empathize.

Chime asked: "Why are you lying to me?"

The darkness seemed to shrink around her. "Because …" she paused, nervous to continue. "Because I'm scared what you will think of me."

Chimes shrunk.

And instead of following up with a question, Treasta held onto the silence, hoping he'd say something to fill the void between them. But he didn't. For some reason Treasta always thought Chimes knew what to say for any occasion, but it seemed this time was different. And after several minutes of silence, she decided to speak.

"I … I'm a thief. So is Davan. So is Elsie—the woman in the cell. And then there's Laine and the Pats. I ran into them in Hayam. That's what happened to my eye. One of the Pats—they're twins," she added when she realized saying "the Pats" probably didn't make much sense. "I … I want the flute so I can trade it with Laine for jewels and other treasures they got. I need it. If I can find the right buyer, I could have enough gold bits to …" Treasta rubbed her stomach. "I just want my old life back," she told Chimes. "I want to go home. I can't go back like this."

Chimes crawled to her in the dark and leaned over her bed, finding her hands clinching the blanket. He weaved his fingers into hers. Where he expected softness were rough pads of skin. His hand tightened, and he rubbed her palm with his thumb.

"I'm sorry," he said.

It wasn't what she was expecting to hear because it was something she didn't hear often.

"I don't care you're a thief," Chimes continued. "Or whether you're with child. The past is the past." A dewy print was left on the back of her hand in place of his lips. "I want to be here for you, do you understand? I've never … I've never felt this way for someone before. And," he drew in a long breath and exhaled as if stalling to find courage, "if maybe …" Ugh, how to say it? Chimes felt his body going numb—or that was the booze. "Can we try me and you? For a bit, maybe? I have feelings for you, Treasta. Feelings that I don't really know what to do with, and I know things have been complicated and difficult, but if it doesn't work, if *we* don't work, we can just pretend it never happened."

Treasta fought against her instinct to withdraw herself. But she eased close to Chimes. The nervousness in his voice brought her comfort and eased her own angst. He rested on his knees leaning over her bedside; she curled closer to better reach his lips.

"You mean that?" she asked.

His breath was hot as he exhaled; she could sense the heat of his body drawing her nearer.

"I need to know you mean that," she added.

Chimes licked his bottom lip as his heart threw itself into its chest wall.

"I'll tell you everything," Treasta said, her voice dropping into a whisper, "but you need to promise me."

"Anything," he said. Her lips—he could have sworn to have felt them just now against his, just for a moment, just long enough he couldn't pull himself away. "What do I promise you?"

"You will never leave me. I don't want you ever to leave me. I don't want to be alone."

"I will never leave you," and he had never tasted such desire before this moment that it was impossible to stop himself from crawling onto the cot with her, taking her body under his. This—*Treasta*—he had never felt such a longing for another body, another soul. He wanted to give her every part of him, share his fears and wants—wanted for her to feel him the way he felt her. Her body, her mind—the way her hair fell over her shoulders and splayed like sunrays, even the way she scowled when upset—he wanted it all.

Treasta took him by the neck, pulling him closer. "Let's not play pretend." She could feel the weight of his pelvis on hers, the heat of their bodies like flames. He kissed her lips then her neck, then unbuttoned her blouse to reveal breasts full and bright in the black of the room. His lips deposited dew drops on her skin, marking the places he admired most, thinking nothing about the roundedness of her torso and coming between her legs to take in every inch.

He bit her thigh, and Treasta exhaled a long moan wrought with an overdue ache. Her leg quivered, and Chimes felt a woman completely giving herself to him.

"Oh, Chimes …," she murmured. Treasta couldn't remember a time she felt so full—not even Davan could tame such primeval instinct. She wrapped her legs around him, digging her nails into his back, grasping his tunic, so hungry, so famished, so …

She couldn't stop herself—she screamed, then groaned, then pulled him into her tighter. She bit into his neck—his pleasure vocalized in low groans was everything she needed for wanting to give him more of herself.

Treasta released a long sigh.

His words were like velvet on her mind: "I have hoped you have wanted me for as long as I have wanted you."

The heat of his body radiated as she ran her hands along his bared chest.

"You really mean it, don't you?"

Chimes' voice simmered, "Every word."

24

IN THE TWO DAYS REMAINING, TREASTA AND CHIMES barely left the others' side apart from fetching the occasional drink and ordering food from the galley. They ate in the cabin, kept the curtains shut so the light was low in the day, so they could exist only in one another's world.

The boat had long eased onto the Great River, so wide it was impossible to see across, and so enraptured were Treasta and Chimes with their own affairs, that neither took in the limitless view of water flowing southward mirroring the cerulean of the sky with such intensity, were it not for the movement of the river, it would be impossible to know where the sky ended.

On the final day, Davan situated himself in the salon, observing the patrons: a woman leaning over the bar belted a laugh as the man she flirted with flashed a toothy grin; four fellows gathered around a table, making bets; two others near the windows, looking out over the water, discussed the view.

From his periphery a figure passed and approached the bar. Davan pulled the hood of his cowl to hide his face. Chimes ordered two drinks. He left without noticing Davan.

Davan followed him from a distance. When Trish mentioned Treasta was here, she failed to mention Chimes, who carried himself with a lilt of delight, an air of confidence. Of course he would. Davan remembered how his knife landed on the ground when he attacked Chimes. He didn't know whether Chimes was a gifted or whether it was something else. A charm or sigil—Davan didn't know much about magic trinkets.

Unbeknown to Chimes, he led Davan to the cabin where Treasta was staying. Chimes slipped inside; the door shut with a click, and Davan stood at it, hand hovering over the handle. But what was he going to say? *Sorry I left you?* It didn't seem right. He wasn't sorry. Maybe he was at first, but not now.

Treasta's laughter could be heard through the door.

Chimes said something, but what, it wasn't clear.

Davan drew his hand away, staring downward, hearing elation in the cadence of Treasta's speech. It was genuine—different than how they had been together over the past few months. He didn't know whether he should feel outraged, dejected, or jealous. He recognized the bitterness entering his heart, the heat under his skin, as his hands began to tremble. Closing his fists tightly, Davan walked off, holding back the impulse to throw open the door, wrap his hands around Chimes' throat and strangle him. As he returned to the cargo hold, he carried the image in his mind of Chimes turning blue, the sound of him struggling to breathe, and the whites of his eyes popping red as they filled with blood.

Inside the cabin, Chimes looked Treasta over, touching the scars on her arms and the symbol branded into her flesh. "What is this?" he asked.

His touch tickled; she grabbed his hand and held it. "It's the symbol of my guild."

"So," Chimes said, "Davan has it too? And that woman in the brig?"

Treasta nodded.

He noticed the "III" etched into her forearm. "And this?"

Treasta was unsure whether she had it in her to recall her childhood. She gave him details here and there of how she and Davan met, of the guild they were a part of before Dubilee, of Davan's undying loyalty to Lodan after he turned on his old guild. She left out the details of how they abused her, saw her as an object despite her being still a child. It was too difficult to recount, and she certainly didn't want Chimes' pity.

"Then Lodan died," she said. "It was sudden. Davan thought he'd take charge. Then the tribe divided itself into factions. Someone traveled to Doar to meet with the leader of a sister tribe and returned with him. Fylle took over as our chief."

"Chief?"

"King? Whatever you want to call it." Treasta explained: "Under the chief are the marshals. Each marshal heads his own tribe. Under the marshals are officers and below them are initiates."

She shouldn't have been telling him all this, but they were hundreds of miles away. It wouldn't matter.

"There are multiple tribes?" he asked.

"Four. All in different towns. Three in Northern Kildore and one in the capital city."

Yes, she was definitely saying too much, but she wanted to share her world with him. "We operate under the name Cleave, but my guild is called Dubilee."

Chimes leaned back, stretching his legs out across the floor and rolling his ankles to loosen the joints after sitting under them too long. He took a swig. Then tapped Treasta with his toes, smiling like a little boy with a crush. Her fingers tickled the sole, and he drew his legs back, laughing. Her eyes seemed to sparkle as the corners of her lips rose into a playful grin.

"I think it's good you left your friend in the brig," Chimes said.

Treasta scoffed. "Elsie is *not* my friend. I think she'd agree."

"She would have gone after Bastan. He'd have done her in the same way he did with the boy in that drawing."

Treasta sat up on the floor and leaned forward upon hearing the graveness in his voice as he mentioned the name. The Andrili warlock had a reputation in the areas surrounding Hatchet, it seemed. The stories of Bastan may even have stretched farther. Her gaze lowered. "What do you mean?"

"He collects souls in portraits."

"So that drawing was a real person? A boy?"

Chimes nodded. "For at least the past century he's ruled over Hatchet—maybe even longer. No one really knows. Anyone who enters the town never leaves. Your friend would have gone after him if you let her out."

Elsie's soul becoming trapped in a portrait was a horrifying thought but not so horrifying that Treasta wouldn't have opposed.

"Again," Treasta said, "she is not my friend. She tried tying me and Davan up in Herra so she could get ahead of us."

"Lot of good that did, huh?"

"Well, we may have also left her for dead in a fire."

Chimes' expression fell. The scar on Elsie's face when she removed the mask … He looked at Treasta and didn't want to believe she would do that to someone. But he should expect no less from someone from a thieves' guild; yet he did because he was so enamored; Treasta was the perfect woman, and a perfect woman wouldn't leave someone to burn to death. His body ran cold. He tried to shake the feeling. He wanted to just let it go.

"Have you …" He paused, searching for the right tone and the right words. "Have you killed someone before?"

Treasta searched his face, watching his countenance shift. Was that fear she saw? She didn't want him to lose her trust, to think that she'd ever hurt him the way Elsie was consumed in flames. "Yes," she finally said. He didn't ask who or why. He finished his drink, stood, and left the cabin.

Treasta shut her eyes, threw her hands to her face, and berated herself with insults, wishing she could take it back. Treasta tried burying her head in her knees but couldn't with how her stomach had grown. She rolled onto the floor, pulled the blanket from the cot, and let it fall over her so she was shrouded in complete darkness.

25

LIGHT SHAFTS SPLAYED FROM BEHIND BILLOWED CLOUDS over the Great Lake. When it became the Great Lake no one knew, except at some point the land the ship had been following rose into tall cliffs, and greenery flourished along its cracks and ridges. Here, the landscape was brighter than anything Treasta or Davan had ever seen, and they observed—albeit at different ends of the boat, neither aware of the other—the landscape's red face and lively vegetation. Both sighed, leaned on the railing and daydreamed of Wesser and remembered home and each other.

Treasta's chest ached. She was angry. But especially she was sorrowful, like a part of herself was absent, and she was beginning to wonder whether she could think straight without him, whether her longing for Chimes was a product of Davan's absence. His lips, the way Chimes took her in and kissed her, everything about him and how he handled her body was new.

Davan didn't understand what Treasta saw in Chimes, and he couldn't shake the idea of them together from his mind. Everything he had been through with her flashed across his vision: the day he found her in the alley, their friendship blossoming into romance as young teenagers, how she always had an answer when he didn't. He really had believed she was his better half; yet he abandoned her, and he tried convincing himself that she'd understand. But maybe that wasn't true, maybe he made the wrong decision. No, stop it. His head fell into his hands, and he tugged at his unkempt hair. She knew him better than he knew himself. It was okay, he thought. Treasta must understand how important this quest was for him. The memory of Treasta astride on his penis, her breasts warm, soft, her arms coming around his neck, so they pressed against him—he adjusted his trousers—then an overwhelming warmth seized him and Oda overtook Treasta's image, then Lorna's pale flesh appeared, her smell returned like a sweet, intoxicating haunt.

Before Davan left Galgaya for Wesser, he met with Lorna under a full moon where the park overlooked the ocean. There, a statue of the goddess Annikah was illuminated by moonbeams, and the stars shone with a special kind of twinkle that appeared only when Lorna was nearby. Secret lovers were they. Her husband knew not of him, and Treasta knew not of her. And solely they existed for the other under the glittering night.

"Must you go?" she had asked.

He tucked curls bright like wheat behind her ears, lifted her chin with his finger and placed a gentle kiss onto her lips. "I'll return," he said.

Lorna dropped her gaze. "Not for months. And what if—"

He hushed her. "No *what ifs*. I promise you, I'll be back, and when I return, yours are the first eyes I want to see"—golden like honey, and she was as sweet.

The blare of the horn interrupted his daydreaming as the steamboat eased along the lake and crept closer to the Great Lake City, which appeared just on the horizon. And as the vessel chugged closer, shapes of the city became tangible—stone buildings constructed with the same red rock of the surrounding landscape, trees extended toward the sky, wealthy with water within their trunks and casting shadows across the busy streets. From here, the dam wasn't visible, as the city was erected along the structure that formed the lake. Buildings towered, their roofs of steep eaves and terracotta shingles, their windows tall and slender to allow light and to better capture the breeze to keep the structures cooler in the summer. Then, there, on the western side of the dam was the citadel, an imposing stronghold of multiple tiers and palace to the city's councilors and magistrate.

Treasta watched the city grow. It was larger than Galgaya, massive in comparison. Cranked lifts powered by wound-up motors carried passengers up and down the dam wall to lower levels of the city, the lowest of which was the docks.

The horn blared. The vessel eased forward, slowing as it neared.

Deckhands lined the dock ready as crew aboard prepared the ropes.

Chimes stood next to Treasta, looking up the dam's wall. Here it was maybe three stories tall, but on the other side, the wall sloped a mile deep to a river, with no parts of the city following its steep grade, nothing but polished, red stone from top to bottom.

The boat's hull hit the dock with a light thud. Its ramp was lowered, and passengers began stepping off, including Treasta and Chimes with their bags slung over their shoulders while others awaited their luggage to be unloaded.

As Davan played the role of deckhand, hauling trunks with other crewmen, he caught a glimpse of Treasta walking with Chimes, then a woman with mouth bound being dragged off by local officers in bright red uniforms and plumed hats. He set down the trunk and followed Elsie.

Davan stayed close, wove through the crowd, and did his best to keep her in his line of sight. They came to a lift; its wooden floor creaked as they stepped on it. Davan watched as the chains took them skyward. He waited for it to return, then cautiously stepped onto the platform with several strangers. The gate closed, and the lake from this vantage looked no different than the views of the Sterling Ocean he knew well.

Atop the dam, the city sprawled along its span, and through the middle cut a wide promenade to the citadel that on days of celebration hosted grand parades. Where Elsie and the officers went, he didn't know, but they couldn't have gone far. So he asked locals where he could find a jail or prison.

A woman pointed east.

Sure enough, as Davan rushed along, he saw the bright color flare through the traffic and Elsie continuing to struggle, trying to break free.

They came to a jailhouse, its stairs running along the lakeside of the dam's wall. A secure location, Davan thought as he peered down the steps to where there was a lone terrace and a door. He could see slats in the wall where jail cells let in light to prisoners. The officers and their Kildorei captive disappeared inside.

It was midday. In approximately five hours the sun would begin to set. He'd wait until night to breach the jailhouse.

Chimes stood alongside Treasta at the docks. He wasn't sure what to say. Neither had spoken to the other until that moment.

"Thank you," Treasta said. "I can pay you when I find Davan. He has our money."

"It'll be difficult to find him," Chimes said.

Treasta inhaled. "I guess I'll have to take that risk. Should we meet at an inn by tonight or morning or something so I can get you your payment?"

Chimes scratched his head. "I … you know what, don't worry about it. You need it more than I do, with …" He caught himself from making any comment about the baby. "Actually, here," he held out a purse stuffed with money; heavily it landed in her hand. She looked at him bewildered, but before she could say anything he said, "You need it more than me."

Treasta's mouth went dry, her words caught in her throat. She stared at the money—Marnie's money and more after his final game gambling with MK—and then looked at the violet-eyed Chimes.

"Good luck," he said and bowed like a gentlemanly stranger. Giving no space for Treasta to say anything, Chimes walked away.

Treasta's mouth hung open. She wanted to tell him to "stop, please don't go" and "I need you; I don't know where I'm going," but getting those words to form on her lips was impossible. He disappeared through the crowd. *But our promise,* she wanted to say. *But you promised you'd never leave me.* And Treasta knew at the moment she would never see him again. Tears flooded her eyes.

The purse, heavy with coinage, weighed the satchel down strapped across her chest. Where to go from here wasn't clear; the golden flute's location wasn't known to her, but surely the locals would have such knowledge over an item known by legend to be hidden in their city.

Treasta grasped the strap with a need to hold onto something as she made her first steps on her own into Wesser. The road brought her to a lift; she watched others ride up as another group of people appeared when it came back down. The gate opened.

The lift operator nudged her, his hand resting on a crank. "Miss, you getting on or what?"

Treasta gave an awkward smile and cautiously stepped aboard. The gate closed. The mechanism creaked as the operator pulled the crank, and the chains clanged around the spool. Stay calm, Treasta told herself as she watched the docks shrink and the lake's blue grow. A chill inched through her body; the edges of her vision went hazy. Deep breaths … in … out … in … out …

The lift jerked to a stop.

"Miss?" Another operator nudged her.

Treasta opened her eyes.

The operator held out his hand and he helped her—the last person to come off the lift—down. She thanked him, then took in the view of the lake before coming into the city's main strip atop the wall. The wide promenade was busy with traffic—foot, carts, horses—packed tightly as everyone moved with the purpose of having somewhere to be.

"Watch it!" a man said as he bumped into her.

"Get out of the way!" said another driving a wagon.

Treasta stumbled backward onto the pavement and off the road. She clutched the strap tighter and searched for somewhere to go, an inn or a tavern, anywhere out of this crowd. She walked through the first door she found.

Skulls of various animals lined shelves; specimen preserved in jars were just out of arms reach at the top of a bookcase, and taxidermy avians were mounted on the wall. A small woman—no, a dwarven woman, Treasta realized—appeared, broad-shouldered, long red hair braided and wrapped in two knots atop her head. She wore rings along her digits with rubies and topaz gleaming in the sunlight striking through the slender windows.

"Welcome in," the dwarven woman said.

Treasta couldn't stop staring. A dwarf. An actual dwarf? She heard tales of their kind, but most folks in Kildore spoke of them like they belonged in myths.

The dwarf rested her hands on her small hips. "Right. So you're not from here, are you?"

Treasta shook her head. "Sorry. No. I'm lost, actually. I'm looking for an inn for the night."

"Ahh, I see, my dear. I suppose you wouldn't be interested in any of my wares?"

"You did this?"

"Ay. I did. It's a hobby," the woman said. "I also trade in jewels. I've got some lovely pearl earrings from the Shardian Waters."

"Shardian Waters?"

"You really aren't from around here. Goodness." And the woman came around a counter fit for her size and unrolled an old map across it. She pointed at the ocean west of Wesserland.

There was more to the world than Treasta could fathom, so much more. And the ocean, the Shardian Waters, was but maybe fifty miles or so from Wesser. She truly was on the other side of the world, beyond the edges of any map her eyes did lay upon.

"Where are you from?"

Treasta held onto the strap for comfort. She looked over the antique map showing more of Cyconis than she knew existed, worn and fragile, at least a hundred years outdated. Kildore had yet to replace the lands of Ceradel and surrounding kingdoms that eventually integrated into provinces after periods of war. Treasta pointed to a city called Athalan resting on the edge of the Sterling Ocean.

The dwarven woman's face shot a look of discontent, then she forced a half smile. "The East Lands?" The name rolled slowly off her tongue. "I'd like you to leave."

"Excuse me? What did I do?" The woman started shoving her toward the exit.

The door slammed behind her, and Treasta was again faced with the overwhelmingly crowded promenade.

By evening, Treasta found lodging, a building prominently featured with multiple stories stacked over the street in such a way that it looked like it could topple over any moment. She entered through a door under a sign that read "The Amethyst Aster Inn." This wasn't any cheap stay by the looks of the establishment—purple wallpaper, pink granite countertops and pillars holding high a vaulted ceiling. Treasta didn't belong here, but she did her best to act like it even if she wasn't quite dressed well enough despite wearing Marnie's clothes. The district she had found herself in was westerly, nearer the citadel and clearly well off.

The innkeeper wore a chemise dyed purple—a color where Treasta was from was reserved only for the royal family and lords to wear. But here, it seemed popular for layfolk.

The man looked her up and down, examining the earthen colors she adorned, the coat too hot for her to be wearing in this temperate region, and the bag slung across her chest. Its leather was fading.

"Can I help you?" An air of judgment was in his voice, and Treasta thought about going somewhere else, but it was getting dark and navigating a foreign city at night didn't seem wise.

"How much for a room?"

He tapped his fingers on the counter, as if impatient she was still standing there. He was expecting her to leave after saying the price. But Treasta set the amount he asked for onto the counter.

The innkeeper slapped his hand over the money and dragged it across the polished stone to count it. Sure enough, it was all there. "Very well," he said as he unlocked a drawer to deposit the payment. "Name?"

"Treana."

"Just Treana?"

"Treana Darius."

He took down her name, retrieved a key from the cubby behind him, and rang a bell. A porter appeared from a back room standing with perfect posture.

"Show this woman to her room," the proprietor said, passing him the key.

The porter approached Treasta. "May I take your bag, Miss?"

Treasta hesitated but passed him her satchel.

"This way," he said, and the porter led her to a staircase, where she followed him to the top floor and down a long hall.

He unlatched a door painted white at the very end, and they entered a round room, a tower with large windows and a clear view of the citadel alight in the evening.

"Can I get you anything else, Miss?"

"No, thank you," she said.

The young man stood there momentarily with his hand out.

"What?" Treasta asked.

And when she didn't tip him, the porter folded his hand into a fist, red-faced with embarrassment and perhaps a bit of disappointment. He took a deep breath, said, "Very well. Good night," and exited.

Treasta locked the door. Her heart pounded into her chest and blood rushed through her veins. Suddenly feeling lightheaded, she sat on the bed. Had she not known this was an inn, she would have thought she was in a palace with the artistically carved beams and posts, the large bed and its canopy. It was more than she ever needed and nothing she ever wanted. She poured water from the pitcher into the porcelain basin, scrubbed her hands and splashed her face. Its coolness eased her anxiety. She needed to figure out where to find the flute.

She rifled through the satchel, retrieved a green knitted poncho detailed with red threads and brass buttons along a v-cut collar. Treasta pulled the long, pointed hood over her head, checked herself in the mirror and felt somewhat pretty in it, glad to see it hid her body. Marnie was a skilled weaver, a talent Treasta never had the honor to learn.

Treasta latched the door behind her when she left the room, her heels pressed silent in the rug running down the hall and stairs. At the counter, the innkeeper was stoic, neither greeting her with a smile nor with a sneer. Maybe it was the poncho. Maybe it was the money. Either way, she silently thanked Marnie.

She explored the grounds some and found connected to the common area a separate gentlemen's lounge where men relaxed puffing on their pipes and discussing whatever they thought was important between them. Down a short hallway was the restaurant, a smaller establishment than she expected from an inn of this size, but its cozy atmosphere attracted a more pleasant crowd than the typical tavern. She ordered wine at the bar. And the bartender listed several different kinds, none of which Treasta had known.

"The Petia arbitas, I suppose," Treasta said, thinking it was easier to pick a random one than ask what the difference was among them.

"This," said the woman, "is crafted from the vineyards near the country village of Petia." She poured a generous amount and passed the goblet to Treasta. "Let it aerate and give it a smell. Then let me know what you taste."

An opulent scent Treasta couldn't quite identify entered her nose. She sipped.

"A hint of vanilla, no? And cherry," the woman said. "It's our most popular dry wine."

Treasta sat at the bar, continuing to sip, trying to understand what she meant by "dry." She played along with the server, smiled and nodded in agreement. Is this what being wealthy was? Treasta savored the drink with what sensibilities she could muster, momentarily transforming into a woman of the upper middle class, going as far as matching the bartender's mannerisms and vocal patterns.

"I am Cherie," the woman said. "What brings you here?"

"I've traveled to visit my husband's family," Treasta said. "We hail from Yeras."

"Ah, a long journey," Cherie said. She topped off Treasta's cup. "What should I call you?"

"Treana Darius." There she went using Chimes' given name as her last name. Before it came instinctively; she said the first name that came to her when checking into the inn, but now she said it knowingly.

"It's wonderful you'll be staying with us Mrs. Darius. Your husband must have found the gentlemen's lounge."

"Not quite," Treasta said. "He's visiting with his grandmother while

I get us settled in here. His grandmother had wanted to meet with him, and his grandfather is seriously ill. We're not quite sure what ails him, but we worried if I came along, it would stress his condition. It's hard right now. Especially with"—Treasta looked down at her bump and rubbed her stomach. "We're expecting."

"Oh, how wonderful!" Cherie cheered. The bright grin on her face, the elation of excitement escaping the woman made Treasta woozy. She didn't understand why she couldn't bring herself to feel the same way, for joy to come so naturally.

Treasta forced a smile. "We're hoping for a boy. It's our first."

"Have you any names picked out?" she asked, leaning over the bar.

"Tytan." The name was said with confidence, because it was one Treasta truly loved the sound of ever since she heard it as a little girl at the orphanage. "Tytan," she said it again, but softer almost melancholic as she remembered the boy who carried the name. He was two years old when he died of fever.

"Lovely. I've never quite heard a name like it," Cherie said. "Well, allow this next pour to be on the house in celebration of your child, sweet baby Tytan Darius. I pray to Alia he is of good health."

Treasta lifted her goblet to cheers.

"Can I ask you something?" Treasta said as she set her cup down. "I met a dwarven woman earlier today, and when I told her where I was from, she rushed me out of her business."

"Must have been Khyari. She owns the oddities shop, yes?" When Treasta nodded, Cherie shrugged and began cleaning the countertop. "And you're from the East Lands. You do not know your own history?"

"What we know of dwarves are in stories passed down from past generations," Treasta said, feeling her faux posh cadence begin to fail. "There are abandoned mines in the mountains north of Kildore and along the cliffs of the Sterling Ocean. I hear of ruins being found within mountains near Yeras, but it is only rumor."

"I see. The legend goes that cursed creatures rose from mud and cast a terrible darkness over the land as they swept over the East Lands and forced the dwarven people into the West Lands," Cherie said. "To Khyari and her people, those cursed people are your ancestors. So ingrained are these tales for Clan Blacthorne that travelers who frequent our town know not to speak of the East Lands. When you meet a dwarf here, you never say from where you hail; it's an unspoken rule."

"Clan Blacthorne?"

Cherie nodded. "The last family of dwarves to dwell within Wesser. Hundreds of years ago, when our rulers' ancestors seized the dam and surrounding lands—spread his empire far and vast from the Shardian Waters, through the Great Canyon, and over the highlands—the other dwarven clans fled north by ship to the After Lands. That is what is told. So forgive Khyari; her people are not well liked by many within the city and to have a wanderer from the East Lands in her shop, well, I'm sure you can understand. For the dwarves of this city, the East Lands are unchanged."

Oh. Treasta felt herself shrink in the stool. She corrected her posture, hoping Cherie didn't notice, but her expression made it seem like she had.

"If this is your first time meeting a dwarf, then I assume the legends of their ancestors are true and that no dwarves have called the East Land home for a millennium."

"You're right," Treasta said. In a way she understood what it was like to be different, but truly she couldn't understand. "I didn't know. These are legends that don't exist in our lands. But we have tales that have traveled as far as Yeras and beyond about the dwarves and about their treasure and ancient ways." She lowered her voice as she continued, "Some say there's a magic flute that turns whoever places his lips upon it into gold."

Cherie laughed, then, puzzled, she placed her finger on her nose, as if to help her think. "You know. I was going to say that I don't think the golden flute is magical, but I've never seen it myself to know."

"So, it is real?" Treasta acted surprised but was truly as intrigued. "In Yeras it is a popular children's story. *Miarani and the Golden Flute.* In the story"—Treasta realized she had Cherie's full attention as the bartender leaned closer—"ten-year-old Miarani and his friend, Issa, venture into the wilderness in search of the treasure said to be kept hidden away in a castle, protected by a greedy ettin whose loneliness consumed him and drove him mad after the second head placed the flute to his lips. To this day, it is believed the ettin to be somewhere in these lands, wandering near his fallen castle with a second head of gold."

"And what of Miarani?" Cherie asked. "What of Issa?"

"They turned to gold," Treasta said. "Such a precious treasure makes its wielder greedy."

"You're a great storyteller. What a wonderful mother-to-be you are."

"And the flute," Treasta stood, "you know of it then."

Cherie laughed. "Yes, of course, everyone knows of it here. The flute is nothing like you say. The Councilor Gustas, I believe, is the keeper of the golden flute. Fascinating it is how stories travel and change. And how sad of a tale. I wished for Miarani and Issa to have succeeded. What would they have done with it, I wonder? Surely they needed the wealth, surely it would have been for the betterment of their village or maybe an ailing mother." Cherie's expression softened. "I quite liked the story. Maybe I'll tell it to my children, too."

"Who is Councilor Gustas?"

"He's one of the Nine under Magistrate Agemon."

"I see. I don't quite know the politics here. In Kildore, we're not ruled under city-states but a monarchy," Treasta said. "And Yeras is stewarded by a lord."

Cherie nodded, understanding. "They may as well consider themselves a monarchy with how the magistrate conducts his business. You didn't hear this from me, but I hear that Councilor Lyra's death wasn't an accident. Tricky business it is to be so powerful. I do wonder," she trailed off, "what it would have been like to live here before the fall of the empire."

"*Bah!* And don't forget the parties," a woman who had been listening from the other end of the bar chimed. "Always with the parties. Must be where all our taxes go. My mother-in-law says they're holding another tomorrow evening, a ball, with hundreds of guests. The wealthiest of families will be there, including from Iragia." The stranger's lips were stained purple with wine.

"Iragia, is that another city-state?"

"It's the kingdom across the Shardian Waters," Cherie said. "They're known for their spices and teas. More expensive than any wine we sell. And only the wealthiest of Wesser can afford it."

"My husband returned from Iragia with an afghan, softest I ever did touch," the woman at the bar said. She pulled a pin from her hair, and her gray tresses fell down her back. "This is also from Iragia." The hairpin was bronze, intricately weaving a knot around a polished onyx cabochon shaped like a diamond.

Iragia, the stranger spoke of it as if it were a land of prosperity. Treasta hadn't finished her final cup when she felt a heavy drowsiness claiming her faculties. She took one more sip and bid the women good night.

In her room, Treasta kept the curtains drawn and the windows cracked to allow in a breeze passing over the lake. She lay in bed able to see from her pillow the citadel alight in the night—the windows, the archer slits, the guards were but a short thought. Too fast did she fall asleep to think about what the next day would bring.

26

DAVAN ASSESSED HIS SURROUNDINGS—the empty streets lit by lamplight, the fading of firelight in homes as residents headed to bed, the gentle gust carried over the lake and along the promenade. He knelt in the alleyway and checked the supplies in his pack. He wished he could have taken more after abandoning the wagon in Maward, but he wanted to keep it light. Davan tightened the straps on his shoulders, the pickax strapped to his waist like one would a sword, and he walked to the jail, then hid when he noticed a guardsman at the stairs.

Clutching the pickax in his hands, he crept along the wall, stalking silently in the moon-cast shadows. Davan adjusted his grip; focused, he patterned his breathing into long, shallow breaths. Crouched just to the guardsman's left flank, Davan readied the pickax and swung. It landed in the man's chest, striking him in the heart. He dropped.

Davan dragged his body into a nearby alley, propping him up along a wall. He positioned his foot on the corpse and tore the pickax from his chest, hearing a cracking from the breastbone permeate the quiet of the night. A river of crimson pooled over the man's bright red coat. Ah, right. Davan forgot about that part. He had wanted the uniform, but it was useless now. Davan unstrapped the boxy, plumed hat from the dead man's head and instead wore that, hoping the silhouette of a Wesserian officer was enough of a disguise.

The stairs were steep, probably to make it more difficult for any escapees to run. It was roughly halfway down the wall when he came upon the door. A light hung next to it, the flame dimmed, on the verge of going out. Davan grabbed the handle; he pushed then pulled. Locked.

Knock, knock, knock!

The window at the top of the door slid open. Davan met with the eyes of an older guard, looking him over through the peep. The plume's feathers atop Davan's head fluttered in the breeze.

"I've been sent to relieve you," Davan said.

The man let out a long sigh of relief. "I was wondering when you'd show up. Alia be damned, the bitch won't shut up."

The window shut, the latch clicked, and the door swung open.

Davan held the pickax at ready and as soon as the guard appeared, he charged.

But the old man was swift. He dodged Davan's swing and drew his blade.

Davan ducked at the man's attack and struck his shins with the blunt top-end of the pickax. The guard screamed, fumbling backward outside the open door. He grabbed the door frame to balance himself, wincing at the immense pain radiating up his legs and through his body.

The pickax struck under his chin, sending him toward the ledge of the terrace. He caught himself on the stone railing. But Davan landed his weapon into the man's side, imbedding it through his torso. The guard coughed blood onto the stone. And as his last breath seemed to escape him, Davan pushed him over the edge.

He shut the door behind him as he walked into the jailhouse, and there, in a holding cell, watching with her one eye, was Elsie.

"You must be the bitch that doesn't shut up," Davan said.

"How did you find me?"

"I saw you getting dragged off the boat. Not a good look, you know." She chuckled and rolled her eyes. "Got me right where you want me, don't you?"

Davan pulled a chair over, straddling it as he sat on it backward. He leaned on the back, setting his hand under his chin as his lips curled into a smile. "I suppose I do. Though, I thought I left you for dead. Pity."

"I narrowly escaped."

Something was different about Elsie. And it wasn't just her wounds he noticed—the burns, the eye stuck partly open—her face seemed long with melancholy. It was a new expression for Davan to see on the otherwise apathetic woman.

"So," Davan said, "were you following me or Treasta?"

"You knew Treasta was aboard?"

"I had an interesting run-in with the Pats, actually."

"The Pats?"

The tilt of her head told Davan she didn't know Pat and Trish had been following Treasta and Chimes. But Elsie didn't address it further. Of course, she had figured others could have made it out to Wesser, but as far as she was aware, she, Davan, and Treasta were the only ones here.

"I was following you," she said. "So, it is true. You and Treasta are no longer together. I've seen the way she looks at the white-haired man. She has a new beau. I'd wager that makes you happy."

The mention of Chimes made his blood boil.

"What do you want? To kill me for trying to kill you?"

Elsie's lips twitched into a wicked grin. "I wanted nothing more than to tear your face off with my bare hands."

"What an honor it would have been," he said.

She rested her head on the bars, arms extended upward, clasping the cold iron. "So, Davan, what do you want? To gloat? To laugh in my face? To look at the work you've done?" And she turned her head so he could see her wound better. "I quite like it. Makes me unapproachable, undesirable. Don't you think? You don't seem to be in any rush to get me out of here."

"Who said I was here to get you out?"

"Well," Elsie crossed her arms, "why else would you be here?"

Davan guffawed. "You know where the flute is, don't you?"

"What give you that idea?"

"Because I know you, Elsie. You're resourceful. I'm betting you've known for quite some time."

"You *do* know me," she said with a sigh.

"So, where is it?"

A smug smirk slinked over her face. "I'd rather rot." And the smile fell.

The legs of the chair released a long screech as Davan stood and dragged it to the table. He folded his hands behind his back, cracked his neck, and closed his eyes with his back to Elsie. A vexation overcame him, aggravated that this could be the end. Discontent, Davan breathed, trying to collect himself. Perhaps he was approaching it wrong. But letting Elsie out of the cell wasn't an option. She'd turn on him in an instant or run. Away from Fylle and the rest of the tribe, no rules kept her from killing him. But, and Davan really began considering it, nothing was stopping him from killing her, either. Stubborn was Elsie. And patient. Waiting was never a problem, as she always would get what she wanted with time. But with Treasta also in Wesser, time he didn't have. He flipped the table, let out a shout—a prisoner from the other end of the jailhouse barked gibberish, and then several others echoed.

"Tisk, tisk," he heard Elsie say from behind. "You done got everyone riled up. That ought to attract some attention."

A piece of unwrinkled paper floated toward the floor. It, along with a mask, had been resting on the table—neither of which he paid mind to until now. Davan picked up the paper. A boy's portrait was sketched on the page. He noticed movement in the child's eyes and then saw the name signed at the bottom.

"Give me that!"

Davan turned to see Elsie straining as she extended her arm toward him through the bars. "This?" The paper flapped as he waved it in her direction. She tried nabbing it, but Davan took a step backward. "Ah, ah, ah."

Face contorted with rage, she bared her teeth.

Davan looked the drawing over, watching the boy's gaze. How can something sketched in graphite seem so lifelike? He recognized the boy, remembered how he held him with a handful of hair in his fist. He looked at Elsie. The boy, had he been traveling with her? Curious as Davan was, he pushed the thought aside.

Elsie grumbled under her breath, cursing Davan, cursing Fylle, cursing this mission. "I know what happened to Lodan," she said, hoping to pique his interest. It worked, it seemed. Davan gave his full attention, one eyebrow raised. "*Give me the drawing.*"

"I've gone this long not knowing," Davan said.

"You should ask Treasta," she said.

At Treasta's name, Davan's eyes narrowed. No, don't entertain it, Davan thought. Elsie was just trying to get under his skin.

"You want to make a deal?" He made sure he had her full attention before continuing. "You help me get the flute, and I'll give you this drawing. You let me keep the flute, and I'll tell you where you can find Bastan."

She gasped. "You know?"

"I don't understand how you got this," Davan said. "I thought I killed him. But ..." then he remembered how the gem had disappeared off his person. He had thought it was the Pats, but maybe it was the kid. But the only time he remembered encountering the boy was in the wilderness near Hayam. In their scuffle, could the boy have slipped his hand in his pocket? Could the gem have fallen out of his pocket? No, that didn't seem right. Davan remembered feeling it through the fabric, remembered the hum it gave off and how it made him feel. Or could that have been all in his head? The doubt he was feeling could drive him mad if he lingered on the thought too long. Either way, at some point Bastan returned between the time Davan ran into the kid and found the drawing.

"I can tell you," he finally said, "but you must give me your word."

"Yes, yes, yes," she said, desperate to get her hands on the drawing. "I am at your beck and call. That drawing is more important to me than any golden flute."

A ring of keys hung near the entrance. Davan fetched them and began trying each one on the lock.

Finally, a click.

The door swung on its hinges.

Elsie didn't move. With what woe she carried on her expression, it seemed at any moment she could collapse. This wasn't the Elsie he had known.

Solemnly, she stepped from her jail cell, picked up the mask from the floor, and donned it. "You have my word."

From on the balcony, overlooking the south side of the wall, a river far below would have been seen were it daytime; at this hour, it was an endless view of black. Davan set down a mug; its thud alerted Elsie, who was looking into the blackness at the terrace wall, that he had returned from the bar.

They were the only ones outside, probably because the night had a chill to it drastically cooler than during the day. The candlelight at the center of the table flickered in a light breeze. Together, they sat at a tavern not too far from the jailhouse. Elsie kept her hood up, paranoid guards may be looking for her. Or maybe they wouldn't bother. Davan had killed two, one of which he had left in the alleyway. She expected the guard would be found by morning. She watched him sip his drink as she wrapped her hands around the cup. Were she a fool, she'd have thought he killed them just for her—were he a woman, she'd have been wooed by such a gesture. But Davan only wanted the flute. Their guildmates always thought Davan was a bit soft, but tonight he proved different. Fylle would be proud.

"So, where is it?" he asked.

Elsie wandered around the terrace some, passing a window through which she spotted a large crowd appearing and becoming rowdier as the night went on, the echo rattling the glass panes. She saw a glimpse of her reflection, momentarily mourning the skin cooked away hidden beneath the mask. She walked back to the table, holding her drink against her chest, and didn't sit down.

"It's in the citadel," she said. "I doubt it will be guarded because the citadel itself is well fortified."

The citadel was massive, overwhelmingly so. And inside it could possibly be more puzzling to navigate.

"What do you purpose?" he asked. "Do you have a plan?"

"Of course I do," Elsie said. She paced around the table. "It's a fortuitous event, truly. I wasn't sure if I'd get here on time." Elsie sat; the drink splashed over its rim as the mug hit the table. "Tomorrow evening a party will take place in the citadel. There will be a parade down the strip. To get inside I was going to hide inside one of the carnival floats."

Davan, intrigued, sat forward. He marveled at the idea of such a pomp and circumstance, trying to conjure what such an event would look like moving along the grand promenade, and the location—to be a spectator must be an inspiring experience. Ah, but serious matters were at hand. His eyes lowered, wondering how Elsie could come across such knowledge. Certainly, she tortured someone somewhere on her journey here. Typical.

"What is a carnival float?" Davan asked.

"It's …," Elsie paused. She didn't know how to describe it beyond something big with decoration. "It's like a platform towed by horses, and it's decorated. Sometimes people are on them, sometimes not." Yes, that seemed like the best explanation. "The parade ends on the grounds of the citadel. With such a grand event commencing, it shouldn't be too difficult to wander to Councilor Gustas' apartment."

"Gustas," he said the name, sitting back and rubbing his chin.

"The councilors' quarters are on the third story."

"How do you know this? How can you be sure?"

She smirked, tapping the table with her finger as she enunciated her words, "A caravan along a highway in the Altan Highlands was escorting a wealthy traveler with wealthy goods inside a lavish stagecoach. Why do blue-bloods always make themselves such easy targets?" A titter escaped her lips as she recalled. "I threatened to slit his throat if he didn't give me the information I needed," and the rich man believed her, too, after she helped him from his coach so he could gaze upon his slaughtered escorts and horses. The rich man's words were caught in his throat as he tried to speak. The memory brought her chills.

Unsurprised, Davan gave a slow nod, not in agreement but because such a tale was of Elsie's character. Never was she one to exaggerate, always to the point. "Resourceful," he said. Davan drank.

Elsie had yet to take a sip. "I'm not going back," she said.

Davan lowered his cup. He searched her face, trying to find any indication of deceit, but Elsie just sat there, her lips rolled inward as she pouted, her gaze low and sad. The paleness of her skin seemed whiter than usual, an effect of her melancholia. Did this have to do with the portrait he kept tucked away in his boot? So desperate was she reaching through bars in the jailhouse with such force she could have torn her shoulder from its socket.

Davan didn't have to say anything for Elsie to add, "I can't go back. Declan—"

The name—Davan could have sworn to see tears in Elsie's eyes. Sure enough she wiped her cheeks. The boy in the portrait. Declan. The boy he held by the hair. The memory of Dana shouting emerged. She was pulling on his arm, trying to get him to let go. He was just a boy. But Davan was too worried about the damn flute to care, thinking the boy could have been from the guild or working with someone from the guild. Apparently, he wasn't wrong, but maybe he wasn't quite right either, something he was beginning to realize after Elsie confessed she had no interest in returning to Kildore.

"Who is the boy?" he asked. "The one in the portrait."

Elsie's wet eyes had dried. The stoicism she held expressed hardship and grief. The silence between them was occupied by roars of merriment from within the tavern. A sharp gust cut through them, and the flame was extinguished. Davan's and Elsie's eyes met in the dim glow radiating from the window as shadows of strangers passing across the glass stroked the light.

"He doesn't hear," Elsie said. "He … he's like me. Comes from a broken home."

That was all she said, and it was enough for Davan to understand that the two had, at some point, created a one-of-a-kind bond, as if cut from the same cloth.

Davan drank until the last drop dripped from the mug. He eyed her untouched drink to which she clung for the sake of having something to occupy her hands. She passed him the cup, uninterested in its liquid touching her lips. And he drank that, too—chugged it, then let out a satisfied sigh as he felt his face flush with warmth and belly become full.

"I thought you and Treasta were in love?" Elsie asked as she sat back and crossed her arms.

The flushing he had been feeling went hot with anger at the mention of Treasta's name.

Elsie smiled widely, pleased to find a way to incite any semblance of fury from him. She especially liked how his brow furrowed. "I get it. You both have come such a long way. It was destined to happen."

He scoffed. "Destined?" Then he laughed. "Destiny … do you believe in destiny?" He laughed again and covered his face with his hands, kicking back. He threw himself forward, landing on the table, face just inches away from Elsie. "Treasta is dead to me."

Delightful. Elsie folded her hands and leaned forward. "And what of that pretty married whore back in Galgaya." She said it slow, took her time with each word, each syllable, each letter and sound, letting their shapes roll off her tongue in such a way that she anticipated the rage. She wanted to push Davan—harden his heart, strip him of any kind of regret or morality left in the marrow of his bones. She held her composure, feeling the twitch of a smile on the corner of her lip. It was difficult to keep in, but watching the emotions rushing through him twisted her face—she could feel the heat of his passion, the desire he had to wrap his hands around her tiny neck and break it. Something about calling his *mistress* a whore—or maybe he was her whore—provoked his humanity. Elsie knew Davan well enough that she saw how he cared, not just about Treasta or his secret lover, but also about his own self-worth and the image he wanted others to know him by.

"Lorna, that's her name, isn't it?"

"How do you know—"

She cut him off. "Everyone knows."

Even Treasta? he wanted to ask. No, not Treasta. She would have said something. Would she have said something? His fist hit the table; the metal of the candle dish shuddering echoed.

His chest expanded as he inhaled.

"Everyone knows about Lorna."

The name coming from Elsie, it felt so foreign to Davan's ears.

Like the last leaf hanging on a tree in autumn just before a storm, Davan clung to his senses, searching for sobriety, but the leaf unlatched from the twig as a flurry ripped through the air. He jumped at Elsie, wrapped his large hands around her throat, gripped it tight, holding back the little bit of strength he needed to snap it as the chair fell to the stone floor.

A twinkle flickered in her eyes. He relaxed, realizing this was what she wanted.

"Where was this Davan before?" Elsie asked, standing. "Treasta holds you back, you know."

He huffed, straightening out his tunic, and throwing his backpack over his shoulders. "I suppose we have some planning to do," he said, composing himself.

A thrill overtook Elsie as she grinned ear to ear, momentarily feeling like she again had a purpose. Declan—she thought to herself as she followed Davan—she promised quietly that she wouldn't rest until she saved him from Bastan's awful curse.

27

After asking the innkeeper where she could find a dressmaker, Treasta set out in the early morning while a mist still lingered in the air. The clime seemed less dry than other parts of Wesserland. Here, a slight humidity stuck to her skin, making the coolness of the hour somehow feel colder than it was. But as the sun rose, the mist parted, and within the hour Treasta found the shop she had been searching for.

As she opened the door, a bell hanging from it rang with a rough jingle. Inside, the walls were tall and dark, cubbies stacked with fabrics ordered from least to most expensive. In the windows were premade gowns for different occasions, and in an adjacent room more were displayed. Treasta walked around, touching the fabrics and rubbing them between her thumb and fingers. Some were softer than others, but all were prettier and cleaner than anything she had owned. While she wandered through the room, a door opened, and Treasta caught a glimpse of several seamstresses hunched in chairs sewing. A woman adorning a gown of blue and green stripes with gold embroidered cuffs materialized.

"Good morning," she said. "I'm Portya, the owner. How may I assist you today?"

This was the first time Treasta had been in a shop like this. She didn't know where to start or what to ask. Her shyness was apparent to the dressmaker.

"Well," Portya said as she circled Treasta. "You must need a dress, yes? Or perhaps need for a tailor? Your clothes do seem a tad loose." She tugged on Treasta's clothes to see where to bring in the waist, and that's when she noticed the Treasta was with child. "Congratulations. You and your husband must be excited."

A thin-lipped, forced smile appeared on Treasta's face. She felt the infant kick then, as if on cue. "Yes," she finally said after a long silence. "We unfortunately arrived later than usual from Yeras, and I haven't had time to order a gown for the party tonight at the citadel. I was hoping you could help me."

"An order so late is impossible to complete before tonight's ceremony," Portya said. She rubbed her chin, thinking. "We could alter one of our completed gowns, but to have it done so quickly would require an additional charge."

"I can pay," said Treasta. "Handsomely." She held out the purse, handing it to the woman. It was heavy as it landed on her palm. "Will this do?"

She loosened the strings, peeking inside to see glimmering gold and silver coins. "A handsome gown you will have," she said, pleased.

Portya showed Treasta through the shop, discussed each gown and its layers, the details, and types of stitching. Of course, to Treasta, any gown would be the nicest attire she would have ever adorned. Portya's descriptions for each outfit held little meaning; many of the words she used to describe pieces were outside Treasta's vocabulary.

"Less is more," Portya said as they approached a silk gown the color of soft cerulean. "A year ago, I would have recommended a crinoline silhouette. Today the most fashionable ladies want high waists and slender figures with soft muslin layers to better catch on the air to appear as if they're floating. The sleeves," she touched the billowing elbow-length fabric decorated with beads and bows, "I expect next year there will be less attention on puffed styles that reshape the shoulder."

"May I try it on?"

Pleased to pique Treasta's interest, she unlaced the gown's back.

Portya helped her into a lightly boned corset, then the dress. Its fabrics flowed gently along her figure, barely bringing attention to the child she carried. Trying to hide the child was becoming more difficult.

Treasta outlined her stomach with her hands, looked herself over in the mirror and the shape of her figure as it appeared from the side. The color matched her eyes, her pallor less snowy than normal and the natural pinks in the apple of her cheeks brightened.

Portya brushed Treasta's locks and pulled pins from her own curly hair to hold up Treasta's. Long blonde strands bounced down her back.

"What does your husband do?" Portya asked, as she adjusted the dress to better accentuate her figure, marking where the fabric needed to be taken in or out.

"He is a trader," she said and added, "in spices. He's well invested in several ports along Aris Bay and hopes to extend his dealings to Wesser and eventually the Shardian Waters and to Iragia." She kept eye contact with her own reflection as if trying to convince herself of the lies, too. "I'm so proud of him. So many said he couldn't do it. We've been fortunate ever since."

"So young," Portya said, "and to have such success. It is admirable." The dressmaker stepped back, examining her work. "What do you think?"

The woman in the mirror wasn't Treasta. Is this what life would be like were she to leave the guild? Or was this life she could have had had she not been abandoned? In the mirror, Treasta found herself in the Atlan Highlands of Wesserland beyond the Great Lake City and beyond the canyon, a world easing into winter's coldest month. Davan at her side, she leaned into his chest to listen to his heartbeat, to remember his body, his breath and smooth, deep voice. She wished she could stop time, go back to when she thought all she ever needed was Davan and all he needed was her. "Are you happy?" she had asked him long ago. "Do you have everything you ever wanted?" And when she had thought he would have said: *of course I do; I have you, don't I?*—he chewed his food, sucked back snot with a sniffle as his nose dripped, and instead said, "What do you mean?" and then "I guess" and then "What is happiness anyway?"

What is happiness anyway? The question lingered.

In the mirror, she looked beautiful, but she felt empty.

Was this happiness? Treasta didn't understand why Chimes left her with Marnie's money, or why he didn't want hers after she promised to pay him. He walked away with no coins on his person, just a satchel of clothes and food. She assumed he'd catch the next ferry back to Maward and return to Hayam for his wagon and horse. She expected within the next week he'd be living his nomadic lifestyle like she never had existed. His pale figure glowed in her memory, his naked body on hers, the charm hanging from his neck, breathing each other's breaths in the same small space that momentarily she didn't think anything else could exist outside the cabin they shared those nights together. She carried the moment with her, thinking about how she reclined in his arms, rubbing his chest and fiddling with the chain around his neck that held the charm protecting him from any kind of metal blade. "My grandmother gave it to me when I was a babe," he had told her.

But what is happiness anyway? Not the woman looking back at Treasta from the mirror. The blue-gowned stranger with child was another Treasta in another life in another universe whom she would never know.

"I think it's perfect," Treasta said. "And I'm sure my husband will love it."

28

Councilor Gustas cuffed his sleeves, leaned forward, and with a concentrated eye looking through a monocle, latched the gear into place. He smiled under his dark beard streaked with white. He had yet to draw the curtains for the day, sitting at the desk focused since he woke that morning. Outside, the city prepared for the parade. Soon enough he'd have to leave to join the rest of the Nine. The responsibility was stressful.

The knock at the door startled him, and the clock he had been working on fell into pieces, save for the smiling face styled with a sun and a crescent moon. His valet poked his head in after Gustas shouted, "What is it?"

"Sir," the valet said, "your son is here."

Gustas dropped the screwdriver he was holding; it nearly hit his foot. He shot a glance at his valet, one that nearly sent him away, but Gustas told him to wait. "Where is he?"

"In the parlor."

"Give me a few. Offer him tea. No, not tea. Offer him lunch. The wild duck pie I ordered for myself should be ready by now. Feed him my meal. And the marzipan cake from last night. Then a glass of our nicest white wine. No the rosé. He prefers the rosé. I think. Just give him everything he asks for, do you understand?"

"Of course, sir. Is there anything I can help you with?"

Gustas waved him off. "No. I'll ready myself. I could use the time to figure out what I should say to my son." Then he faced his valet. "Is he really here to see me? You're sure it's my son?"

"Unmistakably."

"How does he seem?"

The valet shrugged. "I do not know, Sir. Healthy, I suppose."

Healthy. Healthy's good. Gustas folded his hands behind his back. "Go now."

The light from the hall faded as the door shut.

In the quiet, the councilor collected his thoughts as he drew open his chamber's curtains. Light blasted inside. From his apartment on the third floor of the citadel, Gustas could see in the city's haze the shapes of parade floats gathering on the promenade three miles out. He went to the wardrobe, dressed himself, and tied back his long, raven hair, thinking about what he should say to his son after a decade. Instead of leaving, he sat back down at the table, picked up the screwdriver, and continued tinkering with the clock.

Chimes sat on a balcony overlooking a courtyard. Below, children belonging to councilors played, chasing one another as the day waned into afternoon, exhausting themselves so that the youngest of the bunch would sleep well come evening while the older children would attend the party. Chimes broke the crust of the pie open; steam swirled from the wound. He didn't have much of an appetite. After crossing the citadel's threshold, his body had gone numb. He nudged the wound open wider to see the meat inside. The valet came and went from the balcony, setting down more dishes and poured wine in a golden goblet. Rosé, an expensive import no less from across the Shardian Waters.

In the time Chimes waited, his food had gone cold, the goblet still full, the children had long disappeared inside. A crow settled on the back of the wrought iron chair across from him, empty of his father's body, and watched him with an unblinking eye. Nearly a decade, and Gustas hadn't changed, still a disappointment to his only son. Chimes stood. But just as the sharp metallic sound of his chair sliding backwards echoed, Gustas appeared in the doorway.

Standing in silence just feet apart, they stared at one another, searching for the right words. Gustas looked just as Chimes remembered, except his beard was graying, and his hair was longer. The time between ages thirty-five and forty-five didn't do much to change his father except the wrinkles around his eyes that indicated long, stressful, and sleepless nights. If anything his face seemed gaunter, his eyes a little more tired. But Chimes was in his twenties now, still somewhat baby-faced, but the shapes filling out his visage were Gustas'.

"Darius," Gustas' voice was airy, his tone carrying the weight of disbelief.

Chimes sat down. "Gustas."

This felt like a mistake. Chimes' instinct told him to leave, but he kept himself anchored, like a stone in his stomach was holding him underwater.

Gustas took a seat across from his son. "You haven't eaten."

Chimes picked up his fork. The silver tines clinked against the silver plate as he stabbed the pie. He took in a large bite, chewed, and forced it down with a loud gulp, and then took a swig of his drink. "Ahh," he said, acting refreshed with heavy exaggeration.

His father crossed his arms and leaned back in his seat. He searched his son's face for any kind of hint for why he was there. Darius had sworn to his father he wouldn't return. "Darius, I never thought I'd see you again."

"You've been writing Dee, asking about me."

"He says he sees you, but I think he's humoring me."

Chimes gathered food on his fork. "You know he is. So why bother?"

"Why are you here?"

"I can leave if you like."

"That's not what I said." His father sat forward, folding his hands together. Sun rays cut between the buttresses, striking Gustas' golden complexion. "You made it clear you never wanted to see me again. So why now?"

Chimes took a bite, set down his fork, and patted his lip with the napkin. He threw it on the table. "I'm here to protect my inheritance."

"What are you saying?"

"Thieves from Kildore, a band of them are after your treasure."

Gustas guffawed and stood.

"They want the flute," Chimes added.

"You have no interest in seeing me," Gustas said with a sigh. "Of course you have no interest in seeing me." He dropped his head and rubbed the back of his neck as he leaned into the railing. "How many times must I apologize."

"You left her while she was dying." Chimes' voice went cold.

Gustas swiftly turned around, the tails of his coat whipping with force. His voice deepened. "She told me to go."

The wrought iron chair landed on the stone balcony with a heavy thud, the table nearly following as Chimes shot to his feet, pointing at his father. "No, *you* left *her*. She was dying and you left."

"Darius, I don't know how many more ways I can tell you that she told me to go. My coming here, my leaving your mother back in Hayam, it wasn't a decision I made alone. You need to grow up."

Chimes didn't want to believe it. He was five years old when he lost his mother. The only memory of her he still had that was the clearest was the night she took her last breath. When he was old enough to journey on his own, Marnie and Atlas allowed him to travel to Wesser to visit his father. It was the first time he had seen him in more than a decade. Since then, Chimes had been living on his own in the wagon, stopping in to see his aunt and uncle from time to time or visiting Dee in Hayam.

"You were too young to understand," Gustas said. He came around the table and picked up Chimes' chair. "I came here to better our lives. You don't remember much do you? The toys I made for you. You'd help me in the workshop." He set down a windup unicorn made from bronze, tarnished over the years. "We made this together."

Chimes picked up the toy; the smell of old metal entered his nose as he examined it closely. He slumped back in his chair, and a faint memory entered his mind: his father sat on the floor with him, and he wound the toy with its key. A child's giggle lingered in his ears and faded. Winding the toy, the gears struggling, Chimes set it on the stone tabletop; it's four legs kicked as it scooted and then stopped as it fell onto its side.

Gustas watched his son and for a moment saw the little boy he abandoned those years ago. "Your anger toward me," he said as he sat back down, "you have every right to hate me for what I did. I left her, you're right, but not without her blessing."

Chimes shrunk, hiding the tears welling in his eyes behind his hands. But Gustas took his hands, lowering them to meet a firelit gaze icing over with grief.

"Chimes," his father said—it was the first time since Chimes was a child he heard Gustas use that name, "I can't take back what I did. Not being there for you was unfair. But raising you here without a maternal figure would have been unwise. The children who grow up within the citadel, they're not like the children raised in Hayam or in the countryside. Your Aunt Marnie and Uncle Atlas could give you more than I ever could have at that time: more love, more joy and happiness—a *mother and a father*. You're grown now. You can make your decisions about what you think of me. But know, no matter what you feel or how much you despise me, my home is yours."

Chimes lowered his gaze as shame filled his heart. "But why?"

"Because everything I did, I did it for you. And whether you want me in your life or not, I cannot let my work be for naught," his father said. "There is so much on the line. And if you are ready to learn about your inheritance, I would like to tell of its importance."

Gustas came to his feet and stood at the threshold to the parlor. "I would like you to join me at the party tonight. Meet the rest of the Nine. I don't expect you to stay, but I would like for you to be able to be a part of my life if you allow."

Chimes stood. "All right." He held out his hand. "To new beginnings."

Gustas shook it. "To new beginnings."

The door opened into Gustas' chambers, and Chimes walked inside dressed in a suit the color of the night sky with twin tails floating behind him beaded with silver and gold so that when he walked he looked like he drove a chariot of starlight across the sky. Chimes thanked the valet as he stepped inside, adjusted the lapels and fiddled with the gold and pearl pins holding them in place.

Turning from his work bench and wearing a suit similar to his son's but somehow grander with longer tails and sleeves that tapered into delicate points on the back of his hands where a ring, his wedding ring, was seen on his left ring finger, the copper having recolored his finger green from two-decade worth of wear.

He caught Chimes looking at it and said, "I've never taken it off. The other councilors tease me about it, say I'm poisoning myself, but I just tell them if love is poison then let me die loving her. At least then your mother and I would be together."

The afternoon rays splayed through the open doors of the balcony, the curtains drawn to reveal a blue sky, a lowering sun, and plumes of clouds gathering from the west. They looked across the city, and Gustas pointed to the spot where three miles down the promenade dots of parade floats gathered behind the haze.

Chimes took in the city from a view he had experienced only once before, ten years ago, the first and only time he had visited his father after his mother died. Little change could be seen from so high above the city, but he saw at ground level the effects his father's work has had in the twenty years since coming here: the mechanical lifts, the steamboats, the levers and their geared cranks to make drawing up water from the dam's reservoir easier and less labor intensive.

At his work bench, Gustas picked up the clock, about the size of a picnic basket, and opened the door to its back to reveal the mechanisms inside turning. Dropping to his knees, he motioned Chimes to follow him and pointed with an awl as he spoke. "You see here? There, behind that gear"—the up and down movement of a small weight. "That is in that," and he pointed to the longcase clock on the opposite side of the room. "I opened a shop in the city, trained the clockmakers in how to craft them. Imagine what ease it will bring everyone to have a clock, not to rely on the city bells or sundials. And now," he returned his attention to the smaller device before them, "this—it would fit well above a fireplace mantel, don't you think? It's not quite done yet, though. Trying to get the same mechanisms that work in the longcases into something so small, it's not easy. A chamber clock. Or common room clock. I'm still working on what to call it."

"Chamber clock has a nice ring," Chimes said. "The tower in the bailey, the clockface, is that yours as well?"

Gustas smiled. "Ay, it is."

"Why not build it in the city center?"

His father's expression fell. "The magistrate didn't want it there. So bells and sundials it will be for the city folk. Until the longcases of course." He lowered his voice, looking his son in the eye and chuffed, "Agemon doesn't know about the shop. Can't know, you understand? Yes, he will find out eventually. But as far as he's concerned someone leaked the schematics of the clocktower to some clever fellow. Homes across Wesser will have their own clocks in no time, and by the time Agemon finds out, he'll have no choice but to let it go. He has other, more important things to worry about anyway, which reminds me." His father came to his feet. "I think it's time to show you your inheritance, don't you? But," and his father put up a hand, "you must understand that it is not your typical inheritance. And if you decide you don't want it, well, I suppose I would have to make other arrangements ... somehow."

Watching his father's visage shift from excitement to deep concern, Chimes wasn't sure what to expect, except he knew the treasures his father horded in the chamber beneath the foyer stairs, remembered his father showing him long ago, trying to explain what he should know for when he was ready to take up such responsibilities. But at the time, Chimes, too angry with his father to hear another word, discarded his promises and expectations.

Gustas opened the door hidden behind a floor-to-ceiling bookcase lined with old codices and various tomes of study and even a few Gustas had authored himself in the time since he came to Wesser.

"I assure you," he said as they entered the chamber, "my treasures are well secured." Gustas latched the door from the inside where their only light came from window slits too narrow for anybody to fit through. Everything was gilded—the walls, the pillars, the frames, the shelves, the display racks—and the gold leaf reflected enough of the sun's light that the room brightly glittered, forcing the brighter spaces brighter and the darker spaces darker.

Most items were displayed, hanging on wire, or propped up on tables or racks.

"I want to make sure you're well taken care of when I'm gone," he said as he walked around the room. "It is why I left you that charm," he added, not needing to see the necklace hiding inside Chimes' jacket to know it was there.

Chimes brought his hand to his chest feeling the small lump where the charm hung. "Grandmother gave it to me."

"I gave it to her to give to you."

In the hands of a suit of armor, a long sword shimmered in the faint light, it's gold hilt and ruby-set pommel set it apart from any blade Chimes had seen before. Other such weapons were displayed on walls, swords from faraway lands, daggers that belonged to long-ago kings, bronze statues of dwarven royalty from centuries past, ancient rulers of the land. His father even had the tablets containing the history of the dam's construction. A man with his father's intelligence and innovation could trade those skills for just about anything, including rarities such as these. Such items held no value to the nomadic Chimes. He reached into his pocket, grasping the bronze unicorn, feeling its sharp edges and tacked-together frame.

At the far end of the chamber, a wooden case rested on a table. Gustas popped the two latches holding it together, and inside, reclining like a corpse in an expensive red velvet-lined casket, was the flute, shimmering brighter than anything else in the treasure chamber. Its body was long, slender, elegant, and etched with dwarven runes, at the instrument's foot was the head of a griffin with an open beak in a silent screech. The bird-beast's feathers and feet were delicately carved along the flute's body.

"It is our most precious possession. It is very important we care for it," his father said unable to look away from the polished, warm yellow of the rare mineral. "Would you like to hold it?" he asked.

It was cold to the touch, heavier than he expected. He rested his fingers over the holes, held like he would play it, but his father told him his spit could damage the metal, and he grabbed the seven-holed wind instrument from his son.

"Marvelous, isn't it?" Kildore was a long way off, but not so far that what Chimes had told him earlier wouldn't be impossible, just unlikely. "I will have a guard posted," he said. "But, I must ask: how do you know that a *band of thieves* from Kildore wants to steal the flute?"

"I meet a lot of people while traveling. Some overshare."

"And they do not know who you are to me?"

Chimes shook his head. "I almost didn't come. I thought about going back to Marnie's."

Gustas placed his hand on his son's shoulder. "I'm glad you stayed. Truly. And you arrived at a good time. Tonight, I'll be announcing my latest invention. I've been dreaming it up for the past decade. I think you will be impressed.

"Now, are you prepared to learn of our burden? Of your inheritance?"

29

PORTYA WAS TOO KIND TO TREASTA, or maybe it was the sterling bit she carried that inspired such generosity from the dressmaker. Or was it curiosity? Portya had invited Treasta to stay for lunch. She had many questions for the Kildorei, wanted to know the latest fashions in Yeras, and although Treasta couldn't speak on Yeras' mode, it couldn't have been much different than Galgaya; she described the gowns she saw the wealthiest ladies wearing. No hoopskirts or puffy sleeves but long and layered fabrics in several different colors and trumpet sleeves with tails as long as their gowns, square collars that exposed the wealthy ladies' chests and too-tight corsets. Yes, Portya was fascinated, but she chortled.

"Your trumpet sleeves are outdated," she said. "Maybe a hundred years ago …" and she set down her teacup to pick up a biscuit.

"Our cities are months apart by foot," Treasta said. She sipped from her cup. It was too hot, but she forced the tea down anyway, trying not to show any pain on her face. Portya's friendliness might come to an advantage for Treasta—or "Trea," as she had introduced herself. Trea played along.

"But," she said, placing the cup on the saucer and crossed her legs, "perhaps, I could bring the latest Wesserian fashion to Yeras. I know a dressmaker there who has all her hooks in the right people. We can call it the Portya."

It had a nice ring to it, her name the eponym of a trend. She sat back and smiled. "You'll do that for me?"

Trea mirrored her smile. "Of course I would. But I have one request in return."

"What's that?"

"You help me look my best for the party."

"I think that's a fair exchange."

Hair pinned high, dress fitted, lace gloves donned, Treasta glided a woman of wealth to the queue of parade floats. Night had come upon Wesser—the streets now alight from the braziers placed along the promenade. Other decorations along the route had been hung: banners, streamers, garland of the brightest red Treasta had ever seen.

She found an iron-crafted bull, its snout steaming of vapor and eyes glowing of fire. A woman tested the horn—it blared with the same animalistic sound. The woman grinned, and her friend approved with a nod. Around the other side, Treasta came across a young man holding the horses. He was perhaps her age, maybe a year or two younger. Treasta tapped the young man's shoulder, and when he turned to face her, she was met with a youthful, fat-cheeked face.

"Hi," Treasta said. "What's your name?"

He blushed at the pretty woman standing before him, seemingly not used to the attention. "Umm ...," he shied into his shoulders and scratched his head, "I'm Borris," he said.

"Borris, I seem to have caused a bit of a mess over yonder, and I could use your help," Treasta said as she motioned toward an alleyway away from the festivities.

He eyed the direction she pointed and paused, thinking.

"I can make it worth your while," Treasta added with wink.

Borris' face turned red. The blushing young man nodded, eager, and followed her.

"I'm just so clumsy," she said, walking with him.

He looked around the alleyway, hesitant to step beyond where the light failed to touch. The blackness was consuming as she nudged him further along, teasing him with a light touch to his arm and then his hand. Treasta lured him into the darkness—stepping so close, she could smell the onion on his breath from his last meal.

She whispered, "Tell me, Borris, have you ever been kissed?"

But just when he was to answer, he collapsed, passing out. Treasta recorked the open phial she held under his nose while she held her breath and carried on back to the iron bull.

"Excuse me!" she called to the women on the platform. They looked at her, brows raised as if Treasta bothering them was an inconvenience. "Hi. I'm Tina. I've been asked to fill in for Borris. He wasn't feeling well and had to step away."

The women laughed. "You're going to walk three miles in those slippers?"

Treasta peered down at her feet. They were beautiful shoes—beaded, healed, laced, and pinched her toes uncomfortably together. "Well of course. Unless either of you would rather take his place? The festivities must commence, after all."

They looked at each other, one rolling her eyes, the other scoffing, and they shook their heads. "I much prefer my current position, thank you. Your dedication is admirable."

"You must be from House Terrain, then. We're the ladies Corryn and Gayla of House Quinnel. It is a pleasure to meet your acquaintance Lady Tina."

Treasta clumsily curtseyed. "It is wonderful to meet you both. I wasn't quite filled in on Borris' duties. He was to walk with the horses?"

"Yes," said Corryn. Or was that one Gayla? "And don't forget the basket. You're also throwing dried flower petals. We cannot forget the dried flower petals; they're good luck—blessings from our houses to the impoverished."

"It's the least we can do for such unfortunate souls," the other said.

The beating of drums began to echo.

"Hurry," said Corryn. "Get into place. It's about to begin."

Treasta looked around for a basket of dried flower petals and found it not far from where she met Borris. She hooked the handle within her elbow and as the sound of fanfare filled the city, the horses began to take their first steps along the parade route, pulling the float along. The iron bull let out a mighty cry, its eyes flaring and nostril billowing steam. Children ran up and down the route, reaching to catch the dried petals.

From inside a wooden float, Davan and Elsie—donned in black, faces wrapped and hidden, with hoods up and tight around their heads—watched through the spaces between wooden boards as the platform rocked along the promenade. Blaring brass blasted along the procession overwhelmed the cheers and excitement of the large crowds gathered on both sides of the street. So bright was it along the parade that it didn't seem the day had left, and the night had encroached just an hour ago. Neither spoke a word since entering the float, a large ram, with twisting horns and a mouth that opened and closed with the pull of a lever attached on its neck on its outer shell. The ropes and pullies inside the creature moved above the two thieves who waited with patience for the sounds of merriment to fade.

Those who participated in the celebratory cavalcade were the invited houses of Wesser's wealthiest families and important stately figures. Some traveled from as far as Iragia. Their tall stature, short curly black hair that was complicatedly plaited, pale skin, pointed ears, white robes, and fur lapels set them apart from the Wesserians.

"Maybe we should have dressed for the occasion," Davan whispered.

"With this face?" asked Elsie just as quietly.

Davan didn't say another word. Neither knew the layout of the citadel nor what Gustas looked like, but Davan schemed he and Elsie would figure that out with relative ease and proceed from there. Elsie planned they'd find the apartment first, kill a couple guards—maybe—and wait for Gustas to return to his dwelling place. Easy.

The cacophony of such fête coming from the streets pounded against Davan's skull. Get the flute, tell Elsie where she could find Bastan, and return to Galgaya—that was the goal. Being away from Galgaya for months made the idea of returning to the coastal city feel foreign, as if he didn't know where he belonged, a new feeling he had yet to cope with until now. Galgaya was all he had known, aside from a few trips here and there with Lodan to nearby towns. But now, the world was before him; he had seen and experienced things so many people never would—just leaving Galgaya was a feat in itself. It was the same moon, the same stars; it was the same air and same night—going back to Galgaya with or without the flute, he would return a different person. No, he *must* return with the flute. Without it, he would become the joke of the guild. Anyone returning without the prize would be shamed and ridiculed. Many left the tribe in Galgaya to seek new beginnings in other parts of the syndicate. A popular location was within the caves near Doar, old dwarven ruins that had long been dug out. The marshal there was a stern, strict man who hailed from the kingdom of Freasi. Davan had never met him, but the stories he heard were inspiring. He longed to be like the other marshals; he longed to be better. Quiet Davan. Stoic Davan. Secretive Davan. Oh, did he have plans. He and Fylle—and he had told his chief this once in confidence—they would be an unstoppable team. He had learned from the best, after all, as Lodan's favorite underling.

Davan glanced at Elsie who was watching through the slats between boards in the ram's gullet. She truly wasn't the same Elsie who left Galgaya those months ago, who, with a glance, could make blood run cold and without any guilt or empathy could take on the most high-stakes tasks assigned. Sure, parts of her were still there, but then, when they sat in silence, such as now, there was something nurturing about her. The boy—what had she called him? Declan?—he changed her somehow. Nobody in the tribe but her own brother knew her past. Rumors circulated that Elsie killed her parents, gutted them in their sleep. Others said she was the daughter of a duke, a cousin of the king's, that she had run away after her mother fell ill one night and her father killed himself. Then, there were whisperings that she was born in blood, that her father killed her mother just as her mother was giving birth, that the mother's last strength left her body as she pushed baby Elsie into the world; they say her brother found her freshly born on the cement of a back alley road. Nonsense, all of it; everyone knew Ida was younger than Elsie, but the story was exciting and tragic, nonetheless. Did she know, he wondered, what everyone said about her? Murderous Elsie. Blood-lustful Elsie. Born-in-blood Elsie. Ida talked in shrugs and grunts most the time. And when he did speak, he was always angry. Something happened to leave the siblings broken, to bring them both to Dubilee. And everyone had a story of how they got to Dubilee.

Davan braced himself as the float stopped and started again. A child, maybe four years of age, had run into the parade, crossing in front of the iron bull just one place ahead of the wooden ram. She chased after dried flower petals, trying to catch them in her tiny palms. Her mother rushed after her and carried her to safety.

No memory of his mother stayed with Davan. The earliest years of his life were shrouded in shadow. His beginning was as a six-year-old—if that was how old he was—digging through a pile of garbage behind a bakery. The bread was old and stale, but it was the most he could find in days. The baker chased him off a few times, but that night, the night his memory held most clearly, he sat against the wall, nibbling on the rye during a red sunset. An orange cat appeared, his ribs showing through his striped coat. He named the small beastly creature Cat, because he didn't know what else to call the animal by.

Six-year-old Davan snapped his fingers, calling Cat over. He offered the creature bread, but Cat wasn't interested. He dug through the trash heap, found some kind of paste reeking of fish, and held his smeared hand out for Cat to eat. The roughness of his tongue tickled his palm.

"I'm Davan," he had told the cat.

"Meow," and Cat purred, curling up next to Davan against the bakery's wall. Young Davan petted him, and Cat flicked his tail, pleased.

It was the deepest bond Davan ever knew until he met Treasta.

The creaking of wheels went silent as the float came to a stop. The cranking of large doors closing was heard.

"I think we're in," Elsie whispered.

Sure enough, inside the citadel's inner wall, many floats were crammed together, hidden from the public view from the outer wall, as if giving the denizens of Wesser the illusion that the citadel was infinitely large inside. In reality, the festival floats were clustered so that there was little space to walk.

Elsie and Davan watched and waited for everyone to leave.

The citadel bailey was eerily silent save for the hinges of the hatch opening on the underbelly of the wooden ram. Davan and Elsie dropped onto the platform, held their position, crouched low, momentarily assessing their surroundings to be sure no one noticed them. Silent and empty of people—perfect. They were cautious as they stepped from the platform onto the trimmed grass of the courtyard. The citadel's walls were tall around the bailey. During the day, the sun's rays striking the open courtyard was brief in the middle of the winter. But even in the summer months, its rays lingered for but a few hours. Dark and shadowy, it was how the magistrate liked it. Magistrate Agemon wanted the citadel to be otherworldly, set apart from the rest of Wesser, with its skyward walls and multiple tiers, and towers and bastions. His ancestors had built the fortress off dwarven blue prints and with dwarven labor, but he perfected it—an impenetrable stronghold. Inside the bailey the walls were painted black, meant to disorient strangers. And were it not for the torchlight and lamps of floats crammed side by side, Davan or Elsie may not have been able to see too well.

They couldn't enter through the front doors; surely people were gathered on the other side. Tall, slender trees were meticulously planted along the wall near the entrance with low-enough branches hinting to be climbed to the next story. Carefully, Davan and Elsie ascended and slid through an open window on the second floor; they crept along the rafters of the great hall.

The lilting music of harps, lyres, and reed instruments wavered in sweeping crescendos and decrescendos. Clapping echoed of pleased guests satisfied by the musical performance from the quartet on the stage in a corner. The musicians bowed, then began another tune, one easy to become entangled in while mingling during the social hour.

Treasta picked up a crystal glass of white wine, sniffed it the way Cherie taught her to take in the notes. Nothing special, she thought. It smelled like wine. But, Treasta supposed, it was fancier wine. Something about its scent did seem *cleaner.* In fact everything in the great hall seemed clean. The floors were waxed, the gilded beams and frames containing portraits of the council members were polished, and the crystal glass gleamed with such clarity Treasta could have sworn to gained wisdom looking into its sheen.

She wavered through the crowd, following the movement of the music, and sipped with delicate demeanor not feeling much like herself around such prestigious company; yet she appeared no differently than the rest. As she would interact with guests, none seemed the wiser. House Terrain—that was it, she remembered, as she introduced herself—that was the house the sisters assumed she was from. Someone asked where Borris was but she explained he was too sick to attend—puking, she said. "We thought it best he stay behind."

"A real shame," someone said. "I hope it's nothing serious. We can't have a new sickness going about."

"Hmmm," another mused. "It is that time of year, you know? Why must winter bring us the worse diseases?"

Treasta slipped away from the conversation. She needed to be careful. Talking too much to too many people with too many lies, someone would know she was a fake.

The long, tight windows let in a breeze from the bailey. The rafters were shrouded in darkness, away from the bright light of the chandeliers hanging from chains. The flames flickered on their candlewicks. Treasta wasn't sure where to go from here, but she knew she needed to get away from the great hall.

Magistrate Agemon, a tall, tan man with long curly black hair, wearing a circlet decorated with gold and silver leaf motifs, stood above the crowd from the top of a double stairway that slinked to the second story above an archway that lead into other parts of the citadel's first floor. Horns blasted, calling for everyone to turn their attention to Agemon. He stood with open arms, greeting his guests.

"Hear ye!" called one of the trumpeters as the noise of the crowd died with the horns' sound. Everyone, turning, gave their attention to the magistrate and his eight of nine councilors who walked in filed lines to stand along the staircases. They were dressed in expensive silks with squared shoulders, sashes and blues so deep a shade their hue matched a night sprinkled with stars. They wore their hair the same, their beards were cut the same, and they walked and held their posture the same—all to show they were better than everyone else, except the magistrate, of course. Agemon was donned in white shimmering like an iridescent pearl plucked from the fattest clam harvested from the Shardian Waters. He wore strings of pearls to match.

The leader of the Nine prided himself in his festivities, hosting lavish parties that were spoken of as if they were legends in other parts of the world. He thanked such legendary rumors in part to the vastness of Wesserland's desertlike terrain beyond the canyon. Agemon had the most expensive fabrics, trinkets, and jewels imported from Iragia. The wines his guests drink, the food they would consume when the hor d'oeuvres were presented—all of it was Iragian. A large grin shone of white teeth—the whitest teeth of anyone alive—capped with pearls just for the occasion.

"Let us honor," Agemon called, "the god of wine and joy. Alia praise Alvynis." He lifted the wide-brimmed dwarven kylix, painted black and gold with figures telling a story along its sides. It was older than anything else in the room. He waited as everyone raised their crystal glasses, holding their delicate stems.

"Praise Alvynis," everyone echoed. And they lifted their cups to their lips, drinking until the last drop dripped into their mouths.

"Praise our Iragian guests!" he called. "They honor us with their gifts and goodwill."

Echoes of *huzzah* filled the chamber.

"Praise Alia"—heaven—"and the gods who granted us our existence. Praise the moon and the sun, Leo Moarn and Annikah."

And the crowd, again, echoed the sentiment.

"And of course," Agemon's tone softened, "praise such wonderful guests who gather here today to celebrate Councilor Gustas' latest invention. I imagine," he said as he began walking down the stairs, "everyone is excited, perhaps even eager and anxious, to experience Wesser's future.

"Let us gather on the veranda to witness Gustas' vision."

The guests crowded onto the veranda, its wide and open windows brought the outside world inside, its tall ceiling painted like the daytime sky with clouds and birds. It was a large, round structure that overlooked part of the bailey on one side and a decorative courtyard on the other. At the center of the veranda was a pedestal fit with a wide ramp shrouded in a maroon curtain. The councilors and magistrate filed in, standing nearby as Gustas stood above everyone else on the platform. He clutched a glittering tasseled rope, waiting for everyone.

Gustas caught a glance of his son who stood in the back, nearly hidden in a sea of people. He shared a smile with his father.

"Hear ye!" Gustas shouted. "May I have your attention so you may feast your eyes on something I guarantee you have never seen before."

Treasta stood on her toes, looking over heads to catch a glimpse of the councilor named Gustas. She needed to keep him in her sight.

"Now," Gustas said after a pregnant pause, "remember how the lifts changed transportation from the port along Wesser's dam? Remember with what ease it allowed you to travel without having to spend the time and energy following the roads? Remember with what speed the steamboats of our rivers have gifted us not to rely on wind or ore? I consider this next venture an ode to travel, a celebration of sorts." He paused, looked those standing closest to the stage in the eyes to assure he had their attention, that they were intrigued and curious. "I give you"—Gustas tugged on the rope, and the curtain fell—"the horseless steam coach."

A finely dressed female assistant sat on a leather bench, her arms extended as if showing off the steam coach. She uncrossed her legs and stood atop the horseless transportation devise, then leaned over to tug a chain: a horn, like the one on the steamboat, blared.

Everyone ooed and awed, lured by yet another grand brainchild of the great Gustas, trying to look past the person ahead of them to get a better look at the attraction with its smokestack, four wagon wheels, bench, levers, gauges, and gears.

Gustas maneuvered around the machine, firing it up. The billowing smoke became lost in the painted clouds. The councilor ordered the crowd to part, and he and his assistant sat, pulled goggles over their eyes, and let out a celebratory howl. Gustas pulled a large lever, kicking the vehicle into gear, and it chugged with a kick and a jolt down the ramp and into the great hall, then chugging out the open doors to the bailey.

Treasta clapped, fascinated like the others curious to know the ins and outs of its mechanisms, how it functioned—just trying to understand such a machine was hardly believable. Whispers arose into chatter and everyone carried on with the party with Gustas' great steam coach at the top of every conversation.

After setting down her glass, Treasta wandered through the crowd, weaving around people who watched couples dance at the return of the music. If she kept moving, perhaps she'd find the inventor. But several minutes later, she felt her body becoming warm, the heat of hundreds of bodies, her face flushed with wine, overwhelmed her.

At the window, a cool nighttime breeze brought her relief, and she felt her composure return. She caught a glimpse of Gustas who was outside talking to his assistant. Then the front doors opened and—

Chimes?

An unmistakable face, familiar frame, that bright hair, entered the great hall adorned in the nicest clothes she had ever seen him don. She grabbed his arm and threw him on the wall where less people were gathered.

"What the hell are you doing here?" she asked.

He threw up his hands and pushed her away, not realizing it was Treasta who apprehended him. Chimes' eyes widened. "Gods, it's you," he said, reaching out as if apologizing having had shoved her. "What does it matter why I'm here? You and I are done. We're done. I got you to Wesser—that was the deal. Should have known you'd be here," he said, patting his suit jacket and straightening out the creases Treasta caused with her grip. "You look beautiful, if it matters."

She crossed her arms, looking him over with suspicion. "You're the one who left without an explanation. Do you know what it feels like to be mutually wanted and desired by someone, then for that someone, in the next breath, to treat you like a complete stranger?"

His brow furrowed as his eyes lowered. Chimes placed his hands behinds his back, standing straight.

"You have nothing to say about that?" She scoffed. "Of course you don't."

He wouldn't make eye contact, boyishly nervous, boyishly afraid. "Treasta," he said her name, ashamed and low, but struggled to say anything more, not wanting to admit why he left her. "I'm sorry. Maybe everything on the boat was a mistake."

"You …" Treasta's eyes were red with anger and tears. She quaked trying not to cry, her body cold from betrayal. "You don't mean that."

Chimes took her by the arm, but as he tried taking her to a less crowded corner of the room, she yanked herself from his grip. He stood close, whispering, his words sharp knives, "This isn't the place to talk about this."

"I just want to understand what I did wrong."

"You didn't do anything wrong, all right?"

Herbs and spices of his perfume permeated her nose. This man, this version of Darius, he was a stranger.

"Then," Treasta's head fell, her heart aching, "what happened."

"I …," he hesitated, rubbing his face and then his head, "I was scared—*am* scared." As people glided by, he paused, waiting for any semblance of privacy at such a busy occasion. As the music filled the room, crowds gathered around a group of dancers.

Treasta shrunk within herself as she crossed her arms. "Scared of me?"

Chimes shook his head. "Of becoming a different person."

"Darius," Councilor Gustas interrupted as he approached from outside. His gaze passed from Chimes to Treasta. "Who is this lovely lady?" Chimes and Treasta flashed each other the same panicked expression. But she quickly collected herself, grabbed onto Chimes' arm, and held out her hand for Gustas to take. "Councilor Gustas, a pleasure to meet you. I'm Lady Tina, Darius' wife."

As Gustas went to kiss her hand, he paused and looked at his son. "Wife? You are married? My son, married?"

Son? Treasta's jaw tightened. She somehow forced a smile. "I cannot believe he has not told you. He said he would before introducing us tonight so there wasn't any confusion. I know things have been hard between you two." She could feel the muscles in Chimes' arms flexing as he tensed. "And, of course, our big announcement." Chimes' fingers were digging in her skin.

"Oh? An announcement?" Gustas' gaze followed where Treasta touched her stomach. "Oh! An *announcement.*" He looked at his son, unsure what to say, confused why he didn't tell him earlier. But, Gustas supposed, it would be unfair to think Darius owed him every part of his life with their relationship barely rekindled. "A grandchild," he muttered to himself, then began musing all the ways he could do everything over again—but right. A wide smile stretched across his cheeks.

"After the party, let us retire to my apartment for a private celebration, shall we?"

"That is kind of you," said Treasta. She looked to Chimes. "Isn't that kind of him?"

"Kind?" He didn't have much of a choice: Chimes nodded. "Too kind."

And as Treasta held onto Chimes and they followed behind the councilor to mingle, she whispered into his ear. "I'm scared too."

30

DAVAN LURKED ON THE SLOPING ROOF as Elsie lingered behind a planter on a balcony. Elsie was much smaller than Davan; such a hiding place would be revealing for him. And from here, Elsie could hear the chatting of three individuals on the otherside of the open, glass doors.

Sometime between the beginning of the parade and now, the stars had disappeared. It was unclear when the clouds had swept over the citadel, but a sprinkling of rain had begun tapping on the lurking burglars. It had been a long time since either had experienced it, but now wasn't the time to admire the change in weather. If anything, such a shift would hinder the mission by causing Elsie and Davan to drip puddles through the citadel should their clothes become too wet.

Elsie motioned for him to come down. He carefully did and knelt next to her.

She whispered: "They left the room. Not sure where, but they're gone for now."

The sheer curtains made it difficult to see, but Elsie had watched for nearly half of an hour three silhouettes—one female, two male—inside. They had cheered to a marriage then to a pregnancy. The female voice was familiar, but Elsie couldn't quite place it.

"Lady Tina, Darius," Gustas had said, "I hope you will take me up on my offer. There is plenty of space for you here and for your child."

Then he had said something about the future, and what his latest invention would bring for Wesser, and how he could give this Lady Tina, Darius, and the child everything they ever wanted or would need. He was almost begging. It was a pathetic plea.

"Do you think it's safe to go in, then?" Davan whispered.

Elsie crept closer to the curtain, wedging herself between the fabric and wall and sliding inside. She peered from behind the fabric. The sole person in the room, the valet, had his back turned from her. He was tidying up the tumblers from which Tina, Darius, and Gustas had drunk and placing the decanter on a side table. He began snuffing out the candles on the candelabras and left the room. Her hand appeared in the doorway, and she waved Davan inside.

They prowled in the darkened room, feeling their way around. Neither knew what they were looking for, but at the very least they could scout the apartment, learn its layout, before acquiring the bounty. But they needed to be careful. Too loud of a noise echoing down the halls and up the stairs could alert the tenants. They needed to be the ones in control. Davan felt the delicate details of a letter opener under his fingers. He grabbed the small blade. Elsie swiped a fire poker from the fireplace.

The sound of a door opening alerted them. They hid, only able to see the glow of candlelight growing and fading until another door shut.

"Lady Tina?" Chimes set the candlestick on a table.

Treasta was brushing the ringlets out of her hair at the vanity. She softly laughed and shrugged. Then her face turned serious. She set the brush down, pushed her hair behind her shoulders so it fell down her back in thick curls and watched him through the mirror. "So, Councilor Gustas is your father." She stood, turned, and took one step toward him. "Your father is the man who has the golden flute." And another step. "You didn't think you should tell me this?"

Chimes held his ground, his hands balling into fists, ready to brace himself for whatever was to come—physical or emotional. Treasta was but mere inches away, so close he caught a whiff of her smell, the same sweet, yet tangy, scent that filled his nostrils the first night they were intimate. He hated how it made him want her, and her ferocity only fueled his desires. He took a deep breath, trying to calm his fast-beating heart.

"I owe you nothing," he said. "And what was that? Pretending we're married? That that child is mine? What do you expect me to do when you're gone, huh? Don't you think it will look a bit odd that my *pregnant wife* has suddenly disappeared?"

"I was saving your ass," she said. "Or did you have a better explanation for who I was to you? We very clearly knew one another when your *dad*—" Treasta held her breath, holding back. She still couldn't believe this entire time Chimes' estranged father was the keeper of the golden flute. Which meant .... Her eyes widened with realization. And Chimes took a step back before she could grab him as she lunged.

"You know where it is, don't you?"

Chimes shook his head. "I can't say I do."

"Why are you lying to me? I thought we had a deal, you and me, no secrets, yeah?" The upper-class accent she had been mimicking throughout the night had long faded. Treasta pulled off her gloves, throwing them to the floor. "You're going to tell me."

"Or what? You cut me with that knife you keep strapped to your thigh?" He remembered unbuckling the strap and remembered the way she squirmed as his fingers tickled her skin. "You know damn well that you can't hurt me with it."

"And I know damn well that pretty charm you keep tucked inside your shirt is what's protecting you." She remembered tugging on its chain as she rested her head on his chest, twisting the silver links around her fingers the way she and Chimes had been intertwined just moments before. Those nights together on the boat, once surreal, were now but a fever dream.

Chimes flashed his brows and exchanged a taunting smirk, then dodged as she went to seize the buttons on his suit jacket. She was going after his charm; she wanted to be able to press cold metal to his throat so her threats could hold meaning.

They tussled, grappling at the other, one trying to force the other away. Treasta began tearing away the garments of his suit with each available chance. Such strength she had when fueled by her determination surprised Chimes so much so that he wrapped his arms around her waist and lifted her. He threw her onto the mattress.

Snap!

She had weaseled her hand into the collar of his suit, grasping the chain just as he tossed her.

Chimes saw the charm tucked in her closed fist. He jumped onto the bed, straddling her hips and holding her arms over her head, pressing firmly into the mattress.

"Let go," he ordered.

Treasta didn't say a word, only wriggling beneath his body.

His fingernails dug into her arms.

Treasta winced, but she didn't let go.

She felt tiny sharp cuts creasing her skin, imprinting little red crescent shapes as blood gathered beneath the surface.

Chimes held his grip, moving his hands to hold her wrists.

Treasta's chest expanded beneath Chimes. Her furrowed brows relaxed. Her pink lips, pressed inward, parted. He couldn't look away from them. A lingering silence held itself, and what was probably seconds felt like minutes. The flickering light slowed into a gentle lick, rising and extending, its yellow and orange colors waltzing up the green wallpaper like fairies dancing in a meadow at sunset. The sudden sound of pouring rain claimed the silence.

The charm pressed between their palms as their fingers interlocked.

"I didn't think I would see you again," Treasta said. "I thought you hated me. You …," her wet eyes began pooling teardrops, "… you were different after I …," she sucked in a breath, "I told you I killed someone. It was like everything between us was gone."

He leaned over her, his lips coming closer to hers. How Chimes wanted to kiss her, wanted to take her into himself, wanted to reunite with the same intensity he felt the first time their bodies touched.

Chimes was able to take the charm as her hand relaxed. He held the chain in his hand and looked over the magic piece, feeling vulnerable to the world and to Treasta. The gem—a white opal—dangled as he held it over her. She sat up onto her elbows, the charm coming into focus as she examined it.

"Take it," he said.

He lowered it into her palm. It was so light that it was like she was holding nothing, the most delicate piece of jewelry she had ever touched. The precious gem's soft warmth seeped into the pores of her skin and through her body.

Chimes helped her up. Her legs hung off the bedside. "May I?"

She handed him the necklace.

He hooked it around her delicate neck. The charm warmly rested on her chest. She touched it.

But before Treasta could say anything, Chimes retrieved the candlestick and left.

THE CURTAINS HANGING OVER THE BALCONY'S OPEN DOORWAY billowed as a low whistle cut through the apartment carried on the wind. Elsie watched from under a table as someone walked by with a candlestick. It wasn't Gustas. The figure's shape wasn't right, so it must have been Darius. He wasn't as tall as the councilor and a bit slenderer with squarer shoulders. He slipped off his suit jacket. The torn article landed near her. She watched the figure disappear down the hall.

Another set of footsteps approached. The councilor picked up the torn jacket, looking in the direction the figure disappeared. He exhaled a long sigh, muttering, "Darius …"

Elsie followed Gustas.

Davan followed Elsie, having seen her silhouette move across a threshold. He clutched the letter opener.

They squatted at a corner, watching as Gustas appeared at a bookcase parted open. The councilor paused; he shook his head, covering his face with his hand and sighed again with an air of disappointment.

Gustas walked inside, found the candlestick resting on a gilded side table that hosted a display of two crowns from bygone eras set with stones and pearls that held onto time with grace. Chimes closed the flute's case, the latches snapping into place.

"Darius."

Chimes froze, hearing his father's voice. He felt his body turning cold.

"What are you doing?"

Chimes cradled the case. He faced his father, but as he looked up he saw a female figure clothed in black with the fireplace poker to his father's throat. His heart raced. His grip on the case tightened, bringing it into his chest. The only light in the treasure chamber came from the lone candlestick. It's faint glow made it difficult to see anything beyond the shadows of his father's and robber's bodies.

Davan hovered near a pillar, peeking to see a face he would never forget.

"*You.*" Davan stepped into view. "Hand it over."

You? The way the male figure in black said it was like he knew Chimes.

"I'll kill him," threatened Elsie.

"What makes you think I know him?" Chimes asked.

"We're all after the same thing, aren't we?"

"Where's Treasta?" Davan asked.

"Ohhh …" Chimes nodded, realizing who it was. "Good to see you, Davan. Happy trails?"

"Darius …," his father pleaded through his teeth, "what are you doing?"

"I think you know him," Elsie said, pressing the poker into his jaw.

Chimes squinted his eyes, trying to get a better look at the woman. He took a couple steps forward. "And you're the woman from the boat. Huh. This is interesting. You two know each other? Of course you do! I know all about your mission."

"Chimes, hand it over," Davan said. He pointed the letter opener at Gustas, remembering how Chimes was impenetrable. Davan imagined every way he wanted to hurt Chimes.

"Whoa, there," Chimes said, as Davan threatened his father. "Leave him out of this. This is between us." He was stalling, of course, trying to figure his way out of the chamber with the flute and without his father being killed. "I'll give it to you if you put down the poker."

"Darius …" His father's eyes fell to his son's chest, seeing the charm absent from his body.

"Let him go," Chimes said.

"Put the case on the floor," Elsie said.

Chimes carefully set it down at his right side, holding his hands up to show he had no weapons, hoping they wouldn't force him to remove the satchel slung across his body. The guard he briefly relieved should be returning soon. Any moment.

Davan grabbed the case, keeping his eyes on Chimes. "Let's get out of here," he said to Elsie.

She didn't release her grip, holding his neck with her free hand and the poker with the other. "We can't let them live," she said. "He knows who we are. He knows our faces."

"Elsie, let him go. We made a deal," Davan said, each word sharper than the last.

She jammed the poker into Gustas neck then rushed toward Chimes.

Davan threw himself between them, shoving her back.

Chimes attended to his father, who had collapsed on the floor. The fireplace poker had gone up through his jaw, lodging it open. Gustas, gasping, couldn't speak, but his eyes—the blue fading to gray, the flecks of silver seemingly reflecting the iridescent glow of the candle—were wide with fright, telling Chimes to run, telling Chimes to save his wife, to save the baby.

Davan was holding Elsie back. Not because he was protecting Chimes, but because he knew her knives would do nothing against the immune man

—at least he thought.

Elsie managed to break free. She snagged a small dagger from a rack on the wall and threw it at Chimes, it stuck into his arm, and he cried out.

The guard appeared in the doorway. He aimed a crossbow and shot it at Elsie, narrowly missing her head. Davan grabbed the flute case and hid behind a pillar as the guard loaded another arrow.

Chimes ran, darting past the guard, the blade wedged deep in his bone. When he turned the corner, he fell into the wall and yanked the dagger out of his arm. Blood pooled, staining his white tunic.

In the treasure chamber, Elsie tumbled, tripping as Gustas grabbed her ankle. Her foot landed in his side with a heavy kick. She gripped the handle of the fireplace poker, held his eye contact, and as she jerked it from his jaw, a cracking sound split the air. He wailed. The guard took a step back, taking aim. But Elsie charged, driving the poker through his bright red uniform, upward behind his ribs, twisting.

"We need to get out of here," Davan said.

Elsie pried the crossbow from the guards hands and snagged the quiver belted at his waist, strapping it to her own and securing it to her leg. She agreed and grabbed the candlestick. In the foyer, she held the flame against the tomes lining the bookcase.

"What do you think you're doing?" Davan asked, watching the blaze ignite.

Elsie answered: "Creating a distraction."

Outside, thunder rolled as raindrops pelted windowpanes. Flying open, the door slammed against the wall. Chimes, panting, was under the threshold, holding himself up on the frame.

Treasta jumped from the bed, rushing to him—her eyes fixed on his arm. She demanded answers. But Chimes was losing blood; his energy faded. Treasta hurried him inside, briefly searched the darkness of the hallway, and shut the door. The lock clicked. Chimes slid down the wall, a streak of red turning black as it mixed with the green wallpaper. She knelt, stripped him of his tunic, and held up his head, her hands warm on his cheeks, her breath hot, voice near. "Chimes, look at me." His eyes opened. "You're going to be all right. We just need to stop the bleeding. All is well."

All is well. The words echoed in his mind. Sweat dripped from his forehead. "You promise?" he asked with a slight smile. A smile—even as his arm went numb, even as his breath escaped him running to be with her, he found the strength to grin. Her forehead fell onto his, and she lightly kissed him—his lips tasting of salt and hers were the sweet desserts of promise and trust. She tore the seams on the tunic and wrapped his arm, tying it taut, and wiped his forehead of sweat.

"You'll be okay," she said again.

"Yeah," he said, trying to better sit up, "I know, it just hurts like a bitch. We need to get out of here," he said. "Davan is here and that woman from the boat."

Treasta jolted to her feet, her body tensing as she shrunk into herself. "Davan's here?" The syllables of his name sent a chill through her. The flute … She needed to get her hands on it, but—her gaze fell to Chimes who winced in pain as he struggled to his feet. He clutched her wrist. Gentle, but firm. The touch pulled Treasta out of a trance.

"We can't stay here," he said.

"The flute … he'll get it … I can't let him have it."

"Do you trust me?" Chimes' gaze was stern as he held hers.

She nodded—didn't even need to give it a thought.

With his one good arm, Chimes stripped the bed. He wrapped himself in its sheets and waited for her to do the same. They covered their heads with makeshift hoods and crept into the dark hallway.

The valet came rushing up the stairs. "Fire! Fire!"

Chimes and Treasta followed his voice, met him at the staircase where black smoke swelled up the stairwell. The valet shoved them back upstairs, forcing them into a spare room and through a door into the servants' passage.

"Master Darius, follow this passage. It will take you to the bailey," the valet said. "I must find the councilor."

Chimes grabbed his arm. "It's not safe."

"I know," he said. "But I must try."

But before Chimes could say another word, the valet hurried back into the apartment to save Gustas from the flames. What could he say? That his father lay in the treasure chamber likely already dead? He hadn't time to grieve.

He and Treasta ran.

In the rafters of the great hall, Davan opened the flute case.

Their eyes befell red velvet but no golden flute. Davan tore the velvet from the case. Nothing.

"Where is it?" Elsie asked.

He seethed. "That bastard."

"Don't," she said, pulling him back down as he stood. "The fire will force them out."

32

THE NIGHT WANED INTO MORNING; THE SKIES PARTED to reveal blue fresh from the dawn. No one had slept that night. Treasta and Chimes rested in an alley, not knowing Davan and Elsie had been tailing them since they escaped the fire. Elsie held Davan back, told him to wait. "Let them feel safe. Let them think they aren't being followed," she had said. And they kept their distance.

The sheets wet from the rain were abandoned on the street, kicked aside and behind some barrels. Davan watched from afar as Treasta examined Chimes' wound. The way she tended to him, the softness of her movement and demeanor, it wasn't anything Davan had experienced in the years he had known her.

"Must be hard," Elsie said, "watching your lover love another man."

Don't react. She's just trying to get a rise out of you, he reminded himself. Elsie enjoyed getting rises out of everyone—it gave her something to hold over others. But she wasn't wrong.

"New deal," he said. "Kill Chimes, and I'll give you the drawing."

Elsie watched his stern face from the corner of her eyes. "That's it? That's all I need to do?"

Now that he knew Chimes bled, it shouldn't be a problem, and Davan could keep his hands clean, and maybe, just maybe, he could get Treasta back.

Treasta rebandaged the wound. "How's it feeling?" she asked.

Chimes adjusted his shoulder, barely able to lift his arm. He frowned.

"Maybe," she said as she unclasped the necklace, "you need this more than me right now," and clipped the charm around Chimes' neck. She brushed his cheek, then enfolded him within her arms afraid that were she to let go, he'd disappear again. Treasta clutched his tunic as he rested his head to hear her thumping heart.

"I don't know what I'm going to do now," she said. "The Pats were following me. Laine said if I don't bring him back the flute, they'll kill you."

"The Pats …," he mused on the shared name of Pat and Trish—the teenaged guildmates from Galgaya, he remembered her explaining.

Again, she told him about Laine, the deal she had made with him, and the sack of goods. She detailed its contents burned onto her memory: the jewels and gems and pearls and rings and cuffs and crowns and necklaces, gold, gold, gold. *So much gold.* Yes, all this Chimes already knew, but Treasta's need to repeat the information was a reminder to herself about the importance of her goals and for Chimes to understand her seriousness, that this wasn't some fleeting game.

"Hey"—the gentleness of his voice grounded her—"don't worry. We'll get you that bag of treasure. It's not too late. I promise."

A soft kiss to her forehead eased her, and she expelled a long, frustrated sigh, glancing toward Chimes. Treasta had yet to mention the witch, her plan to pay the woman an unnamed sum so the child taking unwanted residence inside her body would disappear. *Tytan.* As her head fell back, an unforgiving anger entered her heart, and she cursed herself for giving the creature a name. With each passing sun, the infant—little baby Tytan—was becoming stronger, and she could feel her life waning as her body became less her own. The weight of Chimes' form as he buried deeper into her chest was a reprieve from reality. Relaxing her chin on his head, she took in his smell; the scent and his warmth of his skin helped her forget—even if momentarily—about the flute, Laine, the Pats, Davan. More than anything, she wanted to turn back time to before she left Galgaya and instead choose to stay at the hideout. Treasta inhaled, drawing on Chimes' smell—like cinnamon. After all, Davan had made it clear he didn't need her. But would she still be pregnant? She thought about the last time she and Davan had slept together—no not while on their journey, but before that. Pinpointing when the child was conceived was impossible; Davan and Treasta's physical intimacy was well known throughout the tribe.

Darkness swept over Treasta at the thought. Recalling the whispering, the stares, the shame the others made her feel invaded the present, and the walls of the alleyway in Wesser transformed into the sandstone brick of the hideout beneath Galgaya. She shut her eyes.

Chimes noticed the shift in her weight, and he barely caught her with his one arm as she was about to faint. He helped her relax against the wall, and they sat together for a while before either said another word. He looked around the alley for any signs of Davan or Elsie, then rested his head against the wall as Treasta adjusted herself to rest her head on his shoulder. She grabbed his hand and placed it on her stomach. The child moved.

"I don't want it," she mumbled. "I … I just … If I could just *erase it*."

Chimes didn't speak, allowing the sounds of the nearby busy streets to fill the emptiness, for Treasta to have the space she needed to cry, and because he didn't know what to say or do. Sitting with her, he hoped it was enough to help her feel a little less alone.

After his father had left him behind in Hayam, while his mother lay dying, Marnie sat with him at her side. She hushed him with a gentle *shhh*, as he looked toward his aunt to speak. The quietness lulled him as Marnie rocked the chair they had shared.

Tenderness filled the silence between Treasta and Chimes as she wove her fingers with his.

Footsteps approached.

From the street an officer appeared.

At first, Chimes thought they must have looked like a couple of tramps still wet from the rain, their clothing—his tunic and her nightgown—clinging to their bodies, their hair attempting to dry in the cool shadows of the alley.

"Darius Gustassan?" the officer said his name with a lowly graveness.

Chimes held his breath as another officer materialized. Of course, he was recognizable; he cursed for whatever unknown reasons the gods made him this way.

Standing with his hand hovering over the hilt of his saber, the officer cleared his throat, cautious, yet trying not to look suspecting of Gustas' son. "The captain"—a pause as he eyed the wet pair—"would like to speak with you at the citadel. Your father, the Councilor Gustas—we have grave news that cannot be spoken about in public."

The other officer took another step forward. "It can be discussed more at the guardhouse," he added.

Chimes felt Treasta squeezing tighter on his hand.

As he stood, his grip slipped from hers. "Of course," he said. But Treasta followed to her feet, occupying his shadow with one palm resting on his shoulder. Her fingers dug into his skin.

The officer grasped Chimes' arm, calling for his partner to apprehend Treasta, but before he had the chance, she swiftly grabbed his blade and sliced through his trouser, cutting deep gashes into his flesh.

The officer ahold of Chimes jumped back and drew his blade.

He swung, but Treasta dodged.

The wet night gown may have weighed her down, her pregnancy may have slowed her, but it was the handling of an unfamiliar sword where she fumbled. Its size, though nothing like a longsword and more like a short sword, wasn't one she was used to. Treasta knew smaller blades: knives, daggers—and even then, rarely did she find herself in combative situations that required such skills. She wasn't good, but what she knew was enough to manage to strike a blow across the officers face and then arm.

Metal resonated on cobble as she threw the saber aside, took Chimes' hand, and ran. Where? She didn't know. And neither did Chimes. The city's roads were unfamiliar, but they knew that they had to gain enough distance to disappear. So they did, and they didn't stop until either of them could hardly breathe—gasping, straining, their lungs struggled, their hearts rushed. Treasta fell over coughing, and that's when she realized they were on a tight road between buildings and a stone fence keeping her from falling over the dam's wall. It was the first view she had of the south side of the dam. One floodgate open, water poured from the mouth of an ancient dwarven king, spewing into what seemed would be a long fall.

Chimes gulped back large inhales, nearly choking on his own breaths. He leaned on the stone fence, glancing at his surroundings. "They were going to arrest me," he said with a cold realization. "My father, they think I killed him, don't they? That I set the fire?"

"Allegedly," Treasta wheezed. She collapsed, resting her head on the cool wall's surface. "But if you weren't a suspect before, you are now."

"You don't understand," Chimes said. "There is no *alleged* here. They'll behead me. They don't care whether I did it or not so long as someone answers for the crime. That's what people want. We need to get out of Wesser. Once we're out of the city, we'll be safer. Law in Wesserland isn't like other places. The wild is lawless. And, here, the magistrate is ruthless."

"Safer? What do you mean safer?" she asked.

"They'll either pin it on someone else or come after me."

Treasta stood. "We better get moving then."

"We?"

"This is a me and you problem, yeah?"

Chimes followed her to her feet and took her hand. "An *us* problem."

"LAINE AND THE PATS, HUH?" ELSIE DIDN'T EXPECT anyone else to have traveled this far into Wesserland, but if anyone had it in him, it would be Laine. Charismatic, smooth-talking Laine. "Let's not waste our time," she said. Davan was watching the sun's setting colors cut golden rays through the buildings and trees. The glow struck his hazel eyes, splaying drops of honey. "We know where they're going now."

Davan crossed his arms. He stood with the posture of a statue. "You going to do it or what?"

"You need to exercise some patience, my friend," she said, patting his arm. "We don't want to rush something like this."

He wondered whether Elsie knew about the pregnancy. At first, as they watched Treasta and Chimes, when he saw the roundness of her stomach on her normally rail-thin frame, when he saw the way the fabric of the wet nightgown stuck to her body, the way she allowed Chimes to rest his hands on her body, the smile—though faint—that appeared on his face as if he sired the babe, Davan didn't know how to feel. But it made him turn to stone, transformed his heart into volcanic glass: black and brittle. His vision narrowed as an intense feeling of violence grew inside him. No breaths, no matter how long and slow, or how controlled he tried to make them, could soothe such vexation. The sensation was like a fire boiling the underlayers of his skin, seizing the tissue and cooking his blood.

Elsie wouldn't notice the magnitude of indignation and jealousy that consumed him. But Davan, already a naturally quiet soul, would become quieter, seemingly disappearing into himself as they began their journey to Hayam, traveling again by steamboat.

That night, they loaded themselves into a crate scheduled for delivery to a town neither recognized. There was little Elsie could do to disguise herself. Certainly the crew wouldn't have forgotten her face. Neither she nor Davan wanted to risk her being recognized, so the first night aboard the boat, after a long twelve hours waiting for the sun to disappear behind the horizon and for the crew, save a man or two, to retire, Davan kicked, and after several attempts to break free, the crate finally busted open. He pried the boards away.

As he reached inside to help Elsie, she slapped his hand and pushed him aside. The vertebrae in Elsie's spine cracked as she stretched. She shrouded her face with a hood, and she and Davan searched for a guest cabin to hunker down in until the boat reached Maward.

WHITE STRANDS OF HAIR LANDED ONTO THE GROUND, shavings from a shadow of scruff that was nearly invisible on his face followed. With the gilded dagger Elsie had thrown at him, Chimes shaved his head and face, then going as far as to shave his brows. The shapes of his visage caught in the light of a nearby window reflected in a barrel of stagnant water from the previous night's rain. A faint reflection of an unrecognizable man stared back. He splashed his face with cool water.

One section at a time, he cut Treasta's golden tresses, temporarily holding the long strands and becoming lost in thought with each chunk.

The first cut: *fireplace poker jammed into his father's disfigured face, jaw displaced, blood everywhere, a man desperate to live gasping.*

The second cut: *I should be mad at her. This is her fault, isn't it?*

The third cut: *no. It's not her fault. Whether she was here or not, this would have happened.* Chimes remembered Treasta explaining the mission bestowed upon them by the thief-king. *But would Father still be alive? He followed me …*

The fourth cut: *clasping the charm around Treasta's neck, sneaking into his father's room, stealing the key to the treasure chamber.*

The fifth cut: *I should be angry.*

Treasta turned around, her eyes downcast as he gently lifted her chin.

The final scrappy cut left a short fringe above her brows. A somber gaze saying everything and nothing met his.

Chimes handed Treasta the dagger to keep.

35

Chimes wasn't too familiar with Wesser, but he knew it well enough to know the neighborhood just east of the harbor and near the lake's edge was where he would need to go to know how to get out of the city, but officers patrolled near the lift, looking for him and Treasta no doubt. They'd have to walk the road's gradual grade.

No announcement it seemed of the chancellor's death had made it to the streets. Nothing on notice boards, no gossiping—the officers were quiet, but it was clear there were more lurking in places where a suspect may try to cross to escape. It was nearly morning when they reached the neighborhood. Neither Treasta nor Chimes slept apart from a moment of dozing while they hid midday.

The buildings, built of lumber, succumbed to the decadeslong wear of the water. An overwhelming smell of fish from the nearby market to open in the coming hour or two wafted along the boardwalk.

Chimes knocked on a door. No one answered. He knocked again.

The sound of the hinges was unkind as the door came ajar. One eye, framed with wrinkles, greeted him.

"I'm looking for Boxley," Chimes said.

Not a word from the stranger and the door eased open.

In their cloaks—stolen from hooks at a tavern the night before—Treasta and Chimes disappeared into the darkness of the room; the faint glow of a single candlestick in the old man's hand was their only light.

"I was sleeping." The old man, cranky over the disruption, shut the door behind them. Indeed, he was dressed for bed, including a night cap over his unkempt gray hair. "Boxley is dead. I go by Bartley now, you understand? Too many of you people coming here expecting things from me—help for this or that—*bah!* Then I get authorities coming around here, seeing if I know so-and-so and whether they went wherever. I've nearly had to relocate. Good that'll do," he said with a scoff. "My clientele wouldn't know where to find me. How'd you find me, anyway?"

Bartley, one eye wider than the others, stared, waiting for Chimes to answer.

"I travel a lot," Chimes said.

"People need to learn to shut their damn mouths sometimes." Bartley sat down.

Neither Treasta nor Chimes followed. They stayed on their feet, both too tired, knowing well that if they sat now, they'd likely fall asleep. But Bartley insisted they sit across from him, and as soon as they did, they felt a drowsiness weigh on them. It wasn't clear for what the establishment in which they presided was meant. From what could be seen in the candlelight, the room could be the front end of an office, but the curtain were drawn shut, the shutters outside latched.

Bartley retrieved what appeared to be a ledger of sorts from somewhere in the black. "Well, out with it," he said, impatient. "What do you need?"

"What's your price," Chimes asked.

The old man gave a smile of a man awake and entertained. Chimes came prepared it seemed, and Bartley's knowledge was not free. "What you got?"

Chimes dug through his satchel hidden underneath the cloak. He set an egg-shaped music box on the table and cranked the key. The gold-crafted latch opened, a dancer—a fairy—rose and began spinning. Another one of his father's inventions. Treasta looked at Chimes with the realization that he had stolen it from the councilor's apartment. She wondered what else he had taken that could be in the sack.

The music box echoed a lullaby in a bell-like sound.

"Oh." Bartley picked up the box to examine the mechanism, curious and fascinated at once. "Lovely."

"We're looking for passage out of Wesser."

"And I take it you can't walk out. Otherwise why would you be here."

"That's right."

Bartley flipped the book open, dust plumes caught in the candlelight. His finger ran across names; he flipped through pages with echoes of "hmmm" and "ahhh" and "nooo" and "well ..." and "here!" His fat finger tapped the page with a thud. "Yes, a merchant you will call Ashen."

"Ashen?"

"Yes, Ashen," Bartley said as he rolled his eyes. He muttered: "Got up to deal with these kinds of questions. Gods smite me."

The old man continued, "He travels with a caravan from a port along the Shardian Waters to Yeras."

"Where can we find him?"

A long, exaggerated sigh escaped Bartley. "He and the caravan usually stop at the H and N Building along Backwater Road. It's a warehouse. Ashen is a stern fellow with red, curly hair. He shouldn't be hard to miss. That is, if he's there. They were scheduled to arrive on the first of the month and depart two days later. May have missed him. But," he said with a finger in the air, "if that's the case, come back. I know of someone who will be in town in two weeks who can get you out of here. Not ideal, I get it, but you pay well, and I like to be sure those who pay well are well treated and get the service they deserve."

Ashen. Red, curly hair. Chimes committed the name and description to memory. *H and N Building. Backwater Road.* He hoped the caravan was there. Waiting two weeks to leave the city, it didn't seem possible. Where they would hide, he didn't know. And his connections in Wesser were none. Chimes spent years avoiding the city to avoid his father. He may not have been angry toward Treasta, but he was furious at himself for returning, for seeing his father, for attending the party, for letting his father's promises—to be there for him as he failed to be—carve themselves into his bones.

36

Treasta didn't know how many more steps she could take. Her body was ready to give in to sleep, and several times, as they carried on down the alleyways—paths that would extend the time it took to get to the H and N Building just to avoid the main roads—she stopped several times, leaning on the wall, pressing into it with her hand or body just to hold herself up.

"I don't know if I can make it," she said. "I feel faint." Her stomach hurt; a deep pain settled into her pelvis.

He grabbed her hand, encouraging her to continue, but the walk ahead of them seemed never to end. "Just keep moving," he told her, as if doing so would help her stay awake. No doubt he was just as tired.

Treasta trailed behind him, but her gait shortened, her stride slowed. She collapsed just at daybreak and as they were attempting to run across the promenade.

Chimes ducked behind some goods. At this hour, the city was coming awake, and people were starting to appear on the streets.

Several souls rushed to her side. They turned her over, saw a woman with short hair, bangs, pallid, and pregnant. The women surrounding her called for help, when Treasta didn't wake. Her dirt-stained nightgown turned red as blood pooled from between her legs. Chimes watched as Treasta was hoisted by two men into the back of a wagon. He had to be careful as he trailed her, but he also had to be swift. The wagon took off, cutting through the city, with the men aboard calling for people to "get out of the way!" He couldn't risk being seen by officers, but he also couldn't afford to lose sight of Treasta. One misstep and finding her would be nearly impossible.

A temple devoted to Alia—the sky, and therefore all gods—was a modest, tucked-away structure with an outer wall. From nearby, Chimes saw the cart carrying Treasta rolling onto its grounds, but then a gate shut. Near the gate was a chapel accessible to the public.

Chimes walked inside the chapel with the hood of his cloak shrouding his face. He held it close. A couple people bowed at an altar, gave a gesture he wasn't familiar with when they were done with prayer, and left. He looked around. He needed to find a way in, but the doors in the back of the chapel were locked.

"Is there something I can help you with?"

Chimes turned to meet the eyes of an older priestess who stood clutching her staff. Atop it was a honing crystal. She watched him with suspicion.

"My wife," he said with no hesitation, "she was taken onto the temple grounds. She's hurt."

The priestess looked him over, observed how he shrunk into himself—a man with little confidence—and the mud caked on what looked to be an expensive pair of boots.

"Your wife is in good care," said the priestess. "I trust she will call for you when she's ready. But until then I cannot allow you onto our grounds."

"She was bleeding. Please," he begged, ready to fall to his knees, "she's carrying my child."

"I cannot. Unless you are here to worship or would like to leave an offering, you cannot loiter. We do not allow …," another judgmental look passed over him, "… loitering of any kind."

"Of course," Chimes said, and he saw himself out, determined to find another way.

How long Treasta had been unconscious, she didn't know, but she awoke to the smell of frankincense burning on a nearby altar. As she sat up, she collapsed too weak even to hold up her head. And her legs felt like gel, and between them was a sticky and crusty sensation as she moved her thighs.

Treasta threw the covers back, then screamed. The panic sent her off the bed and onto the floor with a heavy thud. Startled by the amount of blood, she tried wiping it away with her bare hands, tearing at the fabric. Another cry escaped her lungs as her eyes fell upon her naked pelvis where crimson splotches stained her inner thighs, pubic hair tangled with thick, bloody crust.

A midwife rushed into the room, rushing to Treasta's side.

Treasta latched onto the woman, pulling the stranger to the floor with her.

On the floorboards, the woman sat next to her, slinging an arm around her back and taking her hand as Treasta, shaking, rocked in her arms. "There, there," she said. "Deep breaths. Deep breaths, now." Inhaling and exhaling, she coaxed her frantic patient to relax as they breathed together.

"I'm dying," Treasta muttered. "Gods save me; I'm dying."

"No, you're not dying. And I think baby is all right as well," the midwife said. "Though I won't know for a couple days. If you breakout in fever then, well …" Her gaze fell. "We can worry about that if that comes."

Treasta's body was cold, her chest burned, and sweat trickled from her brow; she dragged the linens to the floor, cradling the fabric for warmth, burying her face within the folds.

The midwife, on her feet, dipped a washcloth in a bowl of water. She lifted Treasta's head and dabbed her face whiter than seafoam. The warmth on her skin eased her.

"I can't stay here," she said with a weak shake in her speech. "Where's Chimes?"

"You came here alone," the woman said.

Alone? Treasta stared at the wooden beams stretching across the ceiling. "What is this place? Where am I?"

"The Confines."

Like a jail? No, that didn't seem right? She was in some kind of infirmary with a midwife and not chained to the bed or being held like a prisoner. No guards were around, at least not what she could see. She watched the midwife who had crossed the room and opened the window to dump the water outside.

"Miss," the woman said, "how are you feeling? Well enough to wash up and change into clean clothes?"

"I don't have anything else to wear," Treasta said.

The midwife knelt and took Treasta's hand, rubbing it as if to soothe her. She was gentle with her words with a gaze absent of judgment. "Do you have a home?"

When Treasta didn't answer right away, the woman patted the back of her hand, and softly smiled, as if taking pity. "It's all right if you don't." Had Treasta been more well, she'd have answered her with a quick lie, said anything more than nothing, anything to blend in with everyday people.

"I'm in between places," she said flatly.

"Well," the woman helped Treasta to her feet, "let's get you cleaned up and see how you fair over the next few days. Then, we can figure out what to do from there to get you what you need. How does that sound?"

Too good to be true, she wanted to say. Kindness always was.

Nauseated, Treasta wavered, her stomach vacant and craving substance. Or, she thought to herself as the sickening ache radiated, I should starve the baby out. Anything to make this end. She held her belly as she bent over and groaned.

The woman took her arm, helping Treasta balance as they walked into an open-aired walkway around a courtyard. "I am sure you can stay as long as you need. What am I to call you?"

Following around the cloister, the woman led Treasta into a hallway with slender windows. A gentle breeze cut inside.

"I'm …," she paused, but didn't have the energy to make up a new name. "I'm Treasta."

"It's a pleasure to serve you Miss Treasta," the woman said. "I reckon with an accent like that you're from the east?"

"Is it that obvious?"

The woman helped Treasta down a hallway. "I'm Kaya. Here we are," and she opened another door.

Inside was a room with folded clothes neatly stacked on shelves and a wash station in the corner with a well pump. She thumbed through the stacks, mostly brown linens and off-white cottons—inexpensive gowns for simple women leading simple lives. As Kaya held up a gown, it unfolded itself midair and looked closer to a burlap sack than a dress.

Right there, in the room with its tiny window, Kaya helped Treasta wash up and change, slipping a chemise and then the dress over her head. She tied it off with a sash around her waist. Treasta never felt more pregnant than now with her stomach so exposed to the gawking gazes and blank stares of strangers.

"Doesn't that feel better?" she asked. "Like a new woman. We can help you, you know. The canonesses, they would be happy to."

"Canonesses?"

"The ladies of the sky, servants of Alia. Now, let's get you back to the infirmary. I can fetch you a hearty meal. You look starved."

"That's too kind of you," Treasta said as the woman helped her back to the room.

In the infirmary, Treasta refused to lie down. She sat in a chair at a table near the window so she could look outside and see the sky. It was sunset. What time exactly, she didn't know, but she saw the stars emerging beyond the tall city buildings scraping the heavens high along the Confines' walls. A single spire to the temple could be seen beyond a roof, but nothing more could be discerned for where in Wesser she was.

Kaya returned with portage, something simple that Treasta could keep down until she regained her strength. As she ate, she watched a hare—barely visible in the light pouring from the infirmary—sneaking through the vegetable garden the canonesses sustained. She envied the hare, how quietly it crept, its cautious demeanor, and keenness to know to steal from the garden in the night. The unsuspecting hare nibbled and carried on its way.

Treasta eventually fell asleep at the table, head resting next to an empty bowl and cup. The midwife came in and nudged her at the day's first light. She looked down at Treasta with pity, an expression Treasta wanted to smack off her face.

She stretched as she sat up, her spine unraveling. She rubbed her stiff neck and winced as the sunlight hit her eyes. Treasta propped her head up as she rested her elbows on the table. She felt herself drifting asleep again, but Kaya's high-pitched voice jolted her awake.

"The high priestess is here," she said.

Treasta rubbed her eyes, slouching back in the chair. She first looked toward the garden, looking for the hare smart enough not to return in broad daylight, then looked at the high priestess, an older woman with hair tied in complicated twists that no woman alone could do on her own. She wore gold jewelry, her stoles matching the shimmering yellow, and robe somehow an even brighter yellow trimmed with black. In her hand she carried a staff with a honing crystal atop it. Priests here didn't seem much different than back home.

"Treasta," Kaya said and, unprompted, pulled her to her feet, "this is the High Priestess Aurana."

The high priestess nodded her head, a minimal acknowledgment. Her gaze scanned Treasta, her head tilted in such a way she had to look down her nose. Treasta knew this look as one that was unwelcoming.

The silence grew between the three.

Then Aurana spoke, "Your *husband*"—a word laced with venom—"is quite persistent."

"Chimes? He's h—"

Aurana lifted her hand, quieting Treasta. Treasta's face flushed hot.

"Let me finish," Aurana said. "We've kicked him off the grounds several times in the past three days."

Three days? Had it been that long? Had she slept nearly all that time? Treasta nearly fell back into the chair, but she caught herself on the table. The high priestess quietly huffed and watched with narrow eyes.

"I think it would be best if you leave," Aurana said.

"High Priestess," Kaya broke in, "I don't advise that. Miss Treasta has been recovering. She nearly lost her child and needs to regain her strength. I can't say whether she's well enough to leave quite yet."

"I would like to leave," Treasta said.

Both women looked at her with surprise, one more upset than the other, but neither expected Treasta's eagerness.

"Then that settles it," Aurana said. "You will go now."

Kaya's jaw hung open. She scoffed and stuttered between her words not quite sure what to say. "No, you can't …"

"Thank you for your help, but I really cannot stay here," Treasta said.

"Your child," Kaya's voice was shaking, her eyes welling, "you could lose your child."

"It's a risk I'm willing to take."

Kaya didn't say another word to Treasta, but she whispered a prayer under her breath. Amid her invocation, she placed her hands on Treasta's pregnant body.

Treasta shoved her away. "Don't touch me!" she shouted. "Do," she took a step toward her, "not," and felt the sudden urge to shove the woman again, "touch," and she did, sending Kaya into the wall, "me."

"That's enough!" the high priestess's voice rang. An unseen force sent Treasta backward, Aurana's staff briefly flashing a bright white light. Treasta skidded across the floor.

Treasta's gaze shot up to see Aurana standing over her like a long shadow. "My … but my child," she said. "You could have hurt it."

"You don't care about that child," the priestess said with a scoff, "and the gods certainly do not care for a bastard child. You're not married. I'm no fool. Now, get out of my Confines you wretched transient whore." Her body seemed to lengthen, the room seemed to darken, and she pointed with her staff toward the door that opened on its own.

Treasta came to her feet, straightened out the wrinkles in her dress, and left with Aurana escorting her closely behind.

"No, no! Please, wait!" Kaya raced after them. "Don't you understand? You could be miscarrying. You could lose your child. It could kill you if that's what's happening."

Treasta paused, looked over her shoulder at the midwife from down the hall, and said, "Then Alia save my soul."

Underneath a window box, Chimes dozed in and out of sleep. The rays of the morning sun striking his face brought him to consciousness, and he sat up, leaning against the wall. He scratched his head through a knitted cap with a long wide brim, shrouding his face from strangers on the street. He yawned and looked around. Luckily the temple's Confines were sequestered away in a less busy area of the city. Since camping outside its walls, no guards or officers marched by in what was an impoverished district. The nearby alleyways were lined with homeless encampments, the residents hopeful for reprieve near the holy grounds of the Confines.

On the first day, Chimes had tried sneaking over the wall, but the high priestess appeared on the other side. She smacked him with the staff, then in a flash, he had found himself at the front gates. Chimes, disoriented, collected himself. He paced the street, scanning the area, the tall walls, the windows that overlooked the Confines, and the clothes lines stretched across the road hanging with drying linens.

That night, he had broken into a nearby shop, climbed to its second floor, but when he dropped into the courtyard, the high priestess was there. She wacked him with her staff, there was a flash, and he reappeared at the Confines' entrance.

The second day, he had wandered the encampments, sat with an old man who shared a portion of his meal he had cooked over a fire. It was a simple meal for a simple man, and the old man said he had dreamed of breaking through the heavens one day, that he dreamed of cloud-walking and sun-dancing, and that he felt Alia calling him there to that very spot in the alleyway.

"It's as close as I can get," he had said. "They won't allow commoners into the Confines, nor will they allow men. It's a congregation of canonesses. Pretty ladies donned in gold."

Just hours later, as the temple bell rang at ten a.m., Chimes witnessed tandem lines of canonesses emerging from the Confines, donned in gold as the old man said, with hoods hiding their faces. As the doors went to close, Chimes had tried sliding in, but the high priestess hit him with her staff, there was a flash, and he stood before the gate with the doors shut.

The old man that evening laughed and hummed a children's rhyme:

Dance around the sun
Merrily little ones, little ones.
Merrily around the sun,
Dance around little ones, little ones …

"My mom," Chimes began, and he pulled his legs in, shrinking into himself, "would sing that to me at night."

The old man took the cap off his head and placed it on Chimes' head. He smiled through missing teeth. "You're head's going to get cold, lad."

Chimes pulled the cap down, then hid his face between his knees, trying to force whatever memories he still had of his mother to his mind. He didn't remember much. But he recalled a time when his ailing mother had sat up in her bed, calling Chimes to her side. Little Chimes had crawled into bed with her, and she quietly sang and held him near her heart and he sank into sleep with the echo of its beat in his ear:

Merrily little ones dance around the sun …

"Merrily, merrily around the sun," Chimes hummed, and he and the old man cheered, clinking together their wooden cups.

He shot back the bitter liquor, unsure what he had just swallowed. Moments later, the shot seized his faculties. Chimes was at the wooden gates, pounding with his fists, kicking the doors, and shouting, "Let me in! Let me in! Let me see her!" He fell into the doors, sliding to the ground and drunkenly sobbed. "I just need to know she's all right."

The old man sat next to him at the gate, put his arm around him and comforted him. "Alia be praised," he said.

The next morning, the high priestess was standing at open doors and nudging the old man and Chimes with the butt-end of her staff. The drunken pair had looked up at the woman, wincing at the daylight's brightness and crawled away to the shadows. Chimes curled into the wedge where the wall and cobblestone met, curling into himself, and falling back asleep. He awoke in the afternoon, a heavy pounding breached the brain, and the old man offered him another drink. Chimes shot it back and drifted into sleep.

The final morning, where he had awoken under the window box, the sun's rays warm on his face were uninviting. He tugged his cap over his eyes, groaning. The hinges of the gate cried in a terrible high pitch as the doors eased open. Treasta emerged from the Confines. Chimes had forgotten he lopped her hair off, expecting to see her long golden locks flowing down her back. She stood there, exhaled, looking around, seemingly nervous to have been abandoned, yet looking for him, knowing he was somewhere nearby.

Chimes jumped to his feet, feeling a sudden soberness, and rushed to her. She hadn't noticed him, and when he took her in his arms, she nearly crawled out of her skin. Treasta eased, recognizing his shape around her. She nuzzled into his body, losing herself in the folds of his tunic as he kissed her.

"You waited for me? You waited three days?"

"I would wait a lifetime if I had to."

The stale alcohol on his breath was sour and unpleasant, but she didn't let that show on her face as they drank in the other with their eyes. Treasta burrowed into his arms.

"Now what?" she asked Chimes. "We can't wait two weeks."

"I know," Chimes said. He had pulled her in his arms, but she pushed him away, too worried about what to do next. Two weeks was a long time with city authorities searching for him. If he lingered too long, it would be no time for them to find him.

37

THE OLD MAN AWOKE TO THE SOUND OF SOMEONE NEARBY. Groggy, he opened his eyes, looking up to see Chimes and a woman at his side. He smiled, "You found your lass," he said.

"I did." Chimes handed him an item wrapped in silk. "For your kindness," he said, and he and Treasta walked away.

The old man, head heavy with a hangover, struggled sitting up. One corner at a time, he pulled back the silk to reveal a gold ring set with large sapphires and emeralds, delicately detailed. The old man looked around the alleyway, then clutched the treasure inside his fist. He fell asleep, smiling.

38

A WHISTLE FROM THE STEAMBOAT SOUNDED over the water as it passed a sister vessel. Passengers waved, exchanged "how do you do," and the boats made their way along the Great River. An attendant was making his rounds, knocking on cabins to check passenger tickets, as was customary. A knock at cabin thirty-three on deck three echoed through the room darkened by pulled curtains, where a man was bound and gagged with his handkerchief. Elsie shook her finger, "No," deterring the man from any attempts to scream.

Davan had thought the cabin was empty, but it turned out the man, instead of retreating to his cabin upon boarding, had gone directly to the bar in the salon with his luggage, shot back a few drinks, had a couple rounds, and wobbled to his room. He had opened an already unlocked door, plopped on the bed without a second thought to why it was unlocked, and moments later was awoken to Elsie and Davan tying him up. Elsie covered his mouth with her hand before he could make a sound.

The drunken man blinked several times, trying to take in what was going on. He gasped at the sight of two unkempt strangers in black now holding him hostage.

"You're not going to scream, you understand," Elsie said.

The man nodded, and she eased her hand off his mouth.

"What do you want from me?" he had asked. "I don't got much."

"Don't talk," Davan had said.

Elsie had kicked open his suitcase, shuffling through his belongings. Clothes, a journal, spectacles for reading, perfume, and pomade. She retrieved the razor, opening the shiny blade, and observing her reflection visible in the light seeping into the room from behind the curtains.

"What now?" Davan had asked Elsie.

She closed the blade and pocketed it. "Well, we could just gag him and leave him here, look for a new cabin that *isn't* occupied."

"It *wasn't* occupied," he said. "Not until five minutes ago, at least." They had spent a good portion of the day in the room before the man arrived. Room thirty-three on deck three was, as far as Davan was concerned, vacant.

"I say we just leave him."

"Just shut up," she had said. "We don't need to go anywhere. We got enough supplies, yeah?"

"It'll be close, but yeah," he had said.

Elsie shoved the suitcase aside and crossed her legs. She smiled at the bound man on the bed. "Then, I guess we just made a new friend," she had said.

Three days had passed. Their supplies had run low. On one evening, Davan ventured out to scout the steamboat. He had spent enough time doing so on the journey to Wesser that it wasn't a difficult task. This wasn't the exact same vessel, but it was similar enough that he was able to break into the galley with no issue and snag food. At the salon, shut down in the wee hours of the night, he grabbed a bottle of bourbon from the top shelf and returned to the cabin.

That night, Elsie and Davan poured themselves drinks and ate well. The man, however, didn't get a morsel, not even a sip. They had earlier that day given him crumbs to silence his whining, but that night they shoved a gag in his mouth and were, believe it or not, merry.

"I underestimated you," Elsie said before hiccuping. "You're determined."

"I know what I want," Davan said. "And when I want something, I get it."

The man banged his head into the wall behind him, rolling his eyes. He tried speaking through his gag, but it was indiscernible. Elsie kicked him.

On the fourth day, the knock came. It was early still, at an hour when most were expected to be in their cabins.

"Where's your ticket?" Davan asked.

The man pointed with his head, nodding toward his jacket. Davan fumbled through the pockets and found the stub. He put on the man's hat and a scarf, cracked open the door, and handed the ticket to the attendant.

The attendant clipped it, made a note on his ledger, and said, "Thank you Mr. Grall. Hope you're enjoying your time aboard the Riverkeeper."

Without a word, Davan took the ticket from him and shut the door. He took the hat and scarf off, throwing the articles at Mr. Grall and relaxed in a chair.

"So you're not returning to the hideout?" he asked Elsie.

Somehow the question felt heavier than it was meant to be. It was a relatively simple yes or no answer, yet her head spun searching for the right words. She flipped the razorblade open and closed.

"That's what you said wasn't it?"

"I don't know. It's complicated." Elsie looked at her reflection in the razor and searched the dead space around her head for signs of Declan or Bastan. Anything, she thought, to give her a semblance of hope that he was alive and that she could find him. "What are you trying to prove, anyway?"

Davan didn't answer.

Later that night, while Davan was away searching the galley for more food, Elsie pulled the gag from Mr. Grall's mouth.

"Can I ask you something?" she said, sitting cross-legged, leaning toward the man with one wide eye. "It's important."

He licked his lips, trying to moisten their cracked layers, and smacked his mouth a few times before hesitating to respond. "I su—su—suppose."

"I su—su—su—suppose," Elsie mocked in a deep voice. "Gods be damned. Get ahold of yourself. We don't plan on hurting you." Then she flashed him a paranoid glance. "Unless you give us a reason to. That's not the case, is it?"

"N—n—n—no, of course n—n—not."

"Good," and she sat up straight with her arms crossed. "I got a dilemma, you see. My friend, he's got something I want, but I promised him I'd, you know"—she ran her thumb along her throat—"another man for him. Would it be unethical to try and take what I want and just, you know, abandon that promise? I could just kill *my friend* instead, you get me?" When he didn't answer right away, she trailed off, "I'm sorry, I'm just a little," she spun her fingers around her head, "overwhelmed with everything going on that it's like I can't think straight. But I *should* just do it, right?"

"Why are you asking me this?" he said.

"Well, you're a stranger, a third-party sort, you know? Who else would be better?"

"Umm ... well, I ... I don't think I would consider killing anyone," Mr. Grall answered.

Elsie rubbed her neck, feeling an awful headache take shape behind her ruined eye. She let out a long sigh then groaned, frustrated. She jumped to her feet, stuffed the handkerchief back into his mouth so deep that he began to gag.

"Come on, get up," she ordered. But he didn't move. She drew the razor blade, flipping it open in his face; its sheen caught his eye. He let out a muffled scream, and a puddle of piss pooled beneath him.

A chair launched across the cabin as she kicked it. "What did I say about asking for the goddamn bucket, huh?"

He scurried to his feet to the best of his ability with bound ankles and knees shaking, with his hands tied behind his back. Tears streamed down the man's face. It was, at least to Elsie, one of the most pathetic sights she had ever seen in a man. But something about him succumbing to her, groveling and sobbing, the way she witnessed his spirit buckle, oh, how it enthralled her. She hadn't felt this excited in a long time.

Elsie shoved the man out the door, and under the stars, outside cabin thirty-three on deck three, she held the blade to his neck. "Jump," she said.

A sharp wind cut between them. She could barely see his eyes in the moonlight, but what she could see from his expression brought her great satisfaction. Elsie smiled, pressed the blade against his throat but not with so much pressure that it cut him, just enough to petrify. Through the gag he tried to scream, but the handkerchief caught most of the sound.

She wielded her arm back, ready to strike across his neck; so frightened was Mr. Grall that his legs, involuntarily of his own actions, sent him scurrying backward until he hit the railing, and the weight of his body sent him overboard.

Elsie looked over the edge of the boat, searching the darkness, seeing but a phantom of a splash in the night. She closed the razor, pocketed it, and retreated into the cabin. A thick stench of piss wafted into her nostrils.

Moments later Davan appeared. He quietly shut the door behind him and placed a small crate of goods on the bureau. "You going to dump the bucket, or what?" he asked before glancing around the room. Then he noticed Mr. Grall's absence.

"Where's he?"

Elsie shrugged as she picked dirt out from her nails with her teeth.

"What the hell did you do?"

She shrugged again. "He got unruly."

Of course, Davan didn't believe her. "I'm sure he did," he said, then popped open a bottle of ale to take in a long drink—anything to numb himself so long as he had to deal with Elsie.

Elsie looked inside the crate. Davan overdid it, per usual. "They're going to notice," she said, "that stuff's missing."

He huffed, took another drink acting like he didn't care; he wasn't planning on listening to any of her advice. No one back at the tribe liked Elsie anyway. Nothing good came of anyone who associated with her. But, she was a good thief, Fylle knew it, and Lodan knew it too. Perhaps it was her lack of empathy, the little thought she gave to the lives of those she affected. Or perhaps it was something else, something Davan couldn't see for himself. He had hoped she wouldn't return to Galgaya, that what she said in Wesser were true. If there was another person Fylle could consider for marshal, it could be her.

Elsie waited for Davan to fall asleep. The headache that crept into her brain had yet to ease. She sat in the darkness of the cabin, her mind spinning with thoughts of the flute, Davan, Declan, of Mr. Grall and the *splash* of the water, of that drawing Davan kept tucked away in his boot. She flicked the razor blade open then closed, open then closed, staring at the soles still on his feet.

Her last day with Declan played out in her head: purchasing the tickets, the snarky upper class women sneering at her. The last thing she remembered before falling asleep the night Declan disappeared was that he was drawing over and over again a fox and a fox-faced boy. The portraits consumed the pages of his journal. She tried recreating the portraits in her memory, but the sketches never held up to Declan's talent.

Davan knew where to find Bastan, but she didn't understand how. She tried connecting the pieces, thinking back to when the demon warlock appeared and a hapless Declan inside the mirror, then remembering at some point in the wild Declan had ran into Davan—the man, as Declan called him, who held him by the hair. She knew this only because Declan had drawn his face. Somehow Davan was connected to Bastan, that was one thing she understood, but what she didn't understand was how Declan was involved.

For a moment she thought about slicing Davan's foot off, sawing through the leather of his boot, then his skin, muscle, and bone. Something about the thought was cathartic. As she scanned him with her eyes, her gaze landed on his neck, vulnerable and open for her taking. How easily she could stand over him and with a single swoop, without a second thought, just end him then and there. The idea brought her a sense of control. In not following through, she felt like she held power over him. He trusted her. Otherwise he wouldn't dare shut his eyes.

Mr. Grall never dared shut his eyes.

39

DAYS AGO, WHEN TRISH PULLED PAT ASHORE, Pat had barely survived, coughing river water onto the banks of the Great River. They were lucky to have been in a spot where the land could easily be reached and for the water's flow to be well mannered. She patted her brother's back, helping clear his lungs.

Neither had expected to run into Davan. Laine wouldn't be pleased, but so long as Davan didn't tell Treasta about the Pats' excursion overboard, perhaps Treasta would still hold up her end of the bargain.

Trish's young naivety had a chokehold on her own personality. She was easy to rouse a reaction from, one that typically was like a bellows on a flame. But she was much more worried about Pat to give even a sterling bit's worth of care about what happened to Treasta and that fellow she was with. Although Trish was certainly intrigued to see Treasta with someone other than Davan.

Pat lay sprawled on the bank. Trish sat at his side allowing him time to collect himself.

"Now what?" he asked.

Trish let out a long, defeated sigh, and placed her chin in her palm as she watched the water's flow. "We go back, I guess. No way we'll find them in a big city like that. No way we'll get there in good time either."

Trish's brother groaned, slapping his hair out of his eyes and kicking his legs in defeat. He felt like a failure, a feeling that haunted him. Trish always outdid him, including as a swimmer, including as a thief and in brains. To be pulled from a river by his own sister—a *girl*—it was humiliating. He stared at the sky, the stars consuming his vision.

"What, you ain't going to thank me?" she asked, then scoffed.

He didn't entertain her need for appraisal and instead became lost in the blazing white twinkling above him, wondering how the stars could look exactly how he remembered them as they were back home in Galgaya.

Would it always be this way, Pat wondered, Trish always out competing him to the extent that he would need to prove himself tenfold? With Trish's guile, it would take moving mountains for Fylle ever to notice; Laine barely acknowledged him most days. Pat was an extension of Trish; never was she an extension of him. He saw his sister sitting on the bank in his periphery. Maybe she should have just let him die were that how the tribe would continue to treat him.

Trish stood, nudging her brother with her foot. "Get up," she said. "We better start walking."

"We don't even know where we're going," he said, unmoved.

"We'll follow the river."

Neither Pat nor Trish slept that night, following the banks, climbing along the cliffs that rose and dropped before them. In the wee hours, not far from the river, they found a village. As they neared it, hoping for some sense of civilization, they discovered it was abandoned. The ghost town boasted crumbling buildings and a water well.

Trish hoisted the bucket up; it dangled on the crank heavy with sludge. Pat slumped over the well's edge, exhaling with disappointment. He stared down into the dark shaft as the bucket disappeared when Trish let go.

Neither had any supplies on them. What they had was on the steamboat somewhere on the Great River headed to Wesser. How far from Hayam they were, they didn't know. The Pats scoured the town, searching for anything that could benefit their journey and aid them. An old bag with a hole in it, its seams decaying with age; an empty, dusty bottle; some kitchenware in an old tavern—they nabbed what they could find.

As they set up for camp, Trish gathered kindling for the fire and Pat ventured off, looking for anything suitable to eat. The twins were starving. They had gone more than a day without food, and continuing under such conditions wouldn't fare either of them well.

As the sun lowered in the afternoon, Pat hunkered behind a rock and observed a lone sheep grazing on some dried grass near a pine. He threw his knife, but the hooved creature skittered away as he missed. As he retrieved his knife he glimpsed a rattlesnake coiling nearby. The rattling of its tail was a sound he had never heard before. Pat momentarily watched with wonderment the critter as it watched him. He adjusted the grip on the knife, lunged toward the venomous snake, clasped it by the neck with one hand and sliced its head clean off with the other. The critter's headless body flopped, and the rattling stopped. Pat, with a triumphant smile on his face, picked up the dead snake and took it back to camp.

Trish had gotten the fire started; over the flames she was roasting a hare she had caught and skinned in the time it took him to kill the snake. He held out the reptile's limp body for her to see, but she scoffed, said, "I'm not going to eat a snake. You're disgusting," and continued roasting the hare.

"You were supposed to just get the firewood," he said.

"Yeah, well, I also happened across a rabbit. What's it to you, anyway?"

"I was supposed to get the meat. *Me.* Not *you.*"

"Shut up and sit down," Trish said, gesturing with a stick. "You hungry or not?"

"I'm not eating your rabbit."

"Fine. More for me."

Pat went to the edge of camp, set the dead critter aside, and gathered his own kindling. He built a tinder bed and stacked twigs and sticks he found nearby. Pat paused. He looked around for the right tools to get a spark, but he didn't have Trish's knowledge. He eyed the blaze consuming the hare, could feel the heat from where he squatted. His sister rotated the animal, letting it cook on all sides, evenly. Pat looked at his dead snake, headless and uncoiled on the cold earth. He split it down the middle with his knife, its dull blade struggled to break through the skin, and he peeled away the scales, pulling flesh from bone. He went to his sister's fire, skewered pieces of white meat, and held it over the blaze, refusing to meet her gaze, but Pat could feel her eyes observing him.

He curled into himself, ashamed not to remember how to light a campfire, and watched from between his knees the snake meat cook.

Days passed and mostly they walked in silence, Pat trailing feet away behind Trish. They stayed as close to the river as they could, but at some point, the banks extended into sharp walls, and the terrain became too rocky to keep on the same path. Should they have walked a few more miles east, they would have found a highway leading to Maward. But neither had a map or compass. At some point—it wasn't clear when—they had strayed away from the Great River and begun to follow the Sarnak.

Come one morning, dark clouds had gathered from the southwest, encroaching like an ominous blue-gray monster. They continued walking, at first not noticing the oncoming storm, and by afternoon, just an hour before dusk, the sky deepened, a violent wind swept through a deep trench the Pats had wandered into with the hope of coming out to the other side before sundown.

But there was no other side, and as they rushed to beat the night and the storm, they found themselves at a dead end where a natural spring pooled from the rock.

Drops of rain hit their faces, at first they seemed harmless and gentle, but in just a matter of moments, a curtain fell upon them, making it difficult to see the other and their surroundings. Pat found the rocky wall of the trench, felt with his hands for grooves into which he could latch the tips of his fingers; his sister tried keeping close, barely able to recognize his form in the storm. She followed up the side, the rock slippery and difficult to hold. Several times she lost her grip but managed to reclaim it.

Then Pat disappeared.

Rain began rushing over the cliffside; a surge of water blasted through the trench, roaring with the same intensity as the clapping thunder. Pat crawled into an alcove out of the rain, hoping he was high enough to avoid the flooding. He grabbed his sister and pulled her inside. They curled into one another, panting, and waiting for the storm to pass.

It seemed endless, and with night upon them, with their only light being the flashing lightning, the Pats were certain they already died, and this became their purgatory. Too wet and cold, too scared the waters would come rushing into their hideaway at any moment, neither slept that night.

When the rain let up, when the clouds carried on northeast toward the highland deserts where the weather would instead deposit a foot of snow, a soft morning glow permeated the alcove. Wide-eyed, never had either Pat or Trish experienced weather so fierce like last night that they thought nature could kill them. They crawled from their hiding place and looked over a trench filled with rainwater.

"What are you doing?" Pat asked as his sister began climbing several yards down.

"Getting us water," she said.

Pat didn't understand how she could be so calm. His heart was still racing; his body shot with adrenaline.

Trish opened the jars from her pack and filled them, closing the lids tight.

They climbed the rest of the way to the top of the trench, finding themselves on a rocky shelf overlooking the Sarnak River. There was nothing for miles.

Continuing along the snaking river, they found themselves at the ruins of a stone building. For what it was used, it wasn't clear, but here they could rest with a feeling of security—the brick walls holding strong save for a roof that long had been taken by the elements.

"Why are there so many abandoned places out here? I don't get it," Pat asked Trish. She was getting a fire going.

"What a stupid question. How the hell should I know?" she said as a spark caught on the tinder bed and flames consumed the kindling. "Think it's easy living out here? You obviously suck at it."

Pat, pulled layers of clothes off and laid them out next to the fire with the hopes of getting the last of the moisture out. He scratched the round burn scars on his breastbone and ribs. Trish glanced at the marks and his bones visible on his malnourished frame. She turned away, so he wouldn't notice her looking.

The Lyonan-born twins had spent the first five years of their lives living in the farming town west of Galgaya. Born bastards to the youngest daughter of a plowman still in her teenaged years, their mother was shamed by her family. Several times she had appeared at her father's door with the twins. But he wouldn't answer her knocking.

Their mother, stone-faced, barely made eye contact with the twins on most days. On the days she was present, she praised the twins, loved them, told them how important they were, but to "stay away from your grandfather's homestead" and to "stay away from your grandfather if you see him in town."

Trish remembered sneaking around town, Pat always following her, and she would spy on her grandfather and his wife—their stepgrandmother. Her mother, when she'd gossip with Leena, the woman they lived with, she would never mention their grandfather's wife by name: she was always "the Woman" or "the Bitch." The Bitch dressed richer than she was, spent their grandfather's money as though they could afford wanton purchases—that's what Trish and Pat had heard their mother say. The Bitch walked with their grandfather, she dressed him more nicely than he was worth, and their fellow townsfolk noticed. Sometimes Trish would overhear someone mention it, something akin to "the dung-fetcher is going to get his silks stained" and "don't worry, his wife will just buy another coat."

The Pats didn't remember when they had arrived in Galgaya, but they remembered their mother being lured to the city with promises of a good life, that she would be able to afford to care for her children without worrying about their health or going hungry or judgment.

Trish and Pat held their mother's hand as they entered a building near the Backwall Slums of Galgaya, not far from the Bazaar district and the road heading down to the docks. "The Stranger," as the young twins called the man, led them through a commons area where other women, their eyes dark and droopy, lay with their bodies lazily slumped over furniture. Their mother's hands tightened around theirs, and she followed the Stranger down a hall to a room with one bed on the floor.

"You said …," she looked at the man, and a feeling of betrayal crossed her face, "… that—" lost for words.

He had poked her with a syringe, and she fell to the bed, woozy and disoriented.

The Stranger looked at the twins, and said, "You two work for me now, you understand?"

They were too young to know what was going on, so they nodded their heads and did everything the Stranger asked of them, cleaning up rooms, pulling sheets, washing the linens every single day, over and over. Men would come and go, passing sacks of gold and sterling bits to the Stranger at the door. Anytime Pat defied the Stranger, he'd burn him with the cigar until, one day, just shy of age thirteen, the twins disappeared, never to return. They had left their drugged mother there in servitude to her pimp.

Neither Pat nor Trish liked the reminder the scars served. The

Stranger never had laid a hand on Trish, mentioning something about keeping her body in perfect condition for when she was old enough to begin working. Their mother coddled her daughter in her drug-induced stupor but criticized her son for not being useful. "The Brat" she had called him, and Trish was her "Darling." Pat had promised Trish he would go back for their mother; it was the only way he could get her to find the courage to leave. Eventually, Trish stopped asking him about their mother and when Pat would fulfill the promise. She realized that her brother didn't have it in him to kill the Stranger, no matter how awfully he treated him, and he feared what the Stranger would do if he ever caught him on his property again. Pat held onto the images of his mother from when they were still in Lyonan, living with Leena, spying on their grandfather and his wife.

Trish stirred the embers with a stick. Flames extended long licks and lapped up air like thirsty hounds. "Why didn't you go back?" she asked. "You promised you'd go back for her."

"What a stupid question," he responded with the same tone she gave him. "Let it go."

She sat up, ready to stand at her feet. "You *said* you'd save Ma."

He slipped on his trousers, tying the waist. "Ma wasn't savable. She wasn't our mother anymore."

Trish mentioning their mother conjured images of her folded in half, holding her knees to her chest in the corner of the room, lightly knocking her head on the wall and humming. Pat knew if they pulled their mother out of the brothel that she'd have gone mad without the drugs in her system, maybe even die, but Trish didn't understand, and it wasn't worth explaining.

His sister stood. "Then why did you lie?"

"You know what was going to happen, right? You would have become like Ma if we stayed there. That wasn't our mother anymore, Trish."

Trish's fists tightened; her eyes filled with anger. The subject of their mother was always a doorway to a fight, and this time Pat wasn't going to entertain it. He didn't respond to her when she mentioned their mother again. But she wouldn't stop. Ma this, Ma that, "of course it's your fault," and "she always hated you anyway."

When he turned his back to her, she shoved him toward the fire. He caught his balance, skipping over the flames, dodging them. He faced his sister. "What is wrong with you?"

She pointed at herself, "*Me?* What is wrong with you? You think you know what's best for Ma, but you don't."

"Gods, Trish, we're too far away from Kildore for me to care right now," his voice bounced off the ruins' brick walls. "There is nothing I could do, anyway." Brat. Brat. Brat.

"That's not for you to decide."

"Oh, you think you can do better?" he asked. "You want to get Ma back, then you can go march into the brothel yourself and get her. See if she follows. I guarantee she won't. I saved you, don't you get it? *I saved you from becoming her.*"

Trish threw herself at her brother, and they wrestled on the ground. She wrapped her hands around his throat, the pressure of her thumb pressing deep into his trachea. He choked back air, fought to grab anything in his reach, and when he found a branch charred on one end from resting in the fire, he hit her in the face.

She fumbled backward, screaming as hot ash fell into her eyes. Unable to see, she cried out. Anytime she tried opening them, it felt like thousands of small shards were tearing into her vision. She rubbed and rubbed, but it only made it worse. And before she knew, it Pat was standing over her, a blurred shadow with his arms in the air and something in his hands. He swung down, bashing her skull between the stone floor and a large brick, almost too heavy for him to have held, but he was seething, and rage guided his actions, fueled an otherworldly strength that, when he swung, he thought nothing of the consequence.

Pat stood over his sister, her head crushed under the weight of the stone. As if coming out of a dark trance, he fell to her side. "No, no, no, no, no. Trish ...?" He collected the pieces—brain bits, skull fragments, chunks of flesh strewn across the floor—and began trying to put her together. "No, no, no, no no no nononono. Trish? *Patricia!*" He fell over her corpse and wailed.

Pat heard his words but with Trish's voice in the wind: *I saved you.*

He awoke to gusts of air forced downward beneath the wide wingspan of vultures gathering around. Pat crawled backward, cowering against a wall, holding his legs. He sobbed, watching the giant birds begin pecking at Trish's corpse, tearing away her clothes in small pieces and digging into her meat.

Patrick. Are you going to just let them eat me like that?

Pat glanced to his left to see a figment of his sister manifesting.

He buried his head in his knees to wipe her from his imagination, and instead the sounds of the winged beasts—digging into her torso, pulling back her bones, coupled with the raspy hisses and grunts of satisfaction—consumed the empty spaces of his mind.

DAYS LATER, PAT RETURNED TO HAYAM. He didn't know how he managed to find his way back—most of the journey he walked with a hazy mind, wavering in and out of consciousness—but the city on the cliffside came into view.

"We made it," he said to his sister, manifesting an image of her to stand at his side as if she, too, were gazing at the city. Trish's image gave a soft smile.

Laine is going to want to know where I am, she said and disappeared.

Pat wouldn't reach Hayam for another thirty minutes or so. The business of the town overwhelmed him; the silence of his journey without Trish was somber. He could feel himself fading into his body as he navigated the streets to the alleyway where Laine had set up at the back of the pawn shop. He rested his knuckles on the door, pausing momentarily, and then knocked in a distinctive pattern.

The door eased open, and Pat walked into a dark room, the sunlight barely providing enough light through the fogged, barred windows. As Pat shut the door behind himself, locking it, he thought about leaving. The guilt and grief he was feeling was pulling him to the snowy desert beyond the canyon, to wander the icy landscape and strip himself bare.

"Why aren't you trailing Treasta?" Laine asked.

Pat leaned into the door, his hand grasping the handle was the only thing holding himself up. He was afraid if he let go, he would collapse. And he didn't want Laine to see him cry.

Buck up, Patrick. I can't protect you now.

Pat swallowed, took a deep breath, and exhaled. He faced Laine who stood about a foot taller than him with scruff on his face and arms crossed.

"We ran into Davan. He was on the boat."

"And where's Trish?"

Pat lowered his gaze but held a stoic face. "Davan threw her into the river. I jumped in after her to save her, but she didn't know how to swim. When I pulled her to shore it was too late. She's … dead."

"That's …," he trailed off, "a shame. She was quite good to have around."

"I'd have gone after Davan, but there wasn't any way I could catch up to the boat. I wouldn't have been able to find them in Wesser if I couldn't stay on their trail. But Treasta, I don't think she knows we're not trailing her. Do you think Davan was following her, too?"

Laine, thumb at his lip while thinking, shrugged. "This is what I want you to do," he said. "You're going to go to Maward and wait for Treasta, then you'll escort her here. If she resists, remind her of our deal. Does she know about Trish?"

His phantom sister leaned on the wall, smirking as she watched him.

"No," he said. Answering anything in connection with his sister was like swallowing stones.

"Good. You'll let her know Trish is watching nearby ready with an arrow should she do anything stupid. Understood?"

"But what if she doesn't return?"

"I'm feeling confident she will. Treasta is always one good for her word."

Trish floated around Pat. *Smart, Patrick, pinning it on Davan like that.* Her laugh echoed in his ears. *If you're going to lie, may as well weave some truth in there. Makes it more believable. Maybe you're not so useless.*

Pat pressed his palms into his eyes and groaned. "Shut up," he said. "Shut up, shut up, shut up."

Laine cocked his head. "Shut up?" He took a step closer and leaned toward him, his face just a breadth away.

"No, no. Not you. Sorry, I keep hearing this buzzing in my ear. I think it's from the river water. Maybe a bug."

Laine straightened. And after a long pause, he said, "What are you still doing here? Go."

Pat hurried, gathering supplies, and left.

His sister's voice ghostly lingered. *Don't worry,* she said, *I'll keep you company.*

40

A STAR-FILLED NIGHT CONQUERED THE DAY; the moon, round with a fullness, hung low near the horizon. Its silvery yellow sheen lit the docks as Treasta and Chimes sneaked—her balance not quite what it used to be, she nearly fell into the lake. Chimes caught her by her sleeve, and swiftly they hid behind a tarp covering an upside-down skiff as footsteps of a nearby watchman echoed. A lantern on his waist, he whistled a tune as he passed by on his round. How many watchmen guarded the boats, they didn't know, so they waited to see if another would pass. Thirty minutes later, a different man showed up, carrying his lantern in his hand. He looked around more cautiously than the other and carried on.

Two watchman and thirty minutes between rounds—that was all they had. Sound carried too easily in the night and across the water; both Treasta and Chimes worried over whether stealing the skiff they hid behind could be possible. They'd have to pull the tarp off, flip it over, and get it into the water without a sound. Impossible. Treasta thought for a moment. They would have to incapacitate at least one of the watchmen; the more laxed fellow, whistling and paying no mind to his surroundings, would be the easier target.

"Wait here," she told Chimes, and crept alone in the direction from where the patrol would come.

Treasta squatted behind a post, waiting for the man to return. A low whistle echoed an unfamiliar tune. She retrieved the phial from the pocket strapped beneath her dress, uncorked it, and as the man approached, he stopped, yawned, and Treasta crept up behind him and reached around his head, placing the phial beneath his nose. Instantly he collapsed. She unclipped the lamp, set it aside, and struggled dragging the heavily limp body behind a stack of crates.

Treasta retrieved the lamp and returned to Chimes. She knelt next to him and dimmed the light until the flame disappeared. "Once the next watchman passes, we'll have an hour to get out of sight."

"What did you do?" he asked in a quiet voice. "You didn't kill the man, did you?"

"You really think I would just murderer someone out right?"

"You said you've killed someone before. So, I don't know, maybe—"

She hushed him. She didn't want to talk about it, not now.

So they waited in silence for the second watchman to make his round. The lake was eerily still, the wind absent. His boots were the only sound as he neared. He moved with a slowness the other watchman didn't have, careful, suspecting of anything and everything; the slightest sound would be enough to draw his attention. There was no way Treasta could get behind him as easily as the other. He would certainly notice her and have her cuffed in no time.

Ten minutes passed since the watchman continued along the docks. Treasta pulled Chimes back down as he stood. "Give it a bit longer. We got to make sure he's far enough away."

He was getting anxious; she could see it in how he fidgeted with the charm's chain, pulling it away from his neck as if it were burning him. His knee uncontrollably shook. She grabbed it, forcing it still, then squeezed to assure him everything would be all right.

After a few more minutes passed, Treasta and Chimes untied the tarp, pulling it back to reveal the rowboat underneath. They heaved it onto its side, rolling it into the water. The light from the watchman's lantern continued along its normal path; it appeared the two remained undetected. Chimes breathed out a long, much needed sigh of relief. He had spent years as a nomad, taking from travelers as he needed, giving away trinkets and goods to those less fortunate. He didn't need his father's inheritance. He never cared about it. Living freely in the wilderness, interacting with travelers, and helping people—those were his passions. Had he taken Treasta's money, he'd have just given away what he didn't need. But this, fleeing a city and being accused of murder, wasn't the same.

Chimes stepped into the skiff first, and Treasta passed him the ores. He took her hand as she stepped carefully into the vessel. Pushing off from the dock, Chimes rowed, and they slipped from the Great Lake City undetected.

The flame behind the glass in the oil lamp came to life as Treasta twisted the key. Far from the city, a great relief washed over them, finally feeling safe from officials hunting Chimes. Treasta watched the shadows in his face reform in the flickering light, wondering what he was thinking behind those violet eyes, how he must be coming apart behind such a well-managed façade. But he wasn't. Chimes had compartmentalized his father's death just as he had done with his father's life. She wasn't sure whether to bring Gustas up in conversation and discuss what had happened over the past week or to let her apology be enough.

In the quiet of the night, an anxiousness overtook her; what had triggered the feeling, she didn't know, but she felt herself fading into her mind, her surroundings becoming blurred and peripheral vision disappearing. It was like looking through a scope with a fogged lens. Treasta closed her eyes, trying to collect herself. Maybe she was just overwhelmed with everything that had happened since leaving Galgaya and since Davan left. Maybe it was her body not knowing how to maintain itself while with child. Or maybe she *was* dying. It had been one situation after another. She didn't know how she had survived this long, with Chimes, with Davan, on her own—the infant squirmed, pressing itself against her organs—and she was beginning to wonder why she deserved Chimes' kindness. Kind. Yes, that was what Chimes was—a simple word with so much meaning, and so unfamiliar to Treasta.

Slowly, Treasta opened her eyes, reacquainting herself with the lamp, the skiff, the ores Chimes tirelessly rowed. Her gaze drifted to the stars, searching the black as if the stars could provide her answers for her feelings, as if they carried knowledge. Treasta could feel herself wanting to withdraw from Chimes, from whatever this reality was, from his kindness.

"It was one man," Treasta said. She hoped talking would distract her from the knot in her stomach. She needed to ground herself, to feel something other than the developing heels of a babe impressing into her insides. Treasta's fingers curled around the bench, the rough woodgrains like sand against her skin. "I only killed one person, intentionally."

Chimes stopped rowing. He gave her his full attention.

"His name was Lodan, and he was the former chief of our guild. Davan loved Lodan like a son does a father. And Lodan doted on him. I'm not sure why. Lodan made Davan do awful things. It was changing him. He was becoming mean. He'd push me around, spoke to me like he owned me. So," she shrugged, "I poisoned his drink. The way Davan was acting, it was unlike him. Or I thought. But now I think that Lodan just brought out the worst in him, a side of him that has always existed. He just didn't know. We don't talk about Lodan in the guild. There are rumors about what happened and who did it, but there's no proof. Rumors they must stay."

Chimes, unblinking, watched the current's resistance against the ores' paddles unmoving in the water.

"You killed a man because you loved Davan," he said, though it wasn't quite clear whether it was meant as a question. But his voice, the flatness, the matter-of-factness chilled Treasta to the point of regret.

"I don't know if I did love Davan," Treasta said, staring into the flame dancing on the wick. "He took care of me when I needed help. And I wanted to take care of him. But I think he's made it clear that he doesn't want that anymore."

Chimes swung his legs over the boat, stepping into shallow water and pulling it ashore, the vessel's bottom scraping on countless stones. It was morning. He rowed far enough that Wesser had disappeared behind a haze. Chimes rubbed the sore muscles in his arms; Treasta collapsed on the riverbank, the water lapping over her hands on the cold shore. She clutched handfuls of rocks and pebbles rounded with time. She was exhausted, and now the sun was blooming in the east, casting long shadows from the outcropping overhang just yards away. She folded into her knees and pulled the stony bank with her.

Treasta shot up, a high-pitched scream echoed across the water; she flung handfuls of rocks, hundreds of ripples breaking its mirrored sheen. She struck the ground with her fists.

Chimes came to her side.

"Do not touch me," she snapped.

He stepped back.

Too furious to move, she clutched the earth. Thoughts of failure rolled through her mind. Davan, Elsie, the Pats, Laine, the golden flute and the baby, Chimes—images flashed so fast she became dizzy. What now? She sat on her feet and held her stomach. Treasta's head fell; she quietly cried.

"I think it's safe to say we're not being followed," Chimes said, breaking the silence. But Treasta didn't acknowledge him.

Chimes sat down next to her, opening his bag, and shuffling through the few items he had taken from his father's apartment before fleeing. He handed her a long item wrapped in red silk.

Treasta wiped her tears on her palms and then her palms on the skirt of her dress. He placed it in her hands. It wasn't heavy, but it wasn't light either—weighty, one might say. She pulled back the silk to reveal a golden-bodied instrument etched with dwarven runes and what appeared to be a griffin. Her jaw hung open without words. The flute. He had the flute this entire time? She looked at him bewildered, a bit annoyed, but mostly in disbelief. Treasta choked up a laugh. She wrapped the instrument and held it to her chest.

"Are the stories true?" she asked. "Will I turn to gold if I play it?"

"You'd be one expensive woman, that's for sure."

They laughed, and then she shoved him. "Why didn't you tell me sooner? Here I thought my life was ruined, and you had it this entire time!"

Chimes shrugged. "I thought it'd be better to keep it tucked away. Didn't need anyone knowing I had it. I know it's not my business," he leaned on his knees and looked across the water, "but if the Pats aren't trailing us, then why are you bothering going back?"

"Something so priceless doesn't hold much value to me," she said. "Laine wants it, and Laine has what I want. I can still pay you," she said, looking at him. "Once I get the treasure, I'll take it to a broker and trade for sacks of gold. So much gold, I could pay you double—no—triple for all your help."

Chimes stood and crossed his arms. Something about how she spoke wasn't right, and he knew she was hiding something. "Do you think I'm helping you for money still?" She gazed up at him with her wide blue eyes and an expression that gave him the answer. He took his hat off, scratched his shaved head, and kicked rocks into the river. "Gods,

Treasta, I don't care about money. You should know that by now. Isn't that obvious?"

She didn't look at him, instead watching the river's smooth flow, and began counting the innumerable stones along the bank. Nervous, she cracked the bones in her hands and wrists, then her neck before burying her face in her palms to hide what was in her heart. But her eyes swelled, and she caught herself whimpering; holding back when her emotions were nearly uncontrollable was becoming more difficult. The chaos in her mind, the sense of self-loathing and defeat, consumed her, despite having exactly what she wanted in her hands. And Chimes … she was frightened, knowing that she would lose him when the time came to find the witch and to go back to Galgaya. He'd tell her to stay with him in Wesserland, but she didn't want that. Wesserland wasn't home.

When he realized something wasn't right, he knelt at her side, put his arm around her, and lowered her hands from her face, holding them. He held her gaze with his, searching for what plagued her thoughts. But Chimes didn't understand. "Did I do something wrong?" He replayed every interaction they had since reuniting at the citadel to his waiting for her outside the temple.

She shook her head, her hands tightening around his. "He promised on his grave he would always protect me. *Davan promised me.* The flute meant more to him than I ever did."

"And what of my promise?" Chimes asked. "What of our promise? Have I left you yet?"

"No," she said quietly. "But that doesn't mean you won't."

"Treasta," her name danced from his lips, "you don't know what you do to me." His hands rested gently on her cheeks, and he looked at her mouth before gazing into her eyes again. "I don't know how to tell you I can't stop thinking about you. I see your face in the reflections of mirrors and lakes and rivers and you make my heart feel as full as the sky is vast. This between us is a fleeting dream, and I have yet to wake. And when I do wake, all of this"—he waved his arms—"none of it will be real. But"—his chest expanded as he inhaled; his breath quivered as he exhaled—"if this is a dream, let me sleep forever."

"You speak like love is something beautiful. How can someone be so earnest?" she said, wanting to taste him as he neared. She pulled him by his neck. "But I'm sorry. It's so hard to think straight right now. I am in no condition to love and be loved."

His forehead fell into hers, his fingers tangling the strands of her hair as he cupped her head at the nape of her neck. "There's nothing to be sorry for," Chimes said.

"So much has happened," she said, trying to fight the lustful pull bringing her closer to him. And so much had happened since Davan left. She had thought the walls of her mind would crumble, and that she'd retreat into its recesses never to emerge. Her life seemed over, but somehow, Chimes' presence soothed her. He made breathing easier, gave her affection in ways Davan never tried, showed her empathy and compassion. Chimes never shied away from his own vulnerability and owned his humility.

Their kiss was gentle, cautious, like they were tasting each other for the first time again. She grabbed the lapels of his tunic, licked her lips, and pulled away. Her face felt hot; a pulsing between her legs made breathing his air intoxicating. "We—" her voice, low, shook with desire, "No." And she grabbed a hand that had slinked under her skirt and up her legs. "The babe … I'm just far too overwhelmed right now. You make it harder for me to think."

His laugh was light and airy, with a hint of playfulness. He adjusted his trousers. "Yes, ma'am," he said. "As you say."

She flashed him an amused glance, her smile and laugh filling his soul. "Ma'am? How old do I look to you?" A gentle nudge sent him rolling onto his back. He pulled her down with him, and they lay, hand in hand, looking at the clouds.

INTERLUDE

THE COOL WHITE OF MOONLIGHT STRUCK AGEMON'S EYES. He held the attention of his councilors who gathered in a hall set with a long table crafted with ivory legs and long-backed chairs, except for one. The men were silent, yet to don their mourning garb in a city that had yet to learn of Gustas' death. His vacant seat, draped in a gray veil, was given space at the head of the table opposite of Agemon's pearl-laden throne. The Eight, along with the magistrate, bowed their heads and honored in private the life of the fallen councilor. They lifted their goblets, asked Alia to forgive Gustas of any atrocities he committed in life and to accept him for all the love and benevolence he gifted the world.

"Gustas was a good man," said the magistrate who stood above the others, goblet in the air. "Let us mourn our beloved councilor, a brilliant inventor who gifted us with immeasurable talent. May he be remembered. As always."

"As always," the Eight echoed, and they waited for Agemon to bring his goblet to his lips before following suit. Together they drank and remembered the brilliant man.

Agemon set his goblet onto the long table, straightened his stoles, and remained standing. "Reports show Darius Gustassan has fled Wesser. Now," Agemon folded his hands behind his back and paced the room, "we must decide: do we pursue Darius Gustassan?" Angry, Agemon clutched his fists. He had many plans, all borne from Gustas' inventions, for Wesser, for the future, and the re-expansion and rebirth of the Wesserian Empire.

One councilor stood. "Magistrate, investigations show that Gustas and his son, Darius, were estranged."

"Yes," said another. "But, Councilor Gustas' wealth—the dwarven artifacts he coveted—had clearly tempted the estranged Darius. Action must be taken."

"We have control over the assets," said the first councilor. "There's no reason to pursue this Darius. It would be a waste of time, resources, money. Let us be honest, only you and I had met him the night before Gustas' death. Why should we bother pursuing a son who wanted nothing to do with his father until the other day?"

"Gustas spoke of his son with love," said the second councilor. "He wanted nothing more than to share his life with Darius. And this is what he gets? What *we* get? Wesser will regress without Gustas' genius. The Iragians will take advantage of our loss. Our empire," he said more quietly, "will fail."

Another shook his head. "I disagree. We have Gustas' blueprints. We own his genius. We simply need to hire another genius to continue his work. Our technological advances will continue so long as we can control what we produce. The Iragians want our technology; they want our weapons and transportation. So long as Gustas' work stays behind these walls, the Iragians are at our beck and call."

"The dwarves' most prized asset is missing. What say you about that?" interrogated someone.

"Only we know it's missing. I say we keep it that way."

Magistrate Agemon quieted the room with a wave of his hand as everyone began talking among themselves. They were worried, scared even, of what could happen without Gustas. "Rumors are spreading," he said, "of Gustas' death. We must announce our loss before we can no longer control the narrative."

A third councilor stood, his fists bashing the table. "Someone must answer to this atrocity, do you not see? If we do not show no mercy, then the laymen of Wesser will take it upon themselves to infiltrate our homes. They will steal from us as Darius did his father. We cannot allow this Darius to become a saintly figure for the downtrodden, don't you understand?"

Another rolled his eyes. "You're acting paranoid."

Agemon leaned on his chair, having yet to sit down. He scratched his chin. "And who reported Gustas' death?"

"The valet," said another.

Khyari dusted the shelves, gently moving skulls of foxes, deer, coyotes aside. Dirt was brought on the wind, sneaking into her oddities shop through open windows and cracks in the door frame.

As she lifted a jar packed with dried herbs, she could see outside the window a crowd gathering near the announcement board. The sound of their curiosity, a cacophony of men and women's voices, rolled inside, drawing customers out of her shop.

The dwarven woman stepped down from her ladder and set the duster on the counter. Khyari watched from the window, curious. The crowd ballooned from the walkway to the street and halted the traffic of horses and carts from proceeding.

She locked up her shop, put a hat on, and went outside to investigate. Some didn't pay mind to the small dwarven woman trying to nudge her way through the crowd to see what news was so important to garner such attention, mistaking her for a child. Others refused to move, even pushed her away, scoffed, muttering something derogatory beneath their breaths. She was one of a small population of dwarven people living in the Wesserian slums—her people forced to the deep underbelly of the city. There were maybe a couple hundred dwarves living in Wesser. The rest of her kind had left these lands hundreds of years ago, and for whatever reason her clan stayed—committed to stewarding the dam their ancestors had crafted with their bare hands and genius minds. Most of them worked in the walls of the dam, keeping its integrity structurally sound, opening and closing the gates as needed. Khyari was one of the few to work within the city itself. And, mostly, things were good.

Towering over her, people shoved by with little care, eager to confirm whether the rumors were true: that Gustas was dead.

The night of the fire, flames could be seen from the city through the storm. Those in the streets stopped and looked toward the citadel aglow, Gustas' apartment in flames.

Khyari managed to wedge her way to the front, slipping through strangers' legs. And she saw it there on a poster that the death of the councilor was true, that there was a fire in his apartment, and that he was killed by a "greedy valet."

Th' valet identyfede as Bas Glennan wil be hangede at dusk at th' cytadele bayl.
Alle Wesseryan denysens ar callede upon.
By ordre of Magystere Agemonne a one-month peryode of mournyng for alle Wesseryans to begynne forthwyth. Any personne not donnyng gray per Wesseryan law wil be subjectede to charge and persecucioun.
Praysen Aliah and may th' godes favour Councellere Gustas Augustassannes soule.

Khyari wriggled from the crowd and returned to her shop, locking the shutters, shunning light from inside, and posting a sign on the door: "Closede for mournyng"—as was the law. With a low head, she dragged herself into her home adjacent to the shop through a back room. Khyari shuffled through her wardrobe and found her gray mourning robe shoved in the back. Dressing, she remembered the first time she had met Gustas, the kindness he extended to her father and the elders, the clear caution on their faces at the man—a Wesserian councilor—who pledged promises and fealty to her people.

"As always," she whispered as she stepped onto the street.

Few businesses would stay open for the next month—only those the magistrate deemed necessary, such as the bakery and the butcher. Taverns would close, but the inns would stay open for travelers. The market would be boarded up. Businesses had until the next morning before authorities would act and begin forcing stores to close. Khyari wasted no time.

At the Amethyst Aster Inn, staff already adorned their mourning garb, flames were dimmed, and the curtains drawn. The man at the front desk rolled his eyes when he saw Khyari walk inside and continued thumbing through the guest ledger, crossing off names of rooms housekeeping staff reported vacant.

At the wine bar, a sign on the door read "closede for mournyng." It was unlocked. Khyari found Cherie cleaning the counter and setting stools and chairs upside down on tables. She looked at her friend, but she didn't smile.

"I was hoping it wasn't true," Cherie said.

Khyari pulled a chair down and hopped up to sit at the bar. Cherie popped the cork on a bottle and poured a goblet for each of them.

"Are you going to the beheading?" Khyari asked.

Cherie shrugged. She took a drink. "Are you?"

"I don't know. The councilor was good to my people. He visited the underbelly often. I wouldn't have my shop if it weren't for his kindness."

A long silence came between them, and they both filled the empty space with swigs. Cherie was deep in thought, and Khyari was saddened, but she was also frustrated; she would lose customers in the coming month with no financial compensation from the city. Growing up, she had wished her clan had followed to the After Lands. Now hundreds of years have passed, and the After Lands were spoken of as legend. Rumor spoke of ships sailing northward along the Shardian Waters, up along the coast to the far north. Something about Gustas' death reminded her of her people's troubles co-existing in the city. But without the dwarves, the dam would be inoperable. Without Gustas, who knows what was to come for them and for Wesser.

Cherie set down her goblet and leaned over the counter. "You know, about ten days ago, there was this young woman in here, blonde girl from the East Lands, said you weren't very friendly with her."

Khyari let out a disgusted laugh, remembering. Forcing the blonde girl from her store brought her great satisfaction—if only she could force her back to the East Lands with that shove. "How do you know the blonde girl?"

"She was here, staying at the inn. Never came back, left all her belongings in the room, including her purse—ten sterling bits and a couple of gold coins."

"Do you think she's dead?"

Cherie shook her head. "She was asking about the golden flute."

"*The* golden flute?"

"Yes, *the golden flute.* The announcement said nothing about it, just a greedy valet." Cherie poured the rest of the bottle. "I would bet my life that girl had something to do with Gustas' death. I bet she wasn't even pregnant."

"Do you think the flute is missing, then?" Khyari asked. "Our elder entrusted it to Gustas. Gustas promised he would keep it safe in the citadel."

"If it is missing, the magistrate and the councilors are keeping it hush-hush, aren't they?"

Khyari's expression was one of dismay. Already the people of the

East Lands had stripped her ancestors of their lands and artifacts, as Agemon's ancestors invaded from the south and forced them to flee to the After Lands.

"I must go," Khyari said. "I'll see you."

"See you," Cherie said, and her friend swiftly left.

The city's slum was the neighborhood farthest from the citadel, near the water but away from the docks. The dwarven population dwelled along the dam's wall in buildings built directly into the structure. Inside this hidden city it smelled damp and old, the sunlight but a faded ambiance of blue reflecting off the lake, the golden glow of fire lighting walls day and night. Gustas gave the dwarves many resources to help the population get by, including his own money he earned from his work. He was their patron, and the elders were grateful.

Khyari, the daughter of an elder, called for her father, where outside the door, a dwarven man stood watch.

"Leave," he said. "The elders are busy."

"Let me in," she said. "I am Elder Darral's daughter, Khyari. And I have urgent news for the elders."

But he wouldn't let her pass. He shoved her away, and she fell to the floor.

The door opened. Her red-bearded father stood at the threshold, his large hand still on the door. "What is this noise about?"

"Father!" Khyari jumped to her feet.

Darral's thick brows turned into a scowl as he looked at the man. "You dare assault my daughter?"

"Sir, you said *no one* was to disturb you," the guardsman said.

Darral helped Khyari to her feet. "My daughter is well-mannered enough to know to only disturb me if it is important." And he and Khyari disappeared into a room with a wide, arching window and a round table where four other elders of various ages sat.

They stood, greeting Khyari with a nod and returned to their seats. It had been a long time since she had seen any of them. The grand elder sat in the largest chair, its log back shadowed by the light from the window behind him. His white hair braided over his shoulders, he placed his arms on the rests and watched Khyari enter with just his eyes, which had faded from blue to gray since the last time she had seen him.

"Khyari, I see you're in your mourning grays," the grand elder said. "Then you know of Gustas' passing."

Darral fetched a chair for his daughter, but she refused to sit, the news too grave.

"What is this about?" another elder asked. "Why do you interrupt our council?"

Her gaze fell. Relaying the information was like announcing another death. "The Oria"—as the golden flute was named—"I believe it to be gone."

A couple of the elders stood.

"Gustas and now the flute? It can't be," one said.

"Do you suppose that is what the valet took? If so, would it not be in the magistrate's care?" another asked.

The grand elder raised his hands and hushed them. "Khyari," he lifted his brows, leaning forward, "are you sure?"

"Yes, Grand Elder," she said. "But I do not believe the valet was responsible. I believe a woman from the East Lands stole the Oria. My friend spoke of a woman staying at an inn who was asking about the flute. It cannot be a coincidence that Gustas is dead."

"We've never trusted the council," Darral said. He stood next to his daughter. "Why should we believe them now?"

"Without Gustas, our people will suffer," an elder said. "He is the one who convinced us to stand down from our attack. He promised to take care of our people in return. I knew entrusting him with our artifacts—and the Oria—was foolish. I say it is time. Agemon would sooner see us fall from the very dam our ancestor's built."

"There are thousands of people in Wesser. What makes you think we could do anything?" Khyari asked. "I agree. The council must pay, but we are few and they are many."

Everyone looked to their grand elder who stood. He grabbed a walking stick and balanced himself with his other hand on his chair. "Let the girl know," he said.

"Khyari," her father placed his hand on her shoulder, "for decades we have been tunnelling through the wall with great care, and not long before Gustas came to the city, we reached the citadel. Gustas said he would take care of our people and in return we would not invade the stronghold. But," he looked to the others as if for confirmation. The grand elder nodded. "They are right. Without Gustas, our situation will worsen. We must act." He then turned his attention to the elders.

Anyone who wasn't already standing came to his feet. "The councilors and Agemon will be distracted tonight during the execution. We must strike while they are weak. There are thousands of people living in Wesser, yes, but there are hundreds of us willing to go against the citadel. Once inside, we will have the upper hand. I say we strike!"

The others pounded their fists on the table, and Khyari felt the rumble moving the floor through her feet. "For the Oria!" she shouted.

"For Gustas!" shouted another.

Darral climbed atop the table. "For Clan Blacthorne!"

"FOR CLAN BLACTHORNE!"

Thousands gathered, shoulder to shoulder, cramming into the bailey and spilling into the promenade leading up to the citadel as the lowering sun kissed the horizon good night, and the sky was stripped of day with streaks of fire splaying from beyond the world's edge.

As the council appeared, eight men plus the magistrate atop a balcony overlooking the bailey, the crowd roared with anticipation. From inside, a man donning a bag over his head was guided to the slab. The chanting of onlookers echoed off the citadel's walls, broke through the streets, and poured over the dam.

Agemon raised his arms, and a wave of silence fell over the crowd, leaving only the resounding caw of crows perched along the walls to echo over the citadel.

Upon seeing the alleged murderer and council, some people whispered among their peers, curious and casting judgment.

"Know we—the Council of Wesser—do not tolerate such crime!" Agemon's voice carried on the breeze. "I, Agemon Tressan, judge of Wesser, condemn Bass Glennan to death for the slaying of Councilor Gustas Augustassan. Punishment: death by beheading."

The valet fell to his knees, the executioner pressing his head against the cold slab.

The executioner lifted his ax, his gaze on the magistrate awaiting the order.

Instead, three guards rushed from the citadel, one whispering in Agemon's ear.

The executioner stood down; the valet was taken away, and the crowd booed.

No one knew what was going on, when officials began rushing everyone from the citadel, many refusing to move as they demanded answers that were then met with threats.

The magistrate and council retreated inside.

Agemon clutched his fist when his eyes befell hundreds of dwarves standing over the bodies of nearly every on-duty guard.

"What is the meaning of this?" the magistrate asked through a clinched jaw.

Darral and the other elders appeared before him, donning finely crafted and polished armor etched with runes and images of their ancestors' stories. They held their weapons drawn at the ready: ancient swords and axes, newly crafted crossbows.

"This citadel," Darral's voice boomed, "now belongs to Clan Blacthorne."

"Clan Blacthorne!" his men echoed.

The unarmed councilors backed into one another, looking to Agemon for answers. Agemon's teeth grinded inside his skull. Here he had been worried about the Iragians when he had failed to consider what the dwarves would plan without Gustas' presence. A coup, of course, but this soon? Yes, Agemon knew of Gustas' partisanship with Clan Blacthorne, but he did not realize to what extent his dead councilor's sway and advocacy extended.

Agemon cleared his throat, straightening his stance as he held the lapels of his suit jacket. "You think we will hand over Wesser to you?"

Darral smirked and cocked his head. "I have men awaiting my orders. Should you resist, expect your precious city and dam destroyed."

"You wouldn't dare destroy something your ancestors have tirelessly maintained."

"You don't understand," Darral said as he stepped forward. "This clan," and he waved his spanning arms as he gestured at the hundreds of dwarves flanking him, "is a collective. The elders do not do anything without their vote. And do you want to know how the people voted if it means their freedom?"

Agemon and his council were silent.

Darral nodded, slowly, his mouth parting as he said, "Ah, that's what I thought."

But half of the council protested, charging toward Darral and the others, their anger and resistance to fall to the dwarves driving their movements. But they stood down as soon as they were met with the sharp points of finely sharpened blades. Darral scowled. The rest of his people, the children and the women, had retreated from the city to higher ground. The elders expected nothing less from Agemon and his councilmen.

Darral shouted in dwarven to his fellow men, "Blow the dam!"

Khyari was at her father's side. "But my friends—there are innocent people," she said. "You can't."

"Casualties for the cause. Honor your friends for their goodness."

Khyari took several steps back, looking her father over, not realizing the severity of his intentions to reclaim Wesser. Tens of thousands of people dead: the thought was paralyzing. She was too distraught to cry, too angry, too confused. Khyari's grip around her blade tightened. She rushed at her father, but he rammed the pommel of his sword into her stomach. Dropping her blade, Khyari fell to her knees, grasping her torso.

This was the plan all along. Regardless of whether Agemon handed over Wesser, the elders had already decided to destroy the dam. They understood that their ancestors' blood and sweat spilled over this city, this citadel, that they had bled for their descendants to be banished into the shadowy underbelly. Their souls were built into the walls of Wesser like some kind of curse. To cling to the dam was to cling to an empty promise for a future their people never had, for a structure they were enslaved to.

A rumble reverberated from deep below, the vibrations shaking the citadel.

"You'll kill us all," Agemon said.

"No," said Darral, "We will kill you. The citadel," his voice lowered, "will be unscathed. Why do you think it was built where it is? Our ancestors were brilliant architects and even more brilliant engineers. You, Agemon, failed to see that. Do you know why Gustas promised to care for our treasures?" Silence. "Because he knew this night would come if anything happened to him."

The councilors looked to one another with widening eyes. Their fear painted their countenances as a series of blasts within the dam went off—one, two, three . . .—becoming increasingly louder with each blow, and the city shook with such intensity that the cries and screams of the people could be heard.

Cracks snaked up the dam's wall. The earth shook. Everyone in the citadel braced themselves; the dwarven women and children who retreated to the high grounds, held one another, watching their home crumble as the mighty roar of the Great Lake crashed through Wesser, the dam, and into the valley below. It would take hours for the lake to drain, and the towns downstream would be swept away in its wake, the land would be reshaped in the night. Casualties for the cause … They would be honored in ceremony, a mass funeral, where all of Clan Blacthorne gathered at the high grounds, dragging with them the councilors and magistrate.

AT DAWN, DARRAL LINED THE WESSERIAN LEADERS, wrists bound behind their backs, along a precipice and pointed with his sword to the crumbled dam below. Gagged, they stared upon the ruins, where dots of survivors gathered along the draining lake's edge. From the center of the destroyed dam, a perpetual waterfall drained into the valley below.

One by one, Darral lowered their heads to the earth.

One by one, he swung down.

Agemon, on his knees, held his composure as his councilors' heads rolled. Refusing to look at the city, refusing to meet the elders' eyes, he fixed his gaze to the rising sun as a blade ripped through his back. Light seared Agemon's vision, and the grand elder split the magistrate down his center.

41

Many suns rose and set before Treasta and Chimes reached the Sarnak. On their journey, they came across little semblance of civilization, stopping where they could find supplies in several abandoned settlements and old mining encampments long picked over by scavengers. Treasta undressed, cleaned, and redressed Chimes' wound. The pain in his arm had yet to ease, made worse by hours of rowing days earlier. Chimes flexed his hand, rotated his wrist, and bent his elbow slowly to keep his limb from stiffening, but the slightest movement caused his arm to ache. She kissed him after each change of bandage.

They settled down just inside the entrance of a mineshaft at the river's edge. Old mine carts were stacked aside, some upside down; broken lamps and mining supplies were scattered along the shaft. While there was some daylight left, Treasta turned items over, looking for anything that could be of use to them. She found some felled boards and hauled those to the entrance. Chimes appeared with a bundle of sticks, and with their combined supplies, they built a fire. The tight walls of the mine helped contain the heat as a cold night crept upon them. Treasta and Chimes held one another for warmth, and she drifted asleep, while he stayed awake most of the night, mind clouded with thoughts of being followed despite knowing they weren't. With each night they rested,

Chimes reined in his thoughts, noting that had the Wesserian authorities been following them, he would have been apprehended by now. He was more anxious over whether Davan and Elsie lurked somewhere in the dark, waiting for just the right moment to strike, again. Chimes knew it wasn't true, that it would have been impossible to pursue them beyond the docks, that Davan and Elsie couldn't have gone undetected on the water. But it didn't stop him from thinking about it.

The image of his father lying on the floor of the treasure chamber consumed his mind, as Gustas' face began to take shape in the shadows cast on the stony wall: the fire poker lodged in his father's jaw, his father gasping, and the fear in his eyes.

Chimes drew a long breath, looked up, shut his eyes, and exhaled. He focused on the warmth Treasta shared with his, her breath breaking through the linen of his tunic, and how her hair splayed across his chest. In and out, he synchronized his breathing with hers. She sighed, muttered something in her sleep, and clutched his shirt. Chimes grabbed her hand.

Treasta sniffled and let out a quiet cry until her sobbing jolted her awake to her tears staining Chimes' tunic. Disoriented she looked around. The crackling sounds of the fire and Chimes' smell helped reorient her. Tiredly, she met his gaze. He hadn't slept, and the days of minimal sleep were showing in the dark circles under his eyes. He passed her a soft smile, and she laid her head down.

"I was dreaming," she said. "I don't remember what, but I feel nothing but utter sadness now, like I relived something awful."

Chimes rested his head on hers. "It was just a dream. Only a dream."

"When I joined the Triple Gang, they were unkind to me in ways I cannot describe," Treasta spoke quietly. "It is when I recall those memories that I feel this kind of sadness, an inescapable sadness bred from terror and hopelessness. I don't know if there was a night I'd not cry myself to sleep. If I'm to cry, I don't want to sleep." She sat up, positioning herself next to Chimes. "You should rest. You need it more than I do right now."

"I don't want to sleep," he said. "I can't sleep."

Her hand was soft on his cheek. "What ails you?"

Chimes looked to the sky. The glare from the firelight hid the stars from his vision. "The other day, you said it's hard to think straight. Well, I'm having the same problem. I can't get the image out of my head. My father was just lying there helpless. He couldn't even scream."

He hadn't spoken about his father since his death. Chimes' voice cracked as he spoke, and he cleared his throat to collect himself as he paused. Treasta was silent, her hands falling to his.

Chimes continued: "She …" Trying to describe the fire poker in his father's jaw was more difficult than he expected. He gestured the motion instead. "Just right through him with the poker. It went right through his jaw." The image was one of the worst things he had witnessed. He thought he could suppress it, believed that if he just ignored the thoughts and his feelings that it would all just go away. Years it took for him to become numbed from his father's absence. And now he truly was gone.

"I need to tell Dee," he said. "He needs to know Gustas is dead."

Resting his head on her chest, Chimes wrapped his arms around Treasta and succumbed to her warmth as he wept.

Sunlight filled the mineshaft, waking Treasta and Chimes. The fire had put itself out at some point in the night. Several crows gathered on a dead tree's branch, chattering among themselves about the dawn, then flapped away as Treasta emerged from the mine. She rubbed her eyes, stretched, and walked to the river to freshen up and hydrate. But as her vision cleared, she saw the river's flow had dropped several feet overnight.

Treasta called for Chimes, and he appeared next to her to witness the dramatic water-level change. A chill ran through his bones.

"What do you suppose happened?" Treasta asked.

Chimes swallowed. "I can't say for sure, but I think the dam failed."

He recalled the conversation about his inheritance with his father just hours before the party. They were again in the treasure chamber, and Gustas showed him his most precious items and explained their origins—nearly all of dwarven make.

"It's more than your typical inheritance, Darius. It comes with responsibility: you would take my place among the Nine should you accept it. And per my will, for you to collect your inheritance, you must because these treasures, they are neither mine nor yours. They belong to Clan Blacthorne."

"Clan Blacthorne?"

"For centuries Clan Blacthorne has endured oppression ever since Agemon's an-

cestors waged war. After Agemon's ancestors took control of these lands, the dwarves fled northwardly by ship to a place they call the After Lands. Clan Blacthorne stayed behind. There are maybe a few hundred or so living and working within the dam.

"When I arrived, I met with the clan's elders, listened and heard their requests and demands. It was more than any councilor had done before me. As I befriended and gained the elders' trust, I learned of their secrets, sat in on their meetings. They wanted to infiltrate the citadel, kill the Nine and Agemon, and destroy the dam. But because I fulfilled some of their requests with the council, the elders agreed to stand down their attack. I promised to continue to advocate on their behalf among the council, and in return the elders agreed to peace.

"I am hoping soon that the Nine will become the Ten. I am working with others who want Clan Blacthorne, the very clan whose ancestors built Wesser, to have a seat at the long table. It may take another year, but the committee is hopeful."

"And my inheritance?"

"Yes, your inheritance is to care for the treasures, to continue my life's work, and to maintain peace between the council and Clan Blacthorne. The elders have entrusted me with their treasures—safer within my chambers are they than in the drab underbelly of the dam.

"And the flute—the Oria—it is their most prized possession."

The dam didn't fail, Chimes knew this, but he never believed his father when he said Clan Blacthorne wanted to destroy Wesser. Gustas was too good for Chimes, too good for any of them, really, and too good for this world.

"The dam failed?" Treasta looked to Chimes who covered his mouth as he yawned. "Like it broke or something?"

"Something like that."

42

It was the middle of the night when Davan awoke to find Elsie sitting on the floor, polishing coins from Mr. Grall's purse, and stacking them in sets of five to count.

"Don't know why people bother with working," she said without looking up. Elsie had heard him stirring on the cot. "Taking things is always easier."

"Not for everyone," Davan said as he sat up.

He went to the mirror and combed through his hair with his fingers, resituating its part and patting the greasy locks down. He tucked his hair behind his ears, gave himself a hard look, and realized he didn't recognize himself—not just physically. Maybe it was because Treasta left him, but he no longer felt like the Davan who left Galgaya those months ago. He ran his hand down his face, felt the valleys and hills of scars along his chin.

Sitting near Elsie, he crossed his arms. "Sometimes we do what we got to do to get by."

"So is this," and she waved her hand around, "is this to get by?"

Davan clicked his tongue and rolled his eyes. "Aren't we all here for the same thing?"

"Joining the guild," Elsie said, looking at Davan briefly, "did you do it to survive?"

"Didn't you?"

She had her hand in the purse, retrieving another coin, when she froze. Elsie ran her tongue along her broken tooth, sharp like a dagger. "I wanted to keep an eye on Ida."

"You and Ida never talk. Why?"

Thirty-six coins she counted. The glimmer of their freshly polished sheen calmed her. But she didn't answer him. Elsie dropped the money into the purse one at a time, listening to each one's plop.

Ida had found his way to the guild long before Elsie. When exactly he joined Dubilee, she wasn't sure. After going on the lam, she had lost track of where her little brother went. The orphanage had no record of him. On three separate occasions she checked, but tired of her loitering they ordered her never to return, threatening to call upon the guards. With nowhere to stay, Elsie had found shelter in Galgaya's Backwall Slums; she lived there for some number of years, unsure of for how many. Time seemed to pass differently.

It must have been a decade when Elsie again saw her brother, a teenaged cadet patrolling with city guards through the slums. Ida was tall for his age, slender. His dark hair was braided down his back, so long that it looked as if he hadn't cut it since childhood. She wouldn't have recognized him if it weren't for half his left eyebrow not grown in because of a scar from an accident he had playing too rough with the neighbor's guard dog. She wondered how the years would have changed him—whether he'd look more like their father or mother as he eased toward adulthood. He didn't look like either of them, though.

Elsie trailed Ida for weeks, following his every move. Some nights he wouldn't return to his adoptive family's townhouse—he was now the son of a city guard. It took some time to figure out where he had been going; until one day, Elsie followed him into an inn at the town square. Ida had gone into the cellar, but when Elsie went to confront him, he was gone. There was nothing but shelves of wine, liquor, and dried goods in the room. She felt around eventually to find hinges tucked away behind a shelving unit. When the door opened, a tunnel appeared before her. But before Elsie had a chance to follow her brother, a man had appeared behind her.

Lodan.

Ida and Elsie never talked.

She was in Lodan's office inside the hideout, waiting alone for her brother to walk inside. But instead, the thief-king appeared without her brother, lowly shook his head as he shut the door behind himself, and told her that for her to stay, she would need to prove herself.

So, she did, one night creeping into the very homestead belonging to the family that had adopted Ida. Late that evening, she slipped inside, slithered up the stairs to find the wife readying for bed and crept behind her, so silent that the woman did not see the bludgeon coming, then to awake bound and gagged in a wardrobe. Elsie, rocking back in a chair, awaited the captain's return. She refused to do it while the man slept. She owed him the courtesy to know his life was ending.

Hearing the echo of the front door opening and shutting from downstairs, Elsie relaxed the chair on all four legs, crossed the crook of her right knee over her left, leaned forward. Snaps and cracks in the floorboards resounded up the stairwell and down the hall. The captain opened the door, cruising across the room without noticing Elsie in the dark. *Thump*—a chest plate landing on the floor. He winced, turned to see if his noise stirred his wife awake then paused when noticing the linens on the made bed undisturbed. He reached for his blade, grasping at air, forgetting he unbelted it in the foyer. His gaze scanned the room, until stopping on a figure, masked in shadow, seated near the wardrobe.

"I wanted to thank you for taking care of Ida," Elsie's voice was low, cold.

His chest expanded as he drew in a long breath as he squinted to see better in the low light. A slight, small woman with long dark hair held out of her face with a pale bandana. "Do I know you?"

Elsie leaned over her crossed legs, resting her arms on her knee. Her hands dangled on delicate wrists free of weapons.

"You're Elisandra."

A brief smirk flashed on her face but disappeared just as quickly hearing the name she had long abandoned.

"Where is my wife?"

She was busy examining him, the wrinkles around his eyes and mouth—she would never forget thinking about how many times a man with such pronounced crow's feet must smile and laugh, laughs he would have shared with boyhood Ida, for such ravines to carve themselves.

"Safe," she said and knocked on the side of the wardrobe.

Hands tightened into fists, he rushed for the wardrobe—*snap!* An iron trap sunk its rusted teeth into a meaty calf, and the captain toppled over, belting out a terrible wail.

Elsie stood. His eyes—the whites exposed, the way he watched in fear as she stood over him—the memory would sear her mind. Living the life she lived, apathy had become second nature, numbness consuming her since the day she killed her father. But this man, who lay cowering below her, cared for her brother in a way she never could have. The barrier containing her empathy shattered in that moment.

Kneeling beside him, she spoke sharply: "You listen to me. Someone powerful wants you and your wife"—untrue, but Elsie needed to say anything to get him to do as she ordered—"dead. You've been good to my little brother—I've been watching—and to take away the life of the man who did what neither my own parents nor I could do, that man doesn't deserve to die."

His cowering expression entangled with a look of confusion and unsureness, certain just a minute ago this gangly woman would have cut his throat.

"Did he call you dad?"

The man nodded.

Elsie sucked in her breath, holding onto her tears. Her lips thinned as she licked them, not able to look the captain of the king's guard in the eye.

Muffled shouts came from inside the wardrobe.

When Elsie drew the doors open, a woman rolled onto the floor.

"Lyra!" the captain yelled, his voice shaking.

"I would have expected you to be braver," Elsie said. "Captain of the guard doesn't seem quite like a fitting title."

She sighed, looking Lyra and her husband over, and drew a well-polished knife, it's edge serrated. "This is what I'm going to do: I need your thumb. Your left one, specifically, to show I killed you." Elsie paused, making sure he understood. "This is what you're going to do: once I take your thumb, you're going to get it and your leg taken care of, yeah? And then you and Lyra here are going to flee to Kaire, and you're going to start over there in the city. It shouldn't be too difficult for you to do that with"—she waved her hand holding the knife around, pointing at the fancy features of his homestead—"your wealth. How's that sound?"

"You're … going to let us go?"

Elsie momentarily sat.

"Who is to say we will do as you say?"

"You will. Because if you don't, I *will* have to kill you; if my big scary boss man finds out I didn't do you in like he ordered, then he's going to do something to Ida. You get me?"

"Yes, yes, yes," the man said with a fast nod.

As Elsie knelt to him, he braced himself, Lyra shouting behind her gag. The captain held his hand flat on the floor, his body already numb from the trap clamping onto his leg. Still, he trembled, his heart racing faster than it already had been as the blade eased toward his thumb. He shut his eyes.

She placed all her weight on his hand, making sure he wouldn't move and began carving into flesh, the skin tearing and peeling between the knuckles until reaching bone. He cried out, turning his head away, as blood pooled on the floor. Elsie stuffed a rag in his mouth.

It was the first time and only time she had ever had to deliberately cut through flesh like that; it was as if she were dismembering hunted game at the butcher's shop, except she hadn't the strength nor the right tools to saw through bone, even as small as a thumb.

Crack!—she violently pulled his thumb in an unnatural direction and broke it at the first knuckle, feeling with her fingers where the softest tissue laid under his skin before finishing the job.

A toe-shaped thumb missing its nail rested bathed in red on her palm. She clutched it into her fist, as if to protect it, as if she were afraid that were she to drop it, it would roll away and she'd never find it.

Sweat beaded down the captain's face, his pallor paled, glowing in the low light.

Elsie stood, pulled the rag from his mouth, and cleaned the knife.

"Remember what I said."

"When you joined the guild, Lodan had you complete a trial, yeah?" Elsie asked Davan, filling the long silence that had fallen between them.

Davan leaned back, crossing his arms. "Yeah. It was bloody." It was all he said of it because it wasn't something guildmates dared to share about themselves.

Elsie didn't meet his gaze, staring at the glimmer radiating off her polished coins, the same sheen that had reflected on the serrated knife.

"I killed Ida's dad," she said. "Twice."

43

Calamity from outside the door brought Davan and Elsie to their feet, both gripping onto a knife, while also bracing themselves as the ship jerked. Neither were sure what was happening, both not wanting to be the first to see what the commotion was about, but Elsie stepped to the door, placed her hand on the handle and looked back at Davan who gave her "a go ahead" with a nod.

Jarring the door, Elsie peeped through the crack to shadows of people rushing along the deck, all heading the same direction as crew members motioned. She threw up her hood, shut the door briefly as she turned to Davan, and said, "They're gathering everyone at the front of the boat.

Davan's first thought was that the vessel had taken on water and that the passengers would be loaded into lifeboats. The Sarnak wasn't a terribly large river, especially when comparing it to the Great River, but it wasn't small either, nor was it shallow. The boat, were it to sink, would be swallowed wholly.

He threw up his hood, and he and Elsie eased out the door, sheathing their blades and carrying their supplies—many of which were stolen from the galley and salon. They melded into the shuffling travelers, following to the front of the ship. It was too dark to see what was going on, but as dusk crept, the faint glow of light revealed a river having run alarmingly low. The boat had run aground not far from the bank some yards above—the shallower river continued around them.

The captain stood atop a crate at the prow, where typically passengers gathered as an outdoor commons area to gossip and meet new people. Crewmen held lamps, standing on the edges of the gathering passengers, blocking them into one place as stragglers continued to show.

The captain, a robust man in his middle-aged years, stood broad shoulder, back straight, hands behind his back—his brimmed velvet navy blue hat shadowed his soft, yet serious gaze.

He spokes through a thick, graying beard, voice loud and strong, catching the crowd's attention. "Listen up!" The chattering passengers, mothers whispering among each other, children clinging at their sides too scared to interact with anyone beside their moms, men standing back, crossing their arms, trying to come up with a solution among themselves or solve whatever problem lay ahead—everyone went silent and gave their attention to the captain.

"We have run aground," the captain said. "For those of you who may not know what that means, it means our vessel is stuck. But worry not," and he grabbed the lapels of his coat. "We are prepared for emergencies and there is a plan in place.

"Men, we will split you in two groups: one group will gather the livestock and rations—my crew will help, of course—while the second group, you will come with me to prepare the skiffs and help row women and children to the nearest shore. This will take some time; we don't have enough boats to do this in one go, so I ask you all to be patient and remain calm."

"You want us to remain calm?" a woman asked, her son's head cradled in her hand, his face buried in her thigh.

The captain rocked on his heels. "We've already run aground. The boat will not sink. Such an unfortunate event is the safest we could ask for. You should feel blessed."

The woman's face reddened, angry and upset. "And what then? Once we get ashore?"

"I hope you wore your walking shoes, ma'am," he answered.

She took a deep breath, exhaling a long, frustrated sigh through her nose, and knelt to her son to tell him everything was going to be okay as she petted his curly hair.

Another mother came to the woman's side, her young daughter following close behind. She placed her hand on her back, leaning close to her to make sure she was all right and to let her know she wasn't alone.

The daughter, who was maybe the same age as the boy, tugged on his sleeve and handed him her wooden doll. "Her name is Sussa, like my grandma, because my grandma's spirit watches over me through her. She can protect both of us, okay?"

The boy, who had been crying, wiped his eyes, and a small smile appeared on his face as he gently took Sussa and hugged the doll.

Elsie turned to Davan. "I'll come with you to help with livestock. I think that would be best for both of us. Something too busy to keep them from looking at us too long."

"But you're a woman," Davan said.

She gave him an incredulous look and spread her arms to reveal her boyish frame. "I don't think they'll notice, do you?"

"You hardly have any breasts, don't you?"

Her judgmental glance shut him up, as she barked, "You're not trying to come onto me, are you? Because you can shove it."

Davan let out a boisterous laugh, throwing his head back. "Absolutely not."

She watched him from the corner of her good eye as she crossed her arms. "Good. I don't need you thinking anything strange since you don't got Treasta no more."

His jaw clenched. "Treasta is dead to me," he said tightly.

"Yeah, you've said that, but I doubt it, since you seem to have a need to tell me again. Plus, I think you're repulsive," she said with a wink.

"Yeah, yeah, yeah," and he started toward the group of men gathering to aid with livestock. "That makes both of us," Davan said. "And by the way, it was a joke."

"Some joke," Elsie scoffed. "Say that to any other woman and see what happens. I bet even Treasta wouldn't have liked it."

"She'd've laughed," he said.

Elsie rolled her eyes. "Yeah, to appease your ass."

THE PALE SKY OF MORNING BROKE, REVEALING THE LONG and boxy steamboat, its paddle wheels jammed with heaps of mud after digging into the shallow bed of the higher banks of the river where the vessel had run aground.

"How far are we from Maward?" someone asked the captain.

Davan heaved a crate onto the shore, helped load carts and latch horses and corral other livestock, all of which after hours were brought ashore. They hadn't enough resources to haul everything. So what carts they managed to salvage from the vessel, were used to transport luggage and other important supplies on their journey to Maward.

The captain placed his hat on his head, rubbed his beard, and examined the scene before him: piles of goods, animals, and most importantly, his passengers. He looked to the young man next to him, answering what everyone was wondering. "Two days, I believe." Maybe more, maybe less—it had been some years since he traveled by road to and from Wesser, and they still needed to find the road, although it wasn't far.

Some stayed behind with the goods they couldn't take, while everyone else followed behind their captain. Davan and Elsie stayed near the back of the line, walking behind a cart, its wheels struggling over the terrain until coming upon the road.

It was a long, slow journey. Crewmen passed out rations, shared water, rested at noon, and carried on until the sunset.

The travelers, exhausted, built campfires and set up tents with the supplies they had. Their voices filled the camp, talking, sharing in their trauma, as the captain walked around to speak with everyone personally, introducing himself, and hearing their thoughts and concerns.

"There is safety in numbers," he told the little boy who held the girl's doll. "Would you like it if tomorrow, you and your mama walked at the front with me?" His gaze passed to the girl and her mother. "All of you are welcome at the front of the caravan. Please don't hesitate." The little boy looked up at his mother who passed him an approving smile. Enthusiastically, he nodded at the captain.

The captain tussled the boys hair and carried along to other campfires.

Elsie kicked back, stretching her legs as she leaned against a stump, watching dots of orange flickering below. She and Davan slipped away from the caravan come nightfall and camped some distance ahead at a higher ground where they could keep an eye on their surroundings.

"I need to know," Elsie said. Davan sat not too far away, sitting on a felled tree with his back turned to her. He, too, watched the dots of orange flickering below. "How do you know the demon warlock."

Davan rested his chin on his hands, leaning forward, gaze shifting from the orange of campfires to the white twinkle of stars. He stood, stretched, and faced her. "You should let it go," he said. "Bastan isn't someone you want to cross."

"I know you hurt Declan," she said. She grasped the hair at the crown of her head and pulled, her expression like stone as she held his gaze.

Davan shrugged. "I don't know what you want me to say. He was sneaking around my camp."

Elsie rolled her eyes. "You know what? Forget it. Don't tell me. Nothing you say is going to stop me anyway."

"You go into that town," he said, "you're not coming out."

"You did," she said. "So I know it's not impossible."

"What's your plan, then?"

"I'll gut him, of course."

Davan lowly chuckled. "Yeah, of course."

After picking up his bag, he lit a lamp he collected from the camping caravan, and kicked out their small campfire, its embers low and poorly fed, with dirt.

"Let's go," Davan said. "We got somewhere to be."

Elsie came to her feet, let out an annoyed sigh, wanting to rest longer, but Davan, determined to intercept Treasta, to kill Chimes, was eager to get to Laine first. The land, dark under the night, the lamp barely enough light to see but feet in front of them, was difficult to trek, but as they came back to the road, it's well packed and worn grooves cut from hundreds of years of wagons and carts and stagecoaches passing through, was far easier to follow under the blanket of night.

"Where do you suppose they are?" Elsie asked.

Davan wasn't sure, so he answered with a shrug.

"And if they get to Laine first?"

"We find Laine and take the flute from him."

"And if we can't find Treasta and her lover boy?"

Davan stopped in his tracks.

"Oh, did I hit a sore spot?" she asked with a pout.

He shut his eyes and cracked his neck, collected himself with a long sigh, a slow exhale to relax his tense body and clouded mind so seized by fury that his sensibilities could easily fail him. Don't react, he reminded himself. You need her.

Davan opened his eyes and looked at her. "Not at all," he said coolly.

A sly smirk stuck on her face as she flashed her brows. She stepped in front of him and walked backward as they continued down the road. "You sure you don't want to ask me what happened to Lodan?"

"He was poisoned," Davan said, refusing to look at her. "Everyone knows how he died."

"But you don't want to know who did it?"

"You're going to tell me Treasta did it just to get under my skin."

"*Hah!*" Elsie stopped with a hand to her chest and blurted another laugh. "You really are in denial over it. Gods, Dav, get over yourself. You want Treasta to be dead to you. Then give yourself a reason for her to be dead. She killed Lodan, Dav. *Treasta killed Lodan.* She's the one who spiked his drink. Why can't you believe that? You've always treated her like some naïve and innocent child, like you can't let the idea of the Treasta you knew years ago go. She's smarter than you, Dav. Always has been. But you held her back, and she held you back. You don't need each other. You *never* needed each other."

Lodan's death had always been laced with rumors. The only bit of truth was that he was poisoned, but that was because the number of witnesses were many: their late chief falling from his chair, convulsing on the floor, foam erupting from his mouth as his eyes rolled back, a gruesome and terrible moment etched into their memories. Everyone present had paused, silence stealing the room. They gathered around Lodan as he shook, head slamming into the cobblestone, foam and blood still pooling even after he stopped moving. Davan rushed to Lodan's side, his chief's skin grayed and eyes dulled. Everyone watched Davan, waiting for him to say something. But he just sat there next to the dead chief, lost. Treasta had come to his side, knelt next to him, her hand rubbing his back as she comforted him, whispering, "I'm here for you. Whatever you need, my love."

As the realization struck Davan, Elise watched fire blaze within his eyes.

44

"SHUT UP, SHUT UP, SHUT UP!" Pat paced along the road between Maward and the fork that led to Hayam, wavering in and out of shrubbery, crossing back and forth to both sides of the road, trying to escape Patricia.

She hadn't disappeared in days. Maybe it was because he was famished, body weak from travel, hardly having eaten anything since he had returned, hardly having an appetite after watching vultures tear through his sister's body.

You need to relax, Patricia's voice whispered from behind.

Fumbling his way off the road, he hunkered behind a tree, finding stillness under branches not far from the Sarnak. He watched the water, now feet lower than the days before, and its flow—what he could see of it—pulling him into a moment of peace so he could collect himself. Pat did not remember picking up the rubble, or lifting it above his head, or even swinging down. Just red splattered around his sister's head, bits of her skull and pieces of brain like an erratic explosion of a crimson star. He searched his mind for anything, something, but the moment between their arguing and Trish's death was blackness.

He sobbed into his knees, pleaded to Patricia with cries of "I'm sorry! I'm so sorry!" as he fell onto his side, curled into himself, deprived of his senses, feeling only the implosion of guilt and anguish within his chest.

Hey, now, Patrick. I'm still here.

Patrick sniveled, hiding inside his shirt. "But you're not real," he whimpered. "Why won't you go away?"

I'm real, Patricia said. *I'm real because you need me to be real.*

The phantom sat next to Pat, placing her hand on his back as if taking pity on him. She leaned on the tree, looking at the river and its now-steepened banks. Patricia rubbed his back, and Pat lulled into a deep sleep.

When Pat jolted awake, his sister's ghost was nowhere to be seen.

He didn't know how long he had slept, but he sat up with a sense of clarity under a gentle sun sharing warm rays on cheeks dried of tears. Pat looked around, the haze he had been living in since Trish died felt distant, though lingered.

Standing, he brushed off the dirt collected on his cheeks and wandered to the road, concentrating on the rocks embedded in the packed orange clay, counting each one his eyes locked with as he distracted himself from thinking about Patricia.

As he came into Maward, he noticed the village shutdown and tents pitched along the road to the dock. The sign near the dock read "CLOSEDE" and the steamboat that was parked there just the other day had drifted to the middle of the river where the water sat low and deep. A cart, arriving from Hayam, unloaded crates of supplies, such as food and linens, as villagers hauled goods into organized stacks along the street. Pat didn't know what was going on, but he remembered the people in Maward gathering along the dock to find the water drained, whispering among themselves before panic arose. At the time, Pat had barely grasped reality. For a while he had stayed hidden in some brush near the dock until a watchman came by and kicked him from the village—something about villagers complaining about a kid talking to himself; apparently his arguing with Patricia perturbed travelers and locals.

But now they were too busy to notice Pat coming and going, muttering to himself, muttering to Patricia.

Pat halted. She was back. For how long she had been floating behind him and he had been muttering, he wasn't sure, but anytime Patricia reappeared, his head thrummed and mouth went dry.

Facing her, Pat tried shoving her away, but he fell through her body, her form dissipating and reforming. Her silent and smug expression taunted him. Pat skidded and rolled over himself on the road, cutting his hands and arms on rocks, as he flew through the apparition.

"Go away!" he yelled, throwing himself at her again.

He continued this, and she continued disappearing and reappearing, hovering over him and casting her appeased grin until, in the center of the village, two strong villagers grasped Pat's arms and dragged him out of town.

Pat sank into half-dried mud, his weight breaking through the crackling surface, as they tossed him out of Maward. On his feet, he faced the men disappearing into town, and he screamed at the top of his lungs until breathless.

He grabbed handfuls of mud, but it splattered on the road behind Patricia when he threw it.

"Why are you doing this to me?"

I'm not doing anything to you.

He bared his teeth, felt an animalistic rage swelling inside his chest.

"I'd kill you again if I could," he spat.

Her chuckle echoed. *Oh, Patrick. Patrick, Patrick, Patrick. You poor boy. Pathetic.*

Pat lunged at Patricia, this time landing into living flesh; tackling her to the ground, he flung balled fists into her face.

A hand clutched his collar, his tunic choking him as he was pulled off Patricia.

"I see Trish didn't let you drown," Davan said as his fingers dug into his shoulder, his grip tight, a sign he wasn't letting go. "You doing all right?"

Blinking several times, reality seeped into his vision as Patricia's cackling phantom barreled over, laughing on the shoulder of the road. He looked at the woman he had attacked.

Elsie.

His face turned pale.

Elsie stood, brushed the dirt off her trousers and shook out the cape of her cloak. She touched her face where he managed to hit her once, the rest landing in the earth near her head. "You need to work on your form," she said, opening and closing her jaw and wiggling her nose. "You hit like a little girl."

Pat gritted his teeth. He kept his mouth shut.

"Where's your sister?" Davan asked, his face nearing his.

Silence.

I'm over here! Patricia tauntingly called. She danced around Pat, her laughter echoing in his head. *Oh, right, they can't see me, because I'M DEAD. Good job, Patrick.*

Pat swallowed air, lips pinched shut, refusing to look at Davan or answer his questions.

"Must not be good," Elsie said as she closed the space between them. "Where's Trish? She hiding in a bush or something?" Grabbing him by the face, her fingers pressed into his cheeks, and she forced his eyes to hers. "Hi, Pat." Elsie flashed a smile. "Usually you're the one hiding. Trish isn't a coward, unlike you."

He landed a kick on her shin—Elsie stumbling backward as pain radiated up her leg—and he jerked from Davan's grip, running.

Elsie darted after him, faster and more agile. She tackled him to the ground, but he wiggled, thrashing out of her arms. But she latched onto his pantleg, and Pat toppled to the ground with a hard slam.

He didn't move.

Elsie nudged him.

Nothing.

As Davan turned Pat over, blood trickled down his forehead from a gash. He pressed his ear to the boy's chest to hear a heartbeat thumping against his ribs.

"He alive?" Elsie asked.

Davan nodded and checked their surroundings to see whether they had drawn attention from the nearby village. He hoisted Pat over his shoulder and carried him away from the road and into the wilderness.

Pat's eyes flickered open to a room darkened by tattered drapes nailed to support beams over a single small window, the day's light beaming through holes in the cloth. He cut the light with a wave of his hand, examining the white glow cupped in his palm. He didn't need to look around to know where he was: back in Galgaya at the pimp's brothel, sitting on a burlap sack stuffed with hay—where he once slept.

He rushed to his feet, hid behind a trunk, his body small and yet to reach puberty, as the door flung open; his mother tumbled inside. A heavy slam shook the room as the door shut.

His brunette mother, youthful features sucked away from years of suffering in this place, muttered something incomprehensible as she stumbled to her bed. She curled into the corner.

Pat, peeking over the trunk, watched her, took in exactly how he remembered her, a living corpse somehow still clinging to this world despite nearly overdosing several times on whatever concoction the pimp shot into her veins each night.

Trish slipped into the room, shut the door behind her and dragged a chair over to jam it under the handle. She fell to their mother's side, curling under her arms and wrapping herself around her.

"I'm here, Mama. You're safe now," Trish said. Safe at least until tomorrow when the cycle started over again: more drugs and more customers to take advantage of her near lifeless frame.

Their mother's head rolled back, her eyes glazed, gaze searching the ceiling but not fully there. "Where's your brother?" she said weakly. "Where's Patrick?"

"I'm here!" Pat raced from his hiding spot. "I'm here, Mama."

He dropped to her side, but his mother groaned, head falling, as she stared with an expression aware and wicked from behind her brows, long tangled curls framing her face. "You left me here," she said. "You said you would come back, but you left me. Stupid boy. Stupid, stupid boy."

"You left Mama," Trish shyly said, hiding in their mother's arms. "You left Mama, and now I'm dead."

"Stupid, stupid Patrick," their voices morphed, filling his head with the continuous chant.

... stupid, stupid Patrick.
Stupid, stupid Patrick.
Stupid, stupid Patrick ...

Pat crawled backward until against the wall, covering his ears and shutting his eyes. He screamed until only red consumed the black behind his lids.

Stupid, stupid Patrick ... Wake up.

They had bound his wrists, tied his body to a tree, and stuffed his mouth with a dirty rag.

Davan was pacing, impatiently kicking a rock back and forth somewhere in the wilderness between the canyon's wall and the road, concealed deep behind trees and brush and boulders that sharply cut toward the blue sky.

Sitting near Pat, who had yet to wake, Elsie opened and closed Mr. Grall's razor. She paused to check her teeth in the reflection and ran her tongue along their ridges.

They had tried waking him, snapping and clapping around his face, shaking him, pouring water over his head, and shouting. Nothing stirred Pat.

Davan placed a finger under the boy's nose, felt a long exhale cascading. Still alive. Growing more agitated, he continued to pace around the small clearing, walking its parameter along the trees and nudging the stone along with him.

"Let's just leave him here," he said, crossing his arms.

Elsie closed the razor and pocketed it. "We need him to find Laine."

"We can find Laine without him."

"And how do you suppose we do that?"

Davan, silent, grunted as the rock shot through the air with a hard kick; a disturbed owl flapped off, its wide wingspan spreading like a black ribbon below the sun, as the stone hit the tree in which the bird soundly rested. He dragged his hand over his face.

A muffled gasp came from Pat; his eyes shot open, and he writhed within his bindings. First, he noticed Davan who stood as a tall shadow over him, the sun just behind his head casting a halo around his silhouette; then he saw the owl settle down on a lone branch hanging onto a dead tree. The creature, its yellow eyes wide and all-knowing, watched him.

Elsie rested her arm on Pat's shoulder as Davan removed the gag.

Pat coughed; his mouth dried from the cloth.

"Hey there, Pat. How's your head doing?" Elsie asked.

Silence.

Davan stepped back, watching as he held a knife tucked behind his back.

"We're not going to hurt you," she said.

Pat watched Davan carefully, saw where he kept his hidden hand.

"What do you want?" he asked.

"Take us to Laine."

"I don't know where Laine is."

With a cold countenance, Davan knelt, brandishing his knife, the sun's light glinting off it and striking his eyes. "We know you know where Laine is because Laine ordered you to follow Treasta. Now," and he grabbed Pat's hand, holding the knife so its tip dug under his fingernail, pressing, "you're going to take us to Laine, or I'll peel your nails off one by one until you do."

A grimace crossed Elsie's expression. Hardly could she look away from the dulled blade's point digging into Pat's nailbed. The boy winced, holding back a scream. Elsie's gaze shifted to Davan; he was so focused, so absent of a soul she no longer recognized him. Her grimace turned into a smirk. Whatever this transformation was, Elsie knew she was looking at Davan's true self, long held back after years coddling Treasta.

"Okay! Fine!" Pat cried. "I'll take you to Laine."

45

A WATERFALL STREAMED FROM THE RED ROCK of the canyon's wall and into a crystal-blue pool where nearby Treasta and Chimes had camped for the night. Now noon, they dipped their bare feet in, felt the warmth of the hot spring tamed by the cool water falling from a gash in the earth ease their aching soles from days of traveling. Chimes' hand crawled toward her hand, and he gently grabbed it. She rested her head on his shoulder, a small smile on her face as she stared into the transparent pool, the sun's rays refracting through its watery surface.

They should get moving, she thought to herself, but she didn't want this moment to escape into the past, knowing what was to come in the next few days when they reached Laine and she exchanged the flute for his treasures. What would she say to Chimes after she got what she wanted? She didn't want him knowing about the witch or her intentions, so she knew she would have to slip away and disappear. She squeezed his hand, held it tighter, not wanting to lose him, but he let go and came to his feet to strip himself down to nothing but the skin on his bones.

Treasta's face flushed pink, somehow shy of his naked body, and averted her gaze toward the earth.

Chimes laughed and slipped into the pool, diving under to emerge, spewing a mouthful of water at Treasta.

She shrieked and rushed to her feet to back away.

"It's just a little water," he taunted, floating to the pool's edge. "Come on, join me."

"It's cold," she said.

"You know it's *not* cold." Chimes laughed and playfully splashed her. He rested his chin on the earth, staring with a begging gaze, eyes wide, puppylike, and bottom lip with a quivering pout. "Please."

Treasta watched his expression and looked at the warm pool, the cool falls, the cerulean midday sky, and low hanging branches of shrubbery dipping their own limbs into the water, how the nearby aspens and pines seemed to lean toward the spring as instinctively drawn to it the way she was drawn to Chimes.

She untied her sash and slipped off the dress the midwife in Wesser had given her, revealing a pale, slender form offset by the child taking residence inside her. Chimes' gentle gaze and soft smile chased away her anxiety, and she felt as relaxed as the trees as she took his hand and slipped into the water.

Chimes caught her by her waist as she bobbed. She balanced on her tiptoes, barely able to touch the bottom of the pool, her hands naturally falling to his chest, her fingers tangling around the charm's chain, the opal glinting. So soothed yet so sad was Treasta that the stillness of the air, the sound of the water pouring from the earth and coolness of its droplets splashing over them felt somber.

He saw the shifting expression on her face, the lowering of her eyes, the way her dimples appeared when she frowned, and placed a hand to her cheek, caressing softly and hoping to calm whatever ailed her mind, no prying, just silently being with her.

Chimes brought her in closer, and she wrapped her arms around him, resting her head on his chest, feeling his heartbeat loud and full. She shut her eyes, her soul finding reprieve in the spring's warmth and his embrace, thinking for a moment her life had been a dream, and he had been her reality this entire time—no Galgaya, no thieves' guild, no Davan.

Just Treasta and Chimes.

THEY DIDN'T CONTINUE ONWARD UNTIL DAYBREAK came on the morrow. Treasta struggled keeping up with Chimes, her body starving, the child growing and needing moremoremore. Such a feeling brought upon her a sickness, and while she could still walk, she was becoming dizzier.

Treasta sat on the ground, Chimes still walking ahead of her, not yet realizing, until he had said something about stopping in the next town, something about supplies, and Treasta didn't answer him.

He looked behind, saw her sat in the dirt and holding her head up. Chimes went to her side, settling down beside her.

"What's going on?" he asked.

"I'm so faint," Treasta said. She tried getting up, but found her strength escaped her.

Chimes frowned, wishing there was something more he could do to help her, so he retrieved a handful of berries; Treasta barely took a bite when an onset of nausea overwhelmed her with their tart taste. But she continued eating, carefully chewing and swallowing until her stomach settled down and her head lightened.

"Think you can walk?" Chimes asked.

"Yeah. I feel much better, thank you."

Chimes helped her to her feet, and they continued until reaching Orrn, a mining town with rows of buildings lining the main corridor. A smaller road jutted toward the canyon's wall where a large mine had sourced silver ore for the past five-hundred years or so. It was a colorful town; its buildings painted bright red with yellow accents and shared motifs of inorganic triangular shapes along the clay-shingled roofs' soffits. Like Wesser, the structures were slender and tall, but not so tall to block the sun, and had skinny windows, glassless and too high to climb into, except for those on the first floor, which let in light through triangular panes. Since the dawn of the steamboat, Orrn's traffic had eased, bittersweet to locals who relied on the steady stream of travelers going to and from Wesser.

The residents of Orrn carried on about their day, people coming and going from shops, stopping and chatting with familiar faces.

Treasta sat down on a bench resting near a general store while Chimes wandered to gather supplies. Taking in the sun, Treasta hadn't noticed she naturally placed her hands on her growing stomach, soothing the child as it moved. Little baby Tytan, a small thing still yet to comprehend existence and all life's complexities and suffering. Little baby Tytan, innocent and unknowing, just simply being and becoming, somehow surviving all this time.

A bitter sorrow entered Treasta's heart as a single teardrop escaped her left eye. She blinked, finding the ground under her heels, the bench on which she rested, the shade swelling as the sun ticked across the sky.

To Annikah she wanted to bend her knees, grovel to the sun goddess whose statue at the altar she, as a newly born baby, was left amid the night those twenty years ago, left cradled in the concaving folds of the goddess's gown swaddled in dirty linens.

"O, Sun Mother. O, Lady of Light. O, Merciful and Dutiful Queen of our world," Treasta mumbled under her breath, remembering the prayer she recited as a young child in the orphanage. "I'm scared," she said. "I'm so, so scared."

Whimpering, she hid her face inside her hands, bending in half. She wanted to collect herself, tried, because she knew she was making a scene, but the swelling of emotion and fear in her chest couldn't be helped. What was this feeling, this stark grieving, sharp and inevitable, crawling in her soul, eating away her spirit? *O, Sun Mother. O, Sun Mother. O, Sun Mother, please … I'm so scared.*

A fuzzy, white glow consumed her periphery; her body felt like it was floating, and her mind seemed to drift, numb of joy, numb of reality. Breaths staggered, lungs gasped, starving of air, Treasta didn't know how long she had left her body, but when she came to, the building's shadow draped her, cooling her face that had reddened.

A woman with long, curly blonde hair, carrying a baby in a sling, sat next to Treasta. Her blue eyes looked upon her child as the babe latched onto her breast, casting a loving gaze as her lips parted into a soft smile.

"How do you do it?" Treasta asked the woman.

But the woman was silent, like she couldn't hear Treasta, and began humming as she coddled the babe, rocking, and brushing back a thick tuff of brown hair on the child's head.

"It'll be all right," she said, not meeting Treasta's gaze. "It'll be all right. I promise. O, Sun Mother. O, Lady of Light. O, Merciful and Dutiful Queen of our world. Her holy servants hear your plea," and the woman's eyes locked with Treasta's; a white, growing haze encroached. "Everything will work out."

Reaching through the whisp of cloud, Treasta's hand hovered over the child's crown, so unassuming of the world beyond the mother's breast. "Tytan?" Treasta whispered the name, and the babies eyes flashed open, wide and wise with wisdom beyond its years. The child's mouth eased off the woman's nipple, gaze shifting and locking with Treasta's.

"It'll be all right, Mama," the babe's voice echoed deep inside her head and rolled with a giant's temblor.

Treasta jumped to her feet, sucking in the haze with a gasp, and reoriented herself as Chimes caught her. Frantic, she looked around, searching for the woman and the infant, but nowhere were they found. Treasta pointed at the bench where the woman sat.

"There was a woman with a baby," she said, looking at Chimes.

"You were the only one here," Chimes said. He felt her forehead and cheeks concerned she was falling ill, especially after the brief spell she had experienced on the road some hours ago.

She batted his hands away, straightened the skirt of her dress, and noticed the mule standing along the side of the road nearby.

Chimes followed her gaze. "Oh, I thought maybe it would be good to get you off your feet. This," and he stepped toward the beast, patting his side, "is Copper. Copper, meet Treasta."

Treasta met the brown eyes set inside the face of a ruddy-coated mule saddled and ready to ride. The gentle creature dug his hoof into the road, breaking clay under his shoe, and shook his white snout as if greeting Treasta with a kind "how do you do."

"You purchased a mule, so I didn't have to walk?"

Chimes shrugged. "It's nothing, really." But he had traded the last treasure he had stolen from his father's apartment: a gold cuff delicately detailed and fashioned with lapis lazuli cabochons, certainly worth more than the mule, but Treasta's comfort was without a price. "Consider him yours."

Hers? Treasta eyed the animal with wonder as her chest swelled.

Sweeping across the sky, a fading twilight painted cooling shades of pink and orange near the horizon as the sprinkling of stars began to brighten above the Great Canyon. The leather of the saddle's horn was smooth under Treasta's hands as she grasped it to steady her balance, but the slightly uneven stride from the beast rocking lulled her.

The shadows from the lamp in Chimes' hand danced, entrancing Treasta whose weariness had her wavering between the realms of awake and sleep, and the vision of the blonde woman and the dark-haired babe had stolen her senses and she returned to sitting on the bench outside the general store, the mother and child next to her. *It'll be all right, Mama,* the babe—Tytan—owl-eyed and without judgment, spoke with clarity as the woman shared a gentle kindness as she smiled at Treasta.

Sweaty palms slipped on the horn as fogginess filled her head, and her chest ached with an intense weight ready to crush her. Treasta called for Chimes, and he eased Copper to a stop. He came to her side. She held her head with both hands, trying to refocus as reality seemed to slip away into a cold darkness wrought with disorientating faces of the woman and babe. All consuming, her mind gripped her throat, choking her airway.

Treasta gasped and gasped and gasped—it was unclear when Chimes had helped her from the mule—as she doubled over onto the road, feeling the sky swell over her and the earth crumble beneath.

Chimes grasped her shaking hands, laid down next to her and tried to find where behind her eyes she had disappeared.

"I'm dying." Treasta's voice was low, childlike with fright. "I feel like I'm dying."

His hand was warm as it caressed her cheek. "Close your eyes. You're going to be all right. I promise. I'm right here. I'm not going anywhere."

A breeze cut through the canyon, its coolness depositing solace in the silence of the night as Chimes' voice soothed her soul. The dark behind her lids danced with colors, swirling and flashing, distracting her from the grip her mind had on her body. Squeezing Chimes' hands, she felt his warmth, realized he was with her in the darkness, lying on the crumbling earth and under the swelling sky.

Her eyes opened; red with tears, the blues of her irises turned green in the firelight, as everything spun around them, and Chimes brought her closer, holding her until the world stopped and she was again grounded.

THE WHITE HULL OF THE RIVERKEEPER AGROUND on a sandbar shone in the moonlight as Treasta and Chimes wavered off the road and toward the Sarnak River, finding a clearing where they made camp for the remaining hours in the night. The vessel, long abandoned, was like a ghost of a once lively river flowing strongly through the canyon to the Great River; Chimes' father's work was sucked downstream and spilled over the broken walls of Wesser's dam. He reclined, watching the low flowing water as he touched the unicorn windup toy he kept in his bag wrapped, its metal containing the coolness on the air. He wound it, set it on the ground, and the toy hobbled along red earth until falling over, legs continuing to kick on the air.

In the firelight, Treasta examined the flute, its markings and details glinting orange and reflecting over her face. Her fingers, resting on the holes, were impressed with circular marks. For a moment, she wondered how the metal would feel on her lips, and how it would absorb the warmness of her skin, that were she to blow a single note, she would become a golden statue, body round and full with child, a memento to motherhood's ailments and solitude reflected in the surrounding landscape of a female figure alone in the wilderness.

Treasta wrapped the instrument in silk and placed it in the bag. The winding motor of Chimes' toy came to an abrupt stop until he wound it again, set it on the ground, and it hobbled with its mechanical wobble toward Treasta.

The toy lightly bopped against her thigh and tipped over. Picking it up, she examined its patina, the tarnished bronze, its sharp edges cut and filed and soldered together, the point of the creature's horn wrapped and twisted with wire. Remnants of paint hinted at a once bright-maned figurine.

"My dad made it for me when I was small," Chimes said. "He gave it to me before he died." His gaze fell as he watched the campfire's hungry flames whip in the air. "I went to see him to warn him about you and the others coming to take the flute. His treasures belonged to Clan Blacthorne. The flute—they call it the Oria—it's their most prized possession. No one knows who crafted it or where it came from, except that it is of dwarven make. My father protected their treasures and advocated for the dwarves to the council. I was supposed to inherit his legacy, to serve on the council, to protect the Oria, and continue his life's work of working with Clan Blacthorne toward peace.

"The dwarves," his voice deepened with a graveness, "they had tunneled through the dam, my dad explained, to besiege the citadel. His advocacy and alliance, his compassion and years of work, had prevented that from happening.

"I think that when my dad died, the dwarves must have followed through with the plan to take the citadel and destroy the dam. Why else would the river run low? Where else could the water have gone?

"My dad wouldn't be dead if I didn't take the flute."

Treasta sat up. "You don't know that. Who knows how long Elsie and Davan were casing the place. Knowing them, they'd have gone after your father, threatened him, maybe killed him to get what they wanted."

The crackling embers consumed the pregnant silence growing between them, Treasta then realizing the words she meant as comforting had only hurt Chimes more as his expression dropped into a sharp frown, unable to look beyond the campfire at her.

"I'm sorry," she said. "I really am so sorry."

"What would you have done if you were Elsie or Davan?"

"I don't know. I knew I needed to find a councilor named Gustas; beyond that I didn't have anything else planned. But I know I would have done everything possible not to have to hurt anyone unless my own life was in danger."

Chimes' intensifying gaze shifted toward hers. "I'd do it again," he said. "I'd steal it again; anything for you."

"Chimes … but your father …"

He crawled to her side, closing the gap between them as he settled down next to her. "I know." His fingers interlocked with hers, his lips depositing a dewy peck on the back of her hand. "Treasta"—he placed another kiss on her soft skin—"I love you."

But Treasta pulled her hand away, setting down the windup toy on the earth next to him as she stood, walking toward the dark edge of camp, her hands covering her mouth. A rush of despair entered her heart as she shut her eyes, tears rolling down her cheeks. Treasta stifled her whimpers, forced her emotions to flee deep inside herself as she wiped her tears away.

"Why would you tell me that?" she asked, keeping her back toward him.

Chimes grabbed the toy, pocking it, and came to his feet. He cautiously stepped toward her, but she drew further away. "Because it's true."

She sucked back air, hands on her hips, looking to the stars. "Chimes … your dad died."

"Can I not mourn him and love you?"

Facing him, she shook her head. "What if I don't want you to love me?"

"What? I don't understand. Why can't I love you?"

"Because we can't be together. I want us to part ways in Hayam, all right? It'll be for the best. ... For both of us."

Too stunned, Chimes hobbled backward. He watched her face, searching for anything in her eyes to tell him she was lying. But Treasta didn't say another word. She lay down on the bedroll, pulling a blanket over her body, head resting on the sack containing the flute and gilded dagger Chimes gave her, and shut her eyes, forcing herself to sleep.

46

THE FOLLOWING DAYS TO HAYAM were filled with silence, neither Treasta nor Chimes speaking to the other unless required, and even then, few words were said.

Chimes remained some yards ahead, Treasta lingering behind atop the mule, her grip tight on the reins as she watched him, her stomach aching with regret, but too stubborn and too afraid to say anything to rectify what had happen just a couple nights ago; to fix it meant to tell him the truth, and she simply didn't have it in her.

Davan's form replaced Chimes'—his brown hair, knotted and dirty, his bronze skin, his shoulders slighter but arms stronger now paced ahead, and her mind was filled with possibilities interlaced with years of memories at Davan's side. And Treasta began to wonder where she would be right now had Davan waited for her, had she told him about the baby.

She imagined being at Marnie's, recovering, Davan knocking on the door, peering inside, and instead of screaming at him to leave her alone, she would say, "Please, come in, my love. Please, come here. I have news that I hope you will be as excited for as I am." And Davan would sit at her bedside, his hands in hers, his eyes alight with curiosity and elation. And he would say, "What is it, my love?" And Treasta would pull his hands to her stomach, show him that what she thought was a bout of sickness bloating her body was actually his child growing inside her, reshaping her insides into a cave. And Davan would smile, surprised and overjoyed, and he would embrace her, and he would say, "Let's forget about the flute; let's forget about Dubilee, start a new life here in Wesserland, just me and you and Tytan."

That was where they would be, she decided. That was the ending she would covet; and they would live like a normal couple in Hayam, who would go about their days as normal people. And Chimes, well, in that universe, he would be Davan's closest confidant and friend.

The fantasy faded as they followed the path along the cliff, riding to the first switchback with Hayam in view, the town bustling in the early afternoon, noisy and echoing into the canyon. Treasta's chest tightened as she clutched the horn of the saddle with one hand and the strap of her satchel with the other. Exchange the flute and find the witch—she repeated her task in her head, trying to keep herself from falling into the dark place that suffocated and seized her mind and body.

Hopping down from Copper, she walked at the mule's side, guiding the beast into the busy town that appeared exactly how she remembered it. Returning to Hayam came with a sense of familiarity—the sun, the buildings cut and carved from the cliff, the deep alleys, and the wide road opening into the town's center. She paused, Chimes still some yards ahead of her, and drank in the view of the canyon, the shrunken river, the tent city along the road near Maward and the steamboat, so small from this vantage, floating in the middle of the Sarnak, and the Great River not nearly as large as when she arrived.

Chimes materialized next to her. He leaned on the wall that separated him from a deep fall, the grains of cement pressing into his palms. "So," he said, gazing at the expanse before him, "this is it, then?"

Treasta was quiet, her expression flattening, lips thinning into a frown as guilt settled in her gut. She tried not looking at Chimes. It was difficult seeing such a beautiful landscape and hearing the bitter tone on his words, the venom of hurt, the feeling of betrayal, like she had squeezed his heart a little too hard and made it burst.

"Chimes …" Treasta inhaled, covering her face, ashamed. "I don't …" But she couldn't get the words out. *I don't want you to go. I want you to stay with me forever. I love you, too.*

"You know what," he said, straightening his back and stretching as he stood upright, "if you want to finish that sentence, I'll be at Dee's."

Chimes disappeared into the crowd.

Blankly staring after him, Treasta froze, feeling her own chest collapsing in on itself.

"I don't want you to go," she muttered, then wiped her eyes, and looked at Copper who stared back at her with one eye.

Pressing through the packed town center, Treasta tied Copper to a hitching post beneath an awning near the alleyway she had followed the Pats into that month or so ago. The passage seemed to stretch more deeply and darker than she remembered, but there was no mistake, as she stepped along the cobble path smudged with mud and dirt, that this was where she needed to be.

Treasta stood at the door, raised her hand ready to knock, and hesitated as she searched the wood for any semblance of sanity left within her soul. The child kicked, and she stepped backward, looking down at her growing body, cradling her stomach.

Knock, knock, knock.

An otherworldly chill rattled her spine as she waited for Laine to open the door. The hinges echoed with a sharp cry; a dark slit exposed Pat's gaze, his face paler than she remembered.

Treasta entered a dark room, lamps dimmed, the sun too far along on its sky journey for its rays to reach the frosted glass of the one window behind her. Each step was met with a creak from the floorboards, the air thick with sweat and body odor, the shadows creeping from the corners and along the walls with immeasurable blackness that she didn't know how large the room was beyond the door and beyond Laine who sat in a torn sofa chair, its fluff spilling from its wounds.

Laine was silent, watching her under red eyebrows with an expressionless gaze. His lip quaked as he went to smile, but his smile didn't stay long. He leaned forward, hands dangling between his legs; his gaze passed over Treasta's shoulder to the door then returned to her, looking her from head to toe, noticing how her body had changed since Galgaya, before hidden under layers and the coat she had held in her arms the last time he saw her.

"Well, do you have it?" Laine's words were tight and tense. "The flute, do you have it or not?"

Treasta reached into her satchel, her fingers grazing the gilded dagger as her hand came around the flute wrapped in silk. But before handing the flute to Pat, she demanded, "The sack of treasure first."

Pat looked to Laine, who nodded his head, and retrieved the goods from somewhere within the shadows. He opened the sack to reveal glinting gold and silver jewelry, a crown, coins, gems, and long strands of pearls.

Just as she reached for the sack, Laine said, "Show me the flute."

Treasta pulled back the silk to reveal the ancient instrument crafted to precision.

He gestured to Pat to continue the exchange.

Treasta placed the flute in Pat's hand and took the sack of treasure, tying it off before slinging it over her shoulder with a hefty heave.

"Pleasure doing business with you Laine. I wish you all the best," she said.

As Treasta pivoted to the door, she froze, face to face with Elsie who twiddled her fingers and scrunched her face into a smile as she waved. "Hi, there. Remember me?"

"How did you …"

"Escape my cell?"

"Where's Chimes?" a dark voice leached from behind Laine, and Treasta turned to see Davan step into the light.

"Dav."

"Where is he?"

"We parted ways," she said, her clammy grip tightening on the sack that was beginning to slip from her hold. He took a step toward her. "I swear it," she said. "We parted ways."

"But you *were* together."

Elsie leaned on the door, preventing Treasta from leaving.

"He's probably at the meadery," Pat said. "He's got a friend there. Dee, I think is his name."

"Pat," Davan said, not taking his eyes off Treasta, "me and Elsie don't know this town too good. Maybe you can show Elsie where the meadery is."

Pat nodded his head, cautiously creeping around Davan and Treasta to disappear out the door with Elsie.

A blast of air hit Treasta as the door slammed shut. She took a step back ready to dart outside, but then she saw the loaded crossbow gripped in Davan's right hand. The bag of treasure eased off her shoulder as she set it at her side.

"You should sit down," Davan said, pointing with the crossbow at a stool to her left.

As she sat, he aimed the crossbow at Laine, who was still holding the flute, its golden gleam shimmering. Laine turned to stone, watching

Davan with just his eyes, looking up the shaft of the arrow.

"Go on, I want to see if its true. Play it," Davan ordered.

Laine's chest expanded.

His breath quickened.

Blood rushed into his face.

"If you don't put the goddamn flute to your mouth and blow air, I'll make sure this arrow lands right in your lung so you die gasping."

Treasta, rigid, grasped the strap of her satchel as she watched Laine bring the instrument to his mouth, its long, slender body running parallel with his own, his fingers hovering over the holes, his eyes, agape, locked with hers. His lips pressed around it; he breathed through his nose a long inhale to delay the exhale.

An isolated, flat, and airy whistle hummed through the Oria.

Davan and Treasta watched Laine who, petrified in his seat, was too frightened to move. He looked at the flute in his hands, then at Davan.

"So it's not true," Davan said with disappointment.

A piercing cry escaped Laine's throat as he jolted to his feet, the flute landing on the faded red cushion of the chair, as he grabbed at his trousers tearing them from his body to reveal his legs glittering of brilliant yellow iridescence down to the finest details in his leg hairs and pores. He took one more step, then found himself anchored.

"Help me!" Laine begged. "You have to help me!"

But Davan, roused with curiosity, just stood there with his mouth open and smiling amused, a low laughter growing from his throat.

His fists held in prayer, his gaping gaze stuck and wide open-mouthed frowning, Laine's encased and statuesque figure was subjugated to a golden eternity.

A ringing filled Treasta's ears, her hand covering her mouth as she gawked at the golden Laine so lifelike and frozen with such a terrifying expression on his countenance that she found herself unable to look away.

Treasta jumped at Davan's boisterous cackle, loud and strong enough to move the earth.

"I did it," he said as he set down the crossbow in the chair. Stepping around Laine, Davan examined the transformation, looking over its detail and running his hand along the surface of what was once Laine's arm under the stiff fabric of a sleeve. "What a pathetic way to go."

Davan smoothly crossed the room to Treasta, his euphoric expression giving life to a man who had become a stranger. His cold, rough palms caressed her cheeks as he guided her to her feet. "We did it," he said.

Treasta didn't know how long she held her breath, but she released a long, shaky exhale, and hid her quivering lip with a clinched jaw. Lips cracked and bleeding, his rough kiss was desperate with longing as she refused to kiss him back.

Davan's hands moved over her body, down her back, up her waist to cup her head at the nape of her neck. His grip clutched a handful of hair, pulling her toward the floor. She let out a scream.

"Why did you kill Lodan?"

"Davan, you're hurting me."

His shadowy face twisted. "I'm hurting you? *I'm hurting you?*"

He tightened his grip, tugging harder, sending her deeper into the floor. "Please," she cried, "I'm pregnant!"

Davan yanked her to her feet, and she let out a yelp as he threw her into a wall. "Yeah, I noticed. Tell me," his heavy steps shook the room as he neared, "did you fuck him?"

Treasta groaned, a sharp pain entering her shoulder blade, as she sat up on the floor. She fumbled into the bag and as Davan lunged at her she brandished the gilded dagger, nicking his side and slicing his arm.

He fumbled backward, grabbing the wound, growling as he shot a monstrous look at Treasta who had scurried to her feet, snatched the sack of treasure, and bolted out the door.

"You bitch!" he called as he chased her down the alley.

But she had untied the mule, slung the bag over the beast, then her leg over the saddle and made haste out of town, clutching the treasure and saddle horn with white knuckles. Davan braced himself on the stone wall, his head pounding with rage as Treasta disappeared.

47

CHIMES HAD MISSED THE SMELL OF HONEY permeating the air, so familiar and comforting, that the early days of his childhood flashed through his mind when he stepped inside the meadery. Sunrays splayed pillars of light through the hexagonal windowpanes, striking Dee's warm, brown skin as he picked up empty mugs and goblets from vacated tables, not realizing Chimes had joined in helping him bus the room until he saw him carrying a bin in his periphery.

Glad to see Chimes, Dee smiled widely. "When did you get back?" he asked, wiping down a tabletop with a towel. "I take it you got that girl where she needed to go."

The clinking of metal clattered inside the bin as Chimes set a plate of half-eaten food atop cups and utensils. He shrugged. "Yeah. I guess we went our separate ways."

"Well, I'm happy you're all right and safe," Dee said. "It'll be for the best. She seemed like trouble, anyway."

Quiet, Chimes dragged himself around the room, cleaning. He hauled the bin into the kitchen, dumping everything in a sink, and without a word, went to the pump outside to draw up water. Inside, he poured the water into a pot over a fire and sat on a short stool, watching it come to a boil.

Dee wiped his hands on his apron, standing behind Chimes. "How about I lock up early. And you and I can relax and catch up."

Steam billowed from the bowling pot. Chimes nodded. Fetching oven mitts, he lifted the pot by its handle and dumped the boiling water into the sink, tossing in a cube of soap, and going outside to fetch fresh water to rinse the dishes.

As Dee placed a sign on the door that read "CLOSEDE" in red letters, he finished serving the remaining patrons, and locked the door after they left. He drew the curtains to cast away the light and lit the hearth in the lounge. Dishes rattled in the kitchen's sink, Chimes aggressively scrubbing, drying, and polishing everything.

Dee had fetched two mugs of mead, placed them on the table in the lounge; Chimes, wiping his arms down and unrolling his sleeves, plopped on the sofa across from him, picking up the mug, his face downcast, expression long and solemn.

"What's bothering you, lad?" Dee asked.

Gulps of mead washed down Chimes' throat, his gullet growling empty and hungry, but he refused to eat, his body weak, his eyes heavy and dark. Dee passed a concerned gaze his direction, watching a young man stricken with melancholia seemingly lost behind his pale-violet eyes.

"I told her I loved her," Chimes said. "And she told me we can't be together." His head fell into his palms, his fingers hooking short strands of hair that had grown in since leaving Wesser. "And …" Chimes covered his mouth; Treasta had consumed his mind so much so that he nearly forgot why he had come to see Dee. "Gustas is dead," he said after a long pause, staring at the blue rug. "I'm sorry. I should have led with that."

Dee, sipping, paused with his lips still on the rim of his cup.

"I visited my dad, Dee. I made things right, and now he's dead. I'm sorry."

Dee's dark eyes narrowed as he set his mug on the table and clasped his hands together as he leaned forward, watching Chimes with seriousness. "You're sure?" When Chimes nodded, he asked, "Does this have anything to do with the river's water level dropping so suddenly?"

Eyes flashing up, Chimes met Dee's gaze, realizing the man who had acted as his uncle since he was born must have known about the dwarves' plan. "Did he tell you about the coup?"

"So it's true? They destroyed the dam?"

Chimes shook his head, unsure. "I can't say. I was long gone after the river dropped. It happened overnight."

Dee came to his feet, carrying his drink with him. "I have something for you."

Chimes followed him upstairs to Dee's private quarters, clutching the mug's handle as the half-filled cup sloshed in rhythm with his steps.

Drawing open the pale curtains, Dee unlatched the window for fresh air to wash into a room he kept tidied and opened the drawer on a side table under the window. His large hands grasped a stack of envelopes held together with a hemp tie.

"These," he said as he passed Chimes the letters, "are from your father. Most of the letters your father sent weren't for me; they were for you."

With furrowed brows, Chimes examined the block of hundreds of sealed envelopes neatly tied together and discolored with age.

Dee took a sip of his drink, patted Chimes' shoulder, and said: "I'll give you some time alone."

8 Annecaan 3299 Leo Ulnis

Dear Darius,

Happy seventh summer, my son.

I promised your mother I would write to you on your birthday, but I know one letter a year simply wouldn't be enough. Your Uncle Dee says he will keep my letters safe until you're older, until you're ready, because you're too young right now to understand why I left, and I'm scared that writing to you will only confuse you. Things will be confusing, but your mother knew your future would be better if you stayed with your aunt and uncle instead of joining me in Wesser.

The city is big. You would be enraptured by such wonder, my son. How such infrastructure can hold up these five-hundred years, it truly is amazing. The city is built on a dam that holds back a lake so big you cannot see across it. You would think it is the ocean. Oh, how I wish I could take you to the ocean. The Shardian Waters is only but fifty or so miles away. When you are older, I would like it if we could travel to the countryside, visit the vineyards, drink wine and be merry together.

Take care, my son. I love you more than you will ever know.

Your father, Gustas Augustassan

8 Annecaan 3300 Leo Ulnis

Dear Darius,

It is your eighth summer. I have failed to write to you and curse myself in the name of all things holy for not taking the time to pick up this quill sooner. I hope you can forgive me.

Do you remember how we used to sit in my workshop behind the dining room? We would open the window to let in the light and fresh air from the canyon as you sat on my lap. Oh, you were so small! Your little hands held my tools so clumsily. Your mother would laugh until she panicked seeing you with the screwdriver. "Never again," she told us and pried it out of your hands. I was thinking about the toys we made together. You used to play with them with your friends a few houses down. Tallon and Eymme. Those were their names, if I remember right. Brother and sister: one a year your senior while the other, I think, was just a few months younger than you. You had a crush on Eymme, always tugging on her braid. I still smile, remembering how happy you were.

I was thinking about making toys again. It would be a reprieve from Agemon's demands. I suppose I haven't told you about him yet. He is the magistrate of Wesser. I serve on his council, along with eight others. It is why I came to Wesser, to accept the position. The council and magistrate were taken with my invention. I call it a steam engine. He wants to see if I can build it bigger and stronger. I begin working with maritime architects in the coming weeks with my new plans. We're going to try to build a transportation vessel that can carry hundreds along the rivers and lake. Imagine, my son, how much faster it will be to travel! Imagine being able to recline and be at leisure instead of caring for a horse and driving a wagon on these uneven highways. We hope to have the first vessel afloat within the next year.

All of this is for you.

Your father, Gustas Augustassan

Chimes sat on the floor beneath the window, opening envelopes and flipping through pages upon pages of letters as the sky carried the sun toward its set behind the canyon. Tears splattered the ink, soaking yearsold parchment. He held his heavy, aching head.

Dee's footsteps were heard as he returned, checking on Chimes, setting a plate of food down next to him and refilling his drink.

"How are you doing?" he asked.

But Chimes just continued tearing open letters to scan his father's words.

28 Moarnaan 3304 Leo Ulnis

Dear Darius,

When you were three years old, you begged every night for me to tell you a story about a little dwarven boy who discovered a spring of water inside the cliffs. That little dwarven boy's name was Hayam, and he saved his people during the great migration from the East Lands. So, they settled in the caves, built towns and cities all over the Great Canyon. When our ancestors arrived from the South Lands, we integrated with the dwarven peoples for a couple hundred years, but then the ancestors of the ruling class in Wesser took hold, casting an empire across the lands, then to crumble under its own power. The same family still controls the city and dam, but during all this strife, the dwarven peoples fled to the After Lands to the far away north.

My son, I have been meeting with Clan Blacthorne, the last family of dwarves to reside in these lands. Theirs are the ancestors who built Wesser. They dwell in the dam, caring for it, operating the levies. But it saddens me to see how they are treated by the Wesserians, cast away into the city's underbelly, few venture into the city because of this. They are angry. And I am angry for them. They have made plans to take Wesser, but I'm afraid their idea of taking Wesser is to ruin what their ancestors built and spent centuries protecting. I do not blame them, of course. I feel for them. But there must be another way.

The elders of Clan Blacthorne have been agreeable. I promised them better lives, lives they deserve to live beyond the dark underbelly of the city. They will cease plans so long as I can fulfill my promise. I must, Darius. I must help them.

Please, pray to Alia, on behalf of Clan Blacthorne.

Your father, Gustas Augustassan

13 Alvynaan 3304 Leo Ulnis

Dear Darius,

I know I wrote only months ago, but as we head into the fall equinox, I can't help but think about your mother. I don't know what your Aunt Marnie has told you about your mother and me, so I must apologize if you already know this story, but you need to know how much I loved her—how much I still love her, may she rest in peace with Alia.

I was young, fifteen, traveling with your grandfather. (You probably don't know this, but you are a mirror-image of him, both cloud children with white hair and violet eyes.) I was staying at the lodge your aunt and uncle now own with my father for a few nights. We were on our way to visit the orchards in the Milnar Valley. Ah, another place I long to take you. It's ripe with fruit during the harvest, and the green valley turns the color of fire. Stunning.

Your mother's parents, as you know, used to own the lodge before passing it down to Marnie and Atlas. As a girl, your mother worked there. I forgot to lock the door and place the occupied sign when I went to bathe, and as I reclined into the tub, your mother comes walking in to clean. I never heard her shriek so loud since. So startled, I splashed her with water, shying behind the tub's wall, so embarrassed. I couldn't believe a girl saw me buck naked, or almost naked. We avoided each other for some time, but when my father and I returned on our way home from the valley, I chalked up the courage to say hi. You should have seen her. So shy and quiet.

That night, we sneaked to the stables. I stuffed a bag full of plums, and we trotted off to the top of the gorge, looking over the highlands and watching for shooting stars as we devoured the fruit, our faces dripping with juice, our clothes and hands stained.

We barely knew each other, but I knew I couldn't wait to see her again. Somehow, I knew she would be my forever.

Darius, guilt eats at me every single day since I left her. I know she gave me her blessing. But what poor timing. I sent letters to Agemon begging to push our meeting. But he returned one letter that said, "You will appear as I ordered when I ordered or consider our deal ended." I remember it clearly because I remember how gutted I felt.

My last day with her, I brought her a plum, but she was too sick to eat it. You ate it instead, and I tried so hard not to cry in front of you, but you were so young, your face dripping with red juice, your smile wide and excited.

It was the last time I saw you both.

I don't know how many ways I can tell you I'm sorry, but I can only hope that one day you will forgive me.

Your father, Gustas Augustassan

His head had fallen back, jaw opened wide as he took in heaps of air into an expanding chest. Chimes' snores rumbled. The cool night air crossed over his body still lounging on the floor, letters in both hands, piles of torn envelopes at his sides.

A loud snort jolted him awake and he gasped. Yawning, Chimes reoriented himself, sitting up with a back stiff and sore. He gathered the letters, folded them, and gently bound them before standing to his feet.

Glancing out the window, a clear night had blanketed the canyon with dazzling stars and a thin waning moon barely visible near the horizon. Chimes latched the window shut, then sat at the bureau where he found writing supplies in a drawer. Lighting a candlestick, he dipped the quill in the inkwell, and wrote:

Dear Dee,

Thank you for my father's letters. I haven't read all of them yet—there's just so many—but I plan to read every mark so I can know my father for the man he actually was, not the man I thought he was for all those years. He was right to ask you to hold onto them until I was ready. I don't know if I would have given these letters the time they deserve should you have given them to me sooner.

I regret not reaching out to him. I regret not asking Marnie more about him and my mother, but I suppose I still have time for that. Maybe were I a more curious child, I would have forgiven him years ago.

By the time you read this, I should be halfway to Marnie's. I hope you don't mind, but I'm short on supplies, so I'll need to borrow some things, including food. I'll pay for whatever I take in labor the next time I'm in town and replace anything else I need to.

See you some day.

Sincerely,
Little Dee

Chimes folded the letter and placed it where Dee would find it the following morning.

48

SITTING ATOP THE FLAT ROOF OF THE MEADERY and huddling outside the open window, Elsie considered sliding over its sill, but when Chimes had started snoring, she peered over the edge barely able to see anything beyond the side table under the window and Chimes' white hair.

She had arrived at the meadery just as the proprietor put up the "CLOSEDE" sign. The last of his customers, full and happy, sauntered outside. Elsie considered trying the front door, thought maybe she should give it a knock, come up with some kind of pathetic reasoning—*Oh, my arm hurts; help, I've been kicked by a horse*—to get him to open the door just wide enough that she'd be able to slip her knife between the crack and pry it open.

No, that would draw too much attention. The streets here were few, which funneled most of the town into its center, and here the meadery, with its white walls, was the most recognizable and easiest to spot when coming into Hayam.

Elsie had lingered near the kitchen's window, listening to the clanking of dishes and sloshing of water within the sink. Chimes sniffled, quietly crying and mumbling under his breath, something about, "I don't understand what I did wrong" and, "Did I misread the situation?"

As Elsie followed them to the second floor, resting under the window where she now stalked, she thought about what Pat would walk into when he returned to Davan, the way the shadows consumed, not just the room, but also Davan's face that had gone dark and rigid. To stoke his ire was an experience she now avoided after weeks of prodding. Treasta's presence was likely a jab in itself, a reminder of what once was and what has recently been. One more poke, Elsie expected that was all Davan needed to lose himself completely.

Chimes snorted awake, stirring in the dark. Elsie quickly ducked when she saw his hand reaching out the window to pull it shut. Its latch snapped closed.

Carefully, she peered inside, watching a groggy, somewhat drunken Chimes find the bureau and fumble through the drawers. Candlelight permeated the dark, revealing the red wood of the desk as the quill sucked ink from the well and Chimes began depositing words onto a sheet of paper. He scratched his head, thinking, then continued scribbling until folding the page in half and disappearing with candlestick in hand.

Elsie followed the soft glow of the light to the next window, losing Chimes momentarily. She sneaked across the roof, climbed to the ground, and crept along the wall until she caught a glimpse of light radiating from the kitchen window.

Through the window she spotted a backpack, supplies piling on the butcher block island at the center of the room, and Chimes returning into the kitchen with winter gear. After he packed his supplies, he snuffed the light and left through the back door.

Quietly, she watched in the shadow of haystacks as Chimes slid open the stable door. Clutching her knife, she crouched closer, drawing in a slow breath and smoothly exhaling. Thoughts cleared from her mind, Elsie focused on the sounds echoing from inside the stable: Chimes unlatching gates, a horse whinnying, hooves clobbering. She eyed him, the pack snug on his back, the shimmer of his hair as he prepared the horse and fastened the beast to a wagon. He was adjusting the harness on a dark-maned mare when she carefully stepped inside. The horse's eyelashes fluttered, gaze casting a warning unnoticed by Chimes as he brushed the beast.

"Let's go home, shall we?" he said.

As he climbed into the driver's seat, she reached with a clawlike grapnel, clutching the backpack, wrenching Chimes to the ground.

The sudden movement startled the mare, and she kicked up a high rear before dashing from the stable, the wagon slamming into the meadery as the beast made an abrupt left down a short road and into the town center.

Elsie retreated outside, around a corner, as the beast flew from the stable, Chimes too disoriented to notice the small figure. He crawled backward, his eyes darting around the stable, frantically searching for whoever had grabbed him as his tailbone and lower spine throbbed.

A jarring cry from his horse echoed the town center. Chimes ran after the beast, skidding across the cobble, to see the mare, half her body hooked over the stone fence, dangling over the cliff's edge.

"Come on," he urged, grabbing the straps of the harness, pulling even as the leather dug into his flesh and rubbed his palms raw. He gripped until his hands were red with blood.

Chimes fell back, his pack catching him from hitting his head on the road. A speeding heartbeat chased him to his feet, as he knew someone was lurking, waiting for the right moment to attack. Hurrying with the haste of a rabbit trying to escape danger, Chimes felt the watchful eyes of the predator as he clumsily unbuckled the harness that strapped the horse to the wagon. The loosening weight of the buggy freed the beast of its burden, but as Chimes helped the creature onto the road, the last buckle broke, and the wagon tumbled, its canvas top tearing and snagging on a tree branch, its boards ripping from their nails, goods spilling, barrels and crates bursting.

He hadn't time to turn around when a hand came over his face, and a knife cut across his neck in a smooth and fast motion.

Elsie stared in astonishment as an unscathed Chimes faced her. "But how?" she asked with a breathy voice. "How are you not dead?"

Exasperated, Elsie's face flushed with fury as she pounced; her knife ricocheting from his chest with such force she felt it through her arm. Metallic clinked on the cobble as the blade bounced. She stared at it dumbfounded, mouth open with disbelief.

Chimes ran for his horse, struggling to climb onto her bare back with the hefty pack. He grasped her mane. The beast cried, threw its ears back, kicking and rearing as a knife planted into her thigh.

Barely landing on his feet, Chimes stumbled backward, his balance escaping him as the weighty pack dragged him toward the stone wall where he felt the lip of it pressing under his buttocks, his arms flailing to catch his footing.

Elsie rushed at him, grabbing his ankles, and yanking with enough strength that whatever stability had kept him from teetering over the edge had been broken.

Chimes disappeared, dropping into the canyon; his body—Elsie watching—crashed through trees and into the rocky cliffside, eventually disappearing within the shrubbery along the road below.

As she turned around, smug smile painted on her face, shutters slammed closed from nearby buildings. Such commotion alerted Hayam's residents awake, some even having come outside with the intent to break up the fight. Too fast it had happened, the townsfolk retreated inside, and gawked from windows. She sprinted down the road and into the alley, escaping watchful eyes.

Davan jumped to his feet, but winced as he grabbed his side, shirtless, dressings soaked with blood exposed on his torso and arm where the dagger had nicked him. The door shot open, crashing into the wall; Elsie stood in the threshold, anger pumping through her, her expression cross.

Coming into the room, she shook her sharp finger. "Did you know that—"

The glint of the golden statue caused her to lose her words, and she found herself walking around a tall figure, praying—no—pleading for his life with a face that belonged to Laine.

Davan waved the flute at her, wiggled his brows with pride. "It works." He laughed. "Can you believe that it actually works?"

"What did you do to him?"

"I needed someone to test it," he said with a shrug.

Elsie swallowed back saliva, or at least what was left in her dried mouth, exhausted after her grapple with Chimes.

Davan came around the statue. "Well, is it done? Did you kill him?"

"Yeah, he's good as dead. Did you know I wouldn't be able to hurt him?"

"What do you mean?"

"I cut him right across the neck. Nothing happened."

Davan stared at her for a long moment, his stoic expression dropping from his face long enough to share his confusion.

"That's why you wanted me to do it, huh? Or were you too sacred to get your hands a little dirty?"

"But he's dead."

"Yeah, saw for myself he fell. Ain't no one going to survive that."

A wry smile forced itself on his face, the corner of his lips twitching as he tried to hold back the joyous surge coming up his throat and escaping as something between a sigh and laughter, but his aching side brought him back to the chair.

"And what happened to Treasta?"

He couldn't bring himself to look Elsie in the eye at the mention of the name. "She got away."

"You didn't go after her?"

Davan flashed her a look of discontent as he kicked off his boot. He pointed. "Consider it yours."

Elsie reached into the worn leather thick with the smell of unwashed socks and monthsold sweat, fishing for Declan's portrait. She threw the boot at him and unfolded it to see smudged graphite barely holding onto the lines in the boy's face.

49

FROM HAYAM, FOLLOW THE ROAD INTO THE CANYON. *Continue past Maward until you find a bridge. Road into the canyon. Find a bridge. Canyon. Bridge.* The directions repeated in Treasta's head as she flew atop the mule still feeling Davan's grip on her hair, his knuckles digging into the base of her skull as he pulled her to the floor. Deeper and deeper and deeper, she descended into an unrecognizable void, the wind against her face the sole reminder that she still breathed. The blackness of the room plaguing her thoughts oozed from its walls over her body, taking her by the arms, entrapping her. Rendered immobile, Treasta felt herself shrinking as Davan's heavy steps beat against the sides of her head, sending shockwaves of terror into her soul.

Copper carried her as far as he could muster in a single sprint, bringing himself to a trot then a steady walk some miles past Maward. Treasta dug her heals into the mule's side, pleading with the beast to keep going as tears cascaded down her face, and she folded in half as defeated and exhausted as the creature. She sobbed into the sack of treasure, staining the burlap with salt.

Treasta wavered somewhere on the edge of reality where the clop of Copper's hooves reverberated with a distant echo, his gentle sway rocking her into a tranquil state as she retreated into the recesses of her mind. She didn't remember the sun falling behind the canyon, or when the violet twilight consumed the sky, or at which point the stippling of stars' twinkling began to shine. A thin sliver of light cast a pitiful smile from the waning moon—the last thing she remembered before a curtain of black fell over her vision.

When she awoke, Copper had halted just short of a bridge, old and worn, the road long faded into a trail barely visible to the naked eye. The river had disappeared into a stream, shallow and flowing fresh, as they had strayed from the Sarnak.

Groggy, Treasta stepped down from the beast, held his harness near the bit, walking with him across the aging wooden structure, pausing as she felt boards bowing beneath her feet. Head still fuzzy, she wasn't sure if this was the bridge Marnie spoke of or whether Copper had carried her somewhere else. Looking across the rocky streambed, she heard the babbling bubbles breaking against stones.

Treasta ran her hand over and around Copper's saddle, feeling for the lamp. She winced as the flame came alight, her head pounding with a terrible ache, her mind still muddy, her body exhausted and sore.

Cross the bridge and follow the riverbank back toward Maward.

Which way was Maward? The cliffs were shrouded in darkness, the night nearly absent of a moon. Treasta came to the stream's bank, knelt to the water, holding the lamp to get a better look at the direction the flow ran and walked with Copper for several miles, her legs turning to gel as she came to a fork in the stream where it met the Little Sarnak River.

As she pulled Copper along, the stubborn mule eventually buckled, refusing to budge one more step without rest.

With the lamp still burning, she draped herself over the mule's side and fell asleep.

A cool breeze cutting from a gorge in the cliffside swooped from the Altan Highlands and into the canyon where Treasta lay. It was early morning, a cornflower-blue sky still awakening with the dawn. Her clothes were damp with dew drops to which the chilly air clung.

She pulled the mule to his feet, felt through a pack for anything he could nibble on, but she had nothing. Treasta rested her forehead against his, scratching behind his ears as she whimpered, "I'm so sorry. I'm so sorry. I'm so sorry," with no food for either the beast or her to satiate their hunger pangs.

"I wish I stayed in Galgaya," she told Copper. "How foolish I was."

His gaze, gentle with compassion, so unknowing of her plight and hardships these past few months, momentarily eased her weariness. But the longer she looked into the mule's eyes, examining the shades of warm earth around pupils that shared the depth of a moonless night and how his brows umbrellaed his red lashes as full and bushy as a freshly bloomed field at spring, she began to weep.

Collapsing to the earth, Treasta curled into herself, holding her head in her arms, hiding from the rising sun as anguish drew her into a forlorn gloom.

Treasta lay sprawled with her arms and legs facing the sky, her growing stomach like a hill rolling over the terrain where on grassy knolls wild horses roamed away from the troubles of the world as they grazed under a crystal sky. One cloud passed her vision, low and full as if disconnected from the blue dome.

Copper wandered into the brush nearby, chewing on branches. The scratching of birds' feet and cooing of quails wandering from within the brush came closer, and their beaks pecked at the fabric of her skirt. Treasta shooed the critters away; they fluttered into the air and settled on rocks near the Little Sarnak. That was when she noticed a stony structure upriver.

Treasta wandered with Copper, each step with a dragging gait, unsure whether her eyes deceived her. A stone bridge, stretching across the Little Sarnak, materialized that had been partially claimed to nature, as shrubs and grass sprouted from the crumbling mortar.

Crossing the bridge, she found the ghost of a trail carved into the earth, walking it until she came upon the tall walls of two plateaus rising skyward. She followed into the smaller canyon, giving little thought to any choices she made as the wild of the wilderness feasted on her senses, the passage covered in fading pictographs and an indiscernible script.

You will know you are there when the land is covered in art.

Marnie's voice entered her ears: *It's been more than twenty years since I sought the witch's aid. Truthfully, I'm not sure whether these directions are right.* The memory of Marnie passing her the directions scribbled on paper entered her head. *You are always welcome here if you ever change your mind.*

A shade overtook the passage as the sun disappeared behind the canyon; the art and script illuminated with a soft rosy glow as a deep humming seemed to come from somewhere deep inside Treasta's mind, as if her presence gave life to a sleeping magic.

The path thickened with vibrant grasses and poppies springing from the earth of myriad hues, vibrant and otherworldly. Anytime Treasta blinked she witnessed the magical veil thinning and reemerging, passing between a barren world of decay and the shimmering fantasy of delight manifesting in the landscape before her. Whatever portal this was, Treasta was too far gone to take heed of the wavering images crossing back and forth as she walked, too far inside herself somewhere dark and distant. For how long she wandered through the passage thickening of phantom vines, it wasn't clear, but at some point the sky had turned to night, the glow of the runes and images her only guide.

A flash—Treasta felt her feet again on solid ground, the path behind her shrouded in mist, and before her a lush grove and grotto recessed inside the surrounding cliffs shimmering with fresh water.

And there, with steep eaves, roof of broken terracotta shingles, walls low, windows tucked deep under the soffits was a cabin succumbing to tangling vines.

Treasta rushed across the grove, fell into the door as she threw her fists into it.

"Hello?" she called. "Hello? Open, please! I need your help!"

She slid toward the ground, heard the clopping of hooves as Copper walked toward her. The bag of treasure slid off his back, landing on a patch of dirt with a heavy thud.

Clutching the sack with one hand, Treasta dragged it to the door. Her heart raced with desperation as she continued to throw her hands into the wood, her knocks going unanswered as she shouted pleas into the ether.

Falling into the door, Treasta's body forced it open, and she tripped over the threshold, skidding across packed dirt, the sack tearing open as it snagged on a dislodged nail in the doorframe, the treasure spilling everywhere. Staring across the floor, vision blurred behind watery eyes, glints of gold, of jewels, of coins distortedly shimmered. Grains clung to phlegm dripping from her nose as sorrow streamed down her face, collecting in small puddles on the floor.

Treasta sucked back her shaky breath, her head heavy like a mountain, her skull throbbing on all sides like something inside her was trying to escape. The numbness began in her face, slithering through her torso and limbs until no part of her being felt like it belonged to her.

In the haze of her vision, Treasta spied boney bare feet, papery and gray like clay. She held herself up, sloppily wiped her eyes and rubbed her runny nose along her arms as she faced the remains of a female figure.

Guttural screams broke the air until her throat could no longer carry the sound.

Hollowed eyes inside thin and fragile folds of mummified flesh gaped at Treasta, the witch's mouth hung open, sharp yellow teeth bared. Her hair, long and scraggly was braided over her shoulders, and around her neck was an emerald amulet next to a silver knife that still stuck inside her chest where her heart once beat.

As she escaped to a place of solace, Treasta's grip on reality loosened. With an all-consuming despondent affect, she mindlessly wrapped strings of pearls like garland around the witch's body, hung golden necklaces laced with jewels around her neck and carefully slipped rings fit for kings onto slim, boney fingers, their gems glinting like stars in the absence of light. Treasta gathered handfuls of gold and silver coins and deposited them in a circle around the dead woman before picking up a delicate crown, the cold of yellow metal seeping into her fingertips.

She sobbed and placed the crown atop her own head.

A breeze passed through the cabin.

Numb.

So numb.

Treasta withdrew the knife from the dead woman's chest, and falling to her knees, she thrusted the blade through her stomach.

Blood pooled at the witch's feet.

Are you happy?

Of course I am. I have you by my side. But are you happy?

The white cliff face of the crag stretched for eternity as a sunless white sky beamed of a radiance that gave the surrounding area and everything within it a shimmering glow; the grass, normally dry and left to decay under snow, waved like a gently rolling sea in the breeze, pale blades colorless.

Wandering the distorted Altan Highlands as she followed perpendicular to the crag, Treasta dragged bare feet through the fields, a numbing mindlessness wholly consuming her; only the tickle of the tall grass extending their delicate touches rippled across her naked form. The sensation was the sole feeling her soul allowed into her heart, its beat like a torn drum struggling to echo.

The air weighed of boulders, somehow containing the weight of countless particulars that held all parts of the before, the during, and the after of anything and everything; the raging fires of burning stars rained of passion and fury; the surging tides of oceans rose with ravenous delight, seeking to consume the bays and fjords, the river deltas and tributaries that stretched for as long as the universe expanded; the pressure of molten earth, millennia-churned, forced against the land's rocky shell, its layers giving to the fullness, the bloat, engorged body ready to burst.

As temblors rumbled, the world crumbled around Treasta, tearing into the blinding whiteness, washing away the unearthly radiance as her figure took on features of the mummified witch who wasted away in the cabin somewhere deep in the Great Canyon of Wesserland.

The distorted Altan Highlands succumbed to the void, the crag the only visible landmark in the black alight in its own glimmer.

A long, airy breath escaped her lungs, sucked into the darkness swirling of night. Treasta felt her bare body, her hands running over her breasts and down her torso where her flattened stomach was slit down the middle to expose the beginning of the universe.

When Treasta looked up, she found herself to have materialized inside a cave. Its wet walls oozing, its floors a shallow pool reflecting light from an anonymous source. Ripples smoothly skipped across the glassy surface from the smooth, gray ankles of a woman standing across from her. Treasta's gaze moved up the naked figure whose ribs were prominent under skin lined with green veins flowing with midnight-blue life.

The woman smiled, her dark gums framing each tooth, long canines prominently flanking a thin, blackish-azure tongue. Yet, her long, ethereal face shimmered with a glint of silver. Her low ears, their double points, were long. Her nails, like claws, were well kept. She bore a gentle gaze with yellow eyes.

"I've been asleep nearly two decades, child," the woman said as she waded steps closer. "Your blood awakens me."

Treasta's voice was crisp as it echoed, "But you're dead."

A soft smile parted the witch's dark lips. "And so are you."

"You're a demon, aren't you?"

"Only your kind calls my people demons, dark ones … We hail from Drynis, yes, but that does not make us evil. Our kind, however, bares a different magic than yours. Your elven folk draw magic from the earth, harness and hone it through the elements, some from the spirit and the sun and moon, while we Andrili take from the soul, our souls and others'."

A sweetness stained the air as the woman spoke, her smooth words slithering with a coo of honesty laced with wisdom. The Andrili's speech danced with a musical cadence, different than anything Treasta had ever before heard. Treasta rubbed her hands together, noticing her palms were unwrinkled and absent of texture. This form, she realized, this silvery white pallor that glittered in the dark, was her soul's manifestation into the familiar shape of a human body.

Guilt entered the place in her chest where her heart once beat. "I just wanted … I just wanted to be me again, to go back to how things were before I came to Wesserland. I just want to go home," Treasta said, her voice shaking, as tears—*tears*—materialized down her face giving manifestation to her grief. "I …," and she looked at her stomach where the gaping entrance to the beginning of the universe exposed itself, "… what have I done?" Water splashed and rippled around her as she fell to her knees. "I was told you could help me. But you, you weren't supposed to be dead."

"Nearly two decades ago, the swirling dark of the In-Between consumed my soul," the witch said. "Two young women appeared to me." Her hand swept through the air, a soft gust disrupted the pool's glassy surface as the image of the two young women materialized. Marnie's countenance was fearful on youthful cheeks, black hair tied tightly in a bun; the second woman, black hair loose, face thin and more mature than Marnie's, was at Marnie's side, soothing her as she rubbed her back, whispering that everything will work out in the end. "She gave me her blood," the witch said as Marnie cut her palm, lifeforce dripping into a bowl of mixed herbs, "and promised me bits of her soul." Marnie, with the other woman holding her close, cupped the bowl in her hands repeating the witch's words: "On this night of the black moon, I am undone."

Treasta found herself mouthing the words, the witch's eyes flashing up lit with fire.

"You know the woman," the witch said. "I can smell her on your spirit, carried through time on your memories. Here, in the In-Between, everything anywhere is here and now."

With another wave of her hand over the water, the ripples revealed a young man, maybe Treasta's age; his heavy dark brows hung serious. Glowering, he crept into the witch's cabin at the midnight hour, rays of the full moon casting inside as the door eased opened. *Atlas.*

"With a blade crafted of pure silver, he cast me into the darkness." A sadness painted her countenance, her dark, thin lips downturned. "Child," the woman's eyes had lost their sheen as she shunned the images of Marnie, the nameless woman, and Atlas away, "I can help you, but I ask you one thing in return."

"What is it?"

"Put me to rest and speak to my god of my death. Ahremnon Culdra is his name."

"But how can you help me if I'm dead."

"What do you desire most?"

Treasta inhaled, thinking carefully as if it were a trick question.

"Imagine," the woman said, "you are still among the living. What would you answer?"

"I just wanted, want …" *Want.* Speak like you're among the living. "I want this baby out of me."

"I will make it so if you promise on your soul you will put me to rest and speak to my god of my death."

"Ahremnon Culdra is his name," Treasta echoed. "I promise."

And from within was a flash—a blast, splitting her trunk in two, and her escaping spirit became the entrails of a star's blazing inferno.

50

A COOL BREEZE CARRIED THE NEW CRY OF LIFE INTO THE CABIN. Treasta opened her eyes, found in her arms a freshly pink babe fully ripened and ... alive? Its sharp cries of its first breaths—*her* first breaths, a girl—pierced Treasta's ear drums.

"No." She shook her head. "No, no, no no no no nonononononono."

I want this baby out of me.

And here that baby was.

So very pink.

Wrinkled.

Wet.

Crying.

Naked.

So distraught, so startled, and so seized by shock was Treasta she nearly dropped the newborn. The child's head, with gaping mouth gasping and howling, was so soft and so small in Treasta's palm, as she balanced the baby—*her baby*—in her arms. Her gaze locked on thick dark hair; she saw hints of Davan's features.

Gasping and howling.

A dark haze consumed the corners of her vision, as if the night oozed into the cabin from the broken windows and door. For how long she had been in the cabin wasn't clear, but when the flash of the witch's magic dissipated, no proof of Treasta's death could be found. Her body had nearly returned to the form she knew before carrying the child. No blood. No knife splitting her body. Just life cradled in her arms.

Treasta took in her newborn's cheeks, the way they creased as she screamed, the white dots speckling her nose, like an artist had caringly stippled each one, the toes small like beans, the strings of red goo, the way the babe's fingers curled into tiny fists so defenseless—gasping and howling, gasping and howling.

Coming to her feet Treasta placed the newborn on the bed, her small form sinking into the dirty linens and straw. Turning to face the witch's mummified remains, she was met with the wide beknowing stare of hollowed out eye holes behind crinkled lids, thin slits wincing with judgment.

Gasping and howling. Gasping and howling.

Treasta's eardrums rattled as a shrill ring pierced her brain like an icicle. Clutching the crown on her head, she flung it at the dead woman, a dry cracking and the sound of metal hitting the dirt-packed floors intermingled as a wail, as sharp as the ringing on her brain, escaped her lungs and she cursed the Andrili, cursed her promise, cursed this gift of life as she yanked the pearls from the corpse, beads scattering across the cabin, bouncing into hidden pockets of shadows under furniture and into corners. Treasta tore necklaces and jewels from the corpse, removed rings and kicked coins, breaking the golden circle of wealth.

"You lying bitch," she hissed, her words sharp and venomous. "You lying *bitch.*"

Gasping and howling. Gasping and howling—Treasta's lungs expanded with the same intensity as the newborn's—gasping and howling. Gasping and howling.

Rushing outside, she slammed the door. The child's demanding wails rolled through broken windows. She ran across the clearing, tucking into the grotto resting near a pool, but the child's demanding wails reverberated through the earth and off the stone and into her skull.

Treasta curled into herself, grabbing her head with clawed hands, wanting to rip her hair from her scalp with the same desire she wished to tear through the papery flesh of the dead witch and leave her remains, flaked skin floating on the air and brittle bones pulled from their joints, strewn across the cabin.

She had made a deal with an Andrili witch. If Treasta didn't fulfill her end of the bargain, there was no saying what would happen, except

Treasta knew one thing: that witch, dead or alive, owned her soul. One promise. Put the demon to rest, speak to her god of her death; Ahremnon Culdra was his name. Ahremnon Culdra, death's true name.

Gasping and howling—Treasta didn't care about the witch or whether she was put to rest or whether her death was spoken into the ether to her god, Ahremnon Culdra—

death death death death death death death death

d e a t h d e a t h d e a t h   g a s p i n g a n d h o w l i n g

g a s p i n g a n d h o w l i n g

gaspinghowlinggaspinggaspinggaspinggaspin g g as p i ng

g a s p i g a s i n g g s i n g

G S

G

A P N

I

H O L N

W I G H O L N

I

W G

G S

G

A P N

I

H O L N

W I G

I O L N

W I G

O N

H L

I

W G

S

G S

G A P N G

I

A P N

I

O N

G S G H L

A P N I

I W G

S

G S G

G A P N G

A P N I

I

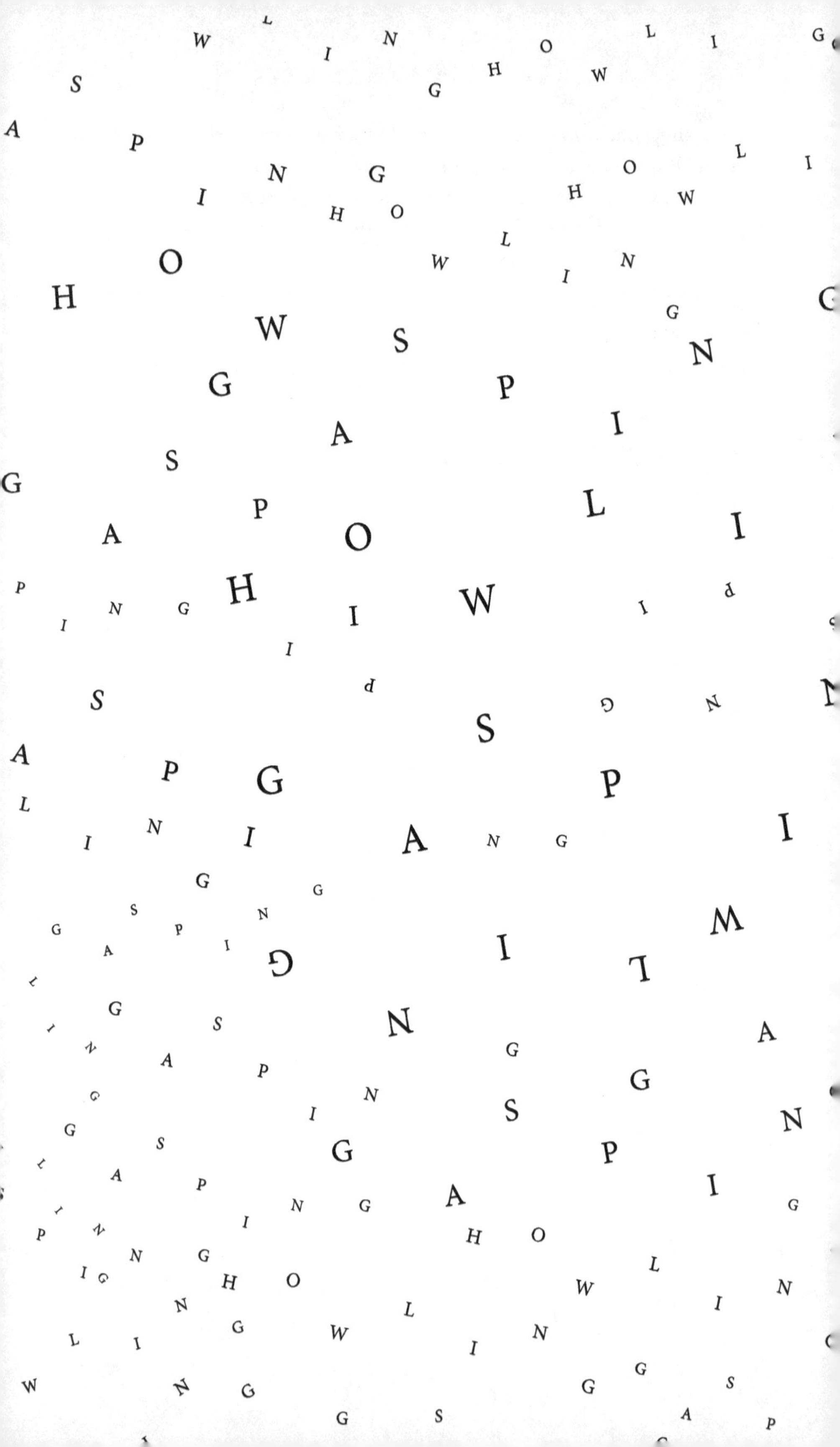

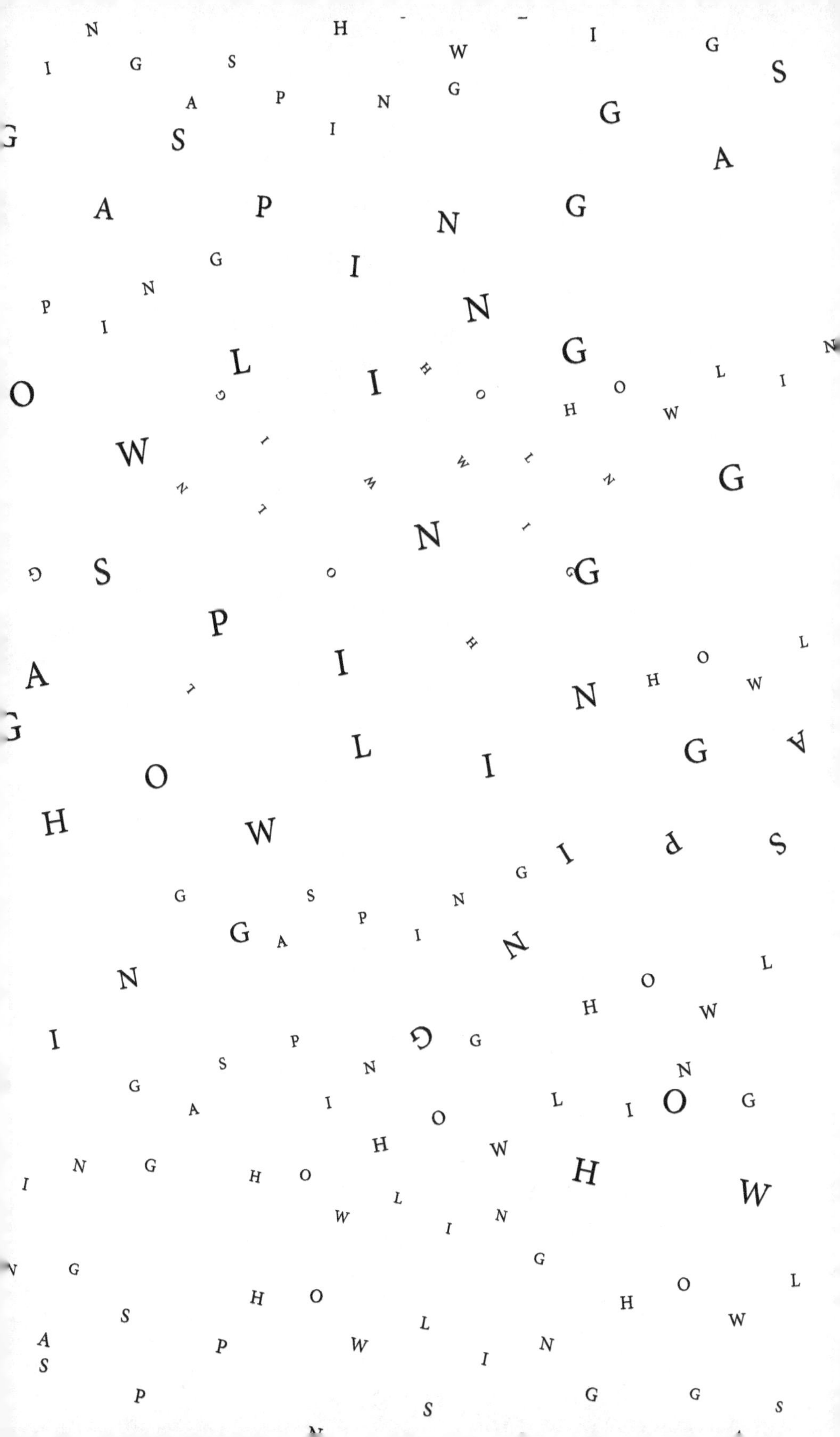

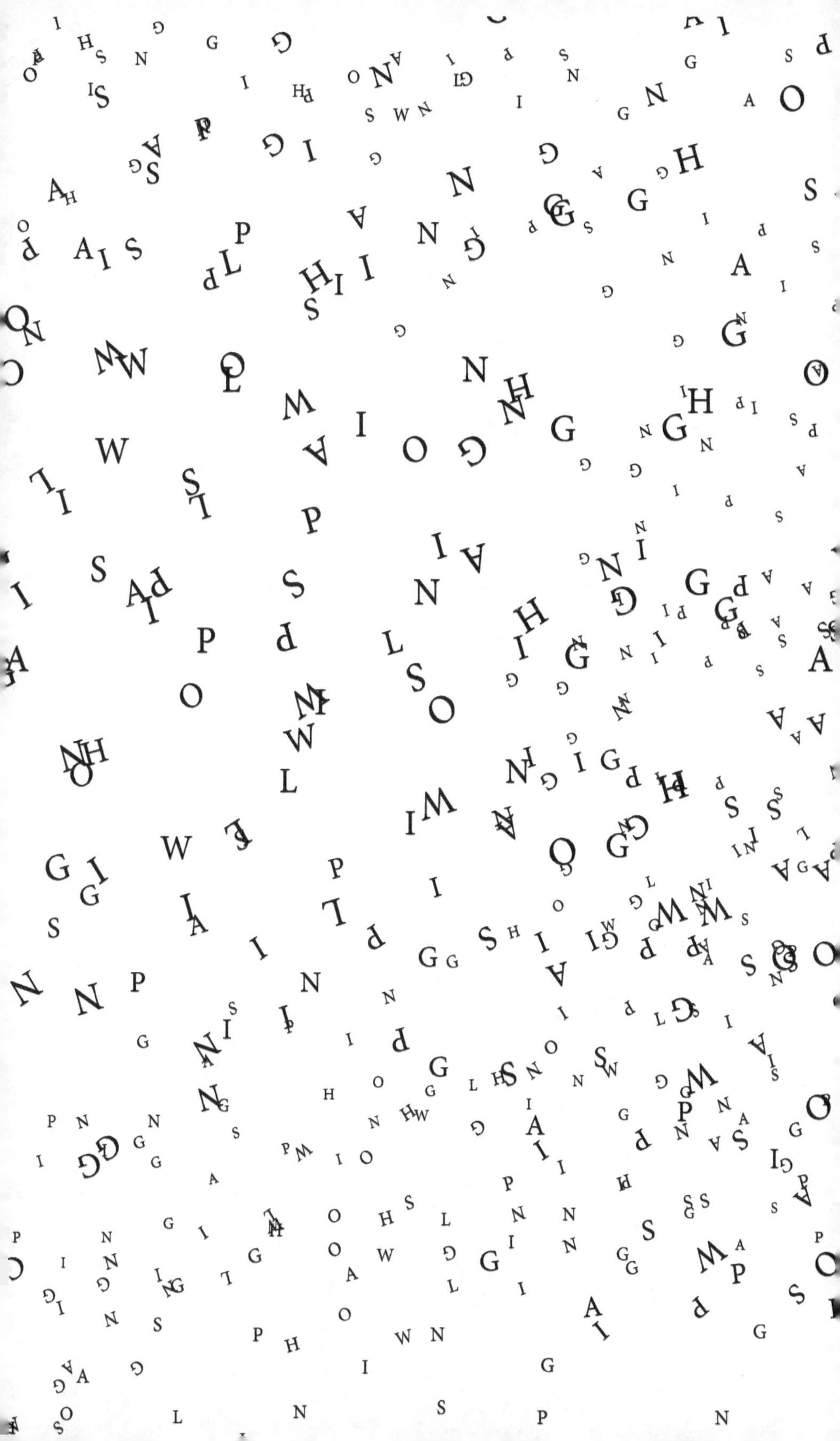

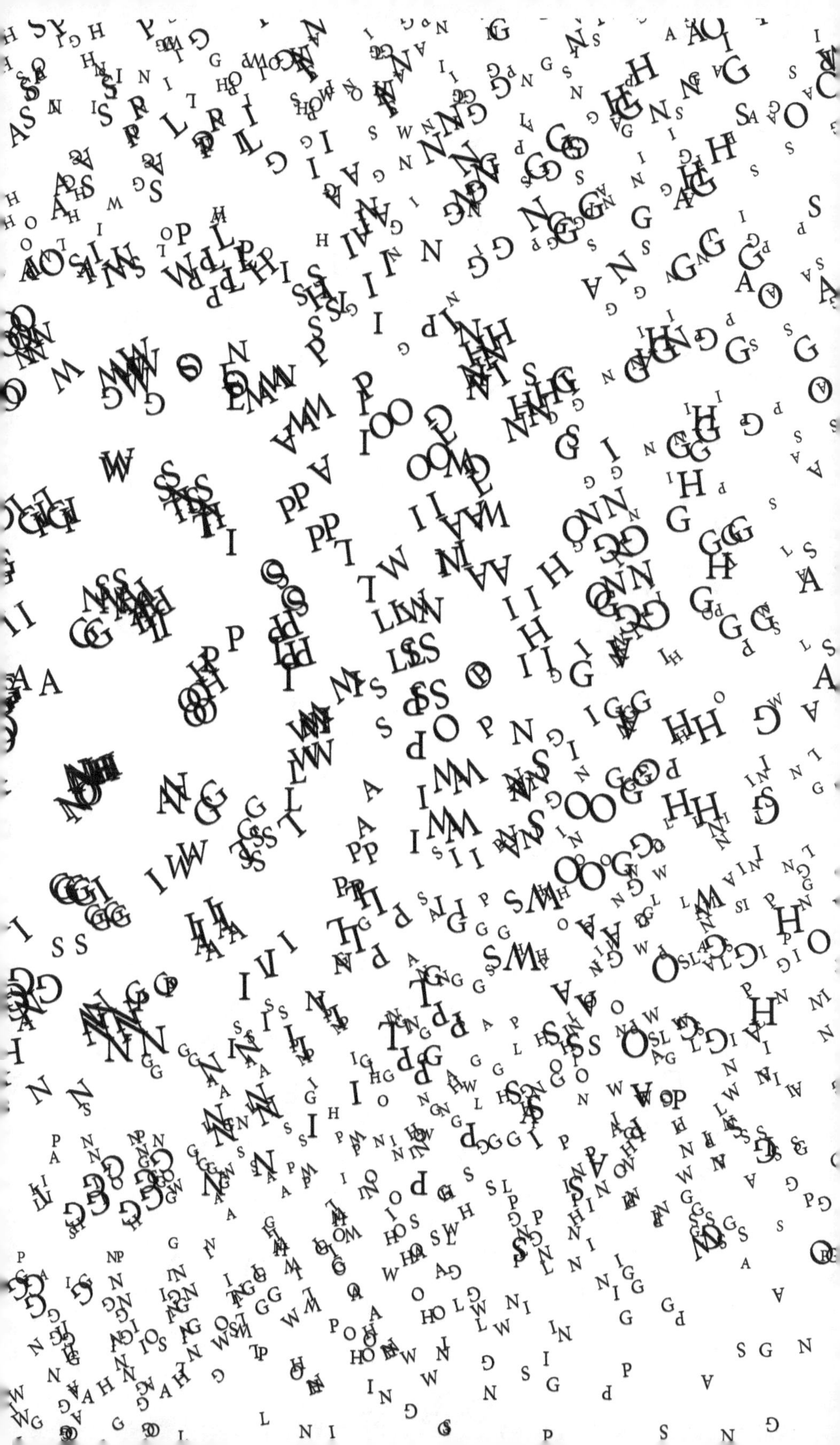

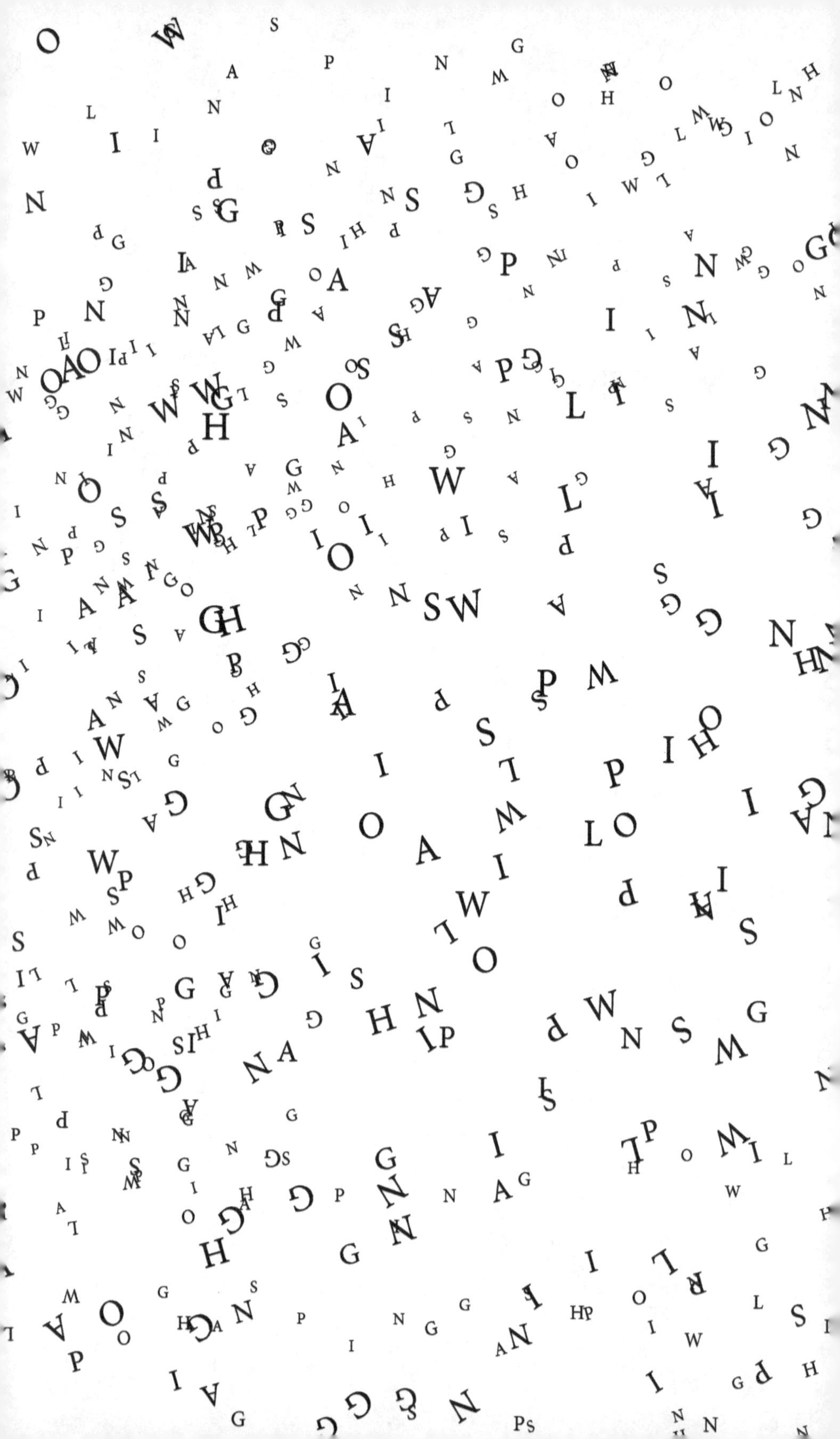

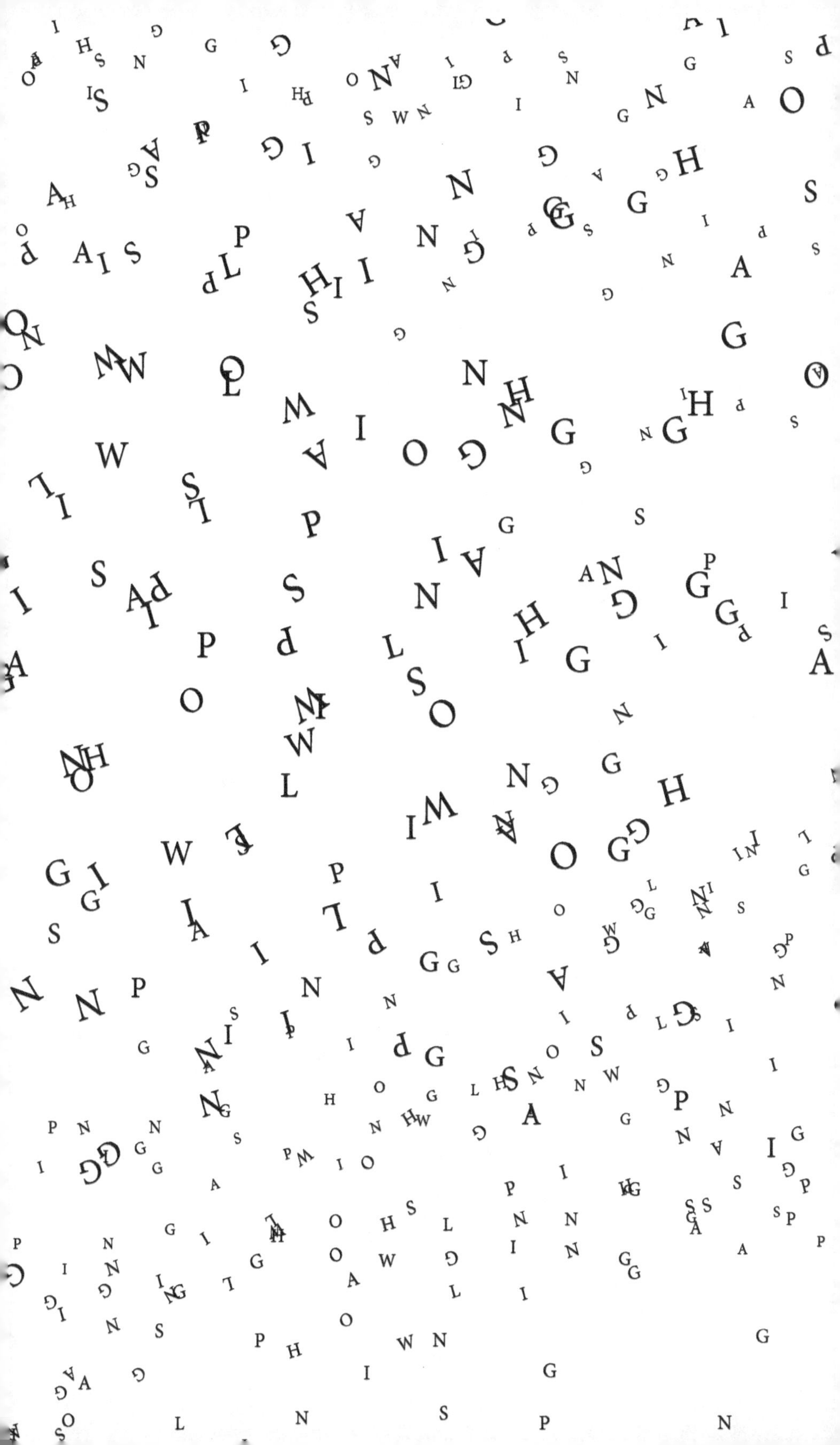

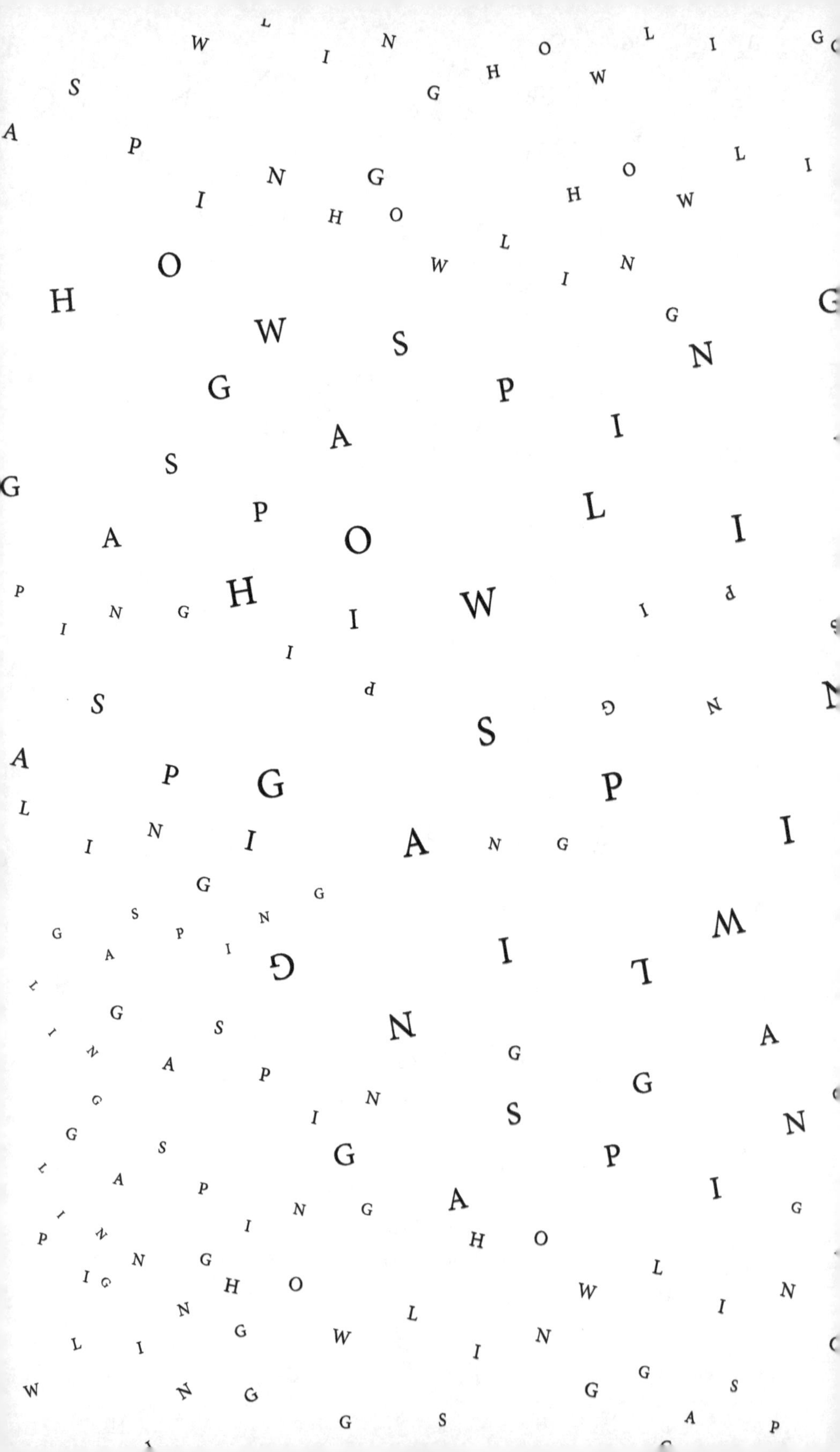

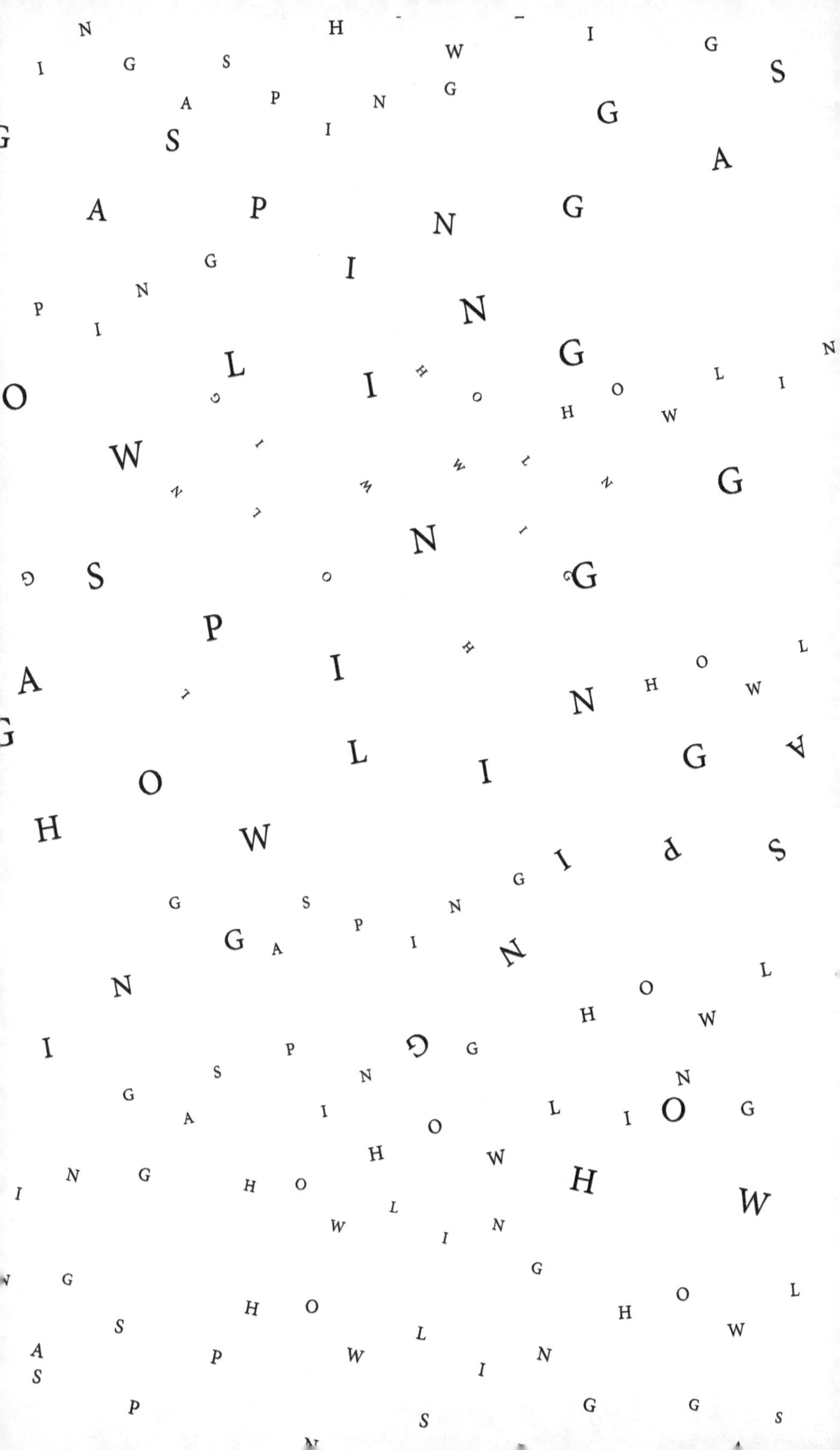

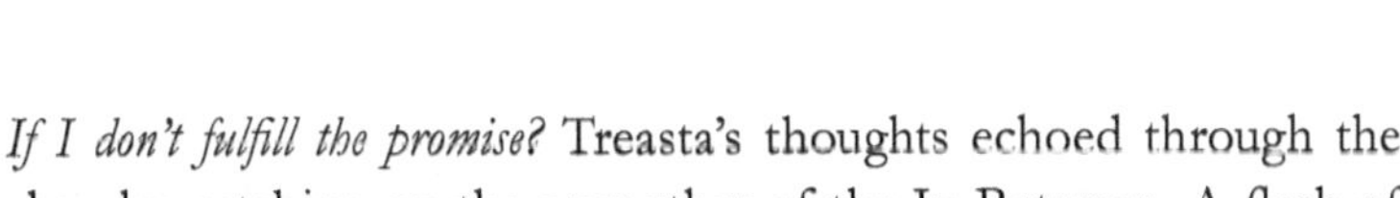

And If I don't fulfill the promise? Treasta's thoughts echoed through the mortal realm catching on the gray ether of the In-Between. A flash of the witch's yellow gaze captured her mind.

You cannot escape Death.

Was this a gift, then? Treasta wondered as the newborn latched onto her breast. *I should be thankful.* But as the babe tugged and pinched on her nipple, she thought maybe, just maybe …

Gasping and gasping and gasping and …

Quiet …

51

FROM OVER THE HILL, DAVAN AND ELSIE GAZED ACROSS the snowy terrain of the Altan Highlands; Pat stood in their shadows under a noon sun, holding the horses.

"I don't know if I'll ever see Treasta again," Davan said, as his gaze scanned the town of Hatchet, the manor somehow intact like everything he had done to help Dana was but a fever dream and this, standing alongside Elsie, was what he had awakened to, as if the last month or so, however long it had been, had never happened.

Clutching Declan's portrait, she looked from the dark manor walls to Davan. "You're sure this is it?"

He nodded, and Elsie heard a weighty exhale escape his lungs as if he were recalling whatever had happened to him in Hatchet; that short time, like a disease, infected him with some kind of madness. That feeling, that deep craze, was exasperating as they stood but a quarter of a mile from the place twisting with demon magic.

Yes, Davan was certain now, seeing the manor's long, dark windows, that this Declan, the boy he had held by the hair in the wilds of the canyon, had stolen the amulet from his pocket. When? He wasn't sure, but the energy of the land radiated with the same ominous feeling he had experienced the day Bastan welcomed him into his halls.

"You go in there, you're not coming out, you know that right?"

A chill ran along his spine. He shook the feeling as he briefly recalled the mazelike halls and vines. "The walls are listening, the mirrors have eyes. The king, that warlock, he's a trickster. He'll try to steal your soul. Traps them in paintings. His magic is connected to the portraits, including his own."

Elsie examined from the distance the small town, the narrow streets, the dots of people meandering them. The deep red stone of the manor as if it were painted in blood, the snow, so pure, so untouched, trying to hide its horrors. "I can handle myself." Crossing her arms, she glanced at Davan. "What happened, exactly?"

"I thought it was just a normal town," he said. "I arrived looking for rest after I left ...," his voice trailed into airiness, and he cleared his throat. *Treasta ... after I left Treasta.* The memory of the way the shadows twisted on Treasta's expression, of the wideness in her eyes, and the sheer terror as she cried, *You're hurting me*, haunted him. The flute in his bag strapped on his back, Laine's golden countenance pleading toward him for help—Davan touched the healing wound in his side where the gilded dagger nicked him. The sound of the blade landing on the floor rang in his ear, the door flying open and Treasta disappearing down the alleyway rushed through his mind. He felt sick thinking about it, but then heard Treasta's words: *why do you always feel guilty, huh?* Davan's jaw tightened as he sucked in his cheeks, trying to gain control over his emotions. "You'll want to sneak in. Bastan has people posted on the road. They bring him travelers passing through," he finally said. "I thought I killed him. But maybe you can't truly kill an Andrili.

"The boy, did he have an amulet?"

Elsie thought back to her time on the boat and when Bastan's naked form flashed before her: a sole green gem had hung from his neck, but she didn't remember Declan having such an item. "I saw an amulet around the warlock's neck when he appeared to me. But I don't know how Declan would have gotten it. Why?"

Davan drew in a breath. "Nothing," he said once he exhaled. "It's nothing."

Elsie faced Davan. "Consider us even."

"Yeah, even," he agreed, and shook her hand.

Starting toward the town, she paused, and looked back. "Hey, Dav," she called. Davan paused next to Pat with the horses. "Don't tell Ida where I am. Let him think I'm dead. It'll be for the best."

Elsie knew her footprints would give her away, so she waited until nighttime when the townsfolk retired before sneaking into Hatchet. She spent the last hours of daylight hunkering behind one of the large rock formations for which the town was named, not far from its border. Watching from this vantage, she witnessed locals wandering the streets floating somewhat ghostlike, their bodies seemingly passing in and out of reality like they were briefly caught in the wind and gently placed back on the road mere feet away.

In the fading twilight, beneath a waxing crescent moon, Elsie smoothed out the wrinkles of the portrait, the graphite smudging across Declan's face, his eyes closed as if he were asleep. No. More like at peace. She wondered if he knew she held his portrait, that she was coming to free him. But what was it Davan said? A sigh of frustration escaped her lungs, remembering Davan's words: he had killed the warlock, or at least he thought, and Elsie began to doubt herself. Free Declan from the portrait—that was all she cared about.

Hours passed after the sun had set, the town finally settling down inside homes and businesses closing for the night. She saw torchlights spark at the town's threshold, a patrol of men guarding the entrance just as Davan warned.

The snow crunched under her feet, the cold seeping into her boots. She had layered her feet, but the night settling over the highlands turned the air to ice. Hunkered behind a town house, she peered around the corner, eyeing the manor down the road and behind a wall of the same red stone to which bared vines, stripped of their leaves for winter, snaked along mortar.

Empty streets, candles and firelight fading, Elsie sneaked along the main street, ducking out of the way as a man passed by. In a town of this size, everyone knew everyone; Elsie had no way of blending in even if she tried.

The dry vines were rough under her palms as she moved along the wall, creeping out of sight of the rest of the town. On the backside of the grounds, she found thick branches that in the warmer months would be bright and lush with life. Elsie gave the branch clutching the wall a tug, assuring its strength, and climbed. Slipping over the ledge, she dropped into a garden at the backside of the manor, landing in the soft snow. No outside lamps were alight, no windows unlatched, no sign of anyone having crossed through the garden before her. The stony stare of a statue—of Bastan, naked—bore into her. As she moved through the garden, she felt its gaze gaping from behind.

Finding a cellar door, Elsie tested it with a light pull. It budged open, the hinges singing, and she stepped into the dark. Her light feet gave little hint of her arrival. A stove beamed of heat, stacks of wood lay across the room in neat piles, and not a single cobweb resided in any corners or cracks or small spaces behind jars and other supplies.

A lamp came to life as she stepped into the kitchen. Elsie paused. She glanced around, looking for any signs of servants, but she was alone.

She followed a staircase to the ground floor, through a dining room, the fireplace blazing beneath a large mirror and vine relief stucco racing along the ceiling and banisters. The emerald-green runner along the table was cleanly pressed, placemats set with dining- and silverware and goblets at each of the eight seats.

The doors swung with an unnatural smoothness as she moved into a corridor that felt unending, where the gazes of portraits moved with her. Elsie's hand tightened around Declan's portrait. More lifelike than she expected were the artworks, their souls bound to each stroke of the paint brush. She turned a corner.

She turned a corner? Elsie looked back. The hall seemed unchanged. She wasn't sure how long she had been walking, but at some point she came to a pair of doors, decorated in leaf motifs. As she touched the carved wood, the portal opened to reveal a vibrant and lively conservatory of plants crawling along the ground and up trees; poppies sprouted from pots and inside planter boxes along the diamond-paned glass walls. The humidity clung to her clothes; the warmth shocked the cold from her body. Rosey runes radiated along the stone floor, creating a path toward a seating arrangement at the center of the room.

As she turned around to leave, Bastan—tall, slender, dressed in furs and gems—smiled just a breadth away.

Elsie stumbled back a step, reaching for her knife, but the emerald amulet around his neck glowed and she felt her hand stiffen. Her skin turned to marble: her nails and scars, even the wrinkles creasing at her joints, looked as if they were carved by a master sculptor.

"Welcome to my home," Bastan said. "I had wondered if we would meet again."

With her living hand, she held up Declan's portrait. "Fix him."

He stared at her, his head cocking as his green eyes looked down his long nose. Raising an eyebrow, he smirked. "I can't fix what isn't broken."

Snake. Trickster. *Demon.*

Elsie clinched her jaw, stepped toward him, and said through her teeth, "You liar."

"You came here to kill me." It wasn't a question. "I don't die easily. And when I do, I come back. So go ahead and try." Bastan stepped back, arms spanning like buttresses holding up a castle. "Go ahead," he prodded. "You still have one good hand. Or are you not left-handed?"

Cautiously, she watched him lower his arms as he scoffed and rolled his eyes.

Bastan folded his hands behind his back. "Well?"

Elsie relaxed her stance but stayed alert. He could have killed her already, she realized. The cellar, it was unlocked. The eyes of the statue in the garden, the portraits, the mirrors, each flame as they came alight—all of it, was him. He knew the moment she stepped onto the grounds that she was there.

"You're an Andrili," Elsie said. "What do you want? My soul?"

"I like it here," he said with a smile, ignoring the second question. "The stars are different, the smells, the weather. There is no snow in Drynis. This conservatory," the hard heels of his shoes clacked as he circled her, "it is a piece of my home world, its forests. What do you think?"

Elsie looked around. "It's very green."

An airy chuckle left his lips. "Right you are. Your Declan is well," he said. "If you come with me, peacefully, I will take you to him and you can then decide whether you still want to kill me or not."

Bastan stood at the door, peering over his shoulder as Elsie stood unmoved in the center of the room. "You and I know the other's true self, so I think it would be best if you didn't act impetuously. Don't you agree?"

With no other option, Elsie followed him, the weight of her stony hand felt heavy at her side. They passed through the foyer where at the first landing hung a portrait of Bastan, perfect in his youth, features flawless, the smell of the oil paints still fresh in the air. She held Declan's portrait in her other hand, more aware of the texture of the paper and its crinkles.

"The people call me their king, but since we will likely be spending eternity together, you can save your breath on any formal titles. If you must call me by anything, I prefer Sir Bastan. But never king. Anything but king. We Andrili save the title for our god," he said. "Elsie"—a chill struck her as he said her name, a name she had never given him—"I truly thought little of you in the days I spent with Declan before he freed me. And, if I'm being honest, yours is a difficult soul to read. So much anger and pain shroud your compassion that I didn't realize the bond you had forged with the boy. He's quite gifted you know. Talented. And not just as an artist, but as a young apprentice of magic. He will make a fine sorcerer one day."

She let him talk as they continued through the manor.

"You will be proud of him," Bastan said. "He's been busy." They stopped just short of a door. "You are perturbed. You do not know what to make of this," he said with a wave of his hand. "You are thinking: why hasn't he killed me yet?"

Elsie gave a slow nod.

"You will see," and with those words, the door propped itself open to reveal a large artist's studio of easels and wooden boards and brushes made from fine wood and boars' bristle. The floors were splattered in colors, the walls not even safe from the mess. And there he was, Declan, sitting at a stool his back to her as he ran a brushstroke along the cheek of a female portrait, the highlight casting light on the bone just below her eyes, in a room that felt completely human unlike the rest of the manor. Familiar eyes—painted a bright azure—looked back at her, and Elsie realized she was looking at a mirror image of herself. As she glanced around the room, firelight cast brightly on several portraits baring her face all with different expressions. She slowly stepped toward him, Bastan staying at the door. Elsie saw a faint smile on the portrait's pink lips, her features soft, her face porcelain and untouched by flame. The boy's portrait slipped from her hand. As she pulled the mask off her face, she noticed her vision changed. The mask hit the floor. She touched her cheeks with her one good hand, felt the soft of peach fuzz where there should have been a scar.

Elsie looked at Bastan, then back at Declan as emotion surged up her throat. The creak of the floorboards beneath her steps bowing alerted him. Lifting the brush off the wood, he lowered it into a jar of spirits before turning around.

Declan gave no pause as he rushed across the room. His paint-covered clothes collided into her leaving smudges on her cloak. Elsie's marble hand flushed with heat as blood flowed through her digits again. She squeezed him in her embrace, cupping his head full of dark hair in her hand and she sobbed into his shoulder.

Declan comforted her, patting her back. He pulled away and began excitedly signing, "I'm so happy you're here."

Elsie wiped her tears from her eyes. "Me too," she spoke and motioned with her hands almost forgetting the words. "You're safe?"

"Yeah!" he said. And she had never seen such joy on his expression before. His gaze shifted to Bastan, and he pulled an amulet hanging inside his tunic, hiding from the onslaught of paint splatter.

Elsie touched the amulet, green like Bastan's. It buzzed in her hand.

"It's Drynite beryl," Bastan said as he approached. "It can be mined only on Drynis."

"It helps me hone my craft," Declan signed. "Do you like it?"

"Are you happy here?" she asked.

He nodded.

"Then, yes, I like it."

Elsie stood to face the warlock, assuring Declan couldn't see her lips as she spoke. "You didn't hurt him."

Bastan laughed. "Of course not. I wouldn't dare harm such potential. Do you still wish to kill me?" he asked lowly.

Elsie glanced at Declan. "Killing you would hurt him."

"Glad we can see eye to eye. I would say that you're welcome to stay here but Declan made that decision long before your arrival."

The portraits. She spotted at least six or seven upon entering the studio. "What do you want with me?"

"Not me," he gestured to Declan who stepped to his side.

Elsie gave Declan her attention. "What do you want from me?" she asked.

He signed one word: "Stay."

"The boy just wants a mother," Bastan said. "And I just want to rule. Think you'd be interested?"

"And, what? Serve you? Help you take souls of innocent travelers?" She noticed Declan was watching her speak. She cleared her throat. "Look, I'm not fit to be a mother, but I can be a big sister."

"Please stay," Declan signed. He must not know what power his portraits held, she realized. Elsie couldn't leave Hatchet even if she tried. "It's safe here."

After a long pause, Elsie nodded. "If that's what you want."

52

THE BLACK MOON WAS UNMOVED, THE DAY ABSENT for who knows how long, yet the clime here, hidden between cliffs, was humid and warm. Treasta dug turnips from a ripe garden, its soil somehow promising of life, and washed them in the pools of the surrounding grotto while the babe slept in the cabin in a makeshift crib she crafted with boards and sheets to keep the child from falling. Her body ached, giving so much of herself to the child, her nipples tender, breasts sore and full. With a heavy head, she dug up more turnips and placed them in a basket. Fatigue kept her chained to some kind of invisible force.

A wail echoed from inside the cabin. Treasta fell into herself on the earth, curling over her knees and groaning into the crevasse between her legs. The echo of her child pierced her brain. Not cries of hunger. No, that was a different kind of howl.

Unmoving, Treasta covered her head with her arms, trying to drown out the sound, wanting to bury herself in the cool loam. Maybe, if she stayed buried long enough, she could sprout a new life, restart from the beginning and go back to the orphanage she had run away from as a child. She remembered her unkempt hair, always refusing to wash it when her turn for the bath on the monthly schedule arrived. The matron saw to her personally, dunked her under the hot water, still simmering from the pot, and ran her fingers through the tangled golden mess atop her head, rubbing the mixture of ash, egg whites, and perfume into her scalp. Treasta fought against the woman, her rough hands, the way she grabbed her by the hair to get her to stop squirming in the burning water. If she could go back, if she could restart, she'd have stopped struggling so much. She would have instead came to the matron's beck and call, slaved over her demands and doted on her the way the matron liked. Then, maybe, just maybe, Treasta thought, by the time she had ripened into a teenaged young adult, she could have found honest work at the castle. She would have been good for it, yes, she was confident about that. And then maybe, just maybe, she could have met a nice young man who would have wooed her and given her everything her heart desired.

In the darkness behind her lids, the smell of earth wafting up her nose, Chimes' image filled her head. The last night they spent together in the canyon as he crawled next to her, as his hand, firm and gentle, took hers, as their fingers interlocked, as his lips left dewdrops on her skin, as his silky voice threaded the air with her name, *Treasta,* as he placed another gentle peck upon her skin—*I love you. I love you. I love you.*

The same rush of despair that had entered her heart then returned and she found herself weeping, her cries drowned out by her child's wailing. *I love you. I love you. I love you.*

Why, why, why would you ever want to love me, a broken woman, a thief, a street urchin, a pregnant unwed whore—a mother, a child who isn't yours? Why, why, why?

Because I love you. I love you. I love you.

His answer wouldn't have changed, and Treasta wasn't sure if she'd ever understand why, but what she did understand was that he was dead because of her. Elsie was always thorough.

Treasta sat up, her gaze shooting toward the sky as tears cascaded down her cheeks. The stars here, they looked different than she remembered them, the streaking colors of the galaxy painting the sky in reds and purples radiated light upon the grove in the moonless perpetuity.

As she came into the cabin, the door fell from its hinges. It's hefty knock against the floor only disturbed the child more, her cries sharpening on the air. A pounding beat against the inside of her skull, and she pressed her palms into her eyes as she screamed.

She had long covered the mummified remains of the Andrili witch with a blanket, the shape of her form somewhat discernable through the fabric. Treasta's bare feet, caked with earth, stepped over the felled door as she crossed the room to the babe in her makeshift cradle near the mattress where Treasta would try to rest. Blotches of mustardy stains colored the cloth she had wrapped around the infant who screamed with discomfort. The smell entered Treasta's nose, and she ran outside, throwing up the boiled turnips she cooked up hours ago. She wiped her mouth on her sleeve, already dirty with spit up and caked-on dirt. Tucking her hair behind her ears, she pulled her shirt over her nose and retrieved her child from the cradle.

Treasta carried the babe to the grassy edge of the pool within the grotto and set her gently on a tuft of leaves under a torn burlap sack. She undressed the babe and herself, and stepped into the water, holding her close to her chest as the spring washed them clean. Treasta sat on a stone, grass blades tickling her ears as she set her head back on the bank and hummed.

Cooing, the baby drifted back to sleep.

She lounged in the pool until she felt herself fading from the awake world and stepped from the water. Laying the child on the bed of leaves, she dried herself and the baby off, then wrapped the child in clean linens before dressing herself.

Bringing her baby back inside, Treasta gently placed her in the cradle and began gathering items into the saddle bags. She readied her mule, fastening Copper with his harness, and giving him a soft rub to the nose.

"I don't think we can stay here," she said to Copper. He bobbed his head, nudging her for more attention. Treasta's sad gaze met his, and as she looked into his eyes, she felt comfort. "Thank you for staying by my side." Returning inside, she could have sworn to hearing the witch's voice on the air and feeling her gaping through the blanket that shrouded her form. Treasta wasn't sure how long it had been since she arrived at the hovel. The unchanging sky made it difficult to discern time. But what she did know was that were she to stay there, she would relinquish herself to a lonely madness that slowly consumed her soul.

Treasta fastened a sling around her body, the child warmed against her beating heart. Carefully, climbing atop Copper, she grasped the reins with one hand and held the baby with the other. She gave a sturdy kick into the mule's sides.

53

When Treasta emerged from the canyon and into the Altan Highlands, she had expected snow, but was met with lush fields of rolling green, sprouted with wildflowers and streambeds flowing fresh with melt.

After leaving the witch's cabin, she found her way to the bridges but couldn't remember exactly how she had gotten there, her failed mental state when she fled from Hayam had disoriented her directions. She had stood at the Little Sarnak River, watched the water rolling southwardly, from where she thought she had come, but instead she followed the river north, stopping to care for the baby and resting. It took her several days to find a road out of the canyon, but eventually she found the ruins of an abandoned watchtower. She housed the mule in the stables, giving him time to rest without the weight of supplies on his back. More supplies and linens aided Treasta in caring for her child. She hauled water from a nearby stream, lit the hearth inside the post, and boiled turnips. It was all she had on her to eat.

The child wailed, her gaping mouth calling for nourishment. Treasta struggled to get her to latch, rocking her in the dancing shadows and firelight as heat radiated from the hearth. "Come on," Treasta soothed. "You can do it. Please."

Finally, the open rosebud of the baby's mouth clamped down. Treasta winced, but relaxed as she carefully sat in a chair, trying not to disturb her. She watched her daughter, so carefree and unbeknown of her own existence, so innocent and so … *beautiful.* Treasta choked back her tears, not wanting to love her.

Her daughter yawned, smacking her gummy mouth. A burp escaped her tiny lungs as Treasta patted her back. "There, there," she said.

Pacing the ground floor of the watchtower, Treasta coddled her daughter, rocking and humming to soothe her to sleep. Tired eyes looked back at her. "Do you think my mother did this for me?" she asked. "I wonder what she was like. I hated her, you know." The child shut her eyes. Treasta whispered: "I hated her for abandoning me. I hope you won't hate me."

As soon as the sun rose and her daughter relaxed into a nap after a long night of crying, Treasta tiredly went to Copper to prepare the mule for departure. She heaved his saddle over him, buckling it into place and tugging to make sure it was safe and secure for her and the baby.

Copper let out a guttural neigh as Treasta gave him a turnip. "Good boy," she said.

The day carried on for more hours than she remembered. Winter, long behind them, had taken the darkness with it. She held her daughter close, keeping her secure in a tight sling as Copper's trot carried them across the green highlands.

A sign at a fork in the road read of the town of Grenna straight ahead and Hatchet to the south. Hatchet, she remembered the name, how Chimes refused to turn north on their ride to Wesser. Chimes … she tried not to allow his visage to reenter her mind as she veered toward Hatchet. Anguish filled her. No, stop. She shook her head, needing to focus on just getting where she needed to go and making sure her daughter was cared for. But her throat felt lodged with a stone, her chest hurting, as he continued to reenter her mind as she traveled.

"Shhh …," she softly hushed as her daughter began to fuss.

Pulling back on Copper's reins, she brought the beast to a halt. She stepped down from the animal, and continued by foot, hoping the change of pace would ease the baby.

Within the following hours, the town came into view, but she decided to follow another smaller, newer road that bypassed Hatchet.

Even as night came upon them, she didn't rest, lighting a lamp she rigged to hang from a stick attached to Copper's back as they walked. She rested when she needed, tending to her daughter and changing the wrappings she was swaddled within, abandoning the dirty dressings along the road with nowhere to wash them.

Sitting on a stone not far from the roadway, she cradled her child in the dip of her closed thighs, holding her head in her hands. Mindlessly looking around, her daughter smacked her lips with content.

The stars shone above them as she bobbed her knees to rock the child. "I won't let you know my life," Treasta told her daughter. "You deserve so much better. But, how about we make a deal?" She paused as if waiting for an answer. "I can give you the love you need for now. In return, I want you to dream of me when I'm gone. Does that sound fair?" Silence. "Yeah, I think so, too."

IT TOOK FIVE NIGHTS AND SIX DAYS FOR THE GORGE to peak the horizon. Fields of wildflowers surrounded the lodge, carriages parked in the stables, horses strapped to posts; the busyness of the spring season brought merchants and travelers flocking for a prime stay.

Holding her daughter closely, Treasta hid her within the sling, as if to protect her from the eyes of nearby strangers whose attention she had caught when trotting down the hill and onto the property. Carefully, she stepped down from the mule, tied him to an empty post near the front door, and lingered at his side to take in the building—diamond-pained windows, doors set under a pointed archway, the flower boxes blooming with life: it was everything she remembered and more. Nervous, Treasta adjusted the sling and crossed her arms over her sleeping daughter before crossing the threshold inside.

The warmth and coziness of Marnie's energy and touches filled the establishment with life and love. A polished countertop at the front desk, waxed floors and tabletops in the dining room, the daily dusted lounge—not a speck of dirt floated on the air smelling of wild roses and herbs gentle on the soul.

Patrons eyed the disheveled and dirty woman as she walked inside with her child. Before, Treasta would have sneered and shrunk inside herself, but now she didn't have it in her to care. She carried herself tiredly across the foyer and into the lounge, looking for Marnie or Atlas, just somebody, a familiar face—*please.*

Her first step inside the restaurant, she froze. Heads of dozens of visitors turned in her direction; the combined smells of her and her daughter disrupted their meals. Then, she saw him at the bar pouring a young man a pint: the white hair glinted silver as the sun shone through the open windows, longer than she remembered it, his body the same slender frame, his arm resting in a sling. His violet eyes flashed up, and he had forgotten he was pouring ale into the man's mug, its brim overflowing with a golden-brown river. He dropped the bottle; its contents spilled across the counter and splashed into the man's lap. The man stood in discontent, but neither Treasta nor Chimes paid him any mind as their eyes drank in the other.

"Atlas!" Chimes called, yet to take his eyes off her, afraid she wasn't real.

His uncle appeared next to him from the kitchen. He followed Chimes' gaze.

"Watch the bar for me, will you?" Chimes asked, and removed his apron before his uncle had the chance to answer.

"I'm so sorry for that, sir. Allow us to wash your clothes for you," Atlas was heard saying to the man soaked of ale.

Stopping himself short of throwing his good arm around her, Chimes' gaze fell to the baby. His hand hovered above the sleeping child's head. He whispered with a smile, "Well, look at that." As he placed his hand in the small of her back, he guided Treasta away from the room of prying eyes, through the lounge, and to the back garden where the well was.

Finding the words was difficult as she looked him over in the sunlight. Alive. He was alive! She sobbed quietly, trying not to wake her daughter. "You," she sucked in a breath, voice quivering, "you're not dead. Elsie … she went after you. I—" the realization of how she had abandoned him after everything they had been through set in, and at that moment, she felt no better than Davan. "I'm so sorry." She fell into him, feeling the babe wiggle between them as she awoke. "I'm so, so sorry. I don't deserve you," she said. "How could you ever want me after I left you like that?"

"Hey now," Chimes rubbed her back, then rested his one good hand on her cheek—the feeling and smell of his skin was exactly how she remembered it. She shut her eyes as her heart filled with guilt. "Maybe if I was dead, I'd feel a little different." His soft laugh comforted her some. "Elsie did come after me, though," he began to explain as they sat on a bench beneath an oak tree that cast its vast shadow over them. "I fell over the cliff. I don't know how I survived exactly, but I remember some of it—the fall mostly, the way everything flashed before me. Yours was the last face I saw before I hit the ground. I remember the sound of hooves and a wagon, feet, and a man's voice. He nudged me, but I couldn't talk. I couldn't move. I remember thinking I had died—that when death comes for us, maybe he comes driving a buggy." He scratched his head, feeling a bit silly at the idea. "I awoke in Hayam at this man's home. He and his wife tended to me. When I was finally conscious enough, I called for Dee. I asked Dee if he had seen you, but he hadn't. I thought maybe Davan killed you, or maybe you went back to Kildore with him. I wouldn't blame you if you did, if you wanted to get back with him." His gaze fell to the baby. "He is her father, after all."

"Davan was waiting at Laine's," Treasta said. "The flute, it truly can turn people into gold. He made Laine play it. I …," she looked away, recalling the horrors. "It was awful, Chimes. Plain awful how Davan was acting. I didn't recognize him. He … he hurt me. Threw me into the wall. It happened so fast. I just remember looking at him and thinking he was going to kill me right there. He didn't care about our child. And he didn't care about me. I got him with the dagger you gave me. I'm sorry," the feeling of the cool metal leaving her hands entered her mind, "I lost it."

"I don't need gold or silver or jewels or gems," he said. "I have you. Gods, I thought I lost you forever." He pulled her closer. "I have all the treasure I'll ever need if you'll have me."

Treasta wiped the tears from her eyes. "I'm so smelly, aren't I?"

"Yes," Chimes said with a smile. "Very, very stinky, but," he massaged her cheek, took in the feeling of her warmth under his palm, the smoothness of her skin, "I think I can handle a little dirt."

"Chimes," her breath was airy as she said his name. "I love you, too. I love you. I love you. I love you."

His lips tenderly pressed against hers.

"How," her hand came to his neck, and he grabbed it, pressing a gentle peck on her palm, "how long has it been?" she asked between breaths. "I …," she didn't want to admit to where she was, "… lost track of time."

Resting his forehead against hers. “Months. Too many months.” He kissed her again, and then looked down at the awake babe. “What is her name?”

Treasta’s expression flattened. “I don’t know.”

Marnie set the candlestick down as she stepped into the attic. An afternoon sun cut through slats in the walls, the daylight barely giving enough for her eyes to make out shapes of crates and sheet-covered furniture.

Chimes helped search the darkness, pulling away and looking under linens until he found it. “Over here!” he called. A plume of dust kicked up as he revealed a bassinet, the wicker hardly damaged—time had been kind.

“That was yours,” Marnie said, “from when you and your parents visited in the fall during the harvest not long after you were born. I bought it for you, so you could be comfortable, and I had secretly hoped I’d have a child one day. She is well?” Marnie asked of Treasta.

“I think so,” Chimes said. “But something is different about her.”

“Children do that,” Marnie said. “We sacrifice our bodies and our minds for them. I’ve got some other things to unpack, but why don’t you take the bassinet to her, and I’ll check on her later.”

Knock, knock, knock.

“Come in,” Treasta called.

Marnie entered to find Treasta rocking her daughter in the wicker bassinet, it’s white paint as bright as the infant’s face. “I’m so happy to see you’re well,” Marnie said. She sat next to Treasta on the bed. “How are you doing?”

“I’m here,” she answered. “But, you know, I’ve felt much worse. The witch,” Treasta’s voice lowered, “she’s dead.” Treasta contemplated telling Marnie that Atlas had killed her. Thought about giving her the silver-bladed knife he drove through the Andrili woman’s heart, but she didn’t need the peace of this place disturbed. “When I got there, I found her like that. Someone had killed her.”

Marnie placed her arm around Treasta, looking at the little girl and her thick dark hair fuzzy atop her tiny crown. "What is her name?"

"Katrin," Treasta said.

"Katrin," Marnie repeated with gentleness. "You named her after Chimes' mother?"

Treasta nodded. "I didn't have a mother to name her after. I …," her gaze fell, "I was wanting to ask you. I mean, I spoke with Chimes about this, and we were wondering …," she cleared her throat. Why was this so difficult? "Would you be her mother? I know I shouldn't ask, but I just can't do it. I can't give her the love and care she deserves—the love you gave Chimes when his mother died."

Little Katrin's fingers curled around Marnie's thumb. Marnie's face came alight, remembering her sister as tears filled her eyes. "I would be honored," she said. "And should Katrin know about you? Will you return?"

Treasta looked at her daughter, sadness entering her heart. "I don't think I ever will return. It will be better that way," she said. "I know you will love her. And should she ever ask about me, tell her I am watching over her in her dreams."

"And the father?"

"Dead," Treasta said with a voice like ice. "Of all the people she should never look for, it's him. He's wicked and selfish." A quiet, shaky sigh escaped her throat. "I wish I could give her more of myself, but I don't think I can. I feel so ashamed. So broken."

"It's all right, my dear." Marnie wrapped Treasta in a tight embrace. "I have enough to give for both of us, okay?"

Treasta melted. "Me and Chimes are talking about leaving after summer. If you mind me staying for a little bit, I mean."

"Stay as long as you like. But where will you two be going?"

"To Kildore."

Six months later …

Dark, wispy smoke danced through the spokes of the wagon's wheels, twisted along the carriage and wrapped around Treasta's ankles. She kicked the smoke away, and it dissipated into nothing, her heart skipping a beat; it wasn't the first time in the past few months that she had seen it, but this was the first time she had felt its cold, wet vapor against her skin.

"Are you sure about this?" Chimes asked as he finished readying the horses. He hadn't seen the slithering smoke. "I don't think it's a good idea. What if Davan tries to hurt you again?"

Still shuddering at the chill reverberating through her body, Treasta cleared her throat.

"There are rules in Dubilee," she finally said and tightened the ties on their bags. "We will be safe." She saw the uneasiness disrupting the handsome features on his face and added, "Remember how I told you I killed Lodan?"

Chimes nodded.

"I didn't just kill Lodan because of what Davan was becoming, I killed him because Fylle made a deal with me and because I truly believed Lodan was a corrupt leader. Fylle wouldn't be in his place of power without me. So, am I worried about Davan trying anything? Not really. In the guild, there is order under our law, *an eye for an eye*. He tries anything, it'll come back to him. Fylle will protect me."

"What about me?" Chimes asked, trying not to sound worried. "He probably thinks I'm dead, you know?"

Treasta smiled, patted his cheek, and kissed him. "And I will protect you."

"I was thinking," Chimes said as he tied a bag of grain to the side of the cart, "what if we visit the orchards in the Milnar Valley. Just for a little bit."

She nodded. "Let's do that. I like that idea."

Marnie appeared in the threshold to the stables, six-month-old Katrin on her hip.

"We've come to say goodbye," Marnie said.

Treasta looked at her daughter and smiled, relieved to know Katrin could have everything she never had. "I love you, I love you, I love you," Treasta said, kissing Katrin on the head. "Remember our deal, all right?

Dream of me when I'm gone. I'll be dreaming of you."

Chimes unlatched the charm around his neck. He placed it over Katrin's head and handed her the windup unicorn. "A gift. To know you're loved and protected. As always."

Marnie drew Treasta and Chimes into a long embrace with Katrin giggling between them. "As always." she said.

Take a peek into the next installment
of *The Legends of Cyconis* series

THE SHATTERED SYNDICATE

A LEGENDS OF CYCONIS NOVEL

MARTINA B. RIVERS

1

"DO NOT STOP." HER BROTHER'S VOICE ECHOED. *"You must keep going."*

Mau didn't need to careen her neck to know the stranger stared with a wild blue gaze; she had noticed him, a wily-eyed man, when the knights bound her to the tree. The knobbed roots beneath added to her discomfort following weeks of fleeing. Were it not for her heightened senses distracting her—the waft of boar roasting over a campfire, the flutter of ash flashing under a starry night sky as a trio of knights waggled their tongues about a thieves' guild and their latest captive, and that gaping stranger—she would have felt the true extent of her soreness.

The soft point of her half-Eldei ears twitched at a whisper.

"I can get us out of this."

Mau peered from the corner of her eye, hearing the stranger's words. With the thumping of her heart a fast and unsteady rhythm, her breath shook as she inhaled.

It was difficult to tell in the firelight whether the red in the stranger's bandanna that held back his dark blonde hair was dye or blood. A single scar cut from his forehead to his cheek over his left eye, a poorly healed gash that must have torn to his bone. And below the scar, he wore a wide smirk hooked deeply into his right cheek.

Mau closed her eyes, trying to ignore the man to gather her thoughts and execute a plan. The knights, now throwing back bottles of—from what she could smell—mead, had caught her crouching near their camp as the setting sun's light spliced through the forest canopy. The scent of food combined with her aching stomach had lured her off the road.

She could still feel the tip of the sword pressed into her spine as a deep voice had rumbled the words "get up." As she had come to her feet, he had ordered her to drop her sack.

Mau eyed her bag that had since been tossed near a heap of supplies several feet away from where the horses were tied. They hadn't found anything suspicious beyond a map of Nateet and Kildore, a half-filled skin of water, and a knife. She had run out of food that morning and had been hiking south from Nateet for hours when they caught her.

"I am not a thief!" she had cried as they detained her with the accusation and something about being with "him"—the stranger.

Hands bound behind her back, Mau watched the sky fade into twilight through the leaves, then night, a full moon peeping through breaks in the wind-rustled canopy.

"You must be one of those half-kinds," the stranger's whisper entered her ear. "You know, like one of those with the elf mom and human dad or something." Elf—it was a conic word, slang really, but Mau, even as a half-kind, wasn't raised among her mother's people, the Eldei of Diresha, so elf wasn't something that offended her the way it might an Eldei man or woman. As a half-kind, there were nastier words she had been called, mostly behind her back.

"I don't need your help," she said.

An empty bottle whistled past her head, a hard clunk hitting the wide trunk of the tree, then a drunken command: "Eh! Keep yours mouths shuts!"

A second knight shoved him. "Oy, don't go damaging the bounty. Got a good reward from the commander for these twos."

The stranger snorted, rolling his eyes, and leaned closer to Mau, his smile turned toothy. "You don't know what they're gonna do to us, do ya?" She didn't answer. "You're not from the guild, I can tell. I know my people. But, you see," and he nodded toward the trio, "they don't care. They're gonna take you to their commander, and you'll get locked in a nasty tower, tortured, and likely killed. Ask me how I know."

"And you're alive, it seems, if what you're implying is you were once locked in the tower, tortured and likely killed."

He chuckled lowly. "Yeah, I am. Guess I'm just lucky like that."

Mau's gaze drifted toward the trio. The ropes on her wrists dug into her skin as she tugged, but even if she broke free, she wouldn't know what to do. They'd come after her if she tried running. The feeling of defeat overwhelmed Mau, dread sinking into her chest. Months of planning with her brother, Torin, to escape Timbol Castle, days of eluding capture in Baene, weeks on foot fleeing the Razorback Mountains and running into Kildore led to this: to be locked in a tower, tortured, and likely killed.

"He is sending me to Asogna," Torin had said.

"But why?"

"The prince's affairs are no longer your concern."

Do not stop.

Mau's head fell, her long, dark tresses slipping from where they were tucked behind her ears. "What do you propose, then?"

"We wait until they sleep and the fire to die out."

AS THE LAST COAL DIMMED, THE ROPES FELL FROM MAU'S WRISTS. The stranger, silent, crept toward the supply heap, shuffling through items until retrieving daggers. Mau, rubbing her wrists, carefully stood, unsure when the stranger had broken free from his restraints. In the moonlight, she noticed he was tall, lanky, and moved with a smoothness. He waved her over.

Cautious, Mau stepped, her vision better than the typical person's in the night. The forest floor was littered with layers of dead brush from last year's winter, packed, and black earth disturbed from when the knights cleared the area for camp.

Snap!

Mau froze as her foot rolled over a twig, her eyes wandering toward the knights who lay snoring on bedrolls, their armor stripped from their bodies. It was the peak of summer in Kildore, humid even at night—their bare chests made them vulnerable to the elements and to the stranger who passed Mau a dagger.

The wily man demonstrated across his neck a slicing motion with his thumb. Alarmed, she attempted to return the blade to him, but he refused, shaking his head and gesturing erratically between the blade and the trio.

"I can't," she whispered.

He shushed her. "Do you want them to wake? *Just do it.*"

Mau felt a stone land in her stomach as she swallowed back air, her face and hands tingling numb. She stepped over one of the men who lay on his back. She adjusted her grip, looking from his neck—one quick swipe—then looked at his pale chest—she could use her body weight to plunge the blade through his heart. In the distance, the rushing waters of the Elna Rapids were faint.

"Follow the river," Torin had said. *"It will take you to Asogna."*

But as she stepped to retreat toward the sound, the stranger stopped her, his grip tight on her arm.

"Where do you think you're going, huh? We're not done here," and he pointed toward the sleeping knight with his dagger. "It's either kill or be killed," his words were like ice.

Mau clutched the blade in her hand. The knight rolled on his side, smacked his lips at the sound of her movement.

She fiddled with the triangular-shaped pendant that hung from an old leather choker around her neck.

Do it.

Do not stop.

The knight's eyes flicked open.

Mau froze.

"Barnes," he muttered, his hand coming to her foot, "yous got girlish feet, don't you? Go back to sleep … sun's comin' … gonna be … soon." He sat up, rubbing his eyes, cursing under his breath. It was at that moment he realized the figure was indeed more petite than he recalled in his stupor.

The knight flew to his feet, wavering forward and back, still drunk. He toppled over Mau. Strong arms wrapped around her legs, and his bulk pulled her to the ground. Eyes flashing up long enough to see the other thief slashing the throat of his fellow knight, his hold around Mau's legs tightened as he shouted.

Kill or be killed.

Mau drove the dagger through the man's throat not once but twice. Blood gushed, and after just a moment he fell limp. She wiggled from his loosened grasp, heart racing, body shaking, forgetting for a moment that there was not only another knight, but the stranger at her side in blood-soaked clothes fresh from his kill.

The commotion had awoken the horses. Their shrill cries echoed through the trees as they kicked and shuffled.

The third knight had come to his feet, his drunken self scrambling for a moment until realizing exactly what was happening. He winced, then saw the aftermath of two dead bodies on the forest floor.

Grasping Mau's wrist, the stranger pulled Mau away from the ground and away from the camp, but he tripped in the woods, the darkness too dark to make out which way was east or west. Mau toppled over him, her face colliding into mulch. She wiped her face, shot a glance over her shoulder to see through the trees some movement.

Mau grabbed the stranger's hands, pulled him to his feet, and said, pointing, "That way."

He looked at her confusedly. But they didn't have time. He let Mau guide him through the woods as the knight, struggling in the darkness, chased after them.

The roaring of the rapids echoed as they approached. Stopping at the riverbank, they searched along the steep embankment for a way to cross. The heavy feet of the knight neared behind them, and they turned to see the half-drunken man catching his breath as he broke through the tree line. The knight adjusted his posture and readied his sword. "I don't gotta bring you in alive," he said. "Bounty's a bounty. I get paid either way."

As the knight rushed them, Mau and the stranger dodged his sloppy swing. But standing too close to the edge, the stranger's balance slipped, and he tumbled down the embankment, splashing into the Elna. Mau caught a glimpse of his head bobbing up and down as the current took him.

The knight turned toward Mau, and she picked up a nearby branch, hefty enough to throw her balance.

Do not stop.

Mau adjusted her footing, braced for the knight to lunge toward her, and when he did, she dipped from his path, came up behind him, and swung the branch against his skull. As he fell, his sword slipped from his grip, and Mau grasped its hilt, lifting the heavy blade and driving it through the knight's back with a scream that echoed beyond the forest.

The knight fell. She couldn't look away from his dying body, his eyes wide, mouth agape, gasping until his chest deflated on its final exhale.

Keep going …

Collecting herself, Mau's eyes searched the river. The stranger was gone. Mau raced with the moon as her only guide along the Elna.

Follow the river …

And then she saw him, the stranger, grasping the dangling roots along the riverbank, clearly unable to pull himself up as he slipped with every effort. His eyes flashed up when he saw Mau lying on the earth, one arm outreached as she offered her hand, the other anchored around a stone. It was only a few feet he needed to climb, but the embankment was slick, his tiring grip struggling to hold onto the wet tree roots. He reached up her arm to pull himself up; Mau let out a cry as her muscles pulled against his tugs. The stranger's fingers latched into the earth, clutching handfuls of dead forest, his feet wedging into the bank as he shimmied onto flat ground. He lay beside Mau, mud-covered, catching his breath.

Mau rubbed her sore arms. Then, she crawled away from the man.

"You," her words were sharp, *"made me do that."*

Her blood-soaked clothes marked her a murderer. Bile shot up her throat and went to the forest floor. Mau wiped her lips on her sleeve, her head faint, her stomach turning. The man just sat there, watching her, as if knowing the spell would soon pass. And after several minutes, it did, and Mau looked at him, feeling so very small with him watching her like that.

"What?" she snapped. "What are you looking at?"

He snorted. "Just someone coping with her first kill."

First kill. The words were heavy. *First and second kill.* But the man was right: it was kill or be killed. Her heart filled with grief. They would have taken her to Asogna. And though she needed to get there, she didn't need her rendezvous with her brother to be met with a rope around her neck.

The man stood, extended a hand for Mau to take, and said, "I'm Julios."

Mau's gaze shifted from his hand to his eyes. She hesitated but took it. He helped her to her feet. "I am … I'm Mau."

"Strange name. Where you coming from, Mau?"

"Nateet," she said.

"Oh. *You're a Natean,*" he said lowly. "I've met a few Nateans when I was coming through Nateet from Freasi a while back. Hey, you guys have that one mountain there, right? Well, I mean, you have an entire range of mountains. I'm talking about the big one with those glaciers on it. What's it called? Wattomna? Or was it Ottamamna …" He trailed off, pondering.

"Ottawamna."

"Yeah, that's what I said. Where are you headed to, princess?"

Princess. Mau scoffed. "Don't call me that."

Julios, amused, laughed. "Uh-huh, sure." Her accent wasn't just Natean, but upper-class Natean. "Maybe don't sound so smartlike, you hear?"

"I don't know what you mean," she said.

Mau followed after him as he started toward the knights' camp. He paused over the dead knight near the river, nodding his head as if approving of the job she did. "Impressive."

"Wait," she called. "Can you help me? I'm trying to reach Asogna."

"Help yourself," he said as he continued through the woods. "I'm not traveling with a blue-blood."

Blue-blood? Mau paused. "I'm not a blue-blood."

His voice echoed through the trees: "Whatever you say, princess."

"I saved your life," she said. "I killed two men and saved *your* life. And you won't help me? That hardly seems fair."

As they entered the campsite, he turned toward her. "Fair, eh?" He let out a long laugh. "Fair? Oh, if only everything could be fair, yeah? I guess lucky for you, I'm headed to Asogna myself. And you sure as hell aren't getting through the gates"—he rubbed the bloody fabric of her blouse between his thumb and finger—"like that. Guess, you're right: it'd be unfair to let you even try. They'd lock you away in a heartbeat. I suppose I could help you."

He was smirking with that same cocksure grin he had when they were bound at the tree. Plenty of meat left on the boar, Julios pulled it from the bone, sat down with crossed legs, and began eating near the simmering coals.

Mau's groaning stomach drove her to her knees. Julios watched her, curious, as she tore into the flesh with the desperation of satiating days of hunger and bit down with tears in her eyes.

About the Author

Martina B. Rivers resides in Washington state with her Chihuahua and two cats. She is an alumna of the University of Alaska Fairbanks and the University of New Orleans. Martina holds a creative writing masters, with select poetry published, and is a twice semi-finalist in Button Poetry's annual chapbook contest.

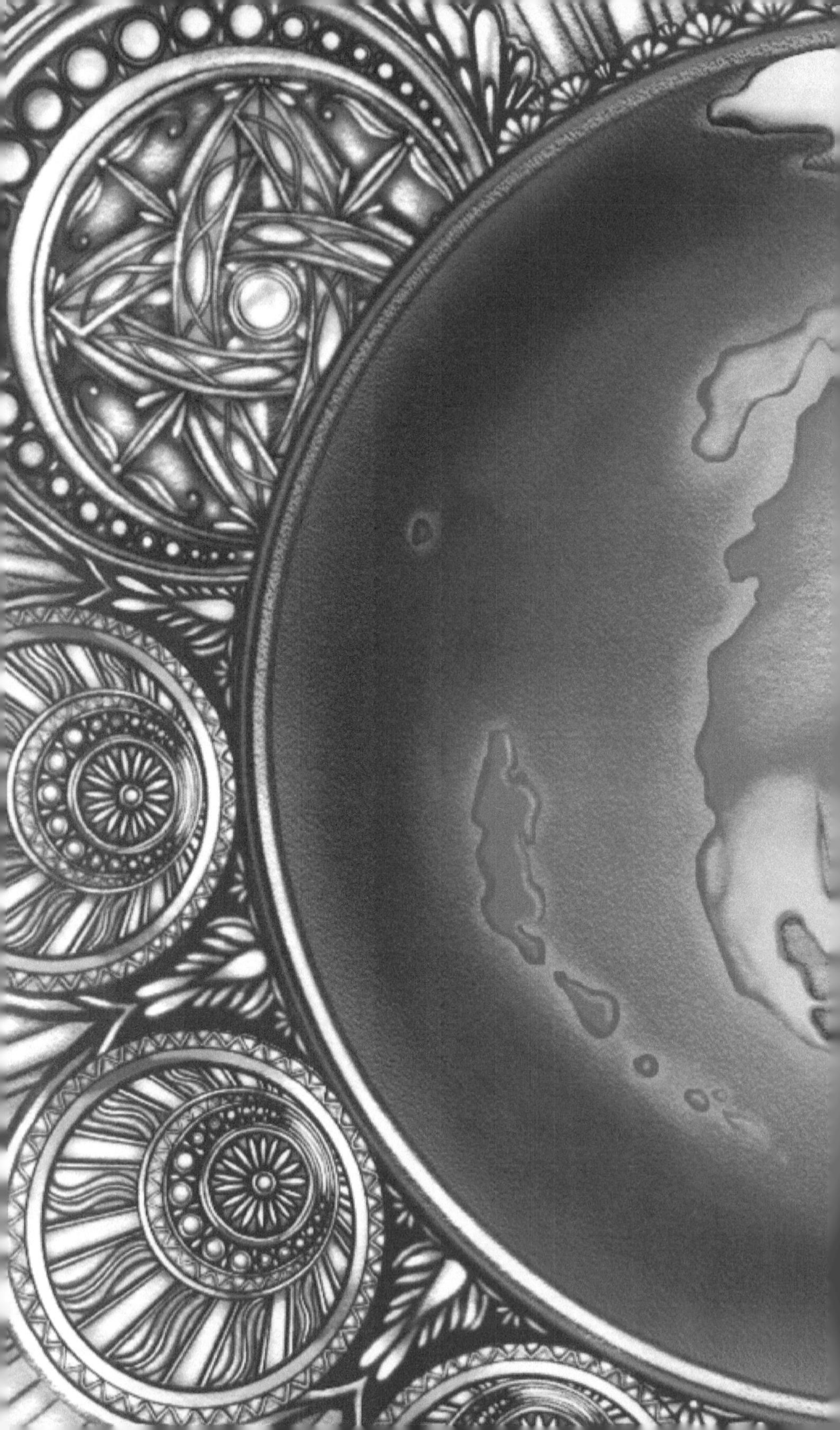

www.ingramcontent.com/pod-product-compliance
Lightning Source LLC
Chambersburg PA
CBHW030335120726
47901CB00007B/1802

* 9 7 9 8 9 9 9 6 2 9 0 0 5 *